The Bitch Tried To Heal

My Husband's Body

ISBN: 1-4196-9367-0
ISBN-13: 9781419693670

Photography:

Cover Model: Alia Bellamy,
aliawinne@hotmail.com and/or BLL670@aol.com.

Photographer: Paul Sirochman
338 West Girard Avenue
Philadelphia, PA 19123
Telephone: 215-629-1119.
www.sirochmanphoto.com

Picture of author, Adrienne Bellamy
Photographer: The Harrison Studio of Photography,
24 Glenside Avenue
Glenside, PA 19038
Telephone: 215-886-0717
Harrison@theharrisonstudio.com.

Hair Stylists:

Cover Model
Stylist: Jennifer Lynne
215-881-6899

Adrienne Bellamy
Stylist: Frank Altomare
Panache Hair Design
205 South 15th Street
Philadelphia, PA 19102
Telephone: 215-545-7166
Cornish93@aol.com

Visit www.booksurge.com to order additional copies.

The Bitch Tried To Steal My Husband's Body

~

A novel by

ADRIENNE BELLAMY

BOOKSURGE
WWW.BOOKSURGE.COM

THANK YOU

❦

Dear God:

Thank you for the blessing of this book. Thank you for allowing and affording me the ability to investigate this matter and for the people you placed in my path to help me along the way. Truly, Lord, they are your angels that watched over and lifted me above the hurdles. Many relationships were also formed because of this novel, which I know came directly from you. I was rescued countless times. Lord, no doubt you were everywhere with me--and I know it was you on that train from New Brunswick to Philadelphia. There are no coincidences. Thank you for giving me the courage to continue on when I ached and was exhausted from injustice. I have learned so much by writing this novel that started off a shot in the dark, but before I knew it you had lit the way for me. I love you even more and am grateful that you are enabling me to share this story with the world.

Adrienne

To My Readers and Fans:

I work with a team. I simply cannot do it alone, so I have to call in the troops. Kudos to my test readers who looked after this novel, edited, and read their butts off. For more information on my test readers, check them out on www.adrienne-bellamy.com. Just click onto the "My Work" key and you'll find them all waiting to meet you. You'll also find a few people on the website and not listed below because they were on time out due to professional and/or family obligations, and could not edit The Bitch Tried To Steal My Husband's Body. They'll be back for upcoming projects.

Mallory Anderson: Virgo
Alia Bellamy: Leo
Deborah "Toni" Edwards: Pisces

THANK YOU

*Linda Etheridge: Libra
Walter Dixon: Libra
Rachel Grossman: Capricorn
Melba R. Guy: Aries
**Regina Bellamy Johnson: Virgo
Lisa Noel: Aquarius
***Arlene Sacks: Libra
****Joquina Somerville: Libra
Ralph Travick: Sagittarius

*She's new to my crew. She comes with a gleaming smile straight out of the Philadelphia School System. Yep, she's teaching me things. Thank you, Linda, for getting onboard and for all your help and advice. I love your gentle spirit and girl, you make some great catches. Thanks for watching my back.

**Special thanks to Regina Bellamy Johnson for remembering, recycling, rehashing and reediting chapters of this novel. You were on overtime, Baby, all the time. I must also give praise to you, Regina for planting the seed which grew into a fantabulous ending to this book. You are the best!

*** Thank you for kicking breast cancer, chemo, keeping my head straight, and working on this damn book while you went through it all. I know there is a hero in this house! I cannot believe you demanded your edits while so ill, and insisted on keeping up with everything. You solve so many problems for me and your thoughtfulness is worth your weight in gold. I cannot thank you enough for being my friend as well as an outstanding asset to my writing. The Libras are ruling, baby!

****Her book club hosted me in 2004 with my novel Departures. She was hooked. She test read my novel Arrivals (which took a backseat to this novel and will be available in December of 2008,) and Joquina has stayed on board with me. She played a special role in The Bitch Tried To Steal My Husband's Body, preparing it for editing by the rest of the test readers. Yep--she had it first.

And now I present to you the people and organizations that also assisted in making this novel happen:

Anthony J. Baratta, Esquire, and the law firm of Baratta, Russell & Baratta, P.C.: For the umpteenth time, you have covered my ass. The calculation and concentration of the Scorpio bore fruit--as usual. I just blew you guys a kiss.

Elinore O'Neill Kolodner, Esquire: Hey, Miss Sagittarius, you're so smart you make my head spin. Thanks counselor, and you know we're not done.

Jerry Murphy. M.D: The Aquarian always knows it before it happens. You continue on an almost daily basis to amaze me. You solve damn near all my problems. I'm literally breathing because of you.

City of Philadelphia, Central Detectives: I'll bet you I know the ropes now because Detective David Smith taught me.

City of Philadelphia, Board of Pensions: Gwen, Tonya and Phyllis--Hooray!

City of Philadelphia, Life Benefits Department: Dorothy Coles, you're one in a million. Capricorns do take care of business, don't they, Ms. Coles?

City of Philadelphia, Department of Marriage Certificates: I told you I smelled a rat.

City of Philadelphia, Department of Register of Wills: What a crew! And you work swiftly, too. Winnie--nice job!

Melody Guy, Senior Editor, Random House: There really aren't any words for you, Miss Libra. Thank you for helping a sistah out on a Sunday night when she desperately needed you. You are my baby!

Mr. Dee: You are by far the best psychic I have ever experienced. You opened up the box and I pulled a rabbit out of the hat.

The Philadelphia Daily News and David Gambacorta: You pointed so many things about me. Thanks for your work on this case. You know I'll be seeing you.

Rhonda Travick Coney: You Cancers sure can get emotional–especially late at night. I am so glad you made me stay awake. Thank you for demanding a thorough search.

Roscoe Coney: I was a damsel in distress. Put an Aries on the job and it's a done deal. Thanks for teaching me all about the *DROP Program*.

Daniel Bishop, Assistant Manager, Citizens Bank: Thank you for your concern and for your patience in taking me slowly through the legal processes of the banking system. You hipped me to a lot of stuff.

Anna and Willie C. Smith: Leo and Pisces Mommy and Daddy: They are my Godparents. They are in Mountville South Carolina bragging their butts off right now. They're telling everybody that "their baby done wrote another book." I love you both. See you in Vegas this fall at Aunt Gladys' house.

Cherry Weiner: She is my former agent. She's given me a lot of great advice, reamed me out big time, many times and she also gave me a gift in 2007. It was the title of this book. Scandalous! Everybody Loves it! Yep, that Cancer named this baby. Go Cherry, Go Cherry, Go Cherry.

Sheldon Price: A good Pisces Man! Thanks for the cover girl and for making me shut up and listen to you. Keep singing, Sheldon, I smell a record deal. It ain't never too late.

Scott Burkett: Capricorn. You saved me---stone rescued me in April of 2008. Thanks, man, for a slamming website! Everybody is loving it! I'm plugging you, baby, www.Burkettphotography6.ifp3.com. You are the bomb! I know worked your last nerve—but hey—that's me. That's what I do. You my love, do great work. You are an excellent photographer and I'm very proud of you and www.adrienne-bellamy.com.

Dr. Anne Highland: We always need a Gemini in the mix. Well, Doc, you said it! You predicted the world would want to know it. You continue to drive me on. Sleep well my love. I miss your face. I know you and God are having some wonderful chats. Thank you for being an angel and my teacher, as well as a hell of a Psychologist.

Janete Scobie and Gentle Pen Editorial Services: The talents of editor Janete Scobie will shine throughout The Bitch Tried To Steal My Husband's Body. I know she put her foot in Departures years ago, editing beyond belief, and my fans loved it. Well, listen up people—Janete has really kicked some ass this time. Had she not had pen in hand to correct and guide me, we all would have been cheated. This Leo worked her butt off, and the Libra author thanks her. The scales don't always balance and the lion roars much too loudly—but when they team up in the pot together, the aroma is a winning novel. You readers can especially thank Janete for the sexiness of the character Dale. She beat him out of me.

And so it began.......

They met in 1977. On this journey as she heads down Rocky Road with her then lover Lenny, this takes him down a familiar road—Adultery Avenue. Lenny and Denise make that left. She and her man traveled together a few miles and make a right turn onto Divorce Drive. He needed to stop there for a moment to get some business straight. A few miles down the road they approached Live-In Lane and bore right on to that. Two blocks down was the intersection of Pregnancy Pike and Childbirth Court. They took Childbirth and went nine blocks down to Maternity Lane. They stopped for a breather. Two miles down and to the right they encountered Wedding Way. They made a right onto that and stopped. Later, a few miles down they continued on and decided to check into Homestead Haven, a comfortable abode. They stayed twelve years resting up before completing their journey. The Homestead Haven faced a strip mall. The businesses sold a variety of items. One of the merchants sold betrayal, passion, lust and desire. His special of the day was "chicks on the side." Lenny purchased all of them. Another small establishment named "The Booty Call" boasted high priced items of Bigamy, Battery, and Broken Hearts and also offered Injured Body Parts at half price. Denise purchased two items and Lenny made a clean sweep walking out with everything. Subsequently, Lenny returned to that shop alone to buy another special of the day and was accosted by a female who was later captured. The charges against her were conspiracy, robbery, receiving stolen merchandise, negligence, reckless endangerment and fraud. The judge had to preside over the chicks on the side. While Lenny's body lay on a slab, one of these wenches continued to masquerade as his wife in drag with a phony marriage license in tow.

Close to a million dollars in insurance proceeds, a lifetime retirement **pension and social security benefits are at stake that Denise Garner refuses** to let a wench take—even though she had lived with Lenny for the past fourteen years.

MEET THE MAJOR PLAYERS

❦

Lenny Garner: He loved the fast life, namely wine, women and song. He ditched his first wife for Denise and became Denise's weak ass, willpower deficient, alcohol and cocaine addicted husband.

Denise Garner: Sophisticated, street smart, and classy, pursued the American dream by marrying the notorious Lenny. She fell head over heels in love with him—just like all the rest.

Noelle Garner: A beautiful mix of her Mommy and Daddy, Denise and Lenny. Their daughter was a troubled teen.

Carolyn Monroe: She was certainly a nurse who looked out for her purse, and her "G" spot. First on her agenda was having Lenny Garner—despite any obstacles, more specifically described as wives and children.

Zena: Lenny's favorite first cousin who blew the whistle on Carolyn Monroe's scheme.

Detective Adam Hartman: A gumshoe that knew. He is determined to nail Carolyn Monroe.

Dr. Relman: The medical examiner who had to answer to Mrs. Lenny Garner.

Theresa Roglich: Lenny's oldest sister who loved him dearly. She is the matriarch of the Garner family.

Tony Marino, Esquire: Denise's attorney who is hell bent on collecting the cash on her behalf.

Angela O'Neill Pelham, Esquire: She is the other half of Denise's legal defense team. This one is an expert on estates and taxes and her mission is to sew the pension board up and keep Denise in check.

Dale: Sexy, seductive, smitten and a soothing soul for Denise—midway through her failing marriage to Lenny. Dale is the star of the steamy chapters titled Shaky Ground, Closing the Door and Showing Up. That thrill is never gone.

Sit back, relax and watch this novel heat up all over the place. Denise Garner, the wifey-poo is gonna burn everybody. Let the court say Amen. Checkmate!

DEDICATION

∾

CONTENTS

∾

Out of Sight   1

The Refrigerator   23

The Chicago Surrender   41

Glitter   58

The Cemetery   77

Shaky Ground   97

Closing the Door   118

Showing Up   143

Devastation   163

The Decision   179

Two Smart Bitches   204

Relentless   223

The Mean Green   236

The Big Payback   250

Room Service   293

Epilogue   330

CHAPTER 1

⁓

Out of Sight

2006

Lenny Garner was a man with two wives
And many people were totally surprised
To find out that he lied and continued to reside
In a boat of sin which would eventually capsize

Denise Garner said "Where's the divorce?"
There must be a decree, of course
So she hunted and searched to find out his worth
While he waited patiently in the morgue

Now who would have thought that Lenny would do
This amazing caper in 2002
But he signed his name and now in 2006 Denise exclaimed
I'm the legal spouse and my benefits are due!

So now Lenny's almost done
And lying here next to the one
Who's come to his rescue and wrote this poem
So we all could have some fun

And wifey-poo Denise is not upset
And she'll get to the bottom of this mess
Not a stone will be left unturned as her husband stays firm
And believe me someone will get burned

As you know I'm a little celebrity
Writing a couple of books as best I could
You all need to know that this funeral will be a show
I'm sending this video tape to Hollywood

If you're someplace you're not supposed to be
Or don't want to be on TV
You'd better ease out the door or crawl on the floor
Because I'm marketing this on ABC

Now our boy Lenny is having some laughs
And those balls of his had to be brass
But one thing I'll say before I walk away
Is my husband is a pain in the ass

I couldn't believe he was dead! The turkey died on Thanksgiving Day. Damn! It was typical of that Negro to screw up my plans during a holiday season. He'd been doing it since the day I met him in 1977. It was my intention to read this hilarious poem at my husband's funeral. I wrote it especially for that occasion after getting the news of his passing. Yep, I was all geared up to have a *fun* funeral.

The man thrived on entertainment, booze and partying, and had done it all of his life, so my idea of a fitting and perfect sendoff was to surround him in his casket with liquor—miniature bottles of Hennessey. I also had Walt and Charlotte download CD's of his favorite music which included *Street Life, Flashlight, Love Overboard, Drop It Like It's Hot, Get Away, What's Going On, Does Anybody Really Know What Time It Is?, Always and Forever, Ain't No Stopping Us Now,* and a bunch of other tunes he loved. Music would be playing during the viewings and repast. I'd also planned to video the entire event. Each guest would be handed little bottles of booze when they arrived and signed the guest book. At the final viewing, just before we closed the casket, mourners could walk by, say good-bye, and put their bottle inside. When his pal Dickie Kendell, found out that I'd ordered three hundred bottles of the spirits for the casket, he said to me," that'll be enough to hold him until he gets where he is going."

But, no—his family wouldn't allow my wishes. They made me back off from all that. I was a bit too creative for them. I only gave in to them out of respect, but I was pissed. His relatives told me that his eighty-two year old Aunt Claudia would indeed have a heart attack and die right there inside the funeral parlor if she heard that poem. That was a whole heap of crap. She got drunk all the time with him. She worked in bars damn near all her life, and my husband was a frequent and faithful customer. He not only patronized her establishment, he was a community and *nationwide hanger outer* and bar owners loved to see him coming. Everybody knew he was no saint, *especially* his family members and I figured—let's be real. I pled my case, but the poem and the booze were eliminated.

It all started the Wednesday before Thanksgiving, 2006. I was having a lot of fun in New Brunswick, New Jersey, celebrating the holiday with my best buddy and test reader, Yolanda Rivers, and her family. I had made the decision to stay at the Hyatt for five days instead of at Yolanda's wonderful house in Somerset. If I had planned to stay with her, she'd be cleaning, food shopping, and doing everything she could to make me comfortable. She'd work herself to death and I wasn't in the mood to be a guest with manners who helped out. I wanted to do whatever I felt like doing, including nothing. Thanksgiving dinner was a scrumptious feast for twenty-three at Yolanda's cousin's house in South Brunswick. I was extremely comfortable with Eric and his wife. They lived in a lovely suburban home. It was the first time I had been in a house with a real movie theater. I was a Black American Princess who was not easily impressed, but Eric's home felt like paradise. After dinner we all sat around and told funny stories. There were some new faces in Yolanda's family that I had never met before, but they made me feel loved and welcome. The gathering reminded me of the times my husband and I were together. Unlike me, he came from a huge family who threw yearly family reunions and holiday get togethers. I actually missed my estranged husband's family more during our separation than I missed him.

My trip to Yolanda's was a well-deserved and refreshing getaway after an array of mishaps, episodes of bad luck, and arguments with my spoiled and ungrateful twenty-two year old daughter, Noelle. I'd purposely left her at home with her boyfriend, Vincent. Thank God he had an apartment in suburban Philadelphia, in opulent King of Prussia, Pennsylvania. Vincent had a college degree and was a mechanical engineer at a great firm. His family was good pedigree and resided in West Chester, another wealthy suburb of Philadelphia. He went to church every Sunday and was basically a nice guy with whom I felt Noelle was safe. Always respectful, he treated her well in the year they had been dating. During that holiday period, he was my babysitter, and Mommy was glad to be having some time away.

I was worn out. I had been through a mini-stroke and pulmonary embolism in my youth and had been plagued with a series of health problems over the past six years. The new year of 2001 started off with a bang, a near fatal automobile accident. I was rear ended on busy Rt. 309 and awakened in Abington Memorial Hospital with multiple injuries and a serious concussion. Noelle was in the car with me and also sustained a concussion as well as other injuries. During my six months recovery, I developed severe pneumonia which left me on a ventilator and in a coma for nine days. I had cheated death again—twice in the same year. Three years down a bumpy road of trying to make ends meet with a sick kid in college, I had cataract surgery that ended horribly. A series of eye infections prevented me from driving at night. The lenses caused me to develop halo problems when I encountered traffic lights and headlights from cars coming in the opposite directions.

In December of 2004, I was rear ended again, this time by an obnoxious drunk driver, sustaining injuries that required surgery to my right wrist. I had torn tendons and ligaments and needed months of physical and occupational therapy. I suffered with severe pain, not allowing me to write and sell a novel. I became terrified of cars and highway driving and was in treatment for months for that phobia. I still haven't recovered from that hang-up.

I had been through it all, and now 2006 was continuing to kick my butt. Everybody always teased me, saying, "Denise Garner, you're a hypochondriac who runs to the doctor for every little thing." I had to admit they were right. In late August, I had what I thought were symptoms of diabetes. I felt I was peeing too much, so I rushed to my doctor and demanded to be tested. It turned out to be nothing, which was usually the case.

In June, I'd finally sold my four bedroom, five bath single-family home that sat on three quarters of an acre of land. I was convinced I'd go broke trying to hold on to that house. I'd been in Elkins Park, an affluent suburb of Philadelphia, for nearly eleven years, and Noelle was now grown and almost never at home. This huge, wonderful fourteen room house was simply too big for the two of us. I was exhausted from finding money to pay people to fix everything from trees falling down or dying, to forking over large amounts of cash to utility companies. I was broke and living on a $1300 disability check from the automobile accident I'd been involved in.

I was a published author, but that was not bringing in the bucks. I was a single mom struggling to put her daughter through college without any help from my detached husband. Hubby Lenny discontinued child support when Noelle turned eighteen in 2002 even though she had been plagued with Crohn's Disease from the age of twelve and was in and out of the hospital. He was ten years older than me and had been enjoying a cozy life in Philadelphia with his girlfriend, Carolyn, since 1992. She was a registered nurse in the skilled nursing unit at Pennsylvania Hospital in downtown Philly. He was a plans examiner for the City of Philadelphia, Department of Licenses and Inspections. We split up fourteen years ago because he liked too much alcohol, preferably Hennessey straight up with water on the side along with a Heineken to chase it all down. In addition to his heavy drinking, Lenny also had a penchant for snorting cocaine and smoking marijuana as well as frequenting every hole in the wall bar and speakeasy in Philly. He'd go to *any* party *anywhere* and had a few extra marital affairs. His many vices were a bit too much and made me fall out of love, and eventually, break up with him. I was convinced that he'd never grow up.

After leaving Eric's house, Yolanda and I went back to her place, staying just long enough for her to pack a bag. She planned to stay at the Hyatt with me that night and watch some TV until we passed out. The next morning, we slept in and had a late breakfast, then spent the day shopping and browsing in downtown New Brunswick. We returned to the hotel around 5:00 p.m. and I decided that I needed a nap. So Yolanda made plans to pick up a friend, Diane, and bring her by the hotel to see me later that evening.

Sleep never came. When Yolanda left the hotel, I called my best buddy,

Zena Garner Tate, who lived in Washington, D.C. She was my husband's first cousin and we had been friends for about twenty-seven years and normally chatted a few times a day. I had been so busy that I hadn't called her since Tuesday night. It was the first time I had gone out of town without letting her know that I arrived safely and giving her a number where to reach me. She picked up on the first ring.

"Hey girl, what's up? I just got a chance to call you. I'm having a ball. How was Thanksgiving?"

"Hey. Are you calling because you got my message?" Zena wasn't her usual chipper self and that was strange to me. I detected something was wrong.

"What message?"

"I left a message for you on your home telephone. I thought that was why you're calling."

The tone of Zena's voice was now distressing to me. My antennas were up. "I don't know how to retrieve my home messages from another place. I haven't had time to talk to anybody. What's going on?"

"You need to come home. *Okay*. And you need to call Noelle."

I became alarmed and thought the worst. I always felt Noelle drove too damn fast and my psychic had told me that she'd be in a car wreck. I imagined her in a mangled car, closed my eyes, and shook my head. I stammered. "Has Noelle been in a car accident?"

Slowly, Zena said, *"No."* Then there was silence. When she didn't say another word, my stomach did a somersault and my gut sent my brain a message. "It's my husband, isn't it? Something happened to Lenny." I waited, hoping I was wrong.

"Yes."

"My husband's dead isn't he?"

"Yes."

I felt my body shutting down, my throat tightening as if I wasn't going to be able to breathe. But I snapped out of it. "What happened?"

"He was cooking Thanksgiving dinner yesterday and had a heart attack. I couldn't find you. I couldn't find your cell number. I was off from work today, but I was planning to go to my office to e-mail Yolanda so she could have you call me."

"I have to get off this phone. I have to find Noelle. I know she is with Vincent. I have to call there." My throat hurt as the words gushed out of my mouth.

"Look," Zena ordered, "don't tell her this on the phone."

"Of course I won't. I'll just tell her I am not feeling well, that I got sick up here and I'm coming home. I'll tell her I need her to pick me up from the train in Philly. I'm leaving tomorrow. Let me get off to call her."

"Well, okay, but Aunt Claudia wants you to call her. She needs to talk to you."

"Okay, but let me find my child first. I'll call you back."

My fingers shook as I dialed Noelle from my cell phone. No answer. I left a message for her to call me right away—it was urgent. Next, I called Vincent's number and left the same message. I recited every number where he could reach me. My heart pounded in my chest. Thoughts raced in my head. How was I going to handle Noelle? I couldn't tell her on the phone that her Dad had died. I needed to find another way. That girl was a Leo. She was not to be ordered around and followed her own will. I would try to get her to meet me someplace and break the news to her. Just thinking about dealing with Noelle made my blood pressure rise, so I concentrated on calling Aunt Claudia, Lenny's aunt, who lived in Philadelphia.

"Aunt Claudia, it's Denise. I just talked to Zena. What happened?"

"All I know is that he was cooking dinner and had a heart attack. The paramedics came and he was dead. That's all I know. Look, Theresa wants you to call her. I'm going to give you her number. Denise, try to work with her. Try to get along. That *is* Lenny's sister and she is upset. You know they just buried his brother Dennis last weekend."

Just the mention of Theresa's name had me reeling fourteen years back when we fell out.

"Listen, Aunt Claudia, I am very upset, too. I've tried to call Noelle and I can't find her right now. I left messages for her and Vincent to call me. I'm coming home. I'll call Theresa and I'll be good with her. Also, let me take a minute to tell you I know how bad you must feel. I know Lenny was your buddy. I am so sorry. I have to go. I'll call you later. I'm gonna call Theresa right now."

Before I could dial her number, I had to give myself therapy on being nice to her. I took a deep breath, hoped for the best, and pressed the phone to my ear.

"Theresa—it's Denise. How are you?"

Theresa asked, "This is Denise Greene Garner?"

"Yes, Theresa." I was wondering why she was being so technical addressing me as *Denise Greene Garner*. I immediately wanted to curse her out. I'd been pissed with her ass for years because she had taken Lenny's side when we separated and ignored her niece the entire time. But I decided not to put on my boxing gloves just so soon.

"Well, my brother passed away," she said.

"Yeah, well, I am trying to find Noelle."

"What do you mean *trying to find her*?"

"Here we go," I thought to myself. I knew it wouldn't be long before I'd be charged with being an unfit mother or something wretched. "Well, she's with her boyfriend in King of Prussia and I cannot find her. I've left messages on their cell phones. I'll be home tomorrow and will tell her then. I'll take care of things when I get home."

"Well, you don't have to worry about anything. We can do the funeral and all. I just wanted to make sure you knew," she said.

A hot sensation spread throughout my body. My blood rose from my feet to my brain.

"What do you mean *I don't have to do anything?* I'm his *wife*. I have to get the body."

"Well, *I* have the insurance policy. *I'm* in charge. You and Lenny never divorced?"

She was warming me up well for a fight. I screamed, "Divorced! No, we never *divorced*. I'm still married to Lenny. Where's the body?"

"I don't know."

"Oh, you are in *charge* and you don't know where the *body* is? Good-bye." I hung up.

At that point, I was enraged and furiously called Carolyn, Lenny's live-in girlfriend. No answer, but I still left the heifer a message. "Carolyn, this is Lenny's *wife*. I've heard the news about my *husband's* death. Here are my numbers. You can call me if you like. I can imagine you may not want to talk to me, but if you do, you can call me. I am out of town, but I am returning home tomorrow to take care of things. I *know* I'll have to take care of things."

After I hung up the phone, I leaned back and let my body sink into the comfort of the bed. I looked up at the ceiling, then closed my eyes as I tried to make sense of how I was going to deal with all of these characters. They hadn't been in my life for years—including my dead husband. If I'd never needed a cigarette before, I needed one now. I flung myself from the bed and called Yolanda's house.

Dammit it was a tape again! I left a detailed message about Lenny's death, then tried her cell. She answered.

"I'm upset. Something has happened and I need some cigarettes. I know I stopped smoking, but I need some cigarettes. You listen to your home tape and call me back. I have to go out for cigarettes. Call me back on the hotel phone."

Before she could answer, I slammed the phone down, grabbed some money from my purse and dashed out. I got on the elevator and ran down to the gift shop. I purchased some Newports, ran through the lobby, and, by the time I hit the driveway, I was already taking my first drag. I marched up and down the front of the hotel inhaling deeply as I kept watch on my cell phone, hoping for a call from either my daughter or the live-in wench. Neither responded. I was impatient, frantic. If I'd waited one more minute, I'd be the one having a heart attack. So, I called both Vincent and Noelle again and left the same message. *Where the hell were they?* When I returned to the room, the hotel phone was ringing. I could tell by Yolanda's voice that she was worried about me, but I reassured her that I was in control. I'm not sure she believed me. In any case, she was on her way to the hotel.

While waiting, I started to think about my own family. I called my brother Jeff. He lived in Ohio, but was in Philly visiting our relatives for the holiday. "Listen Jeff, Lenny is dead!" He was stunned and started asking a million questions. I explained what happened and that I was pissed because Theresa wouldn't tell me where the body was. That didn't matter, I told him. I was going to the City Morgue on Monday. After I got off the phone with my brother, the silence was driving me crazy. I had to talk to someone, so I called Zena back to inform her that I hadn't found Noelle yet or my husband's body. Then I called Aunt Claudia again. "Aunt Claudia, I was nice to Theresa but it did not go well. You know what she told me? That she's is in charge! That's *my* husband and she didn't tell me where the body is."

"Look, Denise, you and him haven't been together for a long time. Just let them handle everything. You know Lenny and Carolyn have been together for a long time. Now, look, you're gonna get his pension and a six thousand dollar insurance policy—just take the money. Don't let this get out of hand. Let Carolyn have the body."

From the way she clearly pronounced her words, I could tell that Aunt Claudia wasn't about to take my side.

"Aunt Claudia, where is his body?" I shouted.

"I don't know. All I know is that the rescue squad went to their house."

"I'll find him!" I swore and hung up the phone. I called Philadelphia City Hall and asked for the morgue. Lenny's body was not there. Then I called the Hospital of the University of Pennsylvania. They had no record of him being there or in their morgue either. This was driving me crazy. Everyone knew Lenny was dead, but no one had the slightest idea where the body was. I was aching for another cigarette. I couldn't smoke in the hotel room. It was a nonsmoking room and Yolanda was coming. She had asthma. I was an absolute nervous wreck. Next I called Pennsylvania Hospital where Carolyn worked thinking she may have taken him there. They had no information on him either. Next was Presbyterian Hospital and, again, I had no luck with them. My phone rang, and finally, it was Noelle.

I had to get this right, so I collected myself and said softly, "Hi, Noelle. I'm not feeling well. My leg hurts and I'm coming down with a cold. I'm coming home early. I need you to pick me up from the train in Philly tomorrow afternoon. I need help with my stuff. I'll let you know what time the train comes in when I check the schedule. I'm really sick. Will you meet me?"

"Are you really sick or are you tricking me?"

"Here we go," I thought. I could feel my plan was already dead in the water, so I told the first lie of the evening, hoping it would buy me some compassion. "I'm sick. Uncle Jeff offered to come, but he has a lot of stuff to do."

"Well, I'm sick, too," she said in a smart-alecky manner.

"Where are you now?"

"I'm in the movies."

"Well, you're not so *sick*. I'll tell you what, you be at that train station."

"I'm not coming."

"If you don't, you'd better be at our house when I get there!" I screamed.

"You're trying to start a fight with me. I'm hanging up."

"Don't you hang up!" I shouted.

"You're stressing me out, Mom, I am hanging up."

I blurted, "Don't hang up! Your Dad is dead! He died yesterday. He had a heart attack. I didn't want to tell you on the phone. That's why I was trying to get you to meet me. I am so sorry." Noelle was silent and then started crying hysterically. I tried to comfort her and whispered, "I am so sorry, Noelle. I just found out late this afternoon from Aunt Zena." Noelle's sobs increased and I couldn't calm her. I yelled, "Put Vincent on the phone!" Noelle continued screaming and I hung up. I waited five minutes, then called her back. There was no answer. I gave up, figuring Vincent could take care of her until I got back to Philadelphia.

I was still shaken up by that call, but, as crazy as it was, I needed to find my husband's dead body. Next I called the City of Philadelphia main number and asked to be connected to the police department for 8319 Union Avenue in Philadelphia. That was the 12th District and covered Carolyn and Lenny's neighborhood. I gave them Lenny's name and address and asked if they had responded to a call on Thanksgiving Day for him. They checked and found no record of any officer or paramedic going to that address. Now I was baffled and frantic. Where the *hell* could he be? A knock on the hotel room door pulled me from my thoughts. It was Yolanda and Diane with Yolanda's three month old Grandson, Xavier in tow. I adored that baby and had adopted him as my grandson. He was so cute and I knew Yolanda had brought him to cheer me up. As soon as she walked in, I reached for the baby and began to unbundle him and kiss his forehead. I hugged Diane and said, "You guys need to know they have hidden Lenny's damn body somewhere. I've called every damn place and I cannot find his dead ass. When I get home, I'm going looking for him on Monday. That damn Carolyn! I know she is behind this shit and Theresa is in it with her. I am pissed. Noelle is a wreck. I can't even talk to her. She's screaming in the movies with Vincent. I cannot believe this shit!"

Yolanda and Diane listened to more of the story and then asked questions. Yolanda still couldn't believe that all this body missing shit had gone down since leaving me that afternoon. They advised me of my rights as Lenny's legal wife. I continued playing with the baby as I took in their advice. He was soothing me. I was chatting, changing his diaper and babbling on about him. Then, like a bitch on a mission, I'd switch back to the Lenny predicament and rant about threatening to have Theresa and Carolyn's asses locked up when I got home and got my business straight. Diane and Yolanda were staring at me and shaking their heads. "Let's order a pizza," Yolanda suddenly interjected to change the subject.

She sifted through the menus that we had brought back with us earlier. "I'm not hungry. Get whatever you want and I'll pay for it," I said. They ordered a pizza for delivery. Another nicotine fit took hold of me. "I have to go out and smoke a cigarette. I'll be back. Here, hold my baby till I get back." I handed Xavier to Yolanda.

"I need one, too. I'm going with you," Diane chimed in.

Yolanda hurried to catch up with us and said, the baby propped on her hip, "I'll go down with you guys."

On the elevator, I growled, "That damn Carolyn. You know, I would have let her have his body. I really would have. You know—since they were together so long. Me and Lenny were okay. We made up long ago. I'd just talked to him at the end of July when Zena and David came to Philly from D.C. for a weekend visit. Zena and I were having breakfast at the West Avenue Grill in Jenkintown when her husband David called her to say he was with Lenny. Lenny talked to Zena but wanted to speak to me, too. He had dreamed about me the night before. We were fighting on a school bus. He said it was so funny.

The memory of that conversation suddenly filled me with deep sadness. He insisted that I call him back with my new address in Jenkintown. An hour after we hung up, David called, rushing us to come to his father's house. Fifteen minutes later, David called again and wanted to know what was taking us so long. When we finally arrived, I dropped Zena off. I had a lot of errands to run that day and didn't have time to go in. As I drove off, my phone rang and it was Zena. I found out why David had been **impatient for our return. Lenny had been waiting for me.**

Yolanda and Diane wanted to say something to me, but words never came to either of them. Instead, Yolanda rubbed my shoulder and Diane attempted a smile. Even the baby was silent. I hadn't turned back because I had errands to run and was tired. I mailed Lenny some great pictures of Noelle's head shots in September and an invitation to my birthday party in October so he could see her. I never heard back from him. That was strange because he had made it a point of asking me to send him my new address and to call him. They were beautiful flicks of her. She resembled a movie star—a Black Ava Gardner. I also included a photo of her and Vincent along with a nice note. It wasn't like Lenny to miss a party, especially at a restaurant where there was food and liquor. He hadn't seen Noelle in such a long time and knew she would be at the party.

Much later, Zena and I talked about Lenny never acknowledging that he had received the pictures and invitation. Zena figured Carolyn had gotten the stuff out of the mail and had never given it to him. I had even called him twice, leaving messages on his home phone to call me. I never heard a word from him. Now his ass was dead. Damn! I couldn't believe it.

We all got off the elevator and Diane and I hurried outside. Yolanda stayed in the lobby with the baby. We smoked in silence, Diane keeping an eye on me while I paced the front of the hotel. I rushed through the cigarette and hurried back up to the room alone. Yolanda and Diane waited for the pizza man. When they returned, I was sitting on the bed. The smell of the pizza didn't increase my appetite. I still didn't want to eat a thing and craved yet another cigarette. In a few minutes in came Danielle and Brian, the baby's parents. They hugged me and gave me their condolences. The atmosphere in the room lightened and we all laughed, talked, and played with the baby. I enjoyed being surrounded by my friends, but I was anxious to get back home. As everyone prepared to leave, Yolanda asked if she should spend the night with me, but it was nearly eleven o'clock at night and I opted to stay alone at the Hyatt.

As soon as Yolanda and the gang left, the hotel phone rang. It was my brother Jeff. "Hold on," he said. My cousin Lynne got on the phone. Lynne Melman Coney was a budget analyst for the Federal Government for thirty years. She was smart as a whip. We hadn't talked to each other for a long time. "Hey," Lynne said, "how you doing, girl?"

"I'm okay. I answered.

"I heard about Lenny. I'm sorry. I know you plan to see about all this stuff on Monday. Jeff told me what's happening about the body. Listen girl, Monday is not good enough. You *listen* to me. You get yourself together. If you are tired, you wake the fuck up right now! You get on the phone and you *find his damn body* as quickly as you can. You cannot let *Carolyn* or anybody else get hold of a death certificate. A death certificate is *power*. By

Monday, she will have that and have his ass *buried*. Lenny has a pension and other stuff. I'll explain all about that later. For right now, you find his ass and tell the people who have him to stay put until you get there. Carolyn could have his ass moved somewhere *tonight!* My take is since he just died last night, they are still running tests on him. A lot of people were off today for Black Friday. You get moving and call me back."

When we hung up, I felt like a doe caught in headlights. Lynne's comments added to my confusion. What the hell was going on! I just wanted my dead husband's body on *Monday.* That's the start of the business week. For Christ's sake, I was in New Brunswick, what could I do from here? Fighting off another deadly cigarette craving, I sat down and put my face in my hands. I didn't know where to start. I called back to the morgue in Philadelphia and asked them to check again. No Lenny Garner. I tried to figure out whose number I had that worked for the City of Philadelphia. I came up with Liz Edwards, a buddy of mine who was a court reporter. I called her immediately. "Liz, listen. Lenny dropped dead of a heart attack last night. I got the news early this evening. I'm out of town in New Brunswick with Yolanda. I've been looking all over for his body and can't find it." I went on to list all the places I had checked. Gasping, Liz was stunned to hear the news. She finally asked, "Where did he die?"

"Well, his aunt said paramedics came to his house and he died there."

"Okay—well, you know he may be at Mercy Fitzgerald Hospital. That's close to his house. Check out there."

"I have no number. Can you get the number and call me back? Here, take my number here at the hotel and my cell, too. I gotta pee." I sat on the toilet thinking about Lenny dying. I envisioned him holding his chest. I thought about him preparing a turkey and washing collard greens and making dressing. He loved to cook and *had* to cook living with Carolyn. He would have been dead a long time ago if she was in charge of the food. He had told me many stories about how bad a cook she was. Even Noelle said Carolyn was lethal with a pot and a pan, but she could make an apple pie. She had stayed three weeks with them one summer when I was sick of her acting like a crazy teenager. I was mad as hell at Carolyn because I figured if the bitch had known how to cook, maybe Lenny wouldn't have had a fucking heart attack trying to make the damn dinner all by himself. I was raging! I thought about Noelle not having a father to walk her down the aisle when she got married, our grandchildren not having a Grandpop.

The hotel phone rang interrupting my mental rant. It was Liz with the number for Mercy Fitzgerald Hospital. I quickly dialed the number and let it ring and ring. No answer. "No answer at a fucking hospital!" I shouted. "Where are these damn people?" I hung up and dialed back, thinking I called the wrong number. No answer again. "Shit," I said lighting a cigarette. At that point, I did not give a hoot if I was in a non-smoking room. I had no ashtray and was looking for one. I spotted an almost empty juice bottle and grabbed it off the hotel table. I called Liz back and we talked. "Look, I don't know what's going on. My cousin is frantic, talking to me about death certificates and stuff. Why does everything have to be done so fast?"

"Well, you know Lenny was in the *DROP program*. I know that from talking to him in the bar."

"What the hell is a *DROP program*?"

"That's a city retirement program wherein an employee voluntarily drops out from working, taking an early retirement. It means he got a lump sum of money to retire and a monthly pension for the rest of his life. It's the Deferred Retirement Option Plan. We call it *DROP*. If he was living with Carolyn at the time of his death and she has a death certificate, being common law and all, she could get *all* that money."

"How much money?" I asked.

"Well, depending on his income, it could be a lot—like over a hundred thousand dollars. Did you get any money when he retired?"

"No. I'm not entitled to any pension money unless I divorce him. At least that's what I thought."

"Well, I don't know all of the rules for married people because I'm not married. I'll find out some stuff on it for you on Monday. I'll also have some phone numbers for you to call. Damn, I can't believe Lenny is dead," Liz said.

"Well, he just came home from Myrtle Beach, South Carolina. He buried his brother Dennis there last weekend."

"What! Damn. Humph. What happened to him?"

"I don't know. He was much younger than Lenny. Lenny is 63. Dennis had some disease, was sick all the time. Something was wrong with one of his organs or something. He was on a lot of medication and he drank a lot of booze. Listen Liz, I gotta run. I'll call you back. Thanks, girl, for everything. Shit. It's damn near two o'clock in the morning. I wonder where Lenny's dead ass is. I'm gonna kill him all over again when I find him. And you know what? If that bitch tries to bury my damn husband real quick and succeeds, I'll have his ass dug up and buried in my backyard. I swear I will. A piece of paper holds a lot of weight."

I hung up and could still hear Liz laughing in my head. My next call was to the police station near Lenny and Carolyn's house. I told the story again, but they had no record of paramedics going from their precinct to get Lenny—dead or alive. I called back to the City Morgue. I was crying and telling the person on the end of the receiver that I could not find my husband's dead body *anywhere*. The gentleman gave me a number that tracks all 911 calls placed from Philadelphia. From there, I was able to find out that Lenny was taken to Mercy Fitzgerald Hospital. That hospital was across the city line and not in Philadelphia. It was in Darby, Pennsylvania in Delaware County. When I tried Mercy Fitzgerald again, they answered the phone this time.

I started in the Emergency Room and was switched to the morgue. From there, I got a supervisor. I explained everything all over again to a woman who said she would have to pull a file and get back to me. She returned my call as promised and took some information. She directed me to another supervisor. I finally got Erin, a medical investigator at the morgue familiar with the file and my husband's dead body. After I explained who I was, Erin informed me that Lenny had been brought in by his wife and granddaughter. I explained again that I was his wife and that Lenny had no granddaughter. Suspect, Erin began to ask me a series of questions about my mother and father-in-law, Lenny's medications, where he was born, where he worked, his Social Security number, and where he resided. She talked to me about Carolyn and I explained that Lenny had been living with her for fourteen years. She also noted on the file that Theresa Roglich was listed as being *next to kin*. Erin was puzzled as to why a *wife*, Carolyn, was listing Theresa as next to kin. She explained that the state of Pennsylvania did not recognize common-law marriages. We talked for a long time and, afterward, she believed I had never divorced Lenny. I didn't know all the medications he was on, but I did know he was taking blood pressure medication and drank heavily. She told me they would run tests on him to find out *everything* that was in his system at the time of his death. I offered to provide her with my marriage license, but she said that it was not necessary. They had another way of checking to make sure I was his wife. They stopped requesting or allowing marriage licenses because, on a prior case, four women had come to claim a body and all of them had marriage licenses. Erin also shared with me that I should contact the Julian Hawkins Funeral Home and gave me a number to call Mr. Hawkins. Carolyn had made arrangements for them to pick up his body. I had to tell them that I had spoken with Erin and that they should not come as scheduled. It was then 3:30 in the morning and she suggested that I wait until 9:00 a.m. to call the funeral home. I agreed, thanked her and hung up.

I couldn't sleep, my mind was too unsettled. I must have checked my watch one hundred times. By six o'clock in the morning, I could not wait any longer and decided to call the funeral director. I explained the situation and advised him not to pick up Lenny's body. Half an hour later, he phoned me back to say he had spoken to Carolyn and she wanted *her* instructions carried out. As planned, he said he intended to go for the body. My voice became stern and I ordered him not go near that body. If he did, there would be trouble in the form of lawyers. I reiterated that I was the legal wife. At the mention of lawyers, Mr. Hawkins changed his mind. I was relieved.

At seven o'clock, I was in the shower and at eight I was packing. By nine, I was back on the phone with the morgue. Erin had finished her shift, so I had to deal with a new person. Thank God he was familiar with the situation, probably having been briefed by Erin. I needed to fax him some identification for his records. All I had was my driver's license and MasterCard, the first registered in *Greene,* and the latter with Garner inscribed on it. I ran down to the hotel lobby and had both copied. I wrote a note requesting the morgue to hold the body and faxed the documents. When Yolanda walked in the door at nine forty-five, I was ready for breakfast. As soon as she looked at me, I sighed and confessed, "I've been up all night."

We chatted as we sipped coffee and juice. I messed over home fries, toast, and fresh fruit. I was antsy, knowing damn well I'd never find my marriage license in all my papers. I would indeed end up at City Hall first thing Monday morning to request a copy. In the meantime, my plan was to go to the morgue as soon as I dropped my luggage off at home. Yolanda and I got my bags together, ordered a bellman, and headed for checkout.

When settling the bill, I was hit with telephone charges in the amount of four hundred and three dollars! It was for calls made after receiving the news of Lenny's death. Prior to that, I had only been on my cell phone since check-in. Unbelievable! I looked at the gentleman's name tag behind the counter. "Gary, I really cannot pay all these charges. This is ridiculous. This is *too* much money for phone calls. As you know, my husband passed away and this is why I'm checking out a day early. As you see from my records, I didn't begin using my hotel phone until after I got the news of my husband's death, which occurred on Thanksgiving Day. Please ask your supervisor if he could reduce the charges. It was due to an emergency that I had made all these calls."

Gary looked at me sympathetically and conferred with his female co-worker. When he returned, he offered to lower the phone bill to $127.00. I thanked him, he gave me his condolences, and Yolanda and I left. I boarded the train to Philadelphia.

Once I got on the train, the most interesting thing happened to me. Ironically, I was sitting in front of two Black guys listening to them talk about their jobs. The more I spied their conversation, I kept hearing the word *drop*. Finally, I turned around and asked if they were Philly City Workers. They were friendly and answered, "yes."

We talked all the way to Philadelphia and they gave me much information. We exchanged numbers, too. They told me to get that marriage certificate early Monday morning and go to the City of Philadelphia Pension Board. They named a few other places to check out, too. The last thing they said to me was not to let anyone get a death certificate. The chance of our meeting was overwhelming for me. I could not believe that those two guys were on that train at the same time as me—God's work and certainly no coincidence.

When I got back home, everything was in an uproar with Noelle. Her condition had deteriorated since our last conversation. Her Crohn's Disease was acting up and she was scheduled to get an infusion the next day. After many years of being on the same medication, her body was not completely responding to treatment. She wasn't feeling well and was staying with her boyfriend.

When I had her on the phone, my maternal instincts sensed she was depressed and that the stress from the news of her father's death inevitably led to a flare up of the disease. She only admitted to me that her stomach hurt and she was upset about her father. But after everything she had gone through with the disease, it had to be much worse. I wanted to run over to Vincent's place to be with her, but I knew my daughter. Time and space was what she needed. I was scared to death, but I decided to stay put.

I called the Delaware County morgue three more times and left messages. Someone finally returned my call and told me that it wasn't necessary to rush out there. I could wait until Monday to pick up the body. They assured me they would not release the body to anyone other than me. I was glad because I was exhausted. The rest of the day was spent telling the story and getting advice from people. My cousin Lynne and her husband, Jerome, stayed on the phone with me the longest on Saturday evening. Jerome Coney was also a former city worker and had retired under the *DROP Program*. He was a wealth of information. He taught me everything I needed to learn about the *DROP Program,* death certificates, and city benefits—things very foreign to me. I still hadn't heard a word from Lenny's sister Theresa. After that conversation, I called the Pension Board even though it was Saturday night. I left messages for three people alerting them that Carolyn Monroe was pretending to be Mrs. Lenny Garner and that Mr. Lenny Garner had passed away on Thanksgiving Day. I added that *I* was his *wife* and would call again on Monday morning to discuss my situation further. I imagined each one of their faces on Monday after hearing my message. I sat back and howled.

The following night, much was on my mind with Noelle and her Dad's death. I was bushed from gathering information, unpacking, and the entire whirlwind from the last three days. I took an Ambien and passed out. Monday was going to be a very busy day and I needed a good night's rest.

Before I left my house the next morning, I called the morgue where Lenny's body was. I was on my way to City Hall for my marriage certificate, but they informed me that they had received one over the weekend from Carolyn Monroe. Lenny and Carolyn married on June 22, 2002! I was in a state of shock! How could he have married that wench when he had never divorced me?

I hauled ass to City Hall and found my marriage certificate on the computer from 1986. Bingo! They tried to get me a copy from the physical file and the entire file was missing. Nowhere to be found. Hunted and hunted. Nothing. They couldn't understand where it was. I swore they had paid somebody a couple of dollars to *lose* that file. I then requested my husband's marriage certificate. Lenny and Carolyn had filled out the application *together* at City Hall on June 3, 2002 to get married. Lenny indicated on the application that he had *never* been married to anyone. Humph. Lenny was married prior to meeting me and divorced after we hooked up. He knew Carolyn about ten years prior to meeting me. Lenny could have been messing around with her when he was married to his first wife. The first wife hated her. Carolyn and Lenny got married in some church in Philly and kept it a secret from his family. It was probably kept a secret so I would not find out. If Lenny and I had divorced, I would have been able to go after the DROP money and pension. If I stayed married to him, the money would be his. If he had dropped me from his medical coverage, I would have found out, filed for divorce to get on the COBRA plan for medical insurance, and attacked the pension, too. That would have affected the DROP lump sum payment to him and his monthly retirement checks. So, they kept the shit quiet. Based on his yearly salary, he was eligible to get about $131,000 from the *DROP Program* as a lump sum payment.

Could Lenny have divorced me without my knowing it? Okay, I had to think quickly. I·knew some shit was going down, so I went to another department that handled divorce decrees. A thorough check was done in 67 counties. No divorce decree ever came up. There had been a divorce complaint filed by me years ago in 1992, but Lenny and I stopped that action and just let it go. After hours of searching, a copy of my marriage license was found in the City file containing my Divorce Complaint. The department gave me two documents with Court seals stating that I had never been divorced and faxed a set of the documents to the medical **examiner holding Lenny's body**.

The Delaware County morgue received everything. As far as I knew, Carolyn never gave the morgue a divorce decree, just her marriage license. This blew their minds. The case was just too big for the morgue's office, and now, they were sending all of our documents over to the Chief Register of Wills in Delaware County to be reviewed. He would make a decision as to who was the legal wife.

After all that drama at City Hall, next was the Pension Board. After I explained my whole story to the clerk, I handed her my marriage license. She wasn't alarmed because Carolyn had never applied for Lenny's pension thus far. Since another wife popped up, the Pension Board decided to have a meeting to discuss it. They planned on sending me papers to fill out requesting documents. The pension board had not known of Lenny's death until I reported it. A pension check would be generated to go to Lenny in three days. No plans were made to stop the release of that check, but they were sending a letter to Lenny's residence stating that checks would be stopped after that. They had to do it that way until they received a death certificate. They informed me that Lenny had picked Option J on his pension, which gave benefits to the spouse after his death for the rest of the spouse's life. He did not indicate a spouse's name. Just checked off *spouse.* If his spouse died after him, I discovered, the benefits would go to a minor child or an adult child with a disability.

I was on a roll! I was *Mrs. Lenny Garner.* My next stop was District Council 33, the Health Insurance Department. I notified them of Lenny's Death and they changed things around to make sure health cards and things like that would come directly to me. I was listed as the wife and was on the insurance until 2009, after which I would move to COBRA. That department had never been informed of Lenny's remarriage or his death.

Next, I went to the post office and had Lenny's mail rerouted to my house. I wasn't leaving anything to chance. I didn't trust that Bitch.

From there, I headed to Social Security Administration and reported Lenny's death. They gave me an appointment to return on the sixth of December with a long list of documents. To show proof that I was Lenny's wife, I had to show my marriage certificate. If I filed at age 60, my benefit would be $944 and $1322 if I filed at 66 or if I were disabled and unemployed. As a widow, I was entitled to an immediate $250 from them.

After all this running around, I spoke to my attorney, Tony Marino. Tony was my former employer and had handled several personal injury cases for me. We had become good friends over the years and if anybody needed to know this shit—it was Tony. He wanted to meet to discuss the matter after I got the *body* stuff straight along with all the other business. The Medical Examiner wouldn't release the body for burial until the legal wife was determined and they heard back from the Chief Register of Wills in

Delaware County. Tony would represent me regarding Lenny's estate until I formally hired an estate attorney. If Lenny had a will, I would have to get a percentage of his assets. I had no idea if there was a will, but I anticipated there wasn't one because my husband was always too busy partying.

I believed Carolyn committed fraud on the marriage application. She indicated that Lenny had no other wives to her knowledge. I could prove her dishonesty. In 1992, Carolyn filed a lawsuit against me, Denise *Garner*. She was trying to obtain $50,000 from me after Lenny moved in with her. She filed the suit for harassment, that I had been calling her house and some other stupid shit. She later dropped it, but the Court kept the records. She was well aware of my marital status because my medical insurance cards were being mailed to her house for years, as Lenny was the subscriber. In the end, she would be burned at the stake.

While I was trying to play Columbo, people, Lenny's friends and family members from all over were ringing the phone off the hook wanting to know the funeral arrangements. They got my phone numbers from Theresa who had become super tight with Carolyn. I simply told everyone the same thing, that I couldn't deal with the funeral at the time because Noelle's Crohn's was in a flare-up and I had to get her infused and healthy again. It came as a surprise to many people, but it wouldn't be for a couple of weeks before I could work on the funeral. I still hadn't talked to Theresa since my return to Philly. She was just as hard-headed as I was and had not called me either since informing me that she was in charge and had a policy.

This thing played like a saga. People were blown away at City Hall and other departments that my dead husband was leading a double life. The Medical Examiner's office confirmed that they were getting a zillion calls on the case of the two wives. People wanted to know when the funeral was. Erin, the investigator for the Delaware County Medical Examiner, and I talked late last night. She believed I was not lying, but procedure was **that the Register of Wills had to get this case. She said that Theresa kept** calling to find out when the body could be released to plan a funeral. At that point, I had not heard from the team of Dumb and Dumber (Theresa and Carolyn) because that was certainly who they were to me. As smart as I was, *I* would end up with his dead body. He was *my* husband, dammit, and after everything he had put me through, in the end, I'd be the chick in charge.

CHAPTER 2

◌

The Refrigerator

Lenny and I had met in the beginning of December 1977 when I was tending bar at a club. I was twenty-four. He was ten years older. At the time, I was seeing an entertainment writer who wrote a column in the Philadelphia Inquirer, a major local newspaper. Alfred Thompson was truly smitten by my pretty face, gregarious personality, and size four tall lanky body. We had met one night when some friends and I were out clubbing. I was unemployed at that time, had very little money, and too much time on my hands. Fearing that he would lose me, Alfred asked a friend of his to give me a job at a club he managed in the Cedarbrook Mall in Wyncote, Pennsylvania.

The very night I started the job, Lenny Garner was on the dance floor doing his thing to the tune *Back in Love Again.* When the record was over, he eased down on the bar stool and checked me out. He liked what he saw behind the bar. "You're pretty cute," he said.

"Hello sir. I'm Denise, what would you like to have?"

"You—on the rocks." Lenny seductively replied.

He was light complected with a beard. I really liked that beard. He had a very small mouth. He was wearing a green knit pullover sweater and a pair of tan corduroy pants. I noticed he had jewelry around his neck, a gold chain with a vertical pendant on the end. On one side of the pendant was an *L* and on the other end were the rest of the letters in his name.

I had an instant attraction to him. "I have someone on ice already, baby. What's your second choice?"

"I don't take seconds," he answered.

I strolled away and waited on another customer. Lenny summoned me when I finished the order and said, "Remy Martin straight up—water on the side."

Once I set the drinks down, Lenny reached into his wallet and handed me a business card. "This is in case you want to melt some ice elsewhere. You can stop in my camera shop some time and I'll take you to lunch in a crowded restaurant where you'll have plenty of protection."

I looked at the card that read *Comet Camera Repair, 1211 Arch Street, Philadelphia, PA.* and placed it into my tip glass. I noticed Mike, my manager, staring at me. He called me over. "Denise, look, baby, this is your first bartending job. Dudes are going to be coming at you from all directions. You've got to be able to handle this. Now, you know I have to look out for you for my man, Alfred. He's my best friend. Don't you get caught up in here. Alfred is in love with you. I know that."

"I'm okay, Mike. I can handle this. I really dig Alfred, too."

"Okay," Mike said as he eyed Lenny suspiciously.

Lenny showed up at the club the next three nights after work, continuing to flirt with me.

A week later, on a freezing afternoon in early December, I was standing on the sidewalk between 11th and 12th and Chestnut Streets in downtown Philadelphia. Without looking, I stepped into the street to cross. A public bus came toward me and halted, just missing me. I screamed. I was petrified. I stepped back onto the sidewalk, nervous and shaking. I ran to the corner and leaned against a building. I closed my eyes, envisioning what could have happened. I could have been killed. I started walking toward Market Street, passed it by and ended up on Arch Street. Lenny's business card suddenly came to mind. I remembered he worked at 12th and Arch. I looked down the street and spotted his store. I rushed in.

"Is Lenny here?" I asked the clerk. I looked around and noticed a row of seats. I sat down and buried my face in my hands.

Lenny came to the counter and saw me sitting there. "Denise?" he said, thoroughly surprised to see me. He looked up, could see I was crying, and **rushed over to me**.

"What's the matter? Why didn't you call me to say you were coming by?" he asked.

"I'm so upset. I came down here to get my daughter some clothes from Wanamaker's Department Store and I almost got hit by a bus. I was so scared. It just missed me."

He seemed very concerned. "Look, stay right here. I'm going to leave and take you to lunch. I'll be right back."

We went to the Reading Terminal and had platters of silver trout, french fries, and string beans. We sipped on lemonade and talked. I found him amusing, soothing and gentle.

"What's the story with you?" I asked.

"I'm a nice guy. I've been unhappily married for a hundred years. I party and all that stuff. I just live my life. Wanna hang out sometime?"

His smile was devilish.

"No, I can't do that. I'm seeing somebody and it's pretty serious. We may get married. He's talked to me about that. I've got to be cool. I do thank you for being so close—I mean being able to rescue me today."

Lenny shook his head. "And another one bites the dust. Damn shame. Hope you make out better than me with the marriage thing. So, you have a daughter?" he asked.

"Yeah, Natasha. She's in kindergarten. A few blocks from my Mom's house. She likes to sing. She's a Chaka Khan fan. She's five years old. You have any kids?"

"Yeah, I have a daughter who is twelve and lives in New York with her Mom. I have a son—well—my *wife* has a son who is sixteen and I adopted him when we got married. He lives in Myrtle Beach with his grandmother, my wife's Mom."

"You and your wife don't have any kids together?"

"No."

"How long have you been married?

"Twelve years."

"Wow—long time."

"Yep. She does her thing—I do mine. Look, I've got to get back to my shop. Do you want to wait there? I'll take you home. We close at five. It's three-thirty now."

I was silent. I was thinking, testing my curiosity, my loyalty to Alfred, my good manners and scruples. "Well, I have to work at the club tonight. My plan was to do some shopping for Natasha and head straight to work. I'm okay. I'll run by Wanamaker's, get some stuff, then catch the buses back up to Mt. Airy."

"Look, haven't you had enough of the buses today? Do a little shopping and meet me back at my shop. I take the train in every day. We'll get the train together. My car is parked at the Sedgwick train station. I'll drop you off at work."

I hesitated, took a breath or the *plunge* and I looked at him. "Okay, let's get out of here and I'll meet you at five."

✳ ✳ ✳

"Hey, Mike. I'm here. I'm a little early," I yelled as Lenny and I entered the club and sat down at the bar.

Mike looked at me in disapproval. "Hi," he said to both of us. He went through the large silver doors to the kitchen. He was pissed that I was with Lenny.

"Mike's a trip," Lenny said as he ordered his drink and offered me one. I didn't drink much at all, maybe only a beer every now and then.

"I don't know what to order. I guess I'll have a vodka and orange juice. That seems simple. A lot of people order that. Yeah, I'll try that."

After I got my drink, Lenny said, "Yeah, like I said, Mike is a trip. You know they robbed this place one night and the bandits put him and the cook in the walk-in refrigerator. He was scared shitless—shit on himself in there. I heard about it. The cook told everybody. The robbers called the cops from a pay phone after that and they came to let them out. Mike's been a nervous wreck ever since then. I know it's not funny, but every time I see him I think about all that shit and start laughing."

"You are *so* bad. That's not right, Lenny. You need to stop," I was cracking up along with him. I wasn't really laughing at what happened to Mike. Lenny's laughter made me start giggling too.

Still doubled over with laughter, he took a breath to say, "I know. I'm glad nothing happened to him. It's just so damn funny to me. You know, since he shit in the refrigerator, you'd better not eat any food in here. Can you imagine—shit in somebody's refrigerator. Damn." We were both cracking up at the bar.

Mike emerged from the kitchen and saw the two of us howling. He addressed me in an authoritative manner, "Baby, you should get your stuff put away. You'll be starting in fifteen minutes. You've got to check your bank."

"Okay, honey. I'm coming in a minute."

"Hey, do you want me to put your bags—your daughter's clothes in my car and bring them by your house tomorrow night or in the morning before I leave for work?" Lenny asked me.

"No, you've done enough for me today. Really, I can make it from here."

"How do you get home on the nights you work?"

"Well, either I call a cab or Alfred picks me up. I don't know how to drive. I'll be okay." Mike was taking it all in, knowing Lenny was trying to pull his best friend's lady.

When I got up from the stool and went to the ladies room, Mike approached Lenny. "Look, Lenny, Denise is a nice girl and so is my boy, Alfred, her fiancé. You know man, there are a lot of chicks around, but she's taken. I'd appreciate it if you would stay away from her. Alfred wants to marry her."

I was walking back toward the bar and saw them talking. I was gathering my bags to take to the back when I heard Lenny say, "Who the fuck are you, the pussy police or the dick detective? You better stay out of my fucking business." I stood cold, listening to this. Mike was trying to smooth it over.

"Look, Lenny, I don't mean any harm, don't get loud, man. It's just that I'm trying to look out for Denise and Alfred," Mike said.

"Come on guys, don't go through a thing about this. Mike, its okay—we're just friends. He did me a favor today. I had almost gotten hurt in town and he was around. Come on, keep it light. There's nothing to worry about." My voice was sweet.

Before Mike could answer, Lenny barked, "You better leave us the fuck alone. Now, Denise doesn't need this fucking job anyhow. Shit. I can pay her whatever you're paying her and then some. Don't you start ordering me around. I'll put your black ass back in that refrigerator."

I was embarrassed and in shock. "Lenny, come on. That's not nice. Stop it." Then Lenny grabbed my face and pulled me toward him. He kissed me—tongue and all. I snatched back from him.

"Now tell *Alfred* that, motherfucker!" Lenny said, looking in Mike's eyes. "Maybe he'll write that in the damn paper."

Mike was flabbergasted and demanded I come behind the bar. Lenny kept shouting obscenities. Then, we all began arguing. Finally, Mike said, "Both of you get the hell out of here! Denise, you don't work here anymore."

I panicked. "I *know* I'm not fired because *he* started all this mess!" I shouted pointing at Lenny. Lenny started laughing and continued to sip his cognac. I was furious.

"Denise, I'm letting you go. I'm sorry. I don't need trouble here," Mike said.

I stared at Mike, then looked over at Lenny and rolled my eyes. I gathered up my bags and put on my coat.

"Looks like you need a ride, baby." Lenny stood up and pulled a wad of cash out of his pocket. He threw a twenty on the bar and helped me with the bags. I strutted off, leaving him with his share of my packages. Guess I'm done here," Lenny coolly said to Mike as he strolled out of the club.

As we walked to Lenny's car, the freezing cold bit into my bones. It was the 11th of December, two weeks before Christmas—and I was suddenly unemployed. Lenny and I argued while putting Natasha's Christmas presents into his trunk. When the two of us got situated in the car and he pulled off, I was still ranting and raving. "Why in the world did you do that? Do you realize you got me fired! You made me lose my damn job! Did you have to curse Mike out? Shit. Do you realize it is two weeks before Christmas? I haven't gotten Natasha's toys yet and I haven't done any shopping for gifts for other people. I live with my mother! I have to pay rent. You've turned out to be a pain in the ass. Maybe I would have been better off getting hit by the damn bus!"

He put an eight track in the tape deck, Parliament Funkadelic's recording of *Flashlight* and placed his hand on my thigh. "Oh come on, baby. It's just a damn bar job. You weren't working at the White House. It's not the end of the world. Hell, I can find you another one of those things in no time. I know a lot of people who own bars. Those jobs are a dime a dozen. Let's go to Tobin's Inn and have a nice dinner. Stop worrying."

I began to protest, but he kissed me. "I've got you covered, baby. We'll go shopping tomorrow night. Be cool," Lenny said.

As soon as we were seated at the restaurant, I told Lenny that I had to make a couple of phone calls right away. I left him at the table and headed for the pay phone.

"Alfred, hey, it's me. Listen, I had some trouble at work with Mike. I need to talk to you."

"Mike called me. Listen you're twenty-four and I'm forty-one. I care a lot about you, but I'm not up for trouble. I've decided we probably need to call it quits. I was always concerned about the age factor here, but I dig you a lot. I don't like what happened and maybe it wasn't your fault—but I'm going to pass." Alfred didn't sound hurt at all.

"Just like that? You're dumping me just like that?"

"It's over," Alfred said and hung up.

I started thinking about plan B for money and immediately called my cousin, Lynne.

"Hey, girl. I'm in a jam. I just lost my job. I can't explain it all, but I need one of your credit cards. I have to Christmas shop. You know I'm good for the money. Which one can you give up?"

"What the hell happened?" Lynne asked.

I explained the entire story. Lynne laughed and said, "Well, at least you've got a man. Maybe it will work out for you. You know Alfred worked a lot and you were complaining that he had little time for you. Everything happens for a reason. My Strawbridge's card is clear. You can have that one to do what you have to do. Come by the house whenever you get a chance. I'll leave it on the living room mantle. You've got keys. See ya."

I went back to the booth. Lenny had ordered drinks for both of us.

"Glad you're back," he said.

"Oh, shut up." I plopped down in the booth, sighing.

"Look, how long are you going to be mad? This is getting boring." Lenny pouted.

"Well, it's not boring to me. I've had a hectic day. Bottom line is— Alfred's done with me. I've been fired twice tonight. You satisfied?"

"Yep." Lenny took a swig of his drink. "Let's order. I'm starving. I want the fried shrimp. Get whatever you want. By the way, George Tobin, who is the son of the owner of this place is in the kitchen. He's a friend of mine and does the hiring here. Used to date my sister. He wants you to call him tomorrow about working here—behind the bar. Here's his number and he'll be over to meet you before we leave. What time do you want to go shopping tomorrow? I can take the day off."

I sat back and stared at him. I was impressed. He was looking out for Natasha and that made me smile. This man worked fast. Look what he had gotten done in a day. "Well, I'm feeling better. I do need a job. I'm really very independent." My voice suddenly turned serious.

"Well, you seem pretty smart, too. Did you ever work at any other places? What else do you know how to do?"

"Well, I actually worked for a clothing wholesaler directly across from your business from 1972 until 1974. I did accounts payable and receivables. I left for a better position and went to work for Delaware Management Company. I was in stocks, doing liquidations and transfers for shareholders. I issued the checks, too."

"That's great. You *are* pretty bright. What happened to that?" he asked.

"I resigned in October. I'm more of a *people person.* I was bored there. I stayed there for nearly four years. I kept getting into trouble for clowning around. I mean, I did the work well, I'm just a character. You know what I mean?"

"I guess you just played around when you weren't busy. Was that it?" Lenny asked.

"Yeah, and I always had something going. I would take naps on my lunch hour, run to my old boyfriend's office over lunch time, and I was always swapping vacation days so I could travel with my man."

"Oh, Alfred did a lot of traveling?" Lenny questioned, perking up a bit.

"No, I just hooked up with Alfred a couple of months ago. I had been seeing a guy named Lenny Sawyer for a couple of years before I met Alfred."

"What happened to that?"

"Well, I was living the fast life with him. It was definitely too wild for me. He's in a group called Blue Magic. You know—the records *Side Show, What's Come Over Me?*"

30

Lenny was impressed. It seemed as if he was seeing me in a different light. "You mean you were hooked up with a guy in *Blue Magic?* I know that group well. And…his name is Lenny, too?"

"Yep—Lenny Sawyer. I was crazy about him, but it wasn't good for me to be with him. Too much traveling and I have a daughter. Too much partying…and we really fell out when I sneaked and had an abortion. I damn near got killed doing it. So, I decided to break it off myself and chill out. I was really in love with him, but I had to go."

Deep inside of me, my heart still burned for Lenny. The memories were still so alive in my mind. That was crazy love. If this Lenny was the same, I was in deep trouble. I needed to change the subject.

"Now, tell me all about you."

"Well, I was born and raised in Myrtle Beach, South Carolina."

"Oh, you're a country boy? That's cute."

"Yep—that's what I am. I moved up here after I got out of the army. I hooked up with my wife—she's also from Myrtle Beach."

"Was she already up here or did you go back for her?"

"She was already up here. I came here because my sister Theresa was living here, she's married to my wife's brother. My wife and I have a really stormy relationship."

I almost wanted to roll my eyes. Married men always said that.

"Why do you stay?"

"I stay because I basically do what the hell I want—and so does my wife. I go out a lot and we don't ask each other a lot of questions. I pay all the bills. We sleep together when I'm home. It's a crazy situation. I make myself happy out here. I like hanging out. That's what I do."

"What do you plan to do with me?"

"I'll get you straightened out, pay your Mama some rent money for you, and get you back behind a bar if you want. Also, I'd like to have a lot of sex with you."

I cracked up and drank half the vodka and orange juice he had ordered for me. "You're a fool!" I said.

Over the next two weeks, I shopped like crazy and the two of us were spending nights together at hotels. I had racked up nearly $1,700 dollars on Lynne's credit card and Lenny made arrangements to pay it. All of Natasha's toys were in the trunk of his car—paid for in cash by Lenny—and we were having a ball together. We were going to restaurants, bar hopping, and damn near killing each other between the sheets. He was the *position* man, flipping me all around in bed. He was sexually open-minded and anything and everything went with him. True to his Leo self, he was rough like a lion. I got a real workout each time. I liked being on top so I could control his wild ass. He was sexually satisfying, but I found him to be more a meat and potatoes man, more sex and not much real romance in bed. If I had one complaint, it would be that he didn't spend enough time on foreplay.

I started to believe that he didn't have a wife because we were spending so many nights in hotels. By Christmas Eve, we had been shopping every night for two weeks and had a ton of stuff stowed in his car for Natasha. To my surprise, Lenny refused to bring the toys to my mother's house on Christmas Eve. I was frantic. My five year old child was expecting Santa that night. He wanted me to come to his home for the gifts. He planned to pick me up and bring me to his place. He had taken the toys inside and stored them in his basement. Humph. What the hell was that man up to? Lenny wouldn't turn over one gift unless I came over, so I agreed he could pick me up. I was scared to death of meeting his wife. I figured he'd told her I was someone he worked with or something, and he had done me a favor by hiding my kid's toys at his place. Hell, I didn't know what to think. While in the car, I asked him what I was supposed to say when we got there—to his wife. "Don't worry about it, she's away," he said, winking at me.

"Away where? At the mall or out of town?" I asked.

"She's out of town for a week visiting her family."

"Okay—let's get my stuff and you get me back home."

We walked into his house and there were people sitting around. He had a nice home, the interior and exterior decorated for the holiday season. I was introduced to a young girl, Lenny's godchild, who lived with them. She seemed about nineteen and had a baby boy. She pleasantly greeted me while putting a toy together. His sister Janete was at the dining room table with a drink and a beer. Lenny mentioned that she also lived with them. She had an eight year old daughter who had gone to the mall with a cousin. I smiled at everyone and waited to be escorted to the basement.

The women didn't seem alarmed or angry by my presence. No one asked me any questions.

"Take your coat off and relax. Are you hungry?" Lenny asked, cool as a cat.

"I'm not hungry. We'd better get the toys and get going," I urged.

"What's the problem? Let me make you some food. Do you want some wine?"

"Look, Lenny, this is not cool. I just need Natasha's things. I've got to go." Although everyone was welcoming, I was not comfortable in Lenny's house. At any moment, I expected his wife to come charging through the door.

Without taking a breath, he recited, "Well, since you don't have a car and you can't drive, and there is ice out there and it's four degrees, your mother doesn't have a car and you live about fifteen blocks away, there is a lot of stuff downstairs and I'm not planning to go anywhere any time soon because Santa Claus is not due until about three o'clock in the morning, and I want to keep you here with me for Christmas, you should get comfortable because I don't think you'll get a cab tonight."

I ended up spending the night, sleeping in Lenny and his wife's bed. It was beautiful, made out of brass and squeaked when we made love. I got back to my mother's home at 6:00 a.m. with Lenny and the toys. We quietly placed them under the tree together. After a night of passionate lovemaking, waking up in a *house* with him instead of a hotel on Christmas morning, I realized that I was totally infatuated with Lenny. He was irresistible and exciting. I loved flying down Lincoln Drive with him late at night in his white Mercury Grand Marquis after closing down a bar. I was intrigued by our relationship, turned on by his sultry demeanor and take charge attitude. Lenny was so damn attractive, always throwing money all over the bars. I was smitten by him. He had a good business and had been established there for years. He was ten years older than me and sophisticated, drinking Lancer's wine and cognac—the best stuff in the world, I thought. I didn't let it bother me that he was married. I talked myself out of that, convincing myself he was in a bad situation and it was all her fault. She should have known how to make him happy. After all, he wouldn't have been out alone if she were doing the right things for him. Of course, he'd been waiting for me all his life. Our relationship was meant to be, so it would work out for us.

It didn't matter that later on I found out he really didn't *own* the camera shop. He had actually just *worked* there for twelve years. He lied to impress me. He was very popular with his boss and was a great employee who showed up for work no matter how hung over he was from drinking, partying, and doing lines of cocaine. His boss liked him so much that he'd even sold him his own house at a great price.

Three months after dating Lenny, he finally did miss a day of work due to an eye problem. During his absence, his boss was looking for some invoices and came across a few receipts revealing that Lenny was stealing from his company. Lenny lost his job.

At the time Lenny got sacked, I had taken an administrative position at Pennocks, a large flower company in the East Falls section of Philadelphia. I had been working full-time during the day and moonlighting a couple of nights a week tending bar. I had managed to get an apartment of my own. I'd been staying at my Aunt Betsy's for the past few months. I never liked living at my mother's because her drinking was stressful for me and she managed money horribly. Even though I paid rent, something was always being shut off and she'd demand more money. Natasha stayed with my Mom, as she attended kindergarten at a school a few blocks from her house. It was easier for me because of my work schedule. Lenny was unemployed and at home during the day while his wife worked. We continued to see each other. He finally secured a job at an after hours club that his cousin Johnny owned in West Philadelphia. We were still hanging tough, hitting speakeasies after the club closed and meeting for dinners and sex a few times a week.

Having an apartment kept us out of hotels and he began to stay the entire night at my place at least one night during the week and always on weekends. My place was only about eight blocks from where Lenny and his wife resided. Lenny kept telling me that things had become pretty rocky between him and his wife. She was disgusted with him. One day, we were riding around in Mt. Airy. At a traffic light, he noticed his wife in the car behind us. "Oh shit. That's Frances behind us!" he exclaimed. Lenny was terrified, having me in the car and his wife following us. He made quick rights and lefts, but couldn't lose her. I wasn't tempted to check out what she looked like and I didn't want her to see my face. She could have been crazy. He finally stopped on a street in front of a strange house. Frances also stopped her car, but did not get out.

"Okay, listen. Just get out here. You have some money, right?" He asked

"Yeah, I have money. What do you want me to do?"

"Just get out and act like you live there," he said, pointing to one of the homes that lined the street. Go up to that house. I'm going to pull off and go home. She'll probably follow me. It'll give her the impression that I was giving you a ride home or something. Look, there's a bar on the corner, too. I'll meet you there in about an hour. Head toward the bar when we are out of sight. I'll come back for you." He sped off while I walked up to the strange house and opened the screen door as if I were entering. When Lenny returned to pick me up, he gave me this account of what happened:

Frances began shouting, "Who the fuck was that bitch in your car!" as soon as they entered their house.

"A friend of mine. I was giving her a ride from the train. She rides the train every day. What the hell is the matter with you? Jesus Christ. You're acting like a maniac. Don't you know how many people I know who ride the train? I only worked in town a hundred years. Leave me alone," he barked back at Frances.

"You think you're so slick. You don't *work in town* anymore, so why are you on the train in the evening? Why are you in town, *period?*" Frances screamed.

"I went down there to apply for a job with the City and hung out in town most of the day. My friend was on the fucking train and I gave her a ride home. Is something wrong with that?"

"I don't believe you. You're never at home anymore. I think the skinny bitch is your woman."

"Yeah, yeah, yeah—*everybody* is my woman," he quipped sarcastically as he walked into the kitchen. He snatched a container out of the refrigerator and put seafood salad he had made the day before on a plate. He grabbed a beer and a fork and sat down at the table to eat.

Frances' nostrils flared. Lenny avoided looking directly at her in fear of egging her on. "I am sick of your shit. You make me sick. I'm footing the bills around here. You need to get out. Do you think I'm dumb enough to believe you don't have somebody else?" Lenny ignored her and kept eating. He got up to turn the radio on. Frances snatched the plug out of the wall.

He walked out of the room with his plate and beer and went into the living room. He turned on the TV and sat on the couch. She followed him. She was hurling obscenities at him while he sat engrossed in the evening news. This infuriated her more and she grabbed a knife from the kitchen. She nicked him on the shoulder and it bled. He shoved her and they began fighting. The next minute, they were knocking over lamps and furniture. She clocked him in the eye and he picked up a brass magazine rack and was about to hit her. Instead, he put it back down on the floor, picked up his keys, and walked out the door.

When Lenny picked me up from the bar, he kept looking in his rear view mirror to see if Frances had followed him. She wasn't there. As he drove, I wondered what the hell I had gotten myself into. I speculated he had brought other women to his house when his wife went away. Maybe I'd picked up a bunch of nuts. For a moment, I thought of dumping him and trying to get my old boyfriend back. We stopped at another bar and had a couple of drinks and then headed to my apartment. As soon as we got settled, he said, "We might have to look for a two-bedroom apartment. It ain't going well at home." That night, we never touched each other.

The next day, Lenny announced to Frances that he was leaving her. He later told me that he had waited for his wife at the kitchen table until she got in from work. She greeted him with sarcasm, saying, "Oh, you're back."

He wasted no time and announced that he would be out by the weekend.

Frances was surprised and not expecting to hear that, he said triumphantly. "Oh, so you're moving in with your bitch? Why do you have to wait until the weekend? Why can't you go now?"

The way Lenny mimicked his wife bothered me for some reason. He denied knowing any *bitches* and had the nerve to tell Frances he couldn't move out until he was paid from the club. His plan, he told her, was to shack up with his Aunt Claudia or one of his sisters. Either way, Lenny knew he would not end up on the streets.

"Do one or the other—quickly," Frances huffed.

Feeling that Frances was testing him, Lenny got up from the table and climbed the stairs to the bedroom. He started packing. Frances came into the bedroom and sat on the bed. As he was placing the clothes in the suitcases, she realized she didn't want him to leave. She walked over to him and put her arms around him. "I don't want you to move. I want to work it out." Resorting to the oldest trick in the book, Frances seduced him. She aroused him and he went for it. They spent the next five hours making up. I showed no emotion when Lenny told me this part. I was hurt, but what could I say. After all, he was her husband.

Lenny spent the next couple of days laying low—staying away from me. He was confused and contemplated the pros and cons of leaving his wife for me. If he left, he would be walking away from his beautiful home and a marriage. He'd have to start all over again and re-establish himself. He considered the fact that he'd only been dating me for four months and didn't know where our relationship was going. He'd never gotten so serious with a piece of ass since his marriage. He usually had some flings that didn't mean anything or take up too much of his time away from home. Also, a big factor was that he didn't have a decent job, and his sister Janete was living at their house with him. He didn't know if Frances would make her move out if he left. If he moved in with me, Frances would eventually find out he was with another woman. Some of his friends and many family members knew all about us because we had been partying with some of them, but they never betrayed the news of our affair.

Lenny confided that Frances was acting better since the sex was happening between them. He figured things would change for the better regarding their marriage. He believed she had even stopped seeing her man on the side in West Philly. He lived on Sansom Street—so Lenny said. He shared with me that she probably hadn't called her lover during the three days they were so lovey dovey. I thought everybody was crazy, including me.

On the following Friday night, at midnight, I took my ass out to the after hours spot where Lenny worked. I had decided that I was tired of talking to the phone. I plopped down on a bar stool, looked at him, and said, "What's the deal?"

"Hey, baby. I'm sorry. I just needed some space. I've been trying to figure some things out." He poured me a glass of wine.

"I took a cab out here. I want my money back for that. I'm leaving here in an hour. You'd better shit or get off the pot. I'm getting sick of you."

"Don't come in here ordering me around. What the hell have you been up to for three days?" He chuckled.

"Nothing—just working. You miss me?"

"Yeah," he said.

"Okay. I'll stay until you get off."

Lenny went home with me and didn't get back to his own house until four o'clock the next afternoon. Frances was furious again. He said they had another gigantic argument. That fight, on top of our sexcapade, killed Lenny. So he took a nap, got dressed, and went to work at the club later that night. I was working the bar at Tobin's Inn until two in the morning and caught a ride to Lenny's club. I walked in looking fabulous and sat down at the bar. I was wearing a new wig because my hair was all sweated out from lovemaking the night before and damn near all day with Lenny. He loved my *other hair*. He strutted over to me, pointed and whispered, "Frances is over there. I didn't know she was coming out here. Be cool. My best cousin Zena is also in town from D.C. She's here too—over there with Frances. Her husband David is with her. I'll introduce you to them later. You look cute."

I nodded my head and ordered a glass of Lambrusco. I lit a cigarette and surveyed the club. It was packed.

The music was blasting in the club. Everyone was demanding drinks and Lenny was super busy behind the bar. I observed his family seated in a couch booth. I was able to figure out which of the three women was his wife. Frances looked average, not overly attractive, seemed to be about a size 14 and was dressed in an outfit that I would never have been caught dead in. She was getting plastered for sure. She was talking and laughing with the others in the booth. I wondered what Lenny was going to do about Frances and me being in the same spot with him. After all, I didn't drive and had no way to get home—or anyplace else, and he knew it.

In about ten minutes, I saw two of the women in Lenny's family party get up from the couch. They walked over to the bar and waited for Lenny. They chatted with him for a few seconds, then made their way through the crowd, walking toward me. I was seated in the middle of the long bar. "I'm Rhonda, Lenny's baby sister. You're Denise and I know about you. This is my cousin Zena." Rhonda pointed at Zena. "Meet us back in the ladies room."

I waited a couple of minutes and then headed to the back. There were a few other women waiting to get in. I walked up and greeted Rhonda and Zena. They both smiled at me. For a moment, I didn't trust them. After all they were Frances's family and were all partying together. I suspected that they wanted to take me in the bathroom to tell me off. In any case, I was going to play it cool. In any case, they'd have to answer to Lenny if they fucked with me.

"So…I hear you and my brother have been quite busy," Rhonda said, giving me the once over. Like Lenny, Rhonda had a light honey complexion. Her jet black, wavy hair was worn off her face in a bun. She was about five foot two and a size eight. She looked very sophisticated and her deep brown eyes were the most striking thing about her. Her mouth, quite voluptuous, could have landed her a job as a model for a cosmetic company. My head sank, then I lifted it up and smiled. "Yep, we've been doing some serious hanging out."

Zena laughed. She was a little taller than Rhonda and had more pounds on her frame. Light complexioned, her skin was flawless and she wore her light brown hair in a fabulous asymmetrical cut. "It's nice to meet you. Me and my husband, David, came in for a few days from D.C. We're staying in West Philly at my father-in-law's house. We'll be here until Monday."

"Nice to meet you, Zena. I know Lenny's wife is over there. I've been trying to figure out what he's going to do about me because she's here. I see she's getting loaded."

Rhonda chuckled. "Yeah, that's my sister-in-law and she's not feeling any pain. I expect her to fall on her face any minute and that's going to be my brother's problem. Look, this is the deal. Lenny is going to take Frances home when he gets off. He has to do that because Chuck and I….Chuck is my husband who's over there at the table with David.....well, we aren't driving all the way back to Mt. Airy to take her home early because she's getting drunk. We're not doing him that big a favor. The plan is that *he* will drive her home. Her car is here and so is his. Lenny is driving Frances back home in his car when he's done. We're leaving here fifteen minutes before closing."

Zena looked at her watch. "That's in about thirty-five minutes."

"Okay," Rhonda went on. "Listen, Denise, in thirty-five minutes, Chuck and I and Zena and David are walking out of here. Once we get up from the couch, you start getting yourself together and meet us outside. We're going to a speakeasy and Lenny knows where to meet us. You're riding with us. My brother wants us to take care of you. If something happens and he doesn't show back up, you're spending the night at my house. We have a spare room. You got that?"

"Comprende," I said and sashayed back to the bar.

CHAPTER 3

༁

The Chicago Surrender

Lenny stood behind me. I was seated at the bar of a lovely basement bar in a private home. He ordered a double Courvoisier and a Heineken for himself and drinks for the rest of the party. He kissed me on the neck as he ordered.

"What took you so long, man?" Chuck, his brother-in-law asked.

"I had to stop in the park. Frances got sick. It was a trip. This whole night has been a nervous wreck nightmare for me. I need a damn drink. Thanks for taking care of my baby." Lenny kissed me on the cheek.

"It was no trouble, she's a riot and pretty cute, too," Chuck joked.

"How'd you get away from Frances, cuz?" Zena asked.

"She thinks I'm outside getting her pocketbook out of the car." They all cracked up.

"You're something else, boy," David added.

"What time are you Negroes going back to D.C. on Monday?" Lenny asked.

"Around noon," David answered.

"What time are you going to Aunt Claudia's later today?" Lenny asked Zena.

"Dinner time—six o'clock. You plan on meeting us there?"

"Yep, even though Aunt Claudia caused all this mess tonight by telling Frances you guys were coming out to the club to see me, I'm still going," Lenny answered.

"What about Frances's car? How is she going to get it? Don't you have to bring her to pick it up?" Chuck asked.

"Nope. You're gonna get your ass up at two o'clock this afternoon and take it to her. You're gonna tell her she left her keys on the table at the club and you picked them up by mistake. Hook up with someone to help you

41

out on that. Call Lester or Johnny. I'm not going home until after Zena and David go back to D.C. I'm going home on Monday. I'll be at Denise's. If I go back home before then, there will be some shit. I'm not having my weekend ruined. My favorite cousin is in town," Lenny said, giving Zena a kiss.

"What are you gonna do about clothes?" Rhonda asked.

"I've got some credit cards. I'll buy some shit—anything to keep from going back there right away.

"Lenny, Frances is going to end up killing you. You already have those stab wounds from four years ago on your chest," Rhonda said.

"I've gotten a couple more since then," Lenny laughed. "I'm a bad cat—I've got more than nine lives. Don't forget—I'm the Leo. King of the fucking jungle." They all laughed and ordered another round of drinks. I didn't find anything funny and had been listening to all this chatter in silence.

"So, how do you like my new baby?" Lenny asked them all, looking at them for approval of me.

"She's as crazy as you," Rhonda said. "Both your asses are gonna end up dead fucking with Frances."

I was beginning to think we could really have a lot of trouble seeing each other. I had just heard the *stab story* and was petrified.

"Denise, how do you stay so skinny? You must be a size 0." Zena, who was a size 10, admired Denise's body.

"Damn if I know. I'm a size 4. I eat everything in sight and never exercise. I was underweight when I was born and stayed that way throughout my childhood. I couldn't gain a pound if somebody taped it on me."

"Well," said Lenny, rubbing his hands up and down my arms, "she might be skinny, but she has a nice ass. Stand up, baby so they can see that ass." I blushed and Lenny's brother-in-law Chuck's eyes opened widely. The large gap between his two front teeth showed.

"Come on, Lenny, you're embarrassing me." I wasn't in the mood for Lenny's antics. I was getting sick of all the drama.

"Oh, stand up for me so my family can see why I go through all this shit just to be with you. Let's show them the reason. Come on, show them." I wouldn't budge.

Lenny pulled my seat back and pulled me onto the floor. He turned me around and squeezed my ass. "See it, yall? This is the ass that has me all fucked up and about to get killed by my wife."

Later, when we were lying in bed, I wanted Lenny to tell me everything that had happened when he took Frances home. I wasn't sure what purpose it would serve, but I needed details. Lenny, sensing that he had better oblige me, recounted the story.

"Frances, please put your other leg in the car. Come on. Jesus—why did you have to drink so much?" Lenny said.

"I drank so much because it was a party. That's why I did it," Frances' words were running together.

"Well, the party's over. We've got to get home. I'm tired. I've been messing with drunks all night. It's stressful."

"Awe, baby, I only had a few drinks. Don't get mad. I had so much fun with Zena and Rhonda. Tomorrow, I am going out to West Philly and we are all going out to lunch after church. Zena got her hair cut. Did you notice it—so sharp. I'm gonna get my hair cut like that. I'm going down to D.C. I'm gonna get Zena to take me to her hair salon."

Lenny could care less what she did to her hair. Some days he didn't even notice her. "Yeah, Frances , Zena looks good," Lenny said. He couldn't wait to get her home and in bed so he could get back to the speakeasy. As they were riding, Frances' head started moving back and forth. Suddenly, she put her hand to her mouth. "I'm sick. I'm gonna throw up. I'm dizzy. The room is going around. Everything is going around."

"Oh, shit, Frances. Damn," Lenny pulled over in Fairmount Park. He jumped out of the car and ran around to her side. He didn't want her to vomit in his car. He snatched her door open and repositioned her body around in the car. He got her out and tried to stand her up. She was wobbling. "Frances, try to get yourself together. If you have to throw up, do it out here. Can you throw up?"

"Well, I'm trying. It's really dark out here. Damn, are we in the woods? This looks like down south. I feel like I'm back in Myrtle Beach," she slurred.

"Frances, please. Will you either throw up or get back in the car. Are you still sick?"

"I can't throw up. It's not coming up. I feel…funny."

Lenny was disgusted. "Shit," he thought.

He was sorry as hell Frances had brought her ass up to that club. Why in the world had his aunt Claudia told her that Zena and David were in town and going to the club? He reached in the trunk and grabbed a towel.

"Frances, put your finger down your throat. That will make you vomit. The stuff will come up and you'll feel better."

She followed his instructions and vomited her guts up. He moved back so it wouldn't get on his clothing. He was gently shoving her body as far away from his car as he could. Finally, it was over. He grabbed a sweatshirt that was in the trunk of his car and cleaned her face and mouth and placed her back in the car.

"Okay, hubby, now I feel better. You were right. Let's go home and freak out in bed. I saw that new porno book hidden in the house. Let's do some of that stuff tonight." That was the last thing he wanted to hear.

They got to their house and he dragged her out of the car. Everybody in the house woke up with all the commotion of him trying to get her upstairs and into bed. She was singing songs as he pulled her clothes off. Once he had her down to her panties and bra, she held out her arms for him. "Come on, baby. I'm glad we made up and you didn't move out. It's show time. Come to mama." She swung her arms back, reaching for something. "Oh, I don't want to forget. The porno book! You love that!" Frances turned over to the night stand. She flipped on her stomach and opened the night stand, trying to go through some magazines in there. She lost her balance on the edge of the bed and fell onto the floor.

"Oh shit. My head. I fell….oh, the room is going around again—like in the park tonight. I'm gonna get sick again," she moaned.

Lenny grabbed a bucket out of the bathroom and threw her a towel. **He left her on the floor. He walked out of the room**.

"Where are you going?"

"I have to get your pocketbook and coat out of the car. Wait here for me. I'll be right back." He went to the car, retrieved her handbag, and threw it on the living room couch. He went into the kitchen to quickly wash his face and hands in the sink and dried them with a paper towel. He jumped in his car and drove back to West Philly to the speakeasy where everyone was waiting for him.

* * *

Over the next seven months, Lenny and I continued seeing each other while he was still living at home. The pattern stayed the same and he lived in two places. Frances was having a fit, but she couldn't keep him at home. I was getting sick of him going back and forth, so I decided to take a trip to Los Angeles to visit my buddies, Candice and Myra. Candice and I had attended high school together in Philly. Shortly after we graduated, she split to California and moved in with her older sister, Myra. After ten days of reminiscing about old times, seeing the sights of sunny California and beautiful downtown Burbank, a little shopping, hitting some discos, and being bossed around and lectured about life by Myra, I returned home to Philadelphia. I boarded my flight and was preparing to take a snooze when the flight attendant interrupted me. "Do you want coffee?"

"Yes, I'll take some." He was tall, a gorgeous shade of a raisin, and fine as he could be.

"Do you want cream and sugar or black like me?" he asked.

I giggled, charmed by him. "Cream and sugar, please."

I never got a bit of rest. His name was Demetrious and he paid a lot of attention to me throughout my flight, relentlessly flirting.

"I'm done work when we land in Chicago," Demetrious said.

"Oh yeah, I have a two hour layover and then I catch a flight to D.C. Then it's on to Philly for me," I said.

"Why don't you keep me company when we land until your flight leaves?"

I looked up at that fine thing and said, "Okay."

Once we got into the airport, Demetrious led me to the parking lot where his car was parked. For some reason, I was not afraid to go with this stranger. He was smooth, funny, and seemed to be a nice guy. I also trusted him because he worked for the airlines and I figured that if he killed me, someone would find out. People had noticed me waiting for him at the gate and many saw me walk away with him. All his co-workers had observed us talking throughout the flight—having a ball—so I knew he'd never get away with doing anything to me.

We got into his car, and he immediately took out a joint. He lit it up and passed it to me. I had smoked a lot of marijuana before when I was hooked up with Lenny Sawyer in Blue Magic. I hadn't had much of the stuff in the three years since our breakup. Lenny had smoked it a lot when we were together, but I had to stop smoking midway through our relationship because it made me paranoid. Also, I accidentally set a trash can on fire once when we were together smoking at my girlfriend's house with other members of Blue Magic. Today, however, I wanted to impress Demetrious by being daring and cool. So, I shared the joint with him.

We kicked back and talked in his car. He was twenty-six, divorced, and had two beautiful daughters. They were seven and five. He showed me pictures of Carla and Sonja. He'd been working for United Airlines for four years and loved his job. He enjoyed traveling and the discounts available to him. He lived at home with his mother and eleven year old sister, Courtney, in Evanston, Illinois, a suburb of Chicago. He had another sister, Karly, who was two years younger than him, twenty-four like me. I dug this guy and told him all about my life. We laughed and joked about the experiences in our lives. I never felt the time pass. Demetrious walked me back inside the airport and checked me in personally for my flight. I was as high as a kite by then. We exchanged telephone numbers and addresses, and he kissed me on the cheek before I boarded the plane.

Once I was settled in my seat, I felt the effects of the marijuana even more. I became jittery. I wasn't frightened of the plane crashing. I was scared because I was traveling on a ticket I had not yet paid for. When I'd decided to go to California I really had no money. I had called the airlines and ordered a round trip ticket. At the time, they mailed tickets out to passengers who, in return, sent in a check for payment. I decided after I **received the ticket to pay for it when I got back with my next paycheck**. This way, I would definitely have a chunk of spending money while in California. It wasn't a bad thing, I reasoned. The airlines had more money than I did and they could afford to wait. I was honest—I'd pay them later. Now, I was sitting in my seat stoned, feeling guilty, and petrified. I tried to relax but was unable to, so I struck up a conversation with the passenger seated beside me. He was a white gentleman, about thirty, and looked kind of plain—almost nerdy. I went on about my trip to California, not that he had asked me anything. I kept chatting away about myself and asking questions about him. After twenty-five minutes of this, he pulled out his wallet and showed me pictures of his wife. I figured he was trying to get rid of me, that he thought I was trying to pick him up. I gave him a break and left him alone.

I was restless and stoned. I glanced about the cabin, observing the passengers. Everyone looked strange. I tried to go to sleep, but was still unable to calm down. I suddenly noticed a gentlemen pacing about the cabin. He was White, too, and when I looked down at his feet, I was alarmed that he had no shoes on. He kept walking up and down the aisle, looking around. This worried me by the second. We were in flight, headed now for D.C., and I imagined he was a hijacker. In fifteen minutes, never taking my eyes off him, I summoned the flight attendant.

"Miss, listen to me," I whispered, as the woman bent down to find out what I needed. "Have you seen that man walking around? See him back there? He's the one with no shoes on."

"Yes, Miss, I see him," the attendant answered.

"Well, he is acting strangely. *Weird*. You know what I mean? I believe he is going to hijack this plane. There's something spacey about him. I'm telling you. We need to check him out. We need to get him controlled." My voice was now slightly louder. At that point, the passenger seated next to me was listening. He glanced at me with a puzzled look on his face and gathered his things. He immediately changed his seat.

I watched him walk away. For a moment, I tried to determine why he was moving. He was either afraid of the man too, or thought I was crazy. I resumed explaining my fears to the attendant.

The attendant listened carefully to me, then went to the front of the plane. She returned in a few minutes and said to me, "Come with me, Miss."

I followed her to the front of the plane and was placed in the first seat in first class, right behind the cockpit door. The flight attendant entered the cockpit. A tall uniformed gentleman with grey hair and kind blue eyes came out of the door and addressed me. "Hi, I'm Captain Feldman. I'm your pilot. I hear you have some concerns. Don't you worry. You just stay right up here with us. We'll take care of you. Do you need anything?"

"No...I'm okay—just worried about that guy. He's creepy. He has to be watched. Maybe he ought to be up here. I can watch him while you fly the plane," I said.

"What's your name?" the Captain asked.

"Denise." I was reluctant to give him my last name, fearing he knew about the unpaid ticket.

"Well, Denise, are you getting off in Washington or are you continuing on to Philadelphia?" Captain Feldman had a taming voice, different from the one we had heard on the loudspeaker before departure.

"I'm going to Philly," I answered.

"Okay, well, we're gonna take great care of you all the way to Philadelphia. You know you have an hour layover in Washington before we take off again, but its only a 27 minute flight from Washington to Philadelphia."

"Yes, I know we have to stop for a while."

"Okay, when the plane lands, you just stay in your seat. I'll be back for you. Okay? I want to thank you for bringing that gentleman to our attention. You're the only person who was able to realize we may have a problem."

"You're welcome. We can't be too careful. There are some crazy people in this world," I added.

For the remainder of the flight, I was spoiled to death in first class. I was glad for the upgrade because I indeed had the munchies and they supplied me with everything. It was much better stuff than I'd ever had on any other flights. The flight attendant kept checking on me and I was curious about what was going on with the hijacker. I wondered if he would be getting off in Washington or if the airlines had alerted security and the police about him. I surmised they had him tied up in a bathroom or something at the back of the plane.

When we landed in D.C. I sat in my seat and watched as the hijacker walked past me and got off the plane unescorted. The pilot came and accompanied me off the aircraft. We were the last ones to leave. I was all set to identify the hijacker and answer questions. Much to my surprise, the pilot kept me with him while he checked in with his superiors. I never saw the strange man and never had to answer any questions. I inquired about him, but the pilot told me the situation was under control and not to worry. He took me everywhere he went and was nice to me. By then, the effects of the marijuana had still not worn off and I was still babbling to the Captain about the hijacker and my visit to California. Upon our return to the plane, he seated me in the same seat back in first class. Although it was a short flight, the flight attendants were going back and forth inside the cockpit and then to the back of the jet.

The pilot announced that passengers should remain seated when the plane landed in Philadelphia. No one was to leave the plane. Immediately after the announcement, the Philadelphia Police Department came on board. Now, I was scared out of my mind. Dammit, I thought. Why didn't I pay for that plane ticket! It was *me* who was going to jail. I wondered if Lenny would get me out on bail. I knew he was pissed with me for going to California. I had cursed him out before I left and hadn't called him the entire time I'd been away. I was truly in a mess.

The police went to the back of the plane. I figured they were going to converse with the flight attendants and then return for me. Nervously, I waited to be taken to jail. As I sat there, I decided to try knocking on the cockpit door and advising the nice captain of what I had done. Yep, I'd surrender. That would be the right thing to do. Since he liked me, maybe he would help. Just as I stood up, the captain's voice came on the PA system. "Ladies and gentlemen, we have a problem. A passenger has been ill and experiencing breathing problems throughout this flight. Please remain seated while this passenger is removed from the plane and taken to a nearby hospital."

I breathed a sigh of relief. The paramedics boarded the plane and took a man away on a stretcher. He looked to be about sixty years old and was clutching his chest when he passed by me. His face was red and I could tell he was in discomfort.

As soon as everyone on board could deplane, I scrambled to get off. I remembered some of my things were in the overhead compartment above my original seat. I waited for all the passengers to leave, then hurried back for them. I saw the flight attendant, who had moved me, staring at me. I became scared again that maybe the authorities at baggage claim were waiting to arrest or take me someplace to interrogate me about the ticket. Now *I* was about to have a heart attack. The flight attendant merely thanked me for flying United and went about her business. I retrieved my belongings and exited the plane, not once stopping to say anything to the captain.

Things went smoothly at baggage claim and I hopped in a cab. I was glad to see my apartment. I went back to work the very next day at the flower shop. When I got paid at the end of the week, I immediately sent in a check for the unpaid ticket. I refused to talk to Lenny the entire week after my return home. He'd called me numerous times, but hung up each time. When the weekend rolled around, I clocked in at the bar at Tobin's Inn. While working, I met a guy named Duane Swann. He worked in advertising. After work, he accompanied me and some other patrons to Chateau, an after hours spot a few blocks from Tobin's Inn. It was a beautiful bar on the second floor of a warehouse with a great lighting and sound system. Duane and I sat and talked while we sipped a glass of wine. Duane was an attractive, single, well-dressed advertising executive and worked for a company in Center City, Philadelphia. He had his life together unlike Lenny. At four thirty in the morning, even though the place was still jumping and the crowd was partying, I decided to leave. Duane offered to take me home. My apartment was about ten minutes from the club. He dropped me off, handed me his business card, and walked me to my door. "Can we get together some time?" he asked.

"I don't know. I'm really busy these days. I have your card, maybe I'll call you. It's late and I need to get inside," I said.

"Can I come up?"

"No—can't do that, sweetie."

"Okay—I understand. Can I have your number?"

"Why don't you let me get in touch with you?" I put my key in the door and left him on the landing.

At six o'clock in the morning sound asleep, I was awakened by the ringing of my doorbell. I peeped out of the window. It was Lenny.

I opened the door to find him as high as a kite. "You still not speaking to me?"

Without answering, I turned around and went up the stairs. I got into bed. He undressed and got in with me. Late that Sunday night, my doorbell was ringing again. I couldn't imagine who it was—Lenny was still in my bed. I went to the door to find Duane Swann leaning against the railing. "Hi." he said. "Surprise. I came back." He flashed a big smile on his face. I could tell he was loaded.

"You've got to go away—and never do this again, Duane. My man is upstairs." I closed the door and got back into bed.

"Who was that?" Lenny asked.

"A friend," I answered. "You've got a *wife* and I have a *friend*. That makes us almost even."

Lenny kept his mouth shut, but he was mad as hell. It was Tuesday night when he left my apartment to go home. He had spent two days there trying to make up with me. He knew he was on borrowed time. First, I darted off to California and he wasn't sure what was going on out there. Now, I have this *friend* showing up at my apartment late at night. He wasn't ready for all this shit.

I was having second thoughts about Lenny. I was also smitten by Demetrious. I couldn't get him out of my head. He was cute and sexy, tall and lean. The time we had together was fun and spontaneous. He had a silly side that I liked. He seemed so free of problems. I was impressed that he had such a glamorous job—flying on planes all the time—seeing so many places. He was also appealing to me because he was *single*. I didn't have to be number two. He was also a great conversationalist and always very candid—he just said it—no matter what. I liked Chicago and had visited there many times. I had a few older cousins, an aunt and uncle who lived there. I'd been in and out of Chicago since I was a child. Yeah, Demetrious was fitting in perfectly, and I had a huge attraction to him.

The moment Lenny left my apartment, I called Demetrious. We had a good laugh when I told him about the incident on the plane with the hijacker. He invited me to come back for a weekend whenever I could arrange it. From then on, we became phone buddies and, often, I would talk to his mom, Agatha, if I called and he was working. Agatha and I became fast friends and she wanted me to come for a visit too. We arranged for me to come for a weekend in May of 1978, three weeks away.

When I arrived in Chicago, that fine ass Demetrious was waiting when I walked off the plane. He gave me a big hug. "You look sharp. I love those pants! Where did you get that bad handbag, girl? Oh my God, look at your shoes! You look fabulous!" He screamed.

I grinned and squeezed him tight. "Hey, Demetrious!" I planted a kiss on his cheek. "You look great, too. Those cowboy boots are sharp! Gucci glasses—Oh Man! And, your little ass is wearing those jeans. Looking good, Demetrious! Give me a kiss so everybody will know whose holding check at O'Hare International Airport." He kissed me deeply. My toes were tingling. "I am so glad to be here. Let's get my bags. What's the plan for tonight?" We walked hand in hand to baggage claim. I had a new man.

"We're going to my house, first. My mom and sisters are waiting for you. My sister, Karly, kind of lives with us. The hook up is that Karly is sharing a basement apartment with my cousin, Susan. You'll meet her. Susan is Aunt Bella's daughter—Aunt Bella is my Mom's sister. Susan's twenty-nine. They cannot wait to meet you. Karly is here from Massachusetts. She's married, but got pissed with her husband and left him. She's sorting things out, trying to figure out if she's going back to him or getting a divorce. In the meantime, she's bunking with Susan. We actually live in a triplex. Me, my mom, and my eleven year old sister, Courtney, live on the third floor. Aunt Bella and her husband, Uncle Charles, live on the second floor, and Susan and Karly are in the basement."

Demetrious was talking a mile a minute, entirely too fast for me. I was struggling trying to keep up with who was who. "Okay, so where am I going to stay? Sounds crowded to me."

"Well, we're going out clubbing. I told some friends of mine all about you. We're meeting them at a club in Chicago. Karly is coming out with us tonight, too."

"So, we're going straight to your house—that's Evanston, right? Then I'm meeting everybody and we're leaving? Okay—I've got that. Just tell me where I'm staying. Am I staying with Karly and Susan in the basement while you stay upstairs with Mommy and Courtney? I can tell you one thing, even as fine as you are, I'm not sleeping anywhere near you with your mother around. That's a no-no for me. You know—the respect thing?"

"Well, I made arrangements for you to stay at a friend of mine—Jocelyn. She's cool and has an apartment in Chicago. Don't let my Mom know that. Just act like you're coming back to the house after the club. Okay?"

"Okay," I said, asking no questions.

The triplex was lovely. It had a giant backyard and was on a charming street. Aunt Bella and Agatha's apartments were beautifully decorated. I met them both and saw that he came from a very loving family. The women were extremely friendly. Aunt Bella was frying fish when I got there and demanded I sit down to eat. Macaroni and cheese was bubbling and just coming out of the oven. Courtney treated me like a big sister from the minute I walked into the house with my bags. She wanted me to bake a cake with her. I thought that was cute. Demetrious' mother, Agatha, held out her arms to me as soon as she saw me and showed me to my room. We had done so much talking on the phone over the past four weeks, that I felt we'd known each other all our lives. Uncle Charles was sweet—and drunk when I arrived.

After dinner, Karly and Susan arrived. They took me to the basement apartment. It was absolutely gorgeous with a thick rust-colored carpet, a bar, two nicely furnished bedrooms, and an elaborate stereo system. There was a small kitchen and living area and it was furnished with taste. They had it hooked up and I was very impressed. Karly went into her bedroom and returned with a zip lock bag of pot. I looked at it, then looked at Demetrious. The two of us began giggling.

"What are you two laughing about?" Karly asked, rolling a joint.

"Private joke," Demetrious said, smiling at Karly.

"Well, I'll just smoke a little of this good stuff and then I'll be laughing along with you two." Karly lit up and took a long drag, then passed it to me.

"None for me. I'm not antisocial. I just cannot handle the stuff. Your brother got me fired up when we met and I'm done with the stuff. Makes me paranoid. If I smoke any of that shit, we won't leave these premises. You got any wine? I can do that."

"Okay, I hear you. I won't force it on you." Karly took an additional drag and passed it to Demetrious. She began rolling another one. Susan headed for the refrigerator and took out a bottle of Kendall Jackson Chardonnay.

As I sat sipping wine and watching Susan, Demetrious, and Karly get high, we began to exchange information about one another. Karly explained that her husband, Chuck, was a nice guy who worked for a pharmaceutical company in Worcester, Massachusetts. They had been married for two years. He was a big teddy bear of a guy, but didn't have sufficient ambition or motivation to meet her needs in a man. He was boring and she was sick of him. She had relocated to Worcester, a small town in Massachusetts, after they got together. She'd met him while visiting one of her friends there. Karly had a job back in Worcester at a place called Nutra Systems—diet stuff. She had taken a leave of absence. She was very tall, big bosomed, and heavy set. Susan was a legal secretary in Evanston for a sole practitioner who was damn near rich.

As they continued to talk, it came out that Demetrious, Karly, and myself were all Libras. Karly and I were actually born on the same date—October 14th.

"Okay—we'd better get started," Demetrious said. "Let's wrap it up and get out of here. I told Jocelyn I'd be at the club by nine. We can wear what we've got on. Let's go. Susan, you sure you don't want to hang out with us?"

"Nope, you guys have got that. I'm not in a clubbing mood. I'll see you all in the morning." Demetrious jumped into his Camaro with me, and Karly went toward her car.

The place was packed when we got there. We all inched through the crowd, searching for a table. We spotted one, grabbed it, and then Demetrious immediately pulled me to the dance floor. He could really move his ass. He was a great dancer. When the song was over, he decided to look for Jocelyn and the rest of his friends. He found them and they came over to the table to meet me. I noticed that many same-sex couples on the dance floor were dancing with each other. Males were boogying with males and females shaking their butts with females. There were some guys dancing with girls. I whispered to Demetrious, "What kind of a club is this? Everybody is dancing with everybody."

"Well, this is the best place in Chicago for partying—you know, a lively group of people. It is sort of a gay club, but we like coming here because it is always bumping. We don't give a shit who dances with who. We like the place," he answered with nonchalance.

I didn't have a prejudiced bone in my body, so I shook my head and said, "No problem. I just asked. I've hung out with gay people in Philly before for a spell. You *can* really party with them. At the gay spots back in Philly, I noticed you can leave your handbag around while you're dancing and it doesn't get stolen. I've been to regular clubs and when people came back to their seats, their stuff was gone."

"Denise, wanna dance?" Jocelyn interrupted.

No matter how open-minded or unbiased I was, I didn't dig dancing with women. I looked at Jocelyn. "We only have Demetrious. Go get another guy and all of us will go out on the floor together. Demetrious can't handle both of us out there." Jocelyn headed for the bar.

I ordered another glass of wine from the waitress and observed the crowd. After a few sips and some conversation, and Jocelyn never returning, I asked, "Where's the ladies room? I gotta pee."

"It's all the way over there. In the back." I followed the direction of Karly's finger.

"Okay, I'll find it. I'll be right back." I gave Demetrious a wink.

I entered the bathroom and checked under the stalls for a free one. In my survey, I noticed two pair of feet in one stall. The heels of their feet were moving up and down slowly. My first reaction was shock then fear. I gasped. I was so upset at what was going on that I could not turn my body around to leave the bathroom. I walked backward out of the ladies room, all the way back to the table. Along the way, I was bumping into people. I found Karly sitting at our table by herself.

I was sputtering and pointing. "Karly—they are in there—doing something? I mean people are in the stall doing something weird—like maybe fucking standing up. Well, I mean they *have* to be fucking standing up. There are two pairs of feet in one stall. The feet were moving. I don't like this shit. This is too much! I want to get out of here. Where's Demetrious? Where did he go? Look, I'm down with almost anything, but not this *bathroom fucking* shit. Oh, no! We gotta go to another place. They are out of control in here! Where's my drink? Oh, there it is. I need a drink." I gulped down the glass of wine. I started to scan the room and thought I was with a bunch of freaks with absolutely no class. I looked back at Karly. "You didn't leave this table and my wine here unattended, did you?" I eyed my glass suspiciously. Someone could have put a Mickey in it.

Karly was trying to keep up with everything I was saying, but she was pretty high. She busted out laughing. "Denise, calm down. Look, Demetrious is out there dancing. He'll be back in a minute. I didn't leave the table and was watching the drinks. Are you okay, now?"

"No. Shit! Hell no. I'm not *okay*. People are fucking in the bathroom, so I am *not okay*. They even had their shoes off! They were getting it on barefoot in the damn ladies room. I wanna get out of here. Do you believe it—fucking in the bathroom? Had to be two women. Yep—two women fucking in the bathroom. No more wine. No more dancing. Somebody better take me out of here!"

Karly sat frozen. It was all too comical to her. She thought I was hilarious. I looked at her, rolled my eyes, and strutted away. I went onto the dance floor walking between the people to hunt Demetrious down. The music was blasting, so I knew it would be no use yelling his name. I spotted him dancing by himself. I yanked him toward me. "Get me out of here!," I screamed in his ear. "We have to leave. I have a problem!"

We all ended up leaving the club and I even had an argument with Jocelyn when we were getting in the car. She wanted me to sit up front with her, but I wanted to sit in the back with Demetrious. We drove back in silence. We got to her apartment and Demetrious stayed there with me. We had sex. It was good—but quick. Although I had a great time with Demetrious and his family, the rest of the weekend was pleasant, but uneventful.

I saw him another time when he flew in to Philly while working. We met at a hotel. He may have meant well, but, that time, he couldn't perform sexually at all. I didn't suspect he was gay, but I should have because he had relocated to San Francisco. We remained friends for over ten years. I really had the hots for him early in the relationship and even got snowed in with him in Chicago for ten days one winter when a blizzard occurred. O'Hare

International had closed and prevented me from returning to Philly. It was then that I discovered he was gay and in the closet. In ten days, he never tried to touch me. In fact, he even disappeared for an entire night. Some of his friends had stopped over to meet me and these men were gay. After that, the attraction fizzed and a friendship flourished.

In the 1990s, he died of AIDS-related complications. His family and I remained close, visiting one another during holidays and other special occasions. While I cared about Demetrious, Lenny still occupied a special place in my heart, despite my best efforts otherwise. With all his vices, and then some, I just couldn't get that man out of my system.

CHAPTER 4

∾

Glitter

Lenny and I were finally together. He left Frances because I had gotten frustrated with him going back and forth. One night, we had a gigantic argument. I'd given him an ultimatum and he knew I was serious. I was going to walk if he didn't shit or get off the pot. He packed his belongings and told her good bye forever. After that, I moved from my apartment and we purchased a house. He hadn't divorced Frances, but I wasn't concerned about that. I felt pretty secure and we weren't having any problems since the move eight months ago.

Zena and I became the best of buddies. In late November, 1983, the two of us were chatting on the phone. Zena and David had a seven year old son, Scott, and now Zena was eight months pregnant. As the conversation wore on, I said, "Girl, my breasts are sore. I wonder what's going on."

"Maybe you're pregnant like me," Zena chuckled.

"No way, Jose. I haven't taken a birth control pill or used a condom in years. I can't have any more kids. I'm certain of that. Maybe I have breast cancer."

"Have you been nauseous? Any vomiting? Are your nipples dark? Have you been dizzy?" Zena questioned, hoping I was pregnant.

I looked down at my nipples. "Nope—none of that. My breasts are just sore."

"Well, when was your last period?" Zena asked.

"Last month. It'll be on in a minute."

"Why don't you get one of those home pregnancy tests? Are the Rite Aids in Philadelphia open on Sunday nights? Go to one right now and buy a test. Maybe you really are pregnant."

"Girl, come on. I'm not pregnant. The doctors told me I'd probably never be able to get pregnant again. I had an abortion back in 1974 and the doctors made a mistake with the vacuum and perforated my uterus. I can't have any more kids. Natasha is *it*. I'm done."

"Well, your titties are sore. Something is up with that. You should get a test."

"Let's change the subject. I'm okay. With my luck, I probably have breast cancer. I'll get a mammogram next week."

When we hung up, I couldn't get Zena's words out of my mind. I got up, went to Rite Aid, and purchased a pregnancy test. As soon as I walked back into the house, I summoned the kids, my stepdaughter, Tara, who was seventeen years old with an eight-month old son, Lloyd, and my own daughter, eleven-year old Natasha. When the girls arrived, I announced, "That crazy Zena thinks I'm pregnant. I bought this pregnancy test. I'm going to do it tomorrow."

"What! Let's do it now," Natasha screeched. "Come on, Mom, let's see."

"These tests are supposed to be done first thing in the morning. *Early morning urine.* It won't come out right if you do it tonight," Tara authoritatively said.

I stared at her and said, my voice filled with sarcasm, "You ought to know. Is this the test you bought when you got yourself pregnant?" Tara rolled her eyes and kept silent.

A very curious and enthusiastic Natasha shot back, "Let's do it anyway." She snatched the box from me and examined its contents. "There are *two* tests in here! We can do it now *and* in the morning. Come on. I want to know!"

The three of us advanced to the bathroom. I peed while they watched. The girls and I nervously waited for the result. It was positive. "Oh my God!" Natasha exclaimed. "You *are* gonna have a baby!"

Tara snatched the vial and stared at it. Then, she glared at us. "No way. This thing is *wrong*. It's ten o'clock at night. This result is not correct. We need early morning urine. We'll try again in the morning." She exited the bathroom with the kit and got into bed with her son Lloyd who was sleeping peacefully. Natasha and I looked at each other, shrugged our shoulders, and retreated to our rooms.

At 6 a.m., Tara shook me on the shoulder to wake me up. I opened my eyes and found her standing over my bed. "Okay, let's go. It's time. Come on in the bathroom," she ordered.

Natasha was waiting by the toilet. We redid the procedure and the test was the same — positive. Stunned, I immediately woke up Lenny, whispering in his ear. "It's your lucky day. Got something to tell you, baby. You're gonna be a Daddy again. I took a test. Yep, I'm pregnant just like your favorite cousin Zena."

Without opening his eyes, he muttered, "Why do you tell lies so early in the morning, woman?" He never even turned over. Lenny was employed by the City of Philadelphia, Department of Licenses and Inspections for the past two years. It was almost time for him to get up for work.

I shook him and pushed the vial in his face. I had his full attention. He couldn't believe it. It had been seventeen years since he had fathered a child, and that was Tara. He actually thought he had become sterile. He had fathered three additional kids with whom he never had a relationship or saw. Plopped in different parts of the country, those children all had different mamas and were older than Tara who had never even met any of them. He'd become a daddy for the first time when he was sixteen while growing up in Myrtle Beach.

"Well, congratulations. I guess I'd better put in some overtime," he said.

I looked disappointed at his reaction. When he noticed my expression, he got out of bed and closed the bedroom door. He decided we'd both be late getting to work after a long session of lovemaking to celebrate the pregnancy.

I was excited when I reported to my job two and a half hours late. I was a paralegal for a small firm that handled personal injury and criminal work. Once settled, I called my girlfriend Charlotte Hilliard, whose three year old son, Darien, was my godchild. "Charlotte, guess what?" I said. Before she could answer I blurted out, "I'm pregnant."

"You're lying. Why are you messing with me this morning?"

"I'm serious. I took two of those home pregnancy tests. Who's your gynecologist? I want to call him. I remember you saying you had a good doctor and I've got to be with somebody who's excellent."

"Definitely, girl. Call Dr. Lilbourn Pratt. He'll take good care of you. You will love him. Call the Hospital of the University of Pennsylvania. His office is there. How did Lenny take it?"

"Well, he's in shock, but happy."

I got a thorough examination by Dr. Pratt and was in good shape. He advised that I needed to be careful and suggested a caesarean section. I had delivered prematurely with Natasha who arrived two months early and had a perforated uterus after my abortion of Lenny Sawyer's baby in 1975. My due date would be August 23rd. I called Zena to tell her the news. She was ecstatic, but calmly said, "I told you."

My couple life couldn't be better. Everyone was happy about the pregnancy, and Christmas was approaching. Zena gave birth to a boy on Christmas Eve, and they named him Brandon. He was born the day before his father's birthday and he was Lenny's and my new godchild. The day after Christmas, Lenny and I were coming from a holiday party at a friend's house. A car attempting to make a left hand turn careened in front of us almost hitting our vehicle. Lenny swerved in order to prevent impact of the two cars. Our car hit a fire hydrant. I was thrown about the car, but felt fine enough not to go to the hospital. I woke up the next day bruised and went to visit Dr. Pratt. He felt I would be okay, but a month later I began experiencing dizzy spells and had trouble breathing. I was diagnosed with panic disorder. I continued to work, driving into Center City Philadelphia every day. One day while out to lunch, I had a panic attack, became dazed and dizzy and fell to the ground. Medics took me to Jefferson Hospital. After examination, I was released to Lenny, who had been summoned to the hospital.

"Do you *have* to run around at lunch time? Why can't you order some lunch and eat at your desk?" Lenny demanded.

"I like to go shopping at lunch time. I have to get out to break up the day. I'll be okay."

"Maybe you ought to stop working. This may be too much with your being pregnant and all. Stay home. Shit. If you stop shopping, I can take care of you. I can pay all the bills."

"Nope, I'm working as long as I can. I have to get a lot of stuff done to the house, the nursery has to be gorgeous. I'm doing the middle bedroom all over for the baby, carpeting and all. And I have to get all of the baby's things. I'm working—that's *that*."

A week and a half later, I had another panic attack and dizzy spell while shopping in Strawbridge and Clothier in Center City during my lunch break. To my surprise, the store had a huge infirmary on the top floor with cots for patients to lie down. When Lenny picked me up, he insisted that I go to the doctor. After examinations by two physicians, my gynecologist, and a psychiatrist for the panic disorder, I was placed on bed rest for the remainder of my pregnancy. I had adequate disability coverage which covered pregnancy complications, so I had an income.

Lenny's sister, Theresa, started up. "You need to sit your ass down someplace. You're going to cause my niece or nephew to be retarded! You've got me worried to death. Do you have to drive us all crazy? I want you to stop working and do what the doctor tells you. Okay, honey."

Theresa was the same age as my mother and was Lenny's oldest sister. She was pretty, smart, and very articulate. With all of that, she still couldn't keep a husband. She was twice divorced with three daughters. I didn't feel like hearing her mouth.

"I am stopping work and staying in bed until August. I can't believe you're making *retarded* calls. You're crazy. I'll be good."

I was bored being at home. My brother, Jeff, moved in with us to wait on me. He also did all the cleaning. Jeff worked at night from eleven to seven, so someone was always home with me. Tara had moved in with a friend of hers and taken her son with her. Natasha got in from school around four o'clock every day. After five weeks of bed rest and staying in the house most of the time, I had cabin fever and was going crazy. I started driving to malls again to shop for things for the baby.

Lenny came home from work one day bubbling with excitement. "Hey, baby, listen to this. Eddie had his living room redone and it is sharp. They have this new thing—glitter ceilings. They are called *Hollywood Ceilings*. They are something else. Even our friends Thelma and Rudy have them. I think I want to get the people who did Eddie's house to do the ceiling in our living room. What do you think?"

I had impeccable taste in furnishings and decorating didn't want any glitter ceiling. "No, that's not me."

"Well, *I* like it. Can't we do it? You always fix things the way you want in the house. I just want the ceilings done." I thought about it and confessed to myself that I'd always done our home the way I wanted and figured that maybe I had been selfish.

"Okay—just the living room ceiling. Okay? Nothing wild. Agreed?"

Lenny's eyes lit up like a child. "Okay. I'll talk to Eddie and get him to set it up. I'll pay the guys myself."

Two weeks later, Lenny was getting ready for work while I was lying in the bed watching *Good Morning America*. "Listen, Denise, the crew will be here about four o'clock to do the ceiling. Make sure you're not out shopping and miss them. There will be fumes from the paint, so you have to stay up here in this bedroom until they are finished."

"Okay. No problem." I said.

They arrived and, again, I was told to stay upstairs with the bedroom door closed until they were finished. I watched TV and stayed in the room, only coming out from time to time to go to the bathroom. The crew was down there for three hours. I thought the workers were taking a long time, but then I figured they had to mix the paint or maybe spackle the ceiling before starting. Lenny hadn't gotten home from work, but I figured he and Eddie were at some bar having a few drinks. It was after all a Friday night. I was scared to go down the stairs, thinking I might have a dizzy spell or something from the paint fumes. I certainly didn't want to get sick with strange men in the house. Anything could happen. Finally, at about seven forty-five, they called up the stairs to tell me they were leaving. I couldn't resist taking a look at the ceiling and rushed down to the living room after they left.

It was pitch dark outside, but there was brightness in the living room without any lighting. The walls were white with silver speckles mixed in the paint. The place glittered all over. Sparkles were everywhere. The walls in the dining and living rooms glistened and the ceilings sparkled too. They had sprayed the fireplace in the living room and the mantle. The place looked like the Wizard of Oz or a discotheque. All it needed was a giant silver ball like the one in the movie *Saturday Night Fever*. I started screaming obscenities. I ran outside of the house looking for the paint crew's truck. They were gone. I was cursing the workers out. I couldn't wait to get my hands on Lenny and Eddie.

Fifteen minutes later, Lenny came strutting home. I was sitting on my living room couch in amazement when he walked in. I was wearing a pair of sunglasses. Lenny had a nice buzz. He and Eddie had been to happy hour at Slim Cooper's on Stenton Avenue. He was in a good mood and Eddie was on his way home.

As soon as he bent down to kiss me, I started screaming at him. "Goddammit, look at my house! Look at this shit! Is this the fucking Wizard of Oz or what? I thought you told me a ceiling? *One* Damn ceiling! You said one damn ceiling! Look at this place. I should kill your ass! You'd better get those damn people back here and get this shit off my walls!"

Lenny stared at the glitter walls in amazement. I wouldn't shut up. I kept babbling.

"Look—I swear I did not know they were going to do this. I'll fix it. I'll call Eddie. Calm down before you have the baby right now," he said. Lenny was pissed. This shit was blowing his high. He'd had such a good time at the bar and hated that he'd had to come home. He walked through the living and dining rooms, shaking his head and touching the walls. He looked up at the ceilings again in amazement and muttered, "What the fuck happened? Did they just get happy with the paint?" He turned to me and I still had on those damn sunglasses. He finally went down to the basement, poured himself another drink, and sat at the bar. I followed him and sat on a stool next to him. He looked at me and started laughing.

"Oh, you think this shit is funny?" You know my baby shower is in two weeks. That shit better be gone. I mean it, Lenny," I snapped.

He lifted the glasses off my face. "I'll get the house fixed. I'll come straight home from work every night and work on it myself. I swear to God I will get the shit off the walls! I'm not letting those crazy motherfuckers back in here. I'll get my tools and work on it. Just shut up about it." Lenny gulped down his drink.

"Where did Eddie find those damn people?" I asked.

"I don't know. Let's drop it."

"Okay. I'm going to start shopping for wall paper. I want the rooms papered when you get that crap off."

"Can we leave the glitter on the ceilings like you promised me? That's not so bad." Lenny turned on his Leo charm.

"I don't care, Lenny. Just get the walls together and the fireplace. I can't believe those assholes spray painted the fireplace. They must have been on LSD. I swear the place looks like a disco. All we need is John Travolta dancing his ass off upstairs and that giant silver ball in the ceiling twirling around. Wait until my brother sees it. He's gonna die."

For the next two weeks, Lenny worked diligently. He was quite successful at transforming the walls. He turned out to be a master at paper hanging. I had purchased gorgeous paper from Atlas Wallpaper at 8th and Chestnut. The house was beautiful for my shower. He had also done the baby's nursery, which was fuchsia, turquoise and yellow wall paper— parachutes with teddy bears in the baskets. I ordered yellow carpeting and lovely furniture, bought a stereo system and soft music tapes, a television set, exquisite comforters that matched the wall paper exactly, and a white grandfather clock that sat on a white wicker nightstand. The clock was a cassette player that played fairy tales. It was divine and everything I had ever wanted for my baby's nursery.

It was a scorching hot afternoon in August and I was on the telephone talking to my best buddy, Joanne. "Look, just bring your butt over here tomorrow. It's Sunday, you're off from work. We're having a hard shell crab party. I'm ordering two bushels of crabs from Dinardo's."

"You're gonna get in trouble with those crabs. Remember what happened three months ago when you went to Boston Sea Party and ate every crab leg in the place. You wound up in the hospital with contractions. That iodine is a bitch in those crabs. The doctor told you if you wanted to go full term—lay off the crabs."

"I cannot stand being pregnant another minute. I want my baby— now. I'm having a crab party and guess what, I'm planning on having this baby by tomorrow night, on Lenny's birthday. Yep, Daddy is going to get his baby on his birthday. All I have to do is eat those crabs, have some good sex, and I'll go into labor."

"Okay Mrs. *Common Law Garner*—go on and try it. You're crazy."

"I'll bet you a hundred dollars I have this baby by tomorrow night. You know I'm having a C-section anyway, so I don't have to waste time in labor."

"Yeah, that C-section is scheduled for August 23rd and I bet that's when you'll have the baby. But, just to please you, I'll take the bet, but only for twenty bucks. See you tomorrow. I'll bring a case of beer and you know you can't have any of that."

"You're on, pal, twenty bucks. I'm hanging up and calling the rest of the gang and then I'm calling Dinardo's. See ya."

I immediately called my sister-in-law, Rhonda, and Demetrious' sister, Karly. Karly and I were now best friends. She and her husband Chuck had reconciled and had been living in Philly for three years when I got pregnant. They were renting a property owned by my cousin Lynne. After I called everybody, I placed the order with Dinardo's in Center City, my best place for crabs.

When I got off the phone, Lenny entered our beautiful basement. Damn he looked like Marvin Gaye! "What are you up to, fatso?" he asked.

"I've decided to have the baby tomorrow," I said emphatically. "It's a crab party tomorrow afternoon and everybody's coming over. You have to pick up two bushels of crabs from Dinardo's at noon tomorrow. Your baby will be born on your birthday—I'll see to that."

"What about August 23rd? You know—the due date—remember that?"

"That's over, darling," I said with a wave of my hand. "It's too hot. I'm tired and I think your baby will be a perfect birthday present. Now give me a little kiss."

"You're a piece of work and I bet this doesn't go down. You won't have that baby tomorrow."

I moved from the bar stool and waddled over to Lenny. I planted a kiss on his tiny lips and purred, "Crabs and sex will send me to the hospital. Wanna bet me? Joanne has already gotten in line to lose twenty bucks."

"I'll pass on the bet. I'll pick the crabs up tomorrow. Wanna go for a drive?"

"Yeah, let's ride out to Aunt Claudia's and see what she's up to. Let's surprise her."

$*\ *\ *$

It was two o'clock in the afternoon on Sunday, the 12th of August. It was Lenny's forty-first birthday. The table was set up in the basement. Mallets and crab eating paraphernalia were in the center of the table. The beer was on ice and the bushels of crabs were out on the patio. A gallon of lemonade in a plastic milk carton sat beside my seat. Rhonda and her husband Chuck – yes, she and Karly were both married to men named Chuck — Karly, and Joanne had shown up. They all sat down to start the feast.

We chatted as we ate the crabs. Rhonda announced to everyone, "I've got some fresh fish I brought over. It's Sea Trout and Spots. Chuck caught them when he went night fishing last night. I put the bag in the refrigerator. We can fry them later." Rhonda and I were pretty tight. She was a great sister-in-law. Rhonda was thirty years old with a pretty face and a slamming body. She was a legal secretary who'd landed a job after I had broken her into that field. Prior to that, she was working as a clerk for the State and was making too little money. I gave her a little training and hooked her up with an agency. Rhonda was as smart as a whip and was making the big bucks now.

"You brought some fish over here?" I asked.

"Yep," Rhonda said.

"Chuck, did you clean the damn things? Me and Lenny will have a fight tonight if I ask him to clean some fish after all the stuff he's done today," I said.

"Oh, don't worry about that. He brought them home already cleaned, wrapped in newspaper, and they're in a paper bag. Everything's done. They had people at the docks cleaning the fish this morning after the boat came back in," Rhonda said.

I cut a glance at Lenny. Lenny was trying not to laugh. He wouldn't look back at me. Chuck never said a word.

"I forgot to take my vitamin. I'm going upstairs to get it. I'll be right back." I headed up the stairs and into the kitchen. I was making noise, rummaging through the kitchen cabinets and slamming doors shut. "Lenny, can you come up here? I can't find my vitamins. Did you clean the cabinet out and put them somewhere?" I yelled down the stairs.

"You can never find anything. I'm on my way."

When he entered the kitchen, I was standing there with the bag of fish in my hand. "That lying sack of shit. *Night* Fishing. *Pleeze*. How dumb can Rhonda be? He *bought* this damn fish. This fish is not fresh out of the water. Smell this bag. Fresh fish does not have a scent like this. Yeah, he was fishing last night—and the rod is between his legs," I huffed.

Lenny examined the fish, heads off and split, and it indeed had an odor. He started laughing. "That damn Chuck is a trip." We both fell in laughter.

"I don't know how Rhonda goes for all his lies. I swear she has rocks in her head. She needs to leave his trifling ass. Remember that story he told her a month ago when he stayed out all night long. He told her he was in New Jersey visiting some friends and, on the way home, he made a few wrong turns and ended up in a forest. He told her he was driving around all night in the woods and couldn't find his way out. She called me up telling me how worried she had been and was thankful he had made it out. His ass got home at eleven o'clock in the morning! He told Rhonda he was scared to death all night that some bears or some other animal would get him."

Lenny cracked up. "Well, she's happy with him—leave my brother-in-law alone. Hell, we've tried too many times to get her to leave him. She can't function without him, so let her ass stay. They've been together eleven years—shit—she must like it." Lenny put the fish back in the refrigerator.

"Well, she can do much better than him. He reminds me of Pinocchio. You know how Pinocchio's nose got bigger every time he told a lie? Well, that gap between Chuck's two front teeth gets bigger every time he comes up with one of his stories. I'm pissed with him."

We returned to the basement, ate crabs, and drank for three hours. I consumed half a bushel of crabs by myself. After everybody left, Lenny and I got into bed, watched some TV, and had some good sex. I fell asleep **certain I would soon be up with pains. I slept through the entire night and** woke up at seven thirty in the morning. Lenny had taken off that day from work.

"Okay, I guess the crabs didn't work. Guess I owe Joanne twenty bucks. I have my doctor's appointment at Dr. Pratt's today at eleven thirty. You going with me?" I asked, unable to mask my disappointment.

"Yeah, I'm going. Let's get some breakfast and get out of here. I have to stop at the bank, too. We're out of money," Lenny sighed.

We stopped at the ATM Machine at 36th and Market and then headed to Dr. Pratt's office. We waited twenty-five minutes before we were escorted in to see the doctor. He examined me as I lay on top of the table. Lenny sat on a chair in the office, watching the doctor. "Denise, something's going on here, dear. You're contracting. I have to arrange for you to be admitted to the hospital. You're going to have this baby today. You know you were supposed to have a C-Section on the 23rd. Well, you're having your baby ten days early. Let's go. Get dressed. I'll get Maureen to set everything up. It's baby time. I'll be at the hospital very soon," Dr. Pratt said.

When the doctor left the room, I bragged to Lenny, "I told you! I told you I could do it! I may be a day late, but I did it! I knew what I was doing. Get my stuff so we can get out of here."

Lenny couldn't believe I had actually pulled it off. It was August 13, 1984 and, for the first time, he would be around to see a child of his come into the world. He was excited and kissed me. I noticed he was also a little nervous. Lenny and I were escorted to the delivery floor of the Hospital of the University of Pennsylvania. Once I was in a bed, he called his co-workers and family to tell them the news. He was grinning from ear to ear. The nurse came in the room with an IV bag and some needles. "Hi, Mr. and Mrs. Garner. I have to place a needle in the Mommy-to-be's back. It's an epidural and will block the pain during the C-section. Let's get started. It'll hurt a bit, but you'll be okay."

Lenny's entire expression changed. He was frowning and getting nervous. He was scared to death of needles. He put his face in his hands. "I've got to leave. Listen, I just need to take a walk. I'll be back." He ran out of the room before me or the nurse could say anything. He vanished.

At 2:50 that afternoon, Dr. Pratt lifted a baby girl from my tummy. As soon as he handed her over for Mommy's inspection, Lenny walked into the delivery room and stood by the door. "I'm back," he said meekly to me and Dr. Pratt.

"Well, we don't need you now. You were really a great help to you wife," Dr. Pratt said sarcastically. "You have a new daughter and she's getting cleaned up. You can wait outside, you big chicken."

Lenny was as high as a kite, having spent the last hour and a half at a bar having four Courvoisier's and two Heinekens. After the drink fest, he had run over to his job to brag about the upcoming baby. "Awe, come on, Dr Pratt. I just got scared. I'm petrified of needles. I'm sorry I ran off. Can I come in?"

"Come on in, you big punk," Dr. Pratt joked.

Lenny looked at his daughter in amazement as she wriggled in the hospital cradle. He was loving her. He looked over at what Dr. Pratt was doing to my stomach and turned his head. He did not want to see that shit. Scared him to death. "How much does she weigh?" he asked the nurse.

"She's six pounds eight ounces and has all her fingers and toes," the nurse replied.

Lenny kept gazing at his daughter. She had a big head just like his and his tiny mouth. He was crazy about her already. "What are you guys going to name her?" the nurse asked. There was silence. Lenny wanted to name her Christina like Christmas since she was a present.

I liked that, but I thought we could be more creative. "How about Noelle? That's Christmassy, but more beautiful than Christina. Noelle, her name will be Noelle, after Christmas. *Noelle*," I said dreamily.

"That's a beautiful name—*Noelle*," the nurse said.

Lenny was flattered, glad it was his idea, and proud. "Yeah, baby, I like that name, too. Let's definitely do that. What about the middle name," he asked.

"Well, let's do Christina, Daddy. Okay?"

Lenny beamed with pride. "I like that. Noelle Christina."

"Happy belated birthday, Daddy," I beamed.

During the hospital stay, I was in a lot of pain. There were gas pains associated with the C-Section. Many times, I wished I'd had a vaginal delivery so I wouldn't have to endure being constantly uncomfortable and **begging for medication. Aside from the fact that Noelle had jaundice,** she was fine. I was worried to death when the nursed explained it was a condition in which there was yellowing of the whites of the eyes, skin and mucous membranes caused by bile pigments in the blood. But she told me it sometimes occurred temporarily in newborn babies whose livers are slightly immature.

In the days that followed, whenever the nurses would wheel Noelle's cradle in my room for feedings, I'd wait until they left to scoop her up and place her in bed with me. Noelle would have her bottle and fall asleep in her Mommy's arms. Those moments together with my newborn daughter were magical. I stayed in the hospital for six days and on Sunday, August 19, Lenny came to pick us up.

"Okay, ladies, time to go home." Lenny was smiling as he entered the room. Noelle was all dressed up in her beautiful pink and white dress that Aunt Joanne had purchased for her arrival home. Aunt Sarah, better known as Munch, another best buddy of mine, had stopped by the day before to drop off a Kanga-Rock-A-Roo infant seat for Noelle to ride home in. I was dressed and ready to go home. Lenny got our bags together and went to load up the car. He returned to the room for his family. A proud Lenny scooped the infant seat up and proceeded down the hall to the elevator. He was as happy as could be with his new daughter. The nurse pushed me in a wheelchair behind Lenny and Noelle. When they got outside, Lenny continued walking toward the car. I was removed from the wheelchair by the nurse. Lenny never looked back and I decided to try to catch up with him and Noelle. I was having trouble walking because of the surgery and was trailing behind them, unable to keep up. Lenny and Noelle were far ahead of me. He still hadn't turned around to look for me. I watched as closely as I could since I had no idea where Lenny parked. Finally, Lenny stopped at the car and carefully placed Noelle's infant seat in the back and belted her in. I finally made it to the car, opened the passenger door, eased in, and tried to get comfortable. Lenny was waiting in the driver's seat for me to get situated. I looked back at Noelle, then at Lenny. "Looks like you don't need me anymore."

He *caught* what I meant and gasped, embarrassed to have left me behind. "Oh, shit. Baby, I'm sorry. I didn't mean to leave you. I'm all excited. Are you okay?"

"I'm okay. Can you two just get me home? I mean, can you two be bothered with a damn near cripple person who recently had major surgery and has had pains shooting through her for the last seven days?"

When we arrived home, Lenny took Noelle out of the car and set her infant seat on the landing of our front steps. He came back for me and helped me out of the car. He had me sit on the steps next to the baby's seat as he removed the bags from the car and placed them on the sidewalk. Before he unlocked the door to the house, he yelled to neighbors who were sitting on their porches and front steps. He went up and down the block ringing our neighbors' door bells to let them know his baby was home. People started to come over to look at Noelle and talk to me. Finally, he took his family into the house. He got us up the stairs to the master bedroom. He set Noelle's infant seat on the floor by our bed.

"She's staying in here, right? We've got to be able to hear her. Maria is coming over soon with her bassinette, she called this morning. She'll be here by four o'clock. I need to check to see if my baby is wet. I have to get the diapers. What time did you last feed her? Maybe she's hungry. I have all the formula downstairs. I got the *Ready to Feed Enfamil* like the nurse said. Maybe we should take her dress off and put her pajamas on. It's hot in here, but do you think we should turn the air conditioner on? I don't want her to catch a cold. She doesn't have to take any medicine for that jaundice thing, right? Tomorrow I have to make an appointment at the pediatrician for her. I'll take her myself whenever it is. I'll take off work for that. I'm staying home tomorrow. Call Zena to see if she needs to tell you anything to do for the baby. Natasha spent the night at Dana's and will be home soon. I called her this morning." Lenny didn't take a breath once.

I meekly replied, "I'm hungry."

"Oh—yeah—I'm going to cook dinner. I'm frying chicken and making some other stuff. Let me get the baby settled in her pajamas and I'll get the food going."

Lenny dashed into Noelle's room, rummaged through the dresser drawers, and returned with a sleeper and a packed diaper bag. As I watched, he undressed Noelle, did the best he could to get the diaper and sleeper on her. I enjoyed seeing Lenny take care of the baby like that. I felt we would be happy forever. "What about her bottle?" he asked.

"**I fed her an hour before you got to the hospital. She's not hungry.** If she were, she'd be crying. She's okay. Do me a favor? Grab me a pair of short pajamas out of the drawer. I need to get out of these clothes. After that, you can do the food. I'm starving, and it's almost three o'clock. Do you have to pick Natasha up or is Cynthia bringing her home?" I asked.

"Cynthia is bringing her. Here's your stuff," he said laying a set of pink pajamas on the bed. Do you need help?" Lenny asked.

"Nope—I'm cool."

Lenny stared at the both of us. He was happy to have us home. He was reluctant to leave Noelle with me because he felt he needed to be there to run things for a while. I was in bad shape, he thought. "Look, I can take her downstairs with me and she can help me cook," he offered.

"Lenny, it's okay. Go do what you have to do. I can take care of Noelle. Maria will be here in an hour. Relax. I've had a baby before and I know what to do—remember Natasha? If I don't understand something, I'll check it out with Maria or Zena or I'll call the hospital. Chill, baby, I'm not gonna screw this up."

Maria was my Italian girlfriend. She arrived on schedule with her twenty-year old niece, Trina and was thrilled to meet her new niece. She set up the bassinette, which had belonged to Andrea, Maria and Frank's four month old daughter, with Trina. Maria and I had met when we both worked at a law firm together. We were like family to each other.

"Thank God you didn't name the kid Wendi," Maria said to me. "I was scared to death you'd do that. I hate that name. I love the name you chose. "Hey, Noelle," Maria cooed as she rocked the baby in her arms. "It's Auntie Maria. You're gonna have fun when you come to my house. You and Andrea are going to be best friends like me and Mommy."

We put Noelle back into the bassinette and the hood toppled on her. Maria and I screamed, thinking it hit Noelle. Trina shrieked. They instantly removed the hood and there was a red mark on Noelle's forehead. They screamed again. I heard Lenny running up the stairs. Maria scooped Noelle out of the bassinette as Lenny charged into the room.

"What happened?," he demanded.

I looked at Noelle and screamed, "Oh my God—it's blood!" I snatched my child out of Maria's arms to examine the wound. I touched it. "This is lipstick! Shit, I was scared to death."

Lenny rolled his eyes at all of us, put Noelle in her infant seat, and headed down the stairs with her, leaving the three of us in the bedroom.

Natasha arrived home at six o'clock. She was thrilled to meet her little sister. She gave Noelle her first feeding at the kitchen table with Lenny supervising. I had taken a pill for the pain and fallen asleep.

I woke up two and a half hours later. Starving, I made it down the stairs and saw no one in the kitchen. Voices echoed in the basement. I went down there and saw a bunch of our neighbors. I surveyed the room. Lenny had a cooler packed with ice against a wall. It contained bottles of beer, wine, and bottles of formula. Noelle's packed diaper bag was next to it, unzipped and displaying diapers, Vaseline, powder, and baby wipes. People were sitting at the bar and in folding chairs. Chatter, food, and drink filled the room. Noelle was perched on the large coffee table in her infant seat with Natasha sitting guard on the couch. The stereo was playing softly and the party was on!

"Hey, baby, glad you're up. I got them all out of their houses—took my baby with me. You hungry? Want me to make you a virgin daiquiri or a Piña Colada? We're having a party for my baby. She's over there—still up. She's a party animal like her Daddy. Two Leo's in the house now, baby. You better buy some No Doze pills from Rite Aid, so you can hang with me and Noelle. We're all going to Happy Hour every Friday night, me and my baby. We'll be partying for the rest of our lives back to back on our birthdays, too—me and Noelle," Lenny said.

* * *

It was ten days before Christmas and Noelle was a little over four months old. I had been shopping like mad for the past two weeks. Santa Claus was coming to town. Natasha wanted a typewriter, so it had to be the elaborate IBM Selectric III—nine hundred dollars and the best model out—along with an array of clothing, music tapes including Natasha's favorite group, New Edition, bath gels and pajamas. I had already had Natasha's entire room redone around the time Lenny was working on Noelle's nursery. Natasha's new digs were beautifully decorated in primary colors and new white carpeting. He had done an excellent job wallpapering it. It was indeed gorgeous.

Now that all the Christmas gifts had been purchased, we needed a tree. It had to be beautiful because we were expecting company from Chicago. Karly and Demetrious' Mom, Agatha, was coming along with Aunt Bella who adored Lenny and me. We'd gone to visit them for Thanksgiving and taken the baby. Aunt Bella's daughter, Susan, was also joining them. The Chicago gang planned to stay at our house for a week.

I managed to talk my sister, Darlene, into coming with me on my tree hunting mission. "Hey Darlene, what are you doing today?" I asked my sister in a phone conversation.

We decided to hit the Willow Grove Mall first so my sister could get the last of her gifts and I could look for some decorations.

The first place we went to was Abraham and Strauss Department Store. I found some tree decorations I liked, but not enough stuff. As my frustration mounted, I noticed a beautiful tree on display in the store. A huge tree with gorgeous ornaments. I loved it. I searched for Darlene and dragged her to the tree.

"I love this tree. This is exactly what I need," I beamed.

"Well, let's just tell them you want the ornaments from the tree. You'll have to pay for each of them. Let's see how much they are a piece." Darlene began to remove ornaments to check the prices.

"That's not what I mean. I want the whole tree. *Decorated. Just like it is.* I want to purchase the entire damn thing. I want it delivered to my house," I said.

Darlene's eyes bulged. "These people aren't doing that. This is the store's tree. You can't buy this thing. I figure they may sell you some ornaments off it, but these people aren't selling this tree. Christmas isn't here yet and this is the display—dummy." Darlene was used to my craziness, but this was the one time she thought I wouldn't get what I wanted.

I ignored her and looked around for a salesperson. I spotted one and walked over to her. "Miss, do you see that tree over there?" I pointed at my newly found masterpiece.

"Yes," the clerk answered.

"Well, I want it. I want the entire tree just as it is—lights, ornaments— everything. I want it delivered to my house. I have an account here and I'm an American Express cardholder."

"Ma'am, I don't think we can do that," the clerk answered.

"Can you make a call to management to find out for sure?" I asked.

∗ ∗ ∗

"It is seven degrees out here and I am freezing! I didn't even bring my gloves because we were supposed to be in the car. I can't believe we have this big ass tree. I swear it's not gonna fit in this car. We need to take the damn thing apart! It's artificial. Shit. We can just put it back together later. It's cold out here," Darlene shouted.

"Look, I took all the decorations off while you were shopping. I did most of the *real* work. We can get the thing in the car. Let's just maneuver it around. It'll fit," I snapped back.

"Denise—dummy—you have the *box*. Let's break it down and put it in the box. I'm freezing," Darlene roared.

"I'm rolling the windows down, we're stuffing it in this car and we're going straight to my house," I shouted.

"You make me sick," Darlene screamed.

During the ride home, cold air was blowing through the open windows to accommodate my great tree. We were frozen to the bone. Darlene cursed me out and shivered all the way back to my place. We finally arrived and the two of us dragged the tree up my steps—stand and all. We stood it up in the living room. "I can't believe you paid eleven hundred dollars for all this shit. It's a good thing you decided to start temping for that legal agency. You're gonna need some money when that bill comes next month. My hands are probably frostbitten." She rubbed her hands together, rolling her eyes at me. "Come on, I need a ride home."

While we were driving back, Darlene asked, "What did you get Noelle for Christmas?"

"Diamond stud earrings," I proudly said.

CHAPTER 5

～

The Cemetery

It was Christmas time again a year later, Noelle's second Christmas. I decided to do my Christmas shopping in New York City. It would be Natasha's first trip to Manhattan, and she couldn't contain her excitement. My friends, Roseanne and Cynthia, went with us on the train along with Cynthia's daughter, Kita, who was the same age as thirteen year old Natasha. Lenny was babysitting Noelle while we were away. The group of us had a ball and put a dent in our credit cards. When we returned, Natasha and I stopped by my mother's house to show her what we had purchased.

After going through the things, my mother, Louise, announced that Ava, my older sister, had met a new guy. They had been dating for the past two weeks. His name was Kenneth. I was glad for Ava. She had a hard time with men all of her life. Her son, Andrew, was eighteen years old and away in the military. Andrew never had a relationship with his father because he had dumped Ava when she got pregnant at age fifteen.

"That's really great, mom. What's Kenneth like? What does he do? Where did she meet him? How old is he?" I was weary about her choice in men and was hoping she had gotten it right this time.

"Well, she met him when he came to the VA hospital for something or other. He's a minister. He's in his thirties." Louise said, shifting her pleasantly plump frame in the chair. Looking at my mother was like looking at a mirror image of myself. We shared the same skin tone and eyes. My mother's graying hair was swept up in an elegant French twist.

"Oh, that's nice. I hope it works out. Where is she today?," I wondered.

"Oh, they're probably off somewhere. I guess you'll meet him some time before the holidays are over." Louise answered patiently.

"I'll have them over to the house for dinner or something. Where's his church?"

"I forgot. She'll probably tell you when she talks to you."

Two weeks later, Ava and Kenneth stopped by our house. Lenny let them in and yelled for me to come downstairs. A beaming Ava introduced me to Kenneth.

For some reason, I took an immediate dislike to the handsome, five foot eleven medium complexion Kenneth even though he had a gleaming smile and was quite friendly. I was cordial to him, asked a few questions about his work with his ministry, and inquired about his family whom he said lived in some city I can't remember. During their visit, I noticed Ava had this *airy* thing about her. Her voice had changed, she seemed aloof and was acting a little stuck up to be in her own sister's house. As I studied her, it reminded me of how women get a man and become "too good" for other people at times. These chicks act like they've been poor all their lives and just struck it rich. All of a sudden, they're too good for the people who have been around their poor asses during the bad times. But this was how Ava had always been. Having a man always changed her and made her start acting like a movie star who just got the leading role. Everyone else in the world could kiss her ass. But her relationships never lasted. The girl was now thirty-five years old. She had been jilted once and every other man had walked all over her—after she took mounds of bullshit off them. Ava was passive unlike her feisty sisters, Darlene and me. Always submissive, gullible, sweet, and accommodating to her men, Ava never learned, and that's why she couldn't manage to keep one.

They stayed a little over an hour and then left. I didn't like Kenneth, but I managed to hide it from everybody and treated him like royalty.

As soon as they left, I began my rant to Lenny. "You know what? There's something about that guy. I swear I don't know what it is, but I can't stand him. I just don't trust him. Humph. I have this bad feeling about him. Ava appears to be head over heels in love with him. This is scary. I wonder what's wrong with me. The man hasn't done one thing to me and for some reason I can't stand him."

Lenny sighed. "Listen. Give him a break. He's probably okay. He'll grow on you, I guess. Who cares? She's just fucking around with the guy.

It's not like she's going to marry him. Relax." Lenny grabbed a beer from the refrigerator and headed down to the basement.

Two weeks later, my mother informed me that Kenneth and Ava were getting married in a month.

"Is she crazy? She just met this guy! She's only been dating him six weeks. She's moving too fast. What do you think about him? I've only seen him once and my antennas went up as soon as I looked at him," I screamed into the phone.

"Well, I swear he seems to be a nice guy. He is in the church and all. You know he is a Reverend. He comes over all the time. I think he's nice." My mother was just as bad a judge of men as Ava sometimes. I wanted to slap them both.

"What church? Where is the church? He told me when he was at the house, but I didn't write it down. I want to go to the church. Find out where it is. I'm calling her now. I've got to go. Bye." I slammed down the receiver and immediately called my sister.

"Hey, mom told me the news. What's this all about?" It was such a feat for me to keep a normal voice.

"Well, Kenneth and I are getting married in March. I'm making all the arrangements now. I've already gotten a lot done. I found a dress I like and I'm talking to people about getting a hall for the reception." Ava reeled off.

"Whoa," I said, "hold up. What's the rush? Where's the fire, baby?"

"Look, this is what we want to do—right away. I don't need a lot of flack from you," Ava snapped.

"Well, don't you have to look for a house and all? Or are you going to move in with him? Does Kenneth have a house? What about Andrew, what's he saying?" I questioned.

"Kenneth is renting a room, so that means he is moving in with me."

"Well, what about Andrew—you know—your son? What's he going to do when he comes home on leave? You know you only have a one-bedroom apartment," I reminded Ava.

"When he comes home, he can either sleep on the couch here at my place—or he can stay at Mommy's. He'll probably stay at your house, that's where he always ended up anyway when he used to come home for the summer and holidays from boarding school. He always liked being over there with you, Lenny, and Natasha. I'm not worrying about that. He's a grown man now, anyway."

I was pissed. Damn. Ava had shipped Andrew off to Milton Hershey Academy when he was a mere eight years old. Many times, he wanted to bring friends home from school during breaks and always brought them to our place so he could show off our house. He knew his Auntie Denise had room for him and anyone else with him. I kept a house full of food and snacks and had people coming to clean my house. Andrew often bragged to his friends, "My Aunt Denise has a maid." When he went to his senior prom, it was me and Lenny who drove from Philly to Hershey to see him off and make a big fuss over him. His own mother felt she had done enough by preparing him with clothes for the affair. I must admit she had spent a ton of money, but he needed more than that. When he enlisted in the Army at eighteen, it was me who sent plane tickets for him to come home to visit so he could save his money. Yep, I love my nephew. In fact, I had named him and taken care of him when he was a baby. Every place his mother lived in since he was born never had a bedroom for him. Ava was working for the Feds and making a ton of money—and hoarding every dime of it. She was a thrifty Cancer. I thought she was being selfish and definitely moving too fast with the wedding plans, but I didn't want to start a fight so I changed the subject. "What are the arrangements for the wedding, sweetie?"

"Well, we want the ceremony and reception to be at the same place. I'm looking at the Merion Tribute House in Lower Merion for everything. I think I'll get that place and the wedding will be on March 23rd," Ava said.

"Well, sis, do what you like. I feel you need more time," I added.

"What do you want me to do, get shacked up like you and Lenny have been doing for the past four years?"

That comment pissed me off. "Yeah, me and Lenny may be shacked up, but we're still together. By the way, since Kenneth is a minister in the church and all, why aren't you two getting married at his church? Aren't you going to be the first lady of the church?"

"He doesn't want to get married at that church."

"By the way," I asked, "where is the church again? I need to go to church myself. I haven't been in a long time. Maybe I'll go with you on Sunday. Wanna do that? Then I can hear my soon to be brother-in-law preach."

"I'll call you back on that. I have to go. I need to call the florist."

In three days I called Ava back. "How are things going with the arrangements?"

"They are coming fine," Ava said, lacking emotion.

"Well, I wanted to ask you something."

"What?," Ava huffed.

"Has Kenneth ever been married before and does he have any kids?"

"No. This is his first marriage and no kids. What else do you want to know?" Ava snapped.

"Well, what am I supposed to be doing for the wedding?"

"Well, the Merion Tribute House is taking care of everything. We don't need any food or anything."

"Well, what about what I'm supposed to wear?," I asked, annoyed. "I have to get my gown or dress or whatever."

"You can wear whatever you want. You've got a ton of clothes. If you want to buy something new, that's up to you."

"What are you talking about, Ava? You know I have to have a bridesmaid dress. Have you made a choice on that?"

"You're not a bridesmaid. I thought it over. You do realize that we aren't really sisters, don't you?" Ava stated her words in a matter-of-fact manner.

It was as if she had punched me in the stomach. "What are you talking about? What are you saying?" I snapped.

"Well, we don't have the same father. Remember that? Have you forgotten that? That just makes you *biologically* my half sister. It's just a *biological* thing. I've decided that my girlfriends, Charese and Donna will be my bridesmaids. You're not in the wedding."

Her words were scathing. Every time I thought of the word *biological*, I imagined a test tube. It hurt and completely crushed me. Tears streamed down my face. I leaned my head against my kitchen wall, test tubes flashing in my mind. Noelle, who was now a year and a half, was sitting on the kitchen floor taking pots out of the cabinet. I hung the phone up and scooped her in my arms. We got into my bed and I held my baby and cried.

When the weekend rolled around, I called my mother to discuss everything Ava had said to me. All three of my mother's daughters had different fathers.

"Well, I don't know what to say. You know you don't like Kenneth, so maybe you shouldn't be in the wedding. Are you sure you just aren't jealous of Ava—her getting married and all? That's what she thinks."

"Mom, I am not *jealous*. If she's got the right guy and he'll treat her well, I'm happy as hell for her. I don't need a piece of paper to seal up anything for Lenny and me. I really don't. There is just something about Kenneth I cannot stand, but I can tolerate him. I'm admitting to that. Do you notice anything unusual about him? I mean, do you like him? What's your take on the situation? Somebody needs to be paying attention to him because you know Ava has no skills on picking men or running a relationship, being as naïve and gullible as she is. Somebody needs to be looking out for her."

"I'm telling you he really is a nice guy. I do like him. There's only one thing I feel is a little weird or strange about him," Louise admitted.

"What's that?"

"Well, he eats dinner over here a lot. They come over all the time. You know your sister can't cook, so I help her out with that. Every time he finishes his meal, he goes for a walk."

"A *walk*? There's nothing weird about that, Mom."

Louise hesitated, "Well, he always walks through that cemetery around the corner. He's usually out there about an hour and you know its dark out when he goes. He said he likes the cemetery."

I was now convinced that I was not overreacting about my ill feelings about him. Something was definitely wrong with him. Over the next few weeks, Ava continued giving me the run around about attending one of his church services and wouldn't tell me where the church was located. She forged on with her wedding plans.

The closer we came to the date, the more uneasy and withdrawn I became about attending. I was wounded about not being part of the wedding and the remarks Ava had made about me only being a *biological* sister to her. Finally, I announced to Lenny and the rest of the family that I would not attend. I simply found it easier to nix the entire affair.

Darlene was also not a member of the wedding party. Throughout the planning of the wedding, I received all kinds of calls from people who had grown up with us. Former best friends of Ava's, who had supported her in friendship throughout her life, were in disbelief they hadn't been chosen to be in the wedding. Numerous friends from the old neighborhood were hurt because they, too, had not even been invited. Even my cousin Lynne, who was really *my* cousin only because she was my father's sister's child, was not invited. That was terrible because the three of us had grown up together playing jacks at my Aunt Ora's house and going to the movies together on Saturdays. Aunt Ora was my dad's sister. We spent weekends with one another as kids and went to the Thanksgiving Day Parades every year, freezing our butts off together. Ava was always accepted by my father's people and always made welcome. Damn, she didn't even invite my father. She could have at least invited Lynne and my Aunt Ora, who'd fed her so many weekends during our visits at her house. I was enraged! Whenever I spent nights with my dad's family or at Lynne's, Ava was there right along with me. Not one member of my dad's family was invited to the wedding. Hell, if money was the problem, I would have paid for each of them.

I sympathized with them all and also felt that Yvonne, Ava's long time friend and godmother to Andrew, should have definitely been part of the wedding party. It was Yvonne and her family who had her back since eighth grade. It was Yvonne and her family who had given her a beautiful baby shower when she wound up pregnant with Andrew at fifteen. It was Yvonne and her family who had always paid attention to Andrew, purchased expensive clothing for him, and never missed giving him gifts for birthdays and holidays since his birth. The Bennett family was a sound support system for my sister. I was angry with Ava for excluding Yvonne. And there was Nadine whom Ava and I had been friends with forever. Nadine was deeply hurt. She figured she had been excluded because of her weight problem. She weighed about two hundred thirty-five pounds. However, she had been through thick and thin with Ava, always sticking by her side.

Three days prior to the wedding, pressure was mounting from family members and friends to forget about what Ava had said and attend my sister's wedding. Lenny was trying to smooth things over and begged me to attend. On Saturday, I gave in at the last minute and Lenny and I got dressed to kill. We showed up, surprising everyone. I paid six hundred dollars for the beige St. John knit dress I walked through the door in. Price never deterred me from buying something I wanted. In fact, I could never hold onto a dollar. However, I was a true fashionista, and they didn't call me Diana Ross for nothing. Lenny, that fine thing, looked like Marvin Gaye—suit, sunglasses and all. Dammit, we *represented* that fucking day if we never had before in our lives.

Ava looked lovely in a beautiful dress, her bridesmaids as stunning in navy blue mid-calf length dresses. The Merion Tribute House turned out to be a beautiful facility in suburban Philadelphia. The room was gorgeously decorated for the affair. Ava had a flute player perform a solo. Andrew had flown in from Louisiana where he was stationed. He was staying with my mother while in town.

People at the reception hall approached Lenny and me, hugging us. They said things like, "We are so glad to see you guys. Thank God you came. Denise, you certainly are bigger than Ava, coming after what she said to you. I'm proud of you. You look sharp, too." Other than greeting us, Ava paid no attention to us. My feelings were hurt, but Lenny didn't let it bother him. He went looking for booze, food, and people to talk with. Lenny was working the room with his Leo charm.

After scanning the room several times, I noticed the guests standing in line waiting for their meal. I hated to see people standing in line for food—anywhere. I hated going to the supermarket for this very reason. I never liked going to restaurants with buffets, either. I always preferred being served by people. I searched the line looking for old friends and relatives. A few approached me. "Girl, I'm starving. They only have hors d'oeuvres. Damn. It's six o'clock in the evening—dinner time. They're only giving you a little bit of the stuff. I wonder why Ava didn't tell us to eat before we came here. Shit, it's a wedding reception and people are used to getting a meal at a wedding." Ava could have done better than that. This was her first wedding and I knew for a fact she had saved a ton of money all her life by bargain shopping, no matter how far she had to drive to save a dollar to get it cheaper someplace else. I was embarrassed even if she wasn't. Lenny walked up to me, complaining. "There's not a drop of Remy Martin or Courvoisier in this place. Damn, if I knew this, I would have brought my own bottle from home." He sucked his teeth and handed me his small plate of food. "Want some? It ain't much, but it will keep you from starving to death." I declined and got through the evening without eating any food. Lenny and I left after presenting my sister with a hundred dollar cash wedding gift. On the way home, Lenny and I dined at a restaurant, ordering a three-course meal.

The next day, we were on our way to New Jersey to stock our bar with some liquor, beer, and wine for an upcoming Easter party. During the ride over, the topic of Ava's wedding dominated our conversation.

"You know what, Lenny? Let's get married. We'll show them how to have a party. The nerve of her—excluding her old friends, acting all uppity in there because she finally got married. She didn't even feed the people a decent meal. Yep, let's get married. You wanna get married?" I asked.

"Well, there's nothing stopping us. You've already made me divorce Frances so you could sleep nights knowing she can't get any part of the house in case I die."

"I didn't make you divorce her. You did it of your own free will," I laughed.

"You're a lying ass. You need to stop it," Lenny chuckled. "You work for damn lawyers. You arranged the whole thing and told me you'd leave me if I didn't divorce her. Remember that conversation?"

"Oh, yeah, I did do that," I admitted. Nobody was going to get my damn house! "Oh well. That's *that*—it needed to be done. I wasn't going to jeopardize my security because you had your name on a piece of paper with someone else. A marriage certificate speaks loudly to the court system. I'm no dummy. Yep. I did the right thing. And look what you've got—me and Noelle." I kissed him on the cheek. "You're a lucky man, Lenny."

"Well, I don't know how lucky I am but, okay—let's do the party—I mean the *wedding*."

"Okay, party animal." I wanted to holler out the window. I was getting married to Lenny Garner!

I began the very next day making the arrangements. I was an excellent organizer and planner. Soon after I got to work, I typed up a memo announcing my wedding and sent it by fax or mail to all my girlfriends. I needed help with everything.

The first thing I did when I got home Monday night was to grab my address books and began making calls. I planned to call Ava's three old girlfriends that I was also fond of, starting with Yvonne.

I asked her if she'd like to be in my wedding. We had known each other for a long time and she had been good to my nephew. I also felt bad about her not being in Ava's wedding. Yvonne hesitated, and, to my surprise, passed. "I thank you, Denise, but I'm okay with what happened with Ava. You don't have to do that," Yvonne said.

"Yvonne, I'd love to have you. I mean it."

"That's so nice of you Denise, but I'd better say no. It'll keep trouble down. But I will definitely be at the wedding. You just let me know when and where. Okay?"

"Okay, sweetie. If you change your mind, just call me. And you won't have to eat before you come to my affair. I'm hauling in the caterers—big time. Your entire family will be invited. I'll let you bring the dog, too!"

The mood lightened and Yvonne gave a hearty laugh. "You're the same old crazy Denise, you never change." Yvonne said.

After we hung up, I telephoned Nadine. I didn't give a damn how fat Nadine was—I loved her and wanted her in the wedding. Nadine agreed to be in the wedding and was thrilled. Then I called Linda, but she declined because she knew I was asking to make up for what her longtime friend Ava had done. She didn't want me to have to do that and felt funny about it. However, she was appreciative I had at least considered her feelings. She planned to come.

Once I got through those phone calls, I started dinner and Lenny arrived **home with Noelle. He had picked Noelle up from my mother's house. She** was babysitting Noelle while we both worked. After dinner, Lenny and Noelle hit the basement and I flipped through bridal magazines looking for invitations and dresses. In between, I took calls from my friends who had by now gotten their faxed memos. They all buzzed with excitement that they were not only included in the wedding, but in the planning of the affair. Natasha was in her room doing homework and listening to New Edition. Natasha was overjoyed about being in the wedding, but from the moment I announced that her favorite group was coming to Philadelphia to do a concert and that Mommy would be taking her along with her best buddy, Dana, she had already forgotten her mother's wedding.

I loved planning our wedding. I was extremely detail-oriented as a result of working for attorneys and performing administrative tasks. I made lists for everything concerning our upcoming affair. The wedding party was receiving memos by fax and mail advising them of developments, giving instructions, and requesting suggestions. At first, we selected a date in August and were going to have a poolside affair, but then decided against that. It was simply too much trouble changing clothes and we were afraid people would get drunk and fall into the pool and drown. My friend Marilyn Sawicky, who worked at a law firm with me, talked us into having our reception at Valley Forge Military Academy. She'd had her wedding there and swore by the place. We set the date for October 4, 1986 and decided on Bright Hope Baptist Church in Philadelphia for the 2:00 p.m. ceremony.

The guest list was one hundred eighty. The bridal party consisted of eight bridesmaids and groomsmen. My godson Darien would be the ring bearer and Gabriella my flower girl. She was the gorgeous five year old daughter of my former boss, Ronald B. Epstein, Esquire. I was crazy about that little girl. She'd be in pink as well as my maid of honor, my sister Darlene. The bridesmaids would be decked out in lavender taffeta.

I bought more bridal magazines in search of my dress. I came across a lovely white, full strapless gown that was very wide and had a crinoline. At the back of the dress, midway to the skirt, was a large bow. With a pair of white pearls, I'd be a perfect princess. I loved it! I immediately snatched it out of the book and mailed it to Zena in Washington for her opinion. I couldn't wait to hear from her. She called me in a few days and I started, "So...you like the gown?"

"Yeah, it's nice. Pretty."

I could tell from the sound of her voice that something was wrong with the dress or she was in a bad mood.

"Okay. What's the problem? You don't like the dress or are you pissed off with somebody? Did I send too many memos this week?"

"Well, the dress is really pretty, but it's not *you*."

"Everybody else loves it. They said the dress looks just like me."

"They only said that because the model in the picture has a haircut like yours, but the dress is not you."

"Well, I'm going to be a princess on my wedding day. That's the perfect dress. I've been Cinderella long enough."

"You're not a *princess*, you're a *bitch*. You need a *bitch* dress. You have no business wearing that nice little dress. I guess you're going to put a tiara on your head, too. Why don't we just have the wedding in Disneyland at the Cinderella castle?"

"Okay, smart ass. I'll look for another dress. I don't feel like fighting with you. I'm already half nuts from planning this thing." I hung up on her.

In three days, I had found another dress in a magazine. The designer was Demetrious for Illyssa and it was unimaginable. It was tight fitting and hugged my little size four ass. It was crème-colored silk satin and hand beaded. The beads glittered like diamonds. The top was sheer from the neckline to the start of the breast line. In back, forty tiny buttons fastened with small loops descended from my neck to my rear end. The train was Italian pleated lace, circular, and entirely beaded. The headpiece resembled a turban and it had a sheer veil attached to it. I called Sukey Rosann's Bridal Shop in Ardmore and they had a sample of it. It was a whopping $2,200 and it was a bad *bitch* dress. The head piece would run me another four hundred. I sent the picture to Zena and in a few days she called me screaming. "*Bitch*, you've done it! I'm proud of you!"

I tried the dress and headpiece on three days later. My heart almost stopped when I saw myself in the mirror.

Next, it was time to do the tuxedo thing. The bridal party was responsible for half the cost of their attire and shoes. Lenny and I were kicking in the other half.

For the music, I called Charlotte who used to sing with a band when the first group I had scheduled cancelled on me. She got her old band to play at the wedding and also agreed to do two solos. We'd chosen *Inseparable* and *Smoking Room*. The church had a piano player for *Inseparable* and Charlotte would be doing *Smoking Room* a acappella. I made sure I picked up the sheet music for both songs well before the event.

Krempf's Florist was in charge of the flowers. I didn't want a carnation in the house. I had an aversion to them. That bill would be fifteen hundred dollars. I had to have the best and Krempf's had done a White House affair. They were my style. Lynne had decided to have a white arch decorated with flowers brought to the church. Two hundred twenty balloons were on order for guests and the bridal party to let go in the sky after the wedding. Some relatives flying in from out of town, who we considered may be hard pressed for money, were sent plane tickets compliments of the soon to be Mr. and Mrs. Lenny Garner. People were flying in from Chicago and Myrtle Beach.

I chose a white Rolls Royce to get me from the hotel to the church and take Lenny and me to Valley Forge Military Academy. I rented it from the former heavyweight champion of the world, Joe Frazer for six hundred dollars. I preferred a helicopter for the ride from the church to Valley Forge, but I couldn't swing that—too much money.

The caterers were a suburban Philadelphia company. We decided on butlered hors d'oeuvres during the cocktail hour which would include Oysters Rockefeller, Clams Casino, shrimp rolls, miniature vegetable lasagnas, pigs in a blanket, chicken fingers, smoked turkey baked in croissants, and jumbo fried shrimp. I wanted waiters wearing white gloves when serving my guests at all times. A beautiful bar would be set up and waiters would deliver drinks to everyone. The sit down dinner would begin with fresh whole pineapples stuffed with fresh fruit and a candle lit at the top. Lights dimmed, the room would only hold the glow of flickering candles as guests arrive at the main ballroom for dinner and the reception. Then there would be served prime rib, asparagus, and scalloped potatoes. Dessert would be raspberry sorbet. Just the food set the bride and groom back a little over seven thousand dollars.

Liquor would be flowing the entire night. Lenny and I had purchased twenty six hundred dollars worth of assorted beer, wine, champagne and every kind of liquor we could find. We picked it all out ourselves and had it delivered to Valley Forge Military Academy the day before the wedding.

The cake I picked out was a masterpiece. It was chocolate chip with butter cream icing, decorated with pink and lavender flowers. That ran four hundred dollars. The invitations were white with pink roses and were mailed on August 20, 1986.

Because you have shared in their lives the honor of your presence is requested at the wedding of Miss Denise Greene and Mr. Lenny Garner on Saturday the 4th of October 1986 at Bright Hope Baptist Church, 1200 North 12th Street, Philadelphia, Pennsylvania 19130 at two o'clock p.m. The reception will immediately follow at Valley Forge Military Academy, 2333 Old Stone Road, Wayne, Pennsylvania 19087 from three o'clock to 7:00 p.m. Kindly respond on or before September 15, 1986.

How Lenny and I got through all the planning and problems without creating mass murder, I'll never know. At the last minute Darlene reneged and dropped out my wedding party. She started an argument with me about her half of the dress and shoe money. I offered to pay the whole thing for her and, still, she was acting mean and made a comment about me **sending out airline tickets. She stayed firm and got out taking her husband** Reggie with her, who was one of the groomsmen. Mindy, my longtime friend replaced her along with her husband Albert with whom I had been in diapers. Nadine dropped out because she ended up feeling self conscious about her weight. My mother and I got into an argument because she wanted my dad to drive her home late at night from my "Everybody Get to Know Everybody" party. She was drunk and I didn't trust the two of them together. His wife was out of town and I didn't want any crap. I absolutely forbade them from leaving my house together. My mother was furious and cursed me out. I kicked her out of my house. My grandfather was supposed to give me away and he got drunk at that party, too, and announced to everyone that he was real happy I had some *white* people there. He wouldn't shut up and continued to drink, so I didn't trust him for the wedding which was in a week. I knew there would be a lot more *white* people there. I imagined him getting plastered and running around thanking them for being white and coming to my wedding. I kicked him the hell out, too. My dad jumped in and took his spot. My wonderful brother Jeff had a wife who had been mad at me for years over some dumb bullshit he did involving me and forbade him from coming from Ohio to attend the wedding. He was supposed to be lighting candles at the altar of the church. He got so disgusted having to choose between us that he got depressed and stayed in Ohio. We were worried that Lenny's brother, Dennis, would get drunk and not show up at all for the wedding. I ran out of money. Karly came by my house and cheerfully threw a brand new Visa card, unsigned and still in its envelope, on my kitchen table with a limit of three thousand dollars—thank God. My friend Ron Sucov, an attorney, bailed me out on the fifteen hundred dollar flower bill three days before the wedding. Every penny I had saved was gone. But I didn't give a shit—we were having the 'wedding of the century.' I'd figure a way to pay everybody back.

The night before the wedding, a bunch of us were at my house folding the cake boxes and getting last minute stuff together. At eleven o'clock, I was bushed and decided to call it a night. I went to the hotel suite to meet my friend Jasmine, who had gotten the room for me. I was in a deep sleep when the phone rang at three o'clock in the morning. It was Zena calling from my house.

"Denise, I'm on my way down to the hotel. I'm sleeping there. Lenny is bringing me. Listen out for me." She hung up before I could ask any questions.

When I opened the door for her she came in with all her stuff. Dazed, I said, "Why'd you come down here? I thought you were staying with David at my house?"

"I cannot stay there. They are carrying on, girl. Everybody is drunk. Dennis is totally wasted, too. I don't know how he's gonna be anybody's best man. I couldn't get any rest there. Even your girlfriend, Tina, the White girl from your job is there and she is wasted, still hanging with them. The bar is packed at your house and those cake boxes aren't all done. I don't know how they are gonna walk down the aisle of the church tomorrow at 2:00. They won't be ready when the limos come for them. Lenny is on his way to the speakeasy in West Philly and dropped me off."

I got on the phone and called my house. Tina answered the phone. I could hear the music blasting. "Tina, I am on my way there. Those cake boxes better be done. You better tell everybody I'll be there in twenty fucking minutes!" Zena looked at me like I was crazy.

"Zena—get in the bed." She began undressing. I got back in the bed and we went to sleep.

The next morning Jasmine said, "Guess what? I got all mixed up with my bags and left all the bridesmaids' clutch bags that you had dyed to match our gowns at my house. I called there and Robb isn't home. I can't go back to Jersey for them." For a moment, I wanted to scream and stomp my feet, but I didn't say a word. By that time, I simply did not give a damn. The preparations and keeping up with everyone had worn me out. I just wanted to get married.

The church was packed, everybody was in attendance and the wedding started a fashionable thirty minutes late. Little Miss Gabriella Epstein stole the show when she traipsed down the aisle, walking too fast as she pitched flowers all over the place. She was gorgeous and too adorable.

After the huge receiving line, we exited the church. The bridal party **and guests released two hundred twenty balloons as Mr. and Mrs. Lenny** Garner got into their chauffer driven white Rolls Royce. The street and curbs were filled with people including neighbors, passers-by, and cars in traffic. It was just like a parade.

The reception went on without a hitch. It may have cost a fortune, but it was well worth it. When it was over, Lenny and I went back to our house armed with about sixty people vowing to party all night. Noelle was there with her babysitter waiting for Mommy and Daddy. As soon I changed out of my wedding dress and got comfortable in the basement, Lenny, The Honorable Paul J. DiBona, a Philadelphia Common Pleas Judge, his girlfriend Pamela Myers, Esquire, our dear friends Dickie Kendell and his girlfriend Lori, surrounded me with peculiar expressions on their faces. "Why do you guys have the *funny* look?" I asked.

"Something happened. We wanted to wait until you got home to tell you. We didn't want to spoil the reception," Lenny said.

I was alarmed. "What happened? Did somebody get hurt or something? Was someone in an accident coming to the reception or the wedding? I saw some name tags on the table at the academy and I know some people didn't show up. Tell me!"

"No, it's nothing like that," Pam said. Pam and I worked in the same suite. She was a brilliant attorney and my buddy Maria was her secretary.

"Listen, Denise, the caterers are thieves. I observed them stealing your liquor. They were heisting it out of the window of the ballroom to members of their crew."

"The crew was loading it up in their vans!" Judge Di Bona added.

"What!" I screeched.

"Yep, Denise," said Lori. "When Judge DiBona noticed it, he went looking for members of the wedding party and friends to tell them. He didn't want to tell you and Lenny. We all ran over, watching them. Also, the caterers were giving full bottles of champagne out to people telling them they could have it to take home. They've got a lot of your liquor. Lori had that "Let's start some shit" look in her eyes.

"We knew better than to tell you in that place. We knew you would have turned it out!" Dickie chimed in.

Lenny took a look at me and Lori and was getting scared. He started pleading. "Baby, don't get too mad. Let's just have a nice time. We've got a whole bar full of liquor here. We can straighten this out on Monday." Lori and I locked eyes. She was pissed. Dickie's gaze shifted from me to her. He knew what me and Lori could do if we put our heads together. That white girl wasn't afraid of anything. He walked away, hunting for a cold beer to enjoy while waiting for the fireworks. I know he and Lenny thought we would jet out the door and probably break all the windows of the catering establishment.

"Denise, you sue those bastards and I'll provide a statement for you. Let's not get all hyped about this tonight. We'll deal with it next week. You have plenty of witnesses. Get your receipts together for the liquor you bought and sent there." Judge DiBona said.

"We sent twenty six hundred dollars worth of liquor, wine, beer, and champagne to that Academy. Nobody driving got plastered because of the winding roads they had to take to get home. I sent memos warning people about them. I can't believe those catering people. Okay, let's forget it for now and party. I know enough attorneys to get my damn money back."

"Well, they didn't get *this*," Lenny said, beaming. He reached on the floor and picked up a beautiful wicker laundry basket. Inside were two bottles of Dom Perignon champagne. The card read: *Congratulations Mr. and Mrs. Garner from your favorite attorney and friend, Ron Sucov and Alicia.*

Prior to our marriage, we had purchased a battery-operated miniature car for two and a half year old Noelle. She liked to ride up and down the sidewalk in it. On our wedding night, we had a celebration at the house after the 'reception of the century' was over. Some members of the bridal party and guests ended up staying over, about nine people. About three in the morning when everyone was asleep, David started running throughout the house screaming that there was a fire in the basement. We all followed him out to the patio and part of it was on fire. Lenny and David tried unsuccessfully to put it out. The gas grill was nearby and likely to explode killing us all. The fire department arrived to quite a scene. David was in his tuxedo jacket and underwear, Lenny clad only in underwear, and I was in a big tee-shirt with no panties. Zena had on one of my nightgowns that was too small for her and David's tuxedo shirt. The firemen were amazed, watching white and black people scurry around the house dressed the way we were. They put the fire out and determined that the wires of the little car had caught fire, causing the blast. Everyone remembered that Tina had been sitting on the car at one point during the party and suggested she could have initiated the problem. The problem initiated, however, from a defect in the wiring of the car.

On the following Monday, I telephoned the company that manufactured the car and also our homeowner's insurance company. I explained the incident to both companies. I told the manufacturer of the car company that I was going to call *Good Morning America* and report it to Joan Lunden, which would bring attention to their company and the defective car. A representative of the company immediately made arrangements to come to Philadelphia to examine the damages and arrived the following day with a helper. I had the report from the fire department. I was furious. I thought about the fact that it could have caught on fire with Noelle in it. Also, I wondered how many of those faulty toy vehicles were out in the world and the number of children susceptible to getting hurt, burned, or killed as a result of this problem. I was grateful and thanked God my family and friends were not killed because that gas grill could have blown up and that would have been *it*. I warned those representatives on the spot that if they didn't cooperate with me and correct the defect in the car, there would be trouble. I also advised them to issue a check to me covering all my damaged items, plus the cost of the car. If not, I would head for New York. They requested to take the car back to Indiana to have it overhauled and I agreed. I warned them that I would diary my tickler system to hear from them in two weeks with their report. I reiterated the *little chat* I would have with Joan Lunden, also a mother of three adorable daughters. That would surely initiate a recall of all those cars. The representative took the remains away.

The insurance company's claims adjuster arrived the following day. I filed a claim for the damages and subsequently collected two hefty checks, one from the manufacturer of the car and one from the homeowner's carrier. With the "hush" money, the money to rebuild our patio, the money to replace damn near everything in the house due to smoke damage, and a new wedding gown because mine had been hanging on the patio and went up in flames, I collected over $40,000. The car was indeed defective and the wiring system had to be redone. Years later, *Good Morning America* aired a story of a Power Wheels car catching on fire. In the documentary, Power

Wheels said it had never happened before. I was pissed and called *Good Morning America* to report what had happened to our house thirteen years prior. No one ever followed up with me. The catering company received a strong letter from Judge DiBona, which must have scared the crap out of them. In a week, we received two checks. One was for $7,000.00 and the other for $2,600.00.

My sister Ava's marriage ended eighteen months after her wedding. Kenneth turned out to be a lying man who was *not* a minister. He was a wife beater and a con artist. It seemed that he had also ripped off the church he attended for a considerable amount of money. When he and Ava separated, he managed to remain at her beautifully furnished apartment and she had to move in with my mother. Six months after they split up, his picture was spotted in Jet Magazine with his new bride. Three months after that, the bride had their marriage annulled. She found out that Kenneth was a bigamist legally married for eight years to another woman—and that wasn't Ava.

CHAPTER 6

∾

Shaky Ground

The wedding was over and so was the honeymoon. Lenny was a pain in the ass and I thoroughly understood why his first wife stabbed him and had another man. He was staying out half the night almost all the time, getting high, and constantly causing arguments between us. I was damn sick of him. My marriage was crumbling. I was taking tranquilizers and seeing a psychiatrist on a weekly basis. I took his ass to the psychiatrist for family counseling and, after one visit with Lenny, the doctor told me that Lenny had a lot of *character* problems—no character. My sex life had dwindled from twice a day to about four times a month, and I wasn't having orgasms. I kept a trich infection and he claimed I was getting it from him not being circumcised. He had a horrible demeanor and was always criticizing me. The more I tried to work things out, the more he drifted. If I wasn't in therapy with the shrink, I was in therapy with my friends—complaining and crying, pissing and moaning. It seemed God wasn't paying a bit of attention to my prayers for change and relief. Maybe he wasn't because what goes around comes around. After all, I did take another woman's husband. I had a feeling God didn't like that crap. I guess I had to pay for it.

One afternoon I picked up my ringing telephone and my girlfriend Nadine was on the other end.

"Hey, Nadine, what's up girl? How are you and Harry doing? Have you killed his ass yet? When you do, come by here and kill Lenny for me."

"Denise, Harry's not half the problem right now. I'm sick of his niece, Erica. She is still at it, running around, doing drugs, and sleeping around. She's been living here for nine months with her three kids now and she's been reported to Department of Human Services for neglecting them. Last week, she left them in a crack house."

"You've got to be kidding—that is really bad news."

"We've had it with trying to help her and the department is coming here in two days to take the kids and put them in foster care."

"You can't keep them?"

"No, I really can't. We're both working and the kids are two months, sixteen months, and three. We can't handle that."

"Yeah, I guess you can't—that's a handful."

"Listen, I called you for two reasons. One being you love kids so much and the other is I wanted you to know that the sixteen month old little boy is Dale's kid."

Dale and I had grown up in the same neighborhood. He was a year older than me, really cute, and he always dressed sharp. He was spoiled to death by his mother, and had three sisters. We had crushes on each other when we were fourteen years old and I was always over his house. His Mom liked me and knew my family well. He never had any trouble finding a girlfriend back then and kept his shit together. When he grew up, the women were still crazy about him. But Dale was like singer Rick James' hit record *Fire and Desire.* He sure did "love 'em and leave 'em— especially if they were giving up the booty. Once he got some, scored, they were considered damaged, used goods and not good enough for him. I didn't go that route with him, so I was a mystery and intriguing to him.

When Nadine told me there was a problem with his son, I didn't hesitate because we'd remained tight over the years even though we only saw each other during the summers when I'd go back to the old neighborhood to visit and attend my old friends' barbeques. He was always the main attraction, a lot of fun, and a barrel of laughs growing up. As Nadine was talking, I remembered how good he looked in his clothes back in the day. "What," I screeched. "Oh, man. I haven't seen Dale in a while. How is he with this stuff?"

"He doesn't know this crap yet. The kids all have different fathers. I thought since you know Dale pretty well, you might want to help. He hasn't had much contact with Erica because she is so crazy. His family tried very hard to help out with Marcus, who is as cute as a button, but Erica wanted a relationship with Dale and kept screwing everything up. She'd get pissed about the *no relationship* thing and when Dale and his family tried to get Marcus, she wouldn't cooperate. I haven't seen or heard from any of the Elliotts in about three weeks."

I told Nadine that she needed to let Dale's family know what was going on. She had no number to reach them, so I gave her their address which was six blocks from her house.

"I'm not sure where *Dale* is living or what *his* circumstances are. I just figured you'd want to know that his kid was about to go into foster care. Are you interested?"

I thought about what Nadine told me. I always liked Dale as a person and after about five seconds, I said, "I'm coming by there tonight."

It was about seven thirty in the evening when seven-year old Noelle and I arrived. Nadine answered and two toddlers were at the door with her. I had to squeeze my way through to get inside the house. Before I could take my coat off, one of the kids grabbed me around the legs and wouldn't let go. I immediately picked him up. He was the cutest child I had ever seen in my life. He had an adorable face and black curly hair. Gorgeous dark brown eyes. He held me tight as I advanced to the living room. I sat him on my lap, and Noelle began playing with him and the other child. I tried to put Marcus down to play with his brother, but he continued clinging to me. I found his insistence to stay with me strange since he'd never seen me in his life. That little boy and I were having a love affair from the moment I picked him up and squeezed him. He was precious.

Nadine led us upstairs to her bedroom and yelled to Erica that I was in the house. She ran into Nadine's bedroom to greet us. This girl was naturally beautiful, a replica of Jayne Kennedy. When I looked at her, I thought, "You could have had it all—and you chose crack and booze?" Her hair was jet black and wavy, her skin a medium toasty brown. Her eyes used to be bright, but were dim and swollen from staying open too long. I felt sorry for her when she walked in. She may have had a better life had she not lost both of her parents years ago. Her Dad was in jail for killing her mother—he had shot her dead on a street when Nadine was eight years old. She was now twenty-five, twelve years younger than me. But she lacked the freshness that I had at that age and her eyes had dark circles around them. She definitely looked worn out.

"Hey Denise, I haven't seen you for a long time. How you doing? Hey Noelle—you little cutie pie—how is school?"

"School's good, I'm on honor roll."

"Good girl. What are you guys doing over here tonight?"

"Just visiting. Erica, you just get prettier and prettier the older you get. Girl you look so much like Jayne Kennedy. So, this is your latest bundle of joy? What's her name?" I asked.

"This is Patrice. I just fed her. Watch this." Erica bounced the baby into the air and caught her. She vomited up the milk.

"Stop that! Erica, are you crazy? Don't do that to the baby!" I screamed.

"Oh Denise, she likes that. Jesus Christ, we do it all the time." Nadine looked at me and shook her head disappointingly.

"You are a piece of work Erica," I said.

"What's been happening with you, Denise?" Erica cheerfully inquired.

"Nothing much. I'm home for a while, I was in an accident and had some injuries, so I'm just chilling out at the doctor's offices. I go to therapy, run Noelle all around, and attend the school meetings."

"How's Lenny?" Erica asked.

"Same shit, different day. We're not terribly happy." Marcus was still clutching me and I started to love this little boy already.

"Listen, Erica, I'd like to take Marcus home with me for a while. I'm not doing too much that I wouldn't be able to handle him. Do you mind?" Noelle's eyes lit up and Nadine looked relieved.

"I don't have any money and I don't want my check affected. You know if you take him, they could take some of my money." Erica balanced Patrice on one hip and had her hand on the other.

"I don't need any money. I'm cool. Just be sure I have his medical card. I want to take him to get a check up. Can you do that? I'll just tell the doctor's office I am his aunt or something."

"Well, yeah, that's cool, but his clothes are all dirty and I'll have to get some diapers together."

"Listen, don't worry about that stuff. Just let me walk with a couple of diapers and I'll stop at the market on the way home. I'll get him some clothes tomorrow. Does he eat everything? What does he like? Is he allergic to anything—you know like tomatoes or anything that you know of?"

"He'll eat *anything*. He's never gotten a rash or gotten sick from anything he ate."

"Does he have a coat or a jacket?"

"Yeah, let me get his jacket."

Erica left the room and came back with a thin, flimsy red nylon jacket. I put it on him, grabbed Noelle's hand, and headed down the stairs, carrying Marcus. Erica and I swapped numbers and she gave me a welfare medical card that I promised to copy and return to her the next evening. I got the kids situated in the car and drove across town to my house. I entered with the two kids. Lenny, who was in the basement after a weekend of partying, looked up at me and the baby with surprise. "Who's that?"

"It may be our new son." I explained to him what had happened. I put Marcus down on the floor and Noelle got him some toys to play with. Lenny rose from the couch, picked him up, and started playing with him.

"Lenny, I have to run to the market to get him some diapers and pick up some food he may like. Just watch him until I come back."

"Okay, go on to the market."

When I came home I found Lenny, Noelle, and Marcus watching a Kids Song Video that Noelle had gotten from her library so Marcus could learn about farm animals. They looked like they'd had a ball.

"You know what, he kind of looks like me," said Lenny. The Leo ego was coming out.

"Might he be yours?" I responded sarcastically.

"Oh come on, Denise, I've never been anywhere near Erica that way. So, she's still one hinge short of a nuthouse door, huh?"

"Yeah, she is. I have to get in touch with his Dad and his family to let them know I have him. I know them all from back in the day. There is no way I was going to let this kid go to a home. I'll work on all that stuff tomorrow after I get Noelle to school. I've also got to get him to the doctor for a checkup. Let's give Marcus a bath and we can all get to bed. I think everybody can sleep in one bed tonight so he doesn't get scared in his new surroundings." Noelle's eyes lit up again and she dashed to me for instructions on the bath.

"Hey, Mom, he can sleep in one of my pajama tops tonight. Do you want me to put the diaper on him?

"Yes, I'll definitely need your help with him. Let's get going."

After the bath and a bedtime story, I placed the kids in my bed. Marcus instantly reached for me and ended up sleeping on top of me, clutching me throughout the night. Noelle was next to us and Lenny on the other side of the bed. The next morning, I made breakfast and was astonished at the amount of food Marcus ate. I had made pancakes, sausage, and scrambled eggs. Marcus ate a little over two small pancakes, an entire scrambled egg, and two pieces of sausage. I dropped Noelle off at school and returned home.

I telephoned my pediatrician and made an appointment for the following morning. Then I put the tape of the farm animals in my VCR and watched it with him, identifying the animals and singing along to teach Marcus the words. He was enjoying it. When it went off, I walked him into the bathroom, sat him on my lap, and explained to him that I had to take a shower. I returned him to my bedroom and placed him on the floor with a few toys. I asked him to stay put and started the tape again, telling him to watch the birds on the TV until I came back from the bathroom. I assured him that I would be back. I dashed in, took a quick shower, and returned to find him smiling and bouncing to the music of Old MacDonald's Farm. I was glad that I had brought him home and introduced him to the calmness of my world, the affection and stability he would have while being with us. He could certainly benefit from collecting a little TLC. We were falling in love with each other.

Marcus and I headed to the mall. *I* had to get him some clothes. I knew Erica had neglected him because of her drug habit. During the ride, I popped in EnVogue's tape and as we grooved to *Who's Loving You.* I drove with one hand and used the other hand to hold his. I was singing to him **and he was loving** it.

The first stop was Gap Kids. I showered him with four new outfits, some toys, and other things he'd need while at my house. Then I picked him up an awesome pair of hot sunglasses so he'd really be sharp and cool.

Next stop was the deli to pick Noelle up turkey and cheese on a Kaiser roll and a Tahitian Treat soda. That was her very favorite thing to drink and she got a bag of chips and a giant chocolate chip cookie for dessert. I hated Noelle drinking soda, but let her have it today because of Marcus staying with us. I wanted to make sure Noelle knew I loved her too and that she was very special to me even though Marcus was in the picture. Marcus and I dropped her lunch off at the school office and headed home singing, *Who's Loving You.* He was quite dapper in his new sunglasses.

As we drove along, I explained the new and unfamiliar sights to him whether I felt he could understand or not. I believed in communication and had read stories to Noelle while she was in my womb. Once I gave birth to Noelle, I always explained to her whatever I did or was involved in at home, whether it was cooking or chores. Many times, she would be in her infant seat on the kitchen table, listening to me talk and watching the tasks I performed. I believe it makes children brighter and closer to you when you communicate non-stop with them. I was sensitive, protective, and had incredible patience with children combining my street and book smarts. I also possessed imagination, excellent parenting skills, and could make a fun game out of anything. Children adored me.

When Marcus and I arrived back home, I announced, "Okay my man, let's go into the house and get ready to find daddy and grandma."

Having Marcus in my life saved me in many ways. I needed to be loved by someone who wasn't trying to capitalize on getting anything else from me, but love. He hadn't known if I had a dime or a credit card when he grabbed on to me, so I knew his feelings were real and genuine. I wanted his spirit around me. I needed to keep him. He made me feel good. I liked the fact that this male child needed me. I knew the Elliotts well and that they would want to keep their grandson, but I was planning to get around that. He'd be well taken care of with his family, but, for once in my life, I was deliberately going to be selfish. If Dale needed me and had the final say, I could convince him to override his family's wishes and let the baby stay with me.

Back on the road again, we arrived at Dale's mother's house. Marcus sure did look sharp in his new outfit and sunglasses. His twenty-five year old aunt Marie answered the door grinning from ear to ear. She was a light skinned beauty. Hot! She had chestnut brown, shoulder-length permed hair that fell just above her shoulders. She wore it straight, the bangs parted on the right side, covering the end of her right eye. And those eyes were pretty and brown, resembling streamlined ovals. Her eyebrows were arched perfectly. Marie was thin, about a size four, and was about five foot four. Lenny knew her and used to tell me that she was one of his fantasies. I knew when she reached for Marcus that I'd have trouble getting out of there with that baby. I cheerfully said, "Hey Marie, how are you? I was at Nadine's last night. She called me yesterday afternoon because there is a problem with the kids." I went on to explain the events.

As she planted a deep kiss on his cheek she said, "Oh man, I am *so* glad you went and got him. He has been spending some weekends here. Dale goes to get him and brings him here."

"Where is Dale?" I wondered what my old flame's situation was. I was curious as to where he was living and if he was hooked up. She told me he was at work. I was disappointed she didn't elaborate more on his personal life. While I was standing there, I reminisced about my younger days when I spent so much time in and out of that house. Marie offered to call him and her mother to let them her know Marcus was there. She called Dale first.

"Dale, listen, Denise is over here with Marcus. Erica is acting crazy. It's a long story, but Marcus stayed at Denise's last night. I'm getting ready to call Mom." Marie passed the phone to me.

"Hey, stranger, what's doing? I've got our kid. You've got to share him with me," I demanded.

"Hey girl, where've you been? I haven't seen you since God knows when. How's your family?"

He was cheerful, his voice still sexy. His words slid into one another just the way a woman liked. Dale sounded exactly like his old self, like we had just seen each other yesterday and we hadn't missed a beat.

"Everybody's fine. Listen, I need to give you all my information so you can see about Marcus. I can take him home with me tonight. He has a doctor's appointment tomorrow for a check up. I'm taking him."

"You're still on the ball, girl, always have been. Give me your information. Is Marcus okay?"

"Marcus is spoiled rotten. Wanna holler at him?"

"Yeah, make it quick, I'm at work and planning to call you later."

"Here Marcus—talk to Daddy." Marcus mumbled something into the phone. I took the receiver and gave Dale my address and telephone number. We hung up.

Marie looked me straight in the eye. "Denise, you know you can leave Marcus here with me. We can keep him. I have to call my mom now, anyway."

I assured her that he was no burden to me and that I wanted to help out. I wanted to make sure she knew Dale should be making the decision. However, I had to be careful. I didn't want her to feel I was ordering her around or trying to take over. I gently said, "You know what, we just love having him around and I have room. I'm home during the day for a while. Let me talk it over with Dale *later* and see what he says to do. Give me the number here so I can stay up with you guys."

Before answering me, she dialed her mother. I stood there worried, thinking Mrs. Elliott would insist I leave the baby there. I listened to Marie explain the situation. I felt myself getting jittery as they spoke and was watching Marie's facial expressions for clues as to what was being said on the other end. Finally they hung up.

"Denise, my Mom thinks he ought to stay here with us, but said to tell you since you made the doctor's appointment to keep him tonight. She said she'll call you later after she talks to Dale."

I didn't know what would happen later, but felt relieved that at least I was leaving there with him. "Okay, let me give him his lunch and then we're out of here. I have to pick Noelle up from school by three o'clock."

I got his lunchbox and took the container of homemade spaghetti and meatballs out. Then came diced apples, crackers, and a thermos containing orange juice onto the kitchen table. I was glad I'd packed a good lunch. It would score points for me. I knew Marie would tell her Mom that and it would help Mrs. Elliott to know that her grandson would be well taken care of by me. She was a divorced single mom who did her best to run her four adult children's lives and stayed in their business.

I carefully watched Marcus eat. We soon left, stopping around the corner at Nadine's to see her and Erica. I returned the medical card as promised. Marcus wouldn't leave my arms. Erica remarked how well dressed he was and also reminded me that she did not want her welfare check tampered with or she wouldn't hesitate to take him back. I assured her. We picked Noelle up and she was thrilled, showing Marcus off to the kids. Finally home, I put Marcus down for a nap and started helping Noelle with her homework.

While I was making dinner, I contemplated the situation with Marcus. It had really made me happy to have him around. I loved babies and always wanted to have another, but couldn't manage to get pregnant. Lenny and I had discussed having another child many times, but we never got pregnant. I was always hyped up at the thought of having another baby, but Lenny was indifferent about the subject. I was forever fighting for kids' rights and crying when I heard stories on the news of kids being abused, kidnapped, or killed. Lenny and I donated toys and clothing to mission societies.

I contemplated cute little Marcus, who had probably never been to the park or the beach, and my heart went out to him. In truth, I was always about rescuing *everybody*. I'd made up my mind to try to persuade Dale to let us keep him. I planned to discuss it with Lenny, but I really didn't give a damn what he said in the end. He was rarely home anyway.

He generally arrived when he felt like it and was usually drunk or high. It was a bad situation, but evidently I hadn't had enough of it because I was still with him. He'd become verbally abusive and could get lightweight physically abusive. Nothing serious—just some smacking around if I nagged him about his hours. He still loved the sauce, the nightlife, doing some drugs recreationally, which amounted to a few days a week, and just plain hanging out. He usually made it in before three o'clock in the morning on weekdays, kept his job, and gave me his share of the money for the bills in the house. He was good with Noelle, but I came to realize what his first wife, Frances, had gone through.

My main problem with him was that he raped me of my self-esteem. I was a beautiful well-dressed, articulate, ambitious bright woman. I had a **gregarious personality and an incredible sense of humor. I was funny and** people liked me. I think he was jealous of my attributes. He constantly told me I was ugly and worthless. He was mean to me and *never* encouraged me.

Once, we had a weekend party because some friends of ours were having some serious financial problems. At the party, I arranged to sell food and liquor, and we'd planned to give them the proceeds. I used my own money to purchase everything and advertised the party all over the neighborhood. I went through my phone book, notifying everyone we knew. It was a huge success, especially the delicious food, and we made a killing. Lenny had helped out all weekend with the party.

Early Sunday morning after the affair was over, about eight people were left sitting at our basement bar having a couple of drinks, laughing, joking, and talking about what a nice party it had been all weekend. I had looked gorgeous the entire time and had purchased the cutest wig especially for the affair because I had so much work to do over that weekend. It looked very natural and I was stunning in it. I was behind the bar chatting and Dale's sister Marie remarked how good I looked in the wig and wanted to know where I got it. Everyone started chiming in, expressing what a fox I was. I was blushing and Lenny was taking it all in. He said nothing. All of a sudden, he reached over the bar, snatched the wig off, and hurled it across the room, revealing my hair, which was a total wreck. Everyone was stunned. Embarrassed, I ran from behind the bar all the way up to our bedroom and lay across the bed crying. Marie and a friend of hers ran after me and apologized. They said they would never have complimented me if they thought it would cause Lenny to react that way.

In the past, Lenny had sat down with me many times to *explain* to me how unattractive I was. Those conversations resulted in my consulting with a plastic surgeon. I was considering having some work done to my face to make me more appealing. I had planned to meet with the doctor when I was financially able to pay for the procedure. In the interim, I took a planned vacation with my Aunt Cecilia to the Bahamas.

While there, I'd met a man who was employed at the elite resort we stayed at and he escorted me and my aunt to the local clubs and took us sightseeing. He constantly told me how beautiful I was. I was surprised he envisioned me so differently than my husband. A few months later, I took a five-day vacation with Lenny to Jamaica. On the second morning of the trip, he and I were having breakfast outside at the resort and the Black waiter came to the table with our food. He stared at me, then switched his gaze to Lenny.

"Excuse me, sir, I mean no disrespect to you. However, I would like to say something to your wife. Is it all right?"

Lenny shrugged and answered, "Sure."

He proudly looked over at me. "Ma'am, I would like to say that you have created quite a stir here since you checked in. We have been wondering if you were a celebrity."

I was flattered and smiled, "No, I'm no celebrity."

"Well, I'd like to say you are extremely beautiful and we are proud that you are one of *us*. Lenny answered before I could.

"Who, her?" He flung his thumb in a backward position pointing at me. He was laughing. "You've got to be kidding."

"No sir, I am not *kidding* and you are quite a lucky man, whether you realize it or not."

I sat there, embarrassed, and said to the waiter, "Thank you very much for such a great compliment." I decided at that point that there would be no surgery.

* * *

At around six thirty, Dale came by for his first visit with Marcus and had a chat with me. As usual Lenny was not at home. "I'm really relieved he is here, " Dale said, watching Marcus play. Dale was his usual self, sharp as a tack with those snake skin shoes on. "I know he'll be well taken care of. Erica is a trip. I can't deal with her. She held the boy hostage for umpteen months. We just started getting him a few months ago. I was with her up until she was about five months pregnant and then she started acting crazy. She was getting high, running around, and all that stuff. I couldn't be bothered. Then she had him in the bed at Nadine's house. Nadine delivered him. She had had no prenatal care. She continued her escapades after he **was born and would call the cops whenever I would find her and try to** take him. She moves around all the time. It's been hell. Maybe it is the best that thing the City got involved because at least all three of the kids will be monitored and get a decent home. They need a break from all her dreadful activities." Dale's voice cracked several times.

"When we first started getting Marcus, he would just walk up to people and hold his hand out for food. I can't believe she left the kids in a crack house. Damn. Well, whatever happens or doesn't happen, I'm not letting her have him back."

"Are you going to go to Court to get him?" I inquired.

"That's *exactly* what I'm going to do. I'm living in a small apartment—nothing like what you have here, but I am working and I can get a sitter."

For some reason, I was relieved he wasn't hooked up in a live-in situation. My eyes focused again at his feet and his expensive shoes. He wasn't wearing any socks—just the way I liked it. I definitely had a "foot thing" and a man's bare feet in good looking shoes turned me way on. I shifted my gaze because I was becoming aroused. "What about your sister, Marie?"

"That won't fly—and don't make me explain why. But trust me, she has a problem, too. Can you help me out with him for a while?"

"I'd love to—just let me talk to Lenny," I said out of respect for my husband.

"How are you guys doing?"

"You want it straight up or do you want me to paint a pretty picture for you so you don't get cold feet about my keeping Marcus?"

"Give it to me straight up."

"Don't ask—shaky ground—but we're together for right now."

"Did he get pissed because you came home with Marcus?"

"Not at all. He likes kids and always had folks living with him before we hooked up. A full house never bothered him."

"How much money a week do you need to play Mommy?"

"Well, just drop me fifty a week. Don't worry about what I buy him on my own. You know how my heart is and I'll do things on my own, too. You'll never get a bill. This is probably the son I never had. You know? He's my new man—I'll enjoy spoiling him to death."

"You're not working. Where are you getting so much cash from, baby?"

"Disability from my car accident. I go to therapy three times a week. In a way, I'm glad it happened because I'm home for Noelle. I go to the school everyday to take her lunch and I pick her up myself. I'll probably be home another four months or so. I have some disc damage."

He reached into his pocket and pulled out some cash. "Okay, here's fifty bucks and I can pick him up every weekend. I'll also stop by twice a week to have dinner with him and put him to bed. I'll bring dinner for all of you when I come or we'll go out. Also, how much do you need for his check up?"

"Don't worry about the doctor. Medical Assistance has him covered."

"Here are a couple of my cards. Give one to Lenny in case he wants to call me to discuss anything. He may want to get a hold of me in case of an emergency. I'm getting ready to split. Hey, Denise, thanks."

"Okay, be sure you call your Mom so she knows the deal."

"I'll talk to you tomorrow." He kissed his son and left.

After dropping Noelle off at school the next morning, I introduced Marcus to an hour of Sesame Street, another learning tool and additional engine of developmental growth. That program had served my Noelle well in her toddler years. Marcus got a clean bill of health and some vitamins at the pediatrician's office. I still needed to get his immunization records to be sure his shots were up to date.

I returned home and called the Department of Human Services informing to them that Marcus was in my custody. I gave them Dale's information. The department set up an appointment for a social worker to visit Marcus in a week. When the woman arrived, she was impressed with his new surroundings and the way he was being cared for. Relieved he was safe, she planned to prepare a report suggesting he remain in my care pending a final decision. She informed me that Erica's other two children, Antonio and Patrice, had been placed in the custody of an aunt in New Jersey and Erica was also living there. The case worker provided me with the address and telephone number of the aunt so I could make arrangements with Erica to visit Marcus. She instructed me to call the Pennsylvania Department of Public Assistance to notify them that Marcus was no longer living with Erica. Any funds Erica currently received for him would be cut by the Philadelphia Department of Public Assistance. When the woman left, I immediately phoned Erica.

"Hey Erica, how are you girl? How are things working out over there for you and the kids?" I made it a point to sound cheerful and upbeat.

"Everything is okay. We're hanging." She sounded depressed.

I cut right to the chase. "Listen Erica, a worker from the Department of Human Services was here today to check on Marcus. She says I have to inform Welfare that you don't have him. They're going to cut your check. I don't want the money, so how are we going to swing this?"

"If they cut my money, I want him back."

"Okay, let's play it this way: I *have* to call them so that's *that*. Whatever money they cut, Dale or I will reimburse to you. Will that work? I'll make sure you get it. I'm giving you my word you'll get the money."

"Denise, Dale can't stand me. He won't give me anything."

"I'll see that you get it—just depend on me. Okay?"

"Okay, I'll try it, but if you screw it up, I'm coming to get him. I mean it. I need my money."

"Erica, listen, by the way, I know about your drinking and drug problems. You are a beautiful girl. Why don't you go into rehab? I'll help you get in so you can get yourself together and raise the kids right. That alcohol and crack is gonna kill you." My heart did reach out to her. Her Dad was doing life, he'd been in jail about twenty years. She'd been from pillar to post since she was ten years old.

"I'm not bad with the drugs and stuff, I don't need to go in there."

"Think about it and give me a buzz. Do you have my information with you?"

"I don't know where I put it."

"I'll hold on and you get a pen and paper."

"Erica, what do you want to do about seeing Marcus? Would you like to set up some days that I can bring him over since you don't have a car?"

"I'll get that together and call you, but I want to talk to Dale. Nadine told me he stopped by her house and he had been to see Marcus at your place. I want to talk to Dale and I want to see him, too. Give me his number at work." Erica sounded demanding and anxious as if something was wrong, but I wasn't giving her his number.

"Let me call him first on that. You know how folks get when you start giving their numbers out. I'll tell you what he says."

"Okay," Erica answered.

I told Erica I'd call her in a day or two and we agreed she would call me back about seeing Marcus. I could tell she didn't like my answer, but there was nothing she could do about it.

I was staring at the copy of the Medical Assistance card and called the Pennsylvania Department of Public Assistance next.

"I'm calling in connection with case number 4582349C and the claimant is Erica Riley. My name is Denise Garner and I would like to speak with the caseworker. I don't know her name."

"Hold on Miss."

"The caseworker is Michelle Ezekiel." She gave me Michelle's direct number because she could not transfer the call.

I had a big smile on my face as I looked at Marcus who was in his high chair finishing his snack. I went over to him and kissed him. "Boy, this is your lucky day."

"Department of Public Assistance, Michelle Ezekiel speaking."

"Michelle—shut up," I said.

"Who's this?"

"Girl, its Denise Greene."

"Oh my God! Where have you been, you crazy thing? I haven't heard from you in five years. I know *you're* not applying for welfare. Everybody and their brother call me when they think they can get on or if their relatives are having a problem."

Michelle and I had gone to high school together and were in a club together when we were teenagers. We often spent weekends together at each other's homes while growing up. "How are you Michelle—what the hell is going on with you?"

"I'm good and John is fine. He's in sixth grade. His dad and I split, but he takes good care of him and treats me better than he did when I was with him. What brings you through to me and how are the kids? Are you still with Lenny?"

"Noelle is fine, seven years old and making straight A's. She's quite the Black American Princess. I have to take her lunch up there each and every day because I'm not working right now. Natasha has an apartment in Germantown. She's eighteen. I can't stay on the phone long because I have to make it up to the school. I'm still with Lenny. Let's get on the phone at night with that story. The reason I'm calling is because I have one of your client's kids."

"So, you're still rescuing folks. Same old Denise. Who do you have that belongs to me?"

"A sixteen month old adorable boy named Marcus Riley. His mother is Erica Riley. You familiar with them?"

"Yep. Erica Riley is a dozy. How did you get her kid?"

"It's a long story, but I know his Dad. DHS was here and said I had to call you." I went on to explain to Michelle where Erica was living and my concern about the check being cut down.

"Well, I have to cut the check, I can't get around that, and damn if you guys are going to make me lose my gig. Now if you aren't going to accept the money for keeping him, then you won't be required to deal with us for visits. I can have the medical card for him issued to you once I get written confirmation notarized that you have him. It shouldn't be a problem since DHS has been there and given you authorization to keep him. Everything looks good to me."

"Okay, Michelle, and I don't need any money. His Dad is going to see that I get money for what he needs. He's a nice guy."

"Yeah, but you know the department here will go after him for what they paid out already on Marcus all this time when Daddy wasn't around. They'll want to be reimbursed. That's court, you know."

"Yeah, Michelle, but the department doesn't know where Daddy is."

"That's right, we don't, *do we*? But you know DHS will inform us down the road when everybody gets their paperwork in order," Michelle said.

"We'll cross that bridge when we come to it. I'll talk to you later. Let's exchange home numbers," I said.

The following day I called Dale. "Hey Dale, I don't want to hold you up at work, but I need you to call me at home tonight."

"Is everything okay with Marcus?"

"Marcus is fine. I just need to run some things by you. I spoke to welfare, DHS, and Erica. We need to talk."

"Okay, I'll give you a buzz tonight."

Dale called me later that night to tell me he'd called Erica at her Aunt Claire's house. He sounded agitated. There was so much racket going on over there that he could barely hear her on the phone. It sounded to him that they had a full house over there. Erica explained that I was keeping Marcus for awhile until she got a place of her own. That was a bunch of horse shit to me. She was twenty-four years old and had never had a place of her own. She wanted to meet with Dale. He refused. Erica still insisted on wanting to talk to him face to face. I knew that heifer was just trying to get Dale back into bed. I played those tricks when I was her age.

"Well, what did you say?" I asked."

"I wanted to talk at that moment, but she remained adamant about meeting me. I was suspicious, thinking she'd try to seduce me and I wasn't up for that. I'm working all the time and had to see the baby a couple of nights during the week. I can't be bothered with her."

I knew from knowing Dale all my life that he was serious because he never turned down much sex. This was a guy who on his wedding day went to bed with a guest who had stopped by his Mom's house after the reception was over and his new wife was asleep. They had a little tryst right then and there.

"Erica had the nerve to ask me if I was angry with her about things that had happened in the past. Shit, I wasn't mad, I just wanted to help get the baby straightened out."

I was in stitches listening to him complain. I thought it was funny.

"All I wanted to know was what the urgency of the call was. So after all this woman put me through she admits to me that she screwed everything up and wants to get back together. Can you believe this, Denise?"

It was hard for me to feel sorry for him because I knew so much raunchy stuff he had done to women in the past. My answer was, "What goes around comes around."

"**Well, I declined and told her I was past all that and merely wanted** to do what I was supposed to for my son. I told her that you would be great for Marcus right now because you were pretty responsible and I asked her to let it go at that."

"Well, Dale, I'd love to keep the baby. You know I'm going to treat him just like he's mine."

"I know you're a good woman. You've always taken good care of your family."

Dale couldn't let it go. He continued on about Erica. "I couldn't give her another shot at us being a couple because it won't work out. You don't know how she handled the pregnancy and all. Jesus, she was running around on me then and, to be honest, I wasn't even sure if Marcus was mine. Neither was she at one point. If he hadn't come out looking just like my nephew, Darius, I would have nixed both of them. I can't hack her way of life—especially the partying and drinking and drugs."

"What's up with her and her baby daughter's Dad? Why doesn't she try to give that a shot?"

"She told me he's violent and crazy and that wouldn't work out. I wanted her to know that us starting over wouldn't work again. Shit, I wonder why he's violent and crazy."

The sarcasm in his voice indicated that he had been through the ringer with Erica. I, myself, was tired from listening to all the shit. I had to get dinner ready, but Dale kept talking, holding me up.

"Since I wouldn't come back to her, she threatened to take Marcus if her welfare check got cut or we didn't come up with her money. She said you and me better know what we're doing. I promised her she'd get her money. She wanted a number to reach me, which I refused. I wasn't giving her any more numbers. She had your number and my Mom's and that's all she needs until this thing is straightened out.

✷ ✷ ✷

Lenny walked into the house at nine-thirty at night. He hadn't called as usual to say he wouldn't be straight home from work. The kids were asleep in separate bedrooms and I was watching television in our bedroom.

"What's up? You look tired," Lenny said to me.

"It's been a busy day," I muttered, noticing he was feeling no pain from whatever he'd been doing.

"I'm going down to get some dinner," I didn't answer.

At some ungodly hour of the morning, he returned to our bedroom and got into bed. He reached for me. I wouldn't budge. I wasn't interested.

As usual, I didn't know exactly where the hell he had been after work and, even if he hadn't been with a woman, I wasn't going to be at his beck and call for sex. Hell, when I wanted it, he was never around or too tired. Also, I'd been thinking about Dale's feet all evening, and that had been enough for me to get my groove on. He kept trying and finally, to avoid an argument, I got out of the bed, stood up, and took my pajamas and underwear off. When I was completely naked, I went into the bathroom and got a bottle of nail polish and got back into the bed. I laid down, spread eagle, and said to him, "You want it, take it, do whatever you want and let me know when you're done." Then I proceeded to paint my nails, extending my hand up in the air so my body would not move. He declined, called me a bitch, and went to sleep without touching me.

In the weeks that followed, Dale kept his word about picking Marcus up on weekends and coming twice a week for dinner. We also kept our word and mailed bi-weekly money orders to Nadine's house payable to Erica Riley in the amount $80.24 to cover the cut in Erica's welfare check. Dale filed the Petition for Custody with the court. Erica resided in New Jersey and Marcus in Pennsylvania. She didn't show up or hire counsel to contest the Petition. Her absence, possession being nine tenths of the law, the judge's observance of happy little Marcus, a sterling recommendation of Denise from Michelle Ezekiel of the Department of Public Assistance, along with favorable reports from the Department of Human Services, and Dale Elliott and Mrs. Denise Garner resembling Dr. and Mrs. Huxtable at the Philadelphia Family Court system hearing all weighed in our favor. Marcus was placed in his father's custody. That evening, everybody met at Chuck E. Cheese's to celebrate.

"Mom, he won't get out of the balls, he loves it in there," Noelle said.

"Well, we've got to get him fed. Let's see if we can drag him out." I walked over to the balls.

When I returned, Lenny and Dale were chatting and Lenny said, "Well, you must feel pretty good today, Dale, winning your case and getting Marcus."

"You got that right. I'm ecstatic. I couldn't have done this without the two of you. Everything *is* okay with Marcus being there during the week, isn't it? Any problems?"

Lenny took a swig of his beer. "No, it's cool. He's no problem and Denise and Noelle are nuts about him. So, Denise, I see you bribed Marcus out of those balls."

Dale proudly corrected Lenny. "No—she *charmed* him. Denise *charms* people. She's been like that all her life. That kid of mine is in love with her. He's a lucky guy and so are you Lenny."

Lenny's face twitched and he seemed uneasy with the comment. I knew right then that Dale dug me. That little flame he had for me back in the day was still lit. His feelings were crystal clear to me and it was scary because I felt I'd be receptive to a relationship with him. I was damn sure sick of being neglected by Lenny. I quickly tried to change the subject and the mood. "Hey everybody, let's order some food, I'm starved." Dale had a look of conquest on his face—like he'd straightened Lenny out.

Dale motioned for a waiter to come and we gave him our order. After that, Lenny abruptly announced that he had to run and would meet me at home. I figured he had a date with something or somebody that I wouldn't have approved of or he was really pissed off. Probably both. My gut feeling was that I was going to be interrogated at a later time by my husband, demanding to know how Dale was such an expert on my personality. I was actually flattered by Dale's comment. Lenny said his good-byes to Dale's family and left.

CHAPTER 7

∾

Closing the Door

Three days after the Chuck E. Cheese's party, Dale appeared for his weekly dinner date at the Garner household. I answered the door.

"Hey girl, what's up? Get the crew together, we're going to eat at the mall tonight—no cooking." I walked away toward the kitchen and he followed me.

"In a bad mood, huh? Okay, I'll take the kids by myself. Is Lenny around?"

"Lenny's not here and, yeah—maybe you should take them. Let me get them together for you." I headed for the basement and he stopped me.

"What's the matter with your eyes?"

"They're red—been crying." He took a long look at me. I could see he felt badly.

"What's the matter? You been diagnosed with cancer or something? A tough broad like you don't cry over bullshit. This must be serious. Come here." He hugged me.

He swayed me back and forth in his arms. "Tell *Uncle* Dale all about it or just hand me a knife and I'll cut the cancer out of you. Is it in your breast? We can start with them." I laughed and cried at the same time.

"You know what? Shit is screwed up here and most of the time I'm just unhappy. Today—bad day for dealing with it."

"What's the problem?" Dale whispered.

"I received a letter today from the police department. They wanted me to contact them regarding a hit and run accident in West Philly a few weeks ago. They got to me through the tag number on my car."

His eyebrows raised, his eyes opened wider. "*You* did a hit and run?"

I explained that, apparently, Lenny did it with my other car and never said a word to me. Now the police department was charging me. Dale questioned me about the registration of the car.

"Oh, that car he drives is yours? It's registered to you?"

"Yeah, and he drives it. I hadn't noticed any damage to it because I hadn't paid any attention to it. It's been parked in the carport for a few weeks. I questioned him about it and he said it needed a new fan belt or something and he wasn't going to drive it until it was fixed. He's been taking public transportation to and from work and I guess getting rides home in the middle of the night."

He contemplated the situation for a moment and looked as if he was trying to figure something out.

"Did you contact the police department yet? Have you called Lenny to let him know you got this letter?"

"I did both today and I went down to City Hall to get a copy of the Police Report. I called the police department and told them it was indeed my car, but that I wasn't at the place of the accident and never hit any car. I had to get out of it, so I told them that Lenny was my old boyfriend and the father of Noelle. My driver's license is in *Greene*—I never changed it. I told them that he comes some days to see her here at my house and that he evidently found my extra set of keys. I told them he took the car without my permission, probably had that accident, and put the car back. By my driving another vehicle, I never went to the carport to check on that car. I had no knowledge of the accident. I also told them that when they find him to let me know because I wanted to make sure he paid for the damage."

Dale was grinning like a Cheshire cat. He thought that was very clever of me and was impressed with how swift, smart, and slick I was. I had even called the man up whose name was listed on the police report and had a chat with him. He told me that Lenny had been so drunk that night he ran into him that he probably didn't even know where he was. The man came by my house earlier in the day to meet me and he really did have some injuries. He was an old man and was limping. I explained everything to him—the story I told the police and he let me off the hook. My insurance company wasn't going to have to pay because Lenny had the car without my permission. He was a nice old man and would vouch that I was not in the car. He actually left my house feeling sorry for *me*. I promised to fix his car and I guess his insurance company would pay for his medical treatment. Dale asked why Lenny did not have his own car in his own name. Lenny couldn't get a driver's license because he had a couple of judgments against him a zillion years ago that he never paid. The state wanted six grand to restore his driving privileges.

"What does Lenny say about all of this?" Dale seemed concerned about me.

"When I called him, he denied everything at first. The more I talked he finally came around and 'fessed up.' He says he'll give me the money to get both the cars fixed—when he can. I'm pissed. He also said it was *my* fault because I could have paid the judgment over the years because I had settled cases and had money and I should have paid them for him."

"Well, you *are* married to the man for *better or worse*," Dale laughed—kind of teasing me.

"Yeah—I am—but I spoke to him many times about the driver's license thing. Heck, I also called the state and got all the info on the payoff. I discussed it with Lenny and told him if he came up with half the money by saving or working part time, I'd help with the balance. He never saved a dime and stays in the street in the bars. I'm a nice person, but you know I'm not a fool."

He gave me a tight squeeze and it felt good. He dragged me over to the sink, snatched a paper towel, wet it, and gently dried my eyes. He looked me up and down and ran his index finger along the side of my face. I felt like I was being taken care of, soothed like a baby. "This shit will work itself out." Dale pulled me into the living room. "Come on, let's go for dinner. I've got something to tell you. I've got problems too."

Over dinner, he explained that Erica was really on his case and was threatening to have a petition filed for custody."

"What's wrong with her?"

"Seems the auntie over in Jersey said they could stay there and feels all the kids should be together in her custody. Auntie would also be able to get a check for all the kids—or something like that. Hell, who knows? Maybe it'll all go away. I've been handling Erica with kid gloves, talking nice to her to keep her from going through with it. She's trying to warm up to me.

120

You know I'm not going back there. It's a pain in the ass right now, but I'm dealing with it."

"What's the take on the baby girl's father? I mean, she hooked up with him *after* Marcus. Seems like she would be after him for a relationship."

"I heard he's schitzo and beat the crap out of her big time just after she had that little girl. She ended up in the hospital for two weeks."

"Wow, she has an eventful and incredible life."

"That's the understatement of the year," he sighed.

✳ ✳ ✳

Things continued to improve at my house with the kids and horribly with my married life. Lenny was creating one problem after another for me and I was stung with pain and aggravation in every occurrence. Two weeks ago, he'd fallen asleep in the kitchen at 12 a.m. in the morning while frying fish and damn near set the house on fire. Had it not been for the smoke detectors, we could have all been dead.

Around 11:00 a.m. on Father's Day, Dale came over for Marcus and asked me to take a ride with him to Willow Grove Mall.

"Listen, Denise,—I've got to tell you something." He was jittery and fumbling for words.

"This sounds serious. Now what?" I demanded. I was waiting for him to tell me Erica was getting custody of Marcus. The words were gonna split me in two, but I sat nervously waiting to hear it anyway. He looked at me and hesitated. He had a troubled look on his face. "I've watched you take care of my son for the past four months. You have impressed me so much, you know—your heart. Things are different. A lot has occurred with me. I have a problem and my problem is that I have fallen in love with another man's wife. That's rough stuff for me." He squeezed my hand and looked deeply into my eyes.

My heart sank. I was grateful, but I did not expect to hear that. Confusion was engulfing my mind and desire was saturating my heart because I really dug him, too. I said to myself, "This shit is gonna be a mess." I put my face in my hands and sat silently for a minute. I was trying to regroup, get some words together. I had to say *something* to the man. He was staring

121

at me and had made such an honest and powerful statement. He deserved to hear *something* back. I couldn't come up with a thing. I simply said, "I can't discuss this with you because I'm all screwed up too—feelings could be mutual, or maybe I'm confused." I appeared cool, but inside, my heart flipped in my chest. I wanted to smash my lips against his.

A look of surprise appeared on his face. He smiled and began to chuckle and shake his head. I knew Dale. He felt he'd made another conquest. He asked me when I first suspected that I really cared for him. I told him he had a way of relaxing me. Every time he had a long talk with me and we'd debate a subject or try to work out a problem, I felt useful, like a contributor, that I was respected, my opinion valued. The mere fact that he took the time to communicate with me, to ask questions turned me on. I didn't get that at home and I didn't get the attention he gave me from my husband. Lenny wasn't a conversation man.

"What are we going to do, Denise?" Dale sat on the base of a huge flowerpot outside the mall with Marcus on his lap.

"Damn if I know what we'll do," I answered, but I was certain that Dale was the perfect sedative for my traumatic marriage.

* * *

Things had been *quiet* with Erica and she was cooperating with Dale and me. I had begun bringing Marcus over to Nadine's house and Erica would play with him for about an hour. I'd then take her to lunch so she and Marcus could enjoy a meal together. After that, I would drop her off wherever she wanted to go, which was usually a bar. Erica often insisted that Dale come to the visits. Occasionally he did if appointments were set up in the evening. Erica began asking Nadine if there was something going on between me and Dale. She was confused because she hadn't observed us **being affectionate to each other. The other thing that threw her off from** being certain was that most people from our neighborhood had this *stick together thing* and they were possessive with each other, always looking out for one another. Erica, absent from growing up with us and not being part of that bond, couldn't be entirely sure what our relationship truly was. She never questioned either of us, but she did suspect that we were more than friends. She *might* have been confused, but she was definitely jealous of the relationship he and I had and my ability to spend time with him.

* * *

It was the first week of July in 1990 and our family was preparing to go on a vacation that had been planned a year ago. It was Lenny and I and our kids, Tara, Natasha, Noelle and grandson Lloyd. We were first flying to St. Maarten for a week and then to Miami for two days. Then, we were going on a Royal Caribbean cruise aboard a new ship, The Empress of the Seas. We'd be heading to the Bahamas for four days. We were all very excited. Noelle and I had cruised before, but this was everyone else's first time on a ship.

Lenny and I were both preoccupied the entire trip—our minds someplace else—definitely not on each other. We weren't arguing, but we definitely weren't the happy couple. We had our own baggage of a failing marriage that we'd brought along, which created a distance between us. Dale was lonely in Philly and would call to check on me. He always sounded like he'd lost his best friend. I missed him, too. When the vacation was over and we arrived back to Philly International, I took the kids and some of the luggage with me and headed home in my car. I left Lenny at the airport, gathering up the rest of the bags. He returned home five hours later with no luggage. He couldn't find the bags at the terminal. He was as high as a kite. He hadn't been back from vacation for a full day and he was already back to his dirty ways. He had demonstrated for the umpteenth time that he couldn't handle the slightest bit of responsibility and couldn't resist taking an opportunity to get plastered. I told him off. Then I sat down at the kitchen table and calmly reminded him of several things.

"Lenny, I have talked to you three times over the past four months to try to work out our differences so we can stay together. I just had a heart to heart talk with you three weeks ago. You know I'm frustrated being in this marriage and I've contemplated leaving. I truly am about to leave you. I'm tired of being unhappy and if things don't change, I'm leaving you."

"Oh, here we go again. Do I have to hear this shit again? You know you're not going anywhere. Why are you trying to start up? The reason

I'm gone all the time is because I have to hear a crock of shit whenever I'm home." He started laughing. "And where are you going—over to your mother's house so she can get drunk every other day and drive you crazy. You may as well stay right here with me." He flipped the channel on the TV to *Wheel of Fortune* and began concentrating on that.

I turned the television off. Lenny's nonchalant attitude and refusal to take me seriously made me fume with anger, but I kept my composure and continued to try to talk to him. After I gave up lecturing and pleading with him, as well as pouring my heart out, he seemed unimpressed and headed for the basement to have a beer. That infuriated me even more. I marched down there and shouted to him. "Tomorrow we were going back to that airport together for the bags!"

I ran up to our bedroom and called Dale. We made arrangements to meet that night. I needed him to tell me everything would be okay. He not only did that, but he told me he loved me and that he wanted us to move in together. That surprised me and made me feel good. I knew then that I really cared for him. At the same time, I was confused by my feelings because, in spite of everything, I was in love with my husband. The next day at the airport, the baggage handlers explained that no one had showed up for the bags and they put them in a storage area. I looked at Lenny and rolled my eyes. This was just another example of my always having to supervise everything. I was not happy.

Two weeks later, one warm summer night at the end of July, Dale telephoned me. He had just received a call from his mother informing him that Erica was in Philly. She wanted me to meet her with Marcus at her old boyfriend's house, Patrice's dad, for a quick visit.

"It's seven-thirty at night, Dale. I don't feel like driving way out there. You said that guy is kind of crazy. I'm not taking the kids out there and Lenny isn't home. I don't like this. Can't she wait until tomorrow and I'll bring him to her?"

"Look, Denise, it's no big thing. Just take the boy out there *now*. She won't want to be around him long. It's okay."

I didn't like this. My antennas were up. I suspected she may even be fucked up on drugs and melancholy. I wondered if she had some of her druggy friends with her. I suggested Dale bring her to my house. He said he'd already offered to do that and she refused. The other two kids were with her and she wanted Marcus to see his brother and sister. Dale began to get impatient and demanded I stop being selfish. He pointed out that Marcus was *her* son. That pissed me off and made me a little jealous that he wasn't really mine. The reality of that frightened me.

"Just let her see him tonight," he begged. Bring him, then you can take him back home with you. You have him *all* the time. Come on, just let her see him tonight for a few minutes. Do you want me to meet you there? Her old boyfriend lives in the 6000 block of Delancey Street."

I hesitated. I did not want to do this. I didn't answer. I was considering everything he was saying and questioning myself, wondering if I was being fair by refusing to take Marcus to his mother. Dale interrupted my thoughts. "Look Denise, either bring him or I'll come get Marcus and take him to her. Come on, it's getting late. I promise you it will be okay." I gathered the kids up drove out there.

✳ ✳ ✳

"Hi, Erica. How are you doing?" I asked after stepping out of the car with Marcus on my hip and Noelle by the hand.

"I'm cool. Look at my man. He sure looks cute in those pajamas," Erica cooed.

"Yeah, he is pretty cute isn't he—looks just like you. I've got him in pajamas because it's close to bedtime and he'll probably fall asleep in the car on the ride back home. "Give Mommy a kiss," I said to Marcus, turning him around to face Erica. Marcus reached over and kissed me. Erica looked at us in disapproval as Dale drove up.

"Hey, ladies. How's it going tonight?" he cheerfully asked. "Where are the other kids Erica?"

"In the house, I'll get them in a minute." She reached for Marcus and he wouldn't go to her. Finally I placed him in her arms. Erica cuddled him and then took a few steps backward. Then she turned around and ran to a car parked at the end of the block. In an instant, she had vanished and I stood screaming in the street, petrified and frozen. I stared at Dale who looked at her in disbelief. Noelle was crying.

After Dale and I argued in the street about why we shouldn't have been there, he said, "No matter what, I promise, I'll get him back. I swear to you Denise, I will get him back."

Dale and I returned to my house and I went through the court papers. I came up with the Order for Custody. We immediately went to the police precinct in my neighborhood. The police officer called it in to the station closest to Nadine's home. Dale, Noelle and I presented ourselves there, and officers from that district accompanied us to Nadine's house to search for Marcus and Erica. Nadine hadn't heard a thing from her and surmised they were in New Jersey at her sister-in-law Claire's house. Nadine suggested we look there for the baby, but we decided not to.

The Philadelphia Police Department had advised us earlier that our papers were in order and recommended we report to Philadelphia Family Court the next day to file emergency papers. Those papers would enable the Philly system to have the authorities in New Jersey search and retrieve Marcus from the aunt's residence. I called Michelle from the welfare office at home late that night to have Erica's check stopped. I figured if Erica had no money, she would be more willing to bring Marcus back and comply with the order. However, I was informed by Michelle that, because Erica was not living in Philadelphia, the Department of Public Assistance had already discontinued payments in Philly and closed her case. The aunt, Claire Foster, had applied for assistance in Gloucester County, New Jersey, stating that Erica had given her custody of the other two children and she was in fact living there herself from time to time.

The next day, we were able to get an emergency hearing at the Philadelphia Family Court. We were granted an Ex-Parte Order, which could be used in New Jersey to recover Marcus from Claire's residence.

After Dale and I made the trip to Jersey late that afternoon, it proved fruitless. The New Jersey Orders had already become effective, ringing **victory for Claire and Erica. The matter would be settled in court at a** later date. At first, no visitation privileges were allowed for Dale because Erica and her Aunt Claire had advised the court that Dale was not Marcus' father. The Court then ordered paternity testing and set a court date for eight weeks. The plan was that the court would notify Claire and Erica by mail of the dates of the upcoming hearing and blood testing.

In the interim, because Dale had a Court Order and was supporting Marcus, they reneged and allowed visitation once a week and every other weekend until the matter reached the court date. I was heartbroken, Dale and his family were absolutely livid, and Noelle was a basket case missing him.

A month had gone by and Marcus still had not returned. Dale and I were missing him terribly. Noelle kept asking questions about when he would be back and even Lenny was concerned. During one conversation, Lenny said he wished I had never let any of us get attached to Marcus. He was sorry I had ever gotten him from Erica. I started working at a temp agency a couple of days a week to pass the time and keep some pocket money. I put Noelle in a summer camp day program. Dale was continuing to work full-time and we were meeting a couple of nights for dinner. He had grown attached to Noelle and would sometimes pick her up from camp for me. Lenny was still up to his usual thing—happy hour day and night. We were just like ships passing in the night. We had mechanical sex—sessions few and far between.

Six weeks after the Marcus kidnapping, the phone was ringing when Noelle and I entered our house after her piano lesson.

"Hello," I answered.

"Hey, Denise, sit down," Nadine said.

I knew there was trouble. I was hoping nothing had happened to Marcus. "What's up?"

"Erica is dead."

"What!" I shrieked. "What do you mean Erica is dead? What happened?" My husband entered the living room from upstairs when I started shouting.

"She was in a horrible car accident last night. Two guys were in the car that she had picked up in Philly at a bar. Drugs were in their car. She died when it hit a pole. Claire called me a few minutes ago."

As the months went by after Erica's death, Dale and I grew closer because of the entire ordeal. The blood tests were taken and he was indeed Marcus' father. The court, however, felt it best that Marcus remain with Claire so he could be raised with his siblings. Claire had taken a two hundred fifty thousand dollar life insurance policy out on Erica, her brother's child, and was collecting payments from the state for all three children including a huge settlement from the automobile insurance carrier of the vehicle she died in. Since Erica legally resided at Claire's house, Claire's own auto insurance company also paid an additional huge settlement to her because Erica died in the accident. She made out like a fat rat.

Dale was granted visitation privileges, but every time we would go to New Jersey to collect Marcus, there would be a confrontation. While I was vacationing in Jamaica with Lenny, Nadine called to tell me Dale was in the hospital. He had been severely beaten by a local hood and had multiple injuries. When he recuperated and resumed his visitation schedule, many times Claire would not be at home at all to give the child to Dale and he would report to the police station and nothing would be done. Most times, he would show up for Marcus, and return to Philadelphia without him. Whenever Dale would actually retrieve the child, Marcus would be filthy and without a change of clothes, causing us to go shopping to send him back with new outfits. We would return him clean and dressed up only to collect him raggedy at the next visitation. Marcus would scream and cry when he was returned to New Jersey. I was aching with grief over this situation.

After months of this and Dale and I paying thousands of dollars to attorneys to try to get the decision overturned, we could not get Marcus back. Finally, we gave up the fight. Dale and I had been spending so much time together running around to hearings and lawyers' offices as well as having dinner together. I saw him more than the husband I did have.

My marriage was still in shambles and Lenny was continuing his outside activities that kept him away from home. Often, he didn't even **know Dale and I were having dinner together because he never called me** to say he'd be late coming home. He merely showed up when he showed up. The marriage had truly deteriorated.

One morning I woke up alone. He'd stayed out all night. That was the last straw. I presented myself at his office. "I have to leave you."

"What?" He asked.

"I'm splitting. I'm telling you straight up that there is someone else. You can have the house and all the furniture, but Noelle and I are leaving. I plan to move shortly. I'll give you a date when I get myself together."

Lenny looked up at me—waved his hand and said, "Here we go again. You drove all the way down here to start some shit on my job?" He hissed, snarled at me.

"Don't raise your voice, Lenny. Everybody doesn't have to know our business. Don't make me turn ghetto down here. You know I can do it. If you'd bring your ass home from work at a decent hour, I wouldn't have had to come down here to tell you this. I'm serious, mister. I'm getting ready to walk for real."

I had his full attention and I watched him become nervous. "Okay— let's go across the street to the bar to talk. Come on," he said preparing to leave from his cubicle.

The last thing I wanted to do was go to a bar with him. This fool thought the bar was the fucking answer to anything and everything. A round of fucking drinks to solve a problem. I was infuriated and growled, "Nope—no bars. I gotta run. I'll talk to you another time if you like, but my mind is made up."

I really hated leaving my home and starting over. I had worked so hard and had such a beautiful place. But I was exhausted from my marriage and I truly believed I'd be happier with Dale. The past months gave me a glimpse of what life could be like with him. I truly wouldn't have to be in charge 24/7 and he would love me like Lenny never could. I was willing to give up everything.

"Look, hold up a minute. Where are you going and who is it?"

My words definitely caught him off guard. Lenny looked jumbled and confused.

"It's *Dale* and you don't need to know where I'm going." I stormed out of his office.

Lenny returned home that evening around ten o'clock. He was high and reeked of liquor. He tried to talk to me, but I ignored him. The will to save our marriage had dissipated. Lenny became more frustrated because I would not talk to him and began shoving me around in the kitchen and throwing furniture. He hurled a chair through the kitchen window. I backed away and went upstairs and got into Noelle's bed with her.

He came up the stairs with a hammer, threatening to cave my brains in. I ran out of the house in panties and a bra. He was chasing me down the street with the hammer and, as I got to the corner of our block, I ran smack into a group of three guys who were walking down the street. Lenny came up behind me and they noticed the hammer. Everybody froze.

One of them gave a throaty warning. "Now, I know, brother, you're not intending to hit this nice lady with that." Another took his shirt off and put it on me.

"This is my wife and I'm gonna kick her ass," Lenny lunged for me.

These were not big guys. They were of medium heights and weights, but there was strength in numbers. They were younger and more energetic than my drunk husband. They roughed him up and scared the crap out of Lenny, then put me in my house and had me lock him out. I offered to call the police, but the guys told me I didn't need them. They positioned themselves on my steps, not letting Lenny in his own house. In two hours, he gave up and went somewhere for the remainder of the night. When I told Dale about the incident, he sat silently taking it all in. His eyes were piercing. He was raging inside. When he finally spoke, he was insistent on having something done to Lenny. I listened patiently and finally calmly ordered, "Nobody better not touch a hair on my husband's head. I mean that."

I needed Dale to just leave me alone for a couple of days so we all could chill out from the altercation between Lenny and I. We needed a breather. During this time, Dale was silent. He didn't even call me. After four days, he showed up at Nadine's house. She and I had previously made a date to get together. When Dale arrived, I figured he had been checking up on me through her. I was glad to see him. He hugged me tight. "Denise, I have to talk to you about money. We're strapped and I've got to do something to get some cash to get us started. I have to be able to take care of you and Noelle."

I was impressed he was trying to get us organized and was relieved that he still wanted me. Over the last four days, I thought maybe he was tired of dealing with me and Lenny. "Well, you're working and I have some money," I answered.

He flashed that gleaming smile and chuckled. "You know that's not enough. I have to try to keep you and Noelle in the same lifestyle. I have a plan."

I started thinking about capers. I wondered if he was planning that we'd rescue Marcus and run off together with both the kids. Or if he was going to rob a bank or something. Was he going to ask me to divorce Lenny and/or sell my house? "What's the plan?" I asked.

He hesitated, then started off slowly. That made me nervous. "Now, I know you won't approve of this, but just hear me out and trust me."

I was impatient to hear about his plan and wanted him to cut to the chase. "Shoot."

For a moment, he went back to his joking self. "You already put a stop to that." I laughed out loud. "Listen, it's illegal and it's wrong, but I just need to do something for one month. Just one month."

I immediately cut him off. I'd never been in trouble before in my life. He wasn't getting me locked up. "No, and I don't want to know the rest."

He patted my thigh and asked me to relax. He squeezed my hand and continued. "Look Denise, just trust me and let me do this. I merely want to turn over one package of coke—just a one time deal and I'll be okay—we'll be okay."

My eyes lit up, my mouth wide open. I caught my breath and said in disapproval, "No. I have never been involved in anything illegal and I'm certainly not going to jeopardize my security, well-being, and Noelle. No."

He continued, speaking clearly and slowly, and stroking me with his words. "Listen, it will work. I have a connection. I won't bring anything or anybody around you or Noelle. I just need to do this to get you out of there."

I protested, "Let me get a *full-time* job."

He sighed and looked at me. He was silent. He was thinking. "Baby, you can't make this much money that quickly on a regular job. I know what I'm doing."

Fear set in my eyes. "You're going to jail. You better call those lawyers asses back up."

He got paranoid. "Don't jinx me Denise—just trust me and I'll have you out of this mess. Where's Lenny, out getting sloshed again?"

"Probably," I shot back.

He kissed me. "I've got to run. I'll call you tomorrow. Are you okay?"

"You'd better rethink that thing."

Two days later, the phone rang at three o'clock in the afternoon. The voice at the other end was moaning. It was Lenny.

"I'm in the subway station. I'm having a really hard time and very mixed up. I can't concentrate."

He was crying out of control. I was startled and immediately worried. My intuition told me to snatch control right away.

"Pull yourself together!" I ordered sternly. He continued to sob. "Denise, I never thought you would leave me. How could Dale do this as nice as I've been about letting his baby stay with us?"

"Lenny, first of all get yourself together. Get out of the train station and I will pick you up and we'll have a talk." I wanted him to meet me at Morton's of Chicago, a restaurant very close to the train station. I made a point of telling him to sit at the bar since he liked bars. I felt he'd leave the train station if I was coming to see him at a bar.

I wanted to make sure I got him out of there, not knowing whether or not he was distraught to the point of jumping in front of a train. I raced downtown praying he'd be okay. Lenny was a pain in the ass, but I did not want anything to happen to him. I had a history with him, a lot of good times and, no matter what, I was compelled to do whatever I could to help, even though I was going to leave him. He was my daughter's father and my husband. He was important to me.

* * *

132

As we sat at the bar, he nursed his drink in bewilderment. He was in critical condition from his ego being shot and I knew he felt like a fool for underestimating me. Despite his love of the party life, he truly did not want to be separated from Noelle and me.

"How in the world can you do this to me? We've been together so long. I know I screw up sometime, but I really do love you. I'll straighten up if you'll let me. Do you still love me?"

He was in pain and probably terrified, but I wasn't going to play games with him or give him false hope. I told him the truth.

"Yes, I do still love you, but you have worn me out. You're entirely too irresponsible. I've had it. I like the way Dale treats me and I swear we did not mean for this to happen. I want you to get a grip and accept it."

"What about the house and all?" Before I could answer, he took a deep breath and exhaled, then put his face in his hands. He placed his hand on my thigh and squeezed it. I removed it. I could have cared less about those material things. "You can have the house and the furniture. I don't care anymore. I can make it."

"I don't need this shit right now." Lenny buried his face in his hands again. He had applied for a new position at his job and had to study for a test. He said he couldn't even concentrate on the material and asked if I could hold off for a while. As usual, he was only thinking about himself. It was all about him and what he needed. I was ticked off. "Lenny, I am moving on. You've gone too far. You drink and do drugs and will probably end up killing yourself. You are not taking me down with you. You should consider getting some help." He refused. "Denise, I've been handling my vices just fine all my life." I was disappointed, but too physically tired to fight. Our ship had sunk.

"Okay, whatever you say. I'm ready to go. Are you coming home, do you need a ride?"

"I'm not leaving right now. I have some stops to make. I'll see you later."

I was not going to *baby* Lenny or plead and beg him to come home. I refused to supervise him that night either.

"If you need any help regarding your problem that you think you don't have, I will help you with that. Just let me know. That's all I can do."

I left the restaurant, filled with emptiness. When I arrived home, the phone was ringing. "I'm going through with my plan to get you out of there. Within a month, we'll be together. Bye," Dale said. I never got the chance to utter a word. An hour after I got home, Lenny walked in the door and headed for the basement to sleep.

The following week, Dale and I were discussing spending a weekend together. I thought about the sex and that made me nervous. In the past couple of months when Lenny and I had sex, I couldn't have an orgasm. I thought something was wrong with me. I was reluctant to sleep with him. I had no sex drive. I explained to Dale that I was having sexual problems and I had even made an appointment to see a sex therapist.

Dale listened intently to what I was saying. His index finger traveled from his chin to his forehead. His face moved up and down. He was silent. Then he took my hand and held it. "Listen, Pal, let's try something different. Let me handle this for you and if it doesn't work out, we'll *both* go to have a chat with the doctor. For right now, let's forget about spending that weekend together. Don't even think about it. No pressure, baby, just relax yourself."

I was reminded again of how totally different Dale and Lenny were. I had told Lenny about my problem a while ago during one of our discussions and his reply to me was, "Well, I'm fine. Yep, there has to be something wrong with you. Don't try to blame that shit on me, too." Having a partner like Dale to work things out with was a blessing in itself. "You mean its okay with you—for real—*about my problem*?" I asked Dale.

"Yes it is."

The following Saturday morning, Dale called. "Let's go to Hershey Park today?"

"Oh wow, we're taking Noelle to get on the rides? She'll love that."

"I'm taking you. Just you."

I fell silent. This man was so sweet. "It's a date," I said.

We had a long, relaxing hour and a half drive to Hershey. Dale had the Johnny Gill cassette playing for me, which was one of my favorites. I loved the entire tape, but the cut *My My My* was my jam. He also played our favorite song, Baby Face's *Whip Appeal.* He had me totally unwound by the time we got there. It was so much fun going on an attraction at the park that taught us all about how chocolate was processed into the candy that we purchased in the stores. Like teenagers, we went on different rides. We even got on the roller coaster and both of us screamed with terror. We dined at the magnificent Hotel Hershey located on the grounds. Stuffed, we then played some games, trying to win a prize, but we lost a bunch of money and headed home. I had a wonderful time. Dale was a very thoughtful, fun, and a creative man. I was hooked all over again.

When he dropped me back at home, I found Lenny in the living room packing. Suitcases were arranged on the couch. I was surprised.

He didn't even look up at me when he announced, "I found a place."

I didn't want a confrontation or for us to get into some long drawn out thing. My mind was already made up about us, so I said, "Okay." I headed up the stairs.

My lack of interest angered him. "Don't you even want to know where I'm going?"

"To be honest, *no*."

I felt he was setting us up for an argument when he said, "That confirms that you really don't give a damn about me."

I stopped, looked at him, and pleaded, "Lenny, I don't feel good. I'm coming down with something. Please don't start with me." I went to bed and when I woke up the next morning, all of his things were gone. I was relieved, but at the same time I ached for his return. Dale called and I explained that I may be coming down with the flu and that Lenny had moved out.

"I'm sorry you're not feeling well. Get some rest and I'll check on you later. Is Noelle helping you out? Do you need me to come to get her? Do you have all the stuff you need in the house to work on the cold?"

"I'm cool and don't need anything. Noelle spent the night at my girlfriend Marcy's house. She's dropping her off at school tomorrow."

"Okay. I'll talk to you later."

I went about my day and that evening Dale called back. "Let's go out and get a bite to eat. Can you make it?"

I was still feeling kind of bad, but maybe it would do me some good to shower and put some clothes and make-up on and get out of the house. After dinner, instead of taking me home, we went to his apartment. It was a second floor walk up located at 28th and Allegheny. The neighborhood was not dangerous, but it was definitely not a vicinity I would live in. When he unlocked the first door leading to the stairs, he stopped and turned at me. "Listen, it's not real nice. I don't have much. Okay?" I felt bad that he was embarrassed.

"Dale, whatever your place looks like—it's good enough for me. Let's go." Upon entering his apartment, the living room was the first room you came to. The floor was covered in an awful shag rug with long, thick fibers of orange, tan, and brown. He had an old couch that was plaid—taupe and orange. Ghastly. There were also two chairs, old but in good condition that didn't match anything. There was a wooden coffee table in front of the couch. Cheap shades covered the three windows. I showed no sign that this room did not meet my approval. He was standing away from me, observing me as I scanned the room. He was scared to death. Then, I noticed an old component set. It had a record player. Thrilled, I ran over to open the top. I noticed a bunch of albums in crates and looked through them. He had everything—The Motown people, Aretha Franklin, The Whispers, Blue Magic, and lots of others! I was having a ball on the floor checking out his collection even though I wasn't feeling well. I noticed Dale relaxing and he said, "let me show you the rest of the place." We advanced to the kitchen, which was a small eat in. It had an old wooden table and two chairs. I looked in the cabinets. He didn't have the Mikasa that I had, but he had some dishes. There were very little staples in the cabinets and a few items in the refrigerator. Then we checked out the bathroom, sparkling and clean as a whistle. We went into the bedroom. The bed was full-size. It had a tan *regular* bedspread, not a luxurious comforter like I was used to. There were two pillows. The sheets were beige and clean. I went over to his dresser and there were pictures of me, him, Noelle, and Marcus that I had given him. They were slipped in the grooves of the mirror and there were more **pictures of me than the kids. I was flattered. A cheap pair of brown curtains** hung from the bedroom window. He worked directly across the street at a hair salon. He was a stylist and had been there for a couple of years. He was such a neat freak! Everything was organized in his dresser drawers. His socks were rolled up in pairs, and I took one out to put on my cold feet. Everything was in its place. There was no dust, dirt, or clutter anywhere.

I was shocked! He was a much better housekeeper than me. Domestic organization was not my forte. Dale's place didn't have nice furniture, but it was just fine for me.

He left me to look around some more. When I found him, he was in the living room, sitting on the floor. Teddy Pendergrass was singing *Close The Door*. The room was dim, a large blanket spread on the floor. Two glasses half-filled with something that appeared to be liquor.

"Umm," I said. Nice atmosphere, but I shouldn't have any alcohol."

"You *should*—it's Rock and Rye. It will help your cold. Come on down and tell me all about it," Dale patted the blanket.

I complied, sat down beside him, and took a sip of my drink. We chatted while we finished our drinks. He began kissing me, deep kisses slowly entwining our tongues. He pulled away and gently caressed my ears with his lips, taking little nips at my ear lobes. His hands were running through my hair while mine fondled his hips and that cute ass of his. I kissed him on his eyelids, cheeks, and his lips. It was all turning to fire as we began undressing each other. He laid me down and cupped one of my breasts in his hand, sucking my nipple. I leaned over and massaged his thigh and advanced to his penis. I was blazing. I got on top of him, positioning myself, so that my clitoris got the full attention of his erected penis. We were both moaning with delight. I eased him into me and shook my ass a little. I hunched my butt in by using my thigh muscle to get it just right. When I made that move, I heard him sigh, *"Damn."* I loved control in any capacity and had full control at that point. My ass was vibrating. So many noises were coming out of me. I was soaking wet, the juices swishing and splattering inside my vagina. Denise Garner had been released. She was no longer held hostage. I climaxed and screamed. He flipped me over and began his work. Like a professional, he was skilled and knew the ends and outs of my vagina like a racecar driver extremely familiar with the twists and turns of the road. It was an amazing experience and left us both naked, breathless, and satisfied on that fuzzy old blanket.

As he gently stroked my face, he said, "Do you still need the doctor?"

In the weeks that followed, my feelings were questionable. Was I in love with him? Had I really fallen in love with him or did I simply love the way he loved me? Was I just overwhelmed because of the sex and the fact that unlike Lenny, Dale seemed to absorb every part of me? Was it that this was such a new and different experience for me—the refreshment of having so much of a man's attention? I got mixed up on a daily basis about what I was experiencing. But one thing I did know was that Dale made me feel like I was *somebody.* He taught me the meaning of the word *relax.* He introduced me to *The Whispers* and their sexy, romantic songs that soothed me many nights. He analyzed my problems. He took time to think about *me.* He was gentle and fun loving and told me I was *worth* something to him. He was a friend and shopped with me—like a *girlfriend.* Most men didn't do that, not having time for that sort of thing. He even accompanied me to *Victoria's Secret* and helped me shop for underwear. Dale made it entertaining. He had patience and appreciated me. Because of my relationship with Dale I came to understand what it was to have someone love you. It was a miracle to actually *experience* being truly and unequivocally loved by a man. If I never had it with my husband or got it again from anyone, at least I was fortunate and blessed in my lifetime to have been introduced to the feeling once. I could go anywhere in this world and meet anybody and I'd be able to *explain* it because I'd *lived* it. The love between us was so strong that, years later, I knew he still loved me.

My confusion continued, but I believed God put Dale in my path for a reason, to show me something. He delivered an experience I needed desperately—the adventure of true love. I ceased evaluating the situation and going back and forth. I finally stuck with my decision and was due to move into a beautiful two-bedroom apartment that Dale and I had picked out together. We were moving in three days. It was a high rise on Lincoln Drive and had an elaborate swimming pool. There were cute shops in the lobby, and I already imagined our daily life.

Lenny moved in with a woman named Carolyn Monroe. She had an apartment in the Eastwick section of Philadelphia, near Philly International Airport. I'd remembered speaking to her on quite a few occasions in the past. The first call I had ever gotten from her was in 1982 when Lenny and I were living together in an apartment. She was a longtime friend, he explained, and was calling because she needed help with her move from Atlanta back to Philly. Carolyn had been in Atlanta attending nursing school. He insisted they were platonic friends. I heard him telling her that he could not help with the move. She had wanted him to come down there to drive her. In the months that followed, she called periodically, but I was never upset with the calls. I had plenty of platonic friends myself and I understood. I was not insecure. Eventually, I did become alarmed when I got a call from her after our wedding. It was on the Monday after we were married. When she asked for Lenny, I was such the excited new bride that I said, "Hold on, I'll get my husband."

Carolyn seemed to have become angry and snapped, "That's not your husband."

"Yes, he is—we got married on Saturday."

She accused me of lying. I had called Lenny to the phone and heard him abruptly answer "yes" and "no." Then, he confirmed that we had gotten married over the weekend. I smelled a rat and hit the ceiling, interrogating him about that woman. He kept insisting she was just a friend and, young and naïve as I was, I believed him.

Dale and I moved into our apartment. Noelle was all charged up about having a pool and a brand new room to show off to her friends. She hadn't worried about missing her Dad because he had talked to her and told her he would spend time with her on the weekends. My house in Philadelphia was left fully furnished and my daughter Natasha moved there. It was perfect timing since the lease to her apartment was about to run out. Dale paid for everything, brand new for our brand new life.

The walls were off-white. The carpeting covering the huge two-bedroom apartment was a splendid shade of mauve. The living room furniture was a floral pattern of soft shades of a pink, mint green, and off-white. We had a huge couch with lots of pillows and big arms. The ensemble also came with the trendsetting oversized *chair and a half*, large enough to cuddle up in, and a love seat. The coffee and end tables were glass perched on off-white wicker bases. Peach, mint, and ice blue ruffles covered the top of the windows allowing light to always shine through. We had a forty-eight inch big screen TV and a glass liquor cart on wheels. It was gorgeous. The dining room table was a light colored wood and had four chairs. The kitchen was bright and we had all new appliances. Our bedroom set was black and the dresser had a large mirror. We had perfect matching end tables on both sides, one for each of us to keep our personal stuff. I purchased seven hundred dollars worth of towels and wash cloths. Noelle had a princess brass bed, a white chest of drawers and mirrored dresser. She had chosen a queen size so her buddies would all fit in it with her during sleepovers. The rest of her room was accented in pastels. The place was so spectacular that the building owners often gave us a discount on the rent because they used it to show potential tenants. Dale was so proud of what I had done to the apartment and had never lived anywhere like it.

Unfortunately, our happiness would be short-lived—two months. I couldn't get used to the way he got his money. His little drug business that he would only be operating for a month had turned into an empire and he was the King. He thought he had a corporation and loved running it. Five people were working for him and he supervised them from his car between the hours of nine and five and was closed on Sundays. When I talked to him about stopping and our agreement, he begged me to let him continue. I was worried sick that we'd all end up dead even though he never brought any drugs into our apartment and none of his workers ever called or came by.

While Dale and I were living together, I began having an affair with my husband. It happened as a result of us simply *missing* each other. It was baffling to us both, but we both longed for each other. And my anxiety over living with a drug dealer was steering me back to my marriage. My husband was a pain in the ass, but he had a legitimate job. That was giving me food for thought. After two weeks of dating, Lenny and I planned to get back together. The excitement of the pool and the new bedroom had worn off for Noelle. It was like a vacation and she was ready to go home. During our separation, Lenny had had a brief affair with a co-worker—a **one night stand which resulted in a pregnancy. He was scared to death of** what that would do to him financially if the child really was his. Lenny swore it wasn't his. I could tell from our conversations that he wanted me in charge of that. He knew I'd get to the bottom of it, ordering blood tests and getting lawyers. It seemed both of us had made bad decisions and the wrong choices. At the time the pregnancy occurred Lenny was living at Carolyn's apartment in Philadelphia.

Lenny and I both returned to our marital residence after our two month separation. Dale was devastated and still very much in love with me. When I left him to go back to my husband, he said, "These arms will always be open. You can come back to me whenever you want to. I love you." He didn't want to keep any of the furniture he'd paid for.

Dale and I never resumed our relationship and he didn't allow me to be his pal or have phone chats. We could not be friends, he said. If I wanted a definite hook up thing, he was mine—forever. I made up my mind that would never happen because I'd have to live life in the fast lane with him. He'd use illegal means to get money to provide for me. I did not want him in trouble or jail. The flip side of it was that I really was in love with my husband. If I was going to try to make it with anyone, I wanted to give my husband and my marriage a shot. The decision was hard for me because there were so many things I would miss not being Dale's woman. I loved the way he checked on me in particular. He'd call periodically during the day just to check in with me, to see how my day was going. He was spontaneous and he paid attention to me, observing things even when I wasn't aware of it. When we were living together, he was planning for Christmas in July. He had a list going of all the things he wanted to buy and do. It seemed he was always planning for the future.

Dale took Nadine and I to Atlantic City one night and tore the crap tables up! Once he cashed in, we sat down in a restaurant. After we ordered, he looked at me and said, "Let's talk about sex. I want to know exactly what you like—everything. I have to be sure I have that completely down." I blushed and fidgeted. No man had ever approached me that way. I was embarrassed and reluctant to answer. Twenty minutes later, I turned into a chatterbox confessing my fantasies. When we left the casino and went to the car, it was early morning, daylight. I started to get in and he stopped me. "Take your panties off." I obediently went under my skirt and handed my underwear to him. He tied them around the antenna of the car. Then, he put me in the back seat and fucked my brains out. Nadine was still gambling and when she got to the car, she saw my underwear around the antenna, blowing from the sea wind. Satisfied, Dale and I were curled up in each other's arms, dozing off. She got in the car laughing and making jokes about us. He drove all the way back to Philly with my panties blowing from that antenna.

One morning as I packed my things, thoughts of Dale flooded my mind. I was crazy to be leaving that man for the one that was still legally mine. Dale regularly took care of my car—had it washed and inspected and kept the tank full. He was great at telling stories and kept me laughing. He was quite the comedian. He left me a daily allowance every day before he went to work—just like I was a child. And he was never missing. I could always find him. A thing he did that blew me away was that he always told people how much he loved me and that he was proud of me. When I made the decision to leave him, my gut told me it was the wrong one. But I did it anyway and, as I suspected, it would turn out that I had truly gone out of the frying pan into the fire.

CHAPTER 8

⌒

Showing Up

Late 1991, four months into our reconciliation, Lenny began drinking at happy hour at 12:00 noon and happy hour at 5:00 p.m. I was taking a lot of shit from him. He lied like a rug, paid bills at our house—his share—and messed up every other dime of his money. Since he'd been running around with me while still married to Frances, I should have known that *what goes around comes around*. He was always *missing* and never called home to say where he was.

He stole money out of my purse and my car—a stone thief. I went to bed at night and hid my money. Sometimes in the freezer, the vacuum cleaner, or anywhere I thought he wouldn't find it. Then he graduated to the ultimate—taking my ATM card and robbing our family in the middle of the night to get coked up. I didn't even realize it. I'd been so upset with everything I was going through that I started to see a therapist. One day, I sat in Dr. Jonathan Morrison's office and explained that I must have been losing my mind because I couldn't keep the checkbook straight anymore. Checks were bouncing all over the place. He told me to bring it in along with the bank statement on the next visit.

When he reviewed the statement, he said, "This is the work of a person who is on drugs." I edged out of my seat.

"What do you mean? Nobody in my house is a drug addict. It's just me, Lenny, and our daughter Noelle in the house. Lenny may be a drinker and may snort a line or two of coke, but no way is he a drug addict."

The doctor paused before continuing. "Look at this statement and the times that this money is being withdrawn from the machine. Look at the pattern, first a twenty-dollar withdrawal, then a forty-dollar one an hour later. Then in the next forty-five minutes another thirty-dollar withdrawal. This is the way people on drugs operate. Have you been checking all your statements? Are you out at night at two, three, and four o'clock in the morning making withdrawals?"

"No," I muttered.

"Well, this is the way it works, and I know because we counsel these people. They start out with a small amount of money. They feel that is all they'll need—just a little bit of drugs. Then they find they need more, so they get a little more money, and they tell themselves that this is the last hit—at the machine and with the drug man. Then they realize they need another hit. They are trying to get that first real potent high—and they can't retrieve it. That's why they run back and forth this way. Your husband is on drugs."

I was shocked. I couldn't imagine Lenny really being a drug addict. Lenny didn't get in that night until about 5:00 a.m. He slept two hours and got up for work. I asked him about the money missing from the checkbook and he denied taking it.

I had to admit to myself that I had a liar, a cheater, and a thief. I knew the three things ran in succession. If you lie, you cheat and you steal. So I announced to my husband that I was going to the bank to explain that my money was missing and that I would demand to see videotapes of the ATM machines. He held to his story that he had never been there. I went to the bank and explained my problem. Bank policy required that I get a signed affidavit from Lenny stating he had not made the withdrawals. They would not replace my money or lift the bounced check fees unless I returned it.

I returned home with the affidavit and waited for Lenny to arrive from work. He showed up about 1:30 a.m. I explained the circumstances and he refused to sign the affidavit. I demanded my money back from him, but he told me he was not giving me shit. The following morning, I waited until he left and took a shower. I gave Noelle her breakfast. It was Lenny's payday.

I got Noelle dressed in mismatched clothes, pulled her hair out all over her head, and wet it up so it would dry without combing or brushing and would look a wreck. I deliberately did not put shoes on the child. Then I got myself dressed in purple Dr. Denton pajamas and leopard high heel shoes and put on my six-year-old mink coat. We headed for Lenny's office.

"May I speak with Lenny Garner? I'm his wife, Denise," I said to the receptionist. I had carried Noelle in and placed her on the floor. The receptionist eyed us, astonished at our appearance.

"Just one moment," she said as she paged Lenny to the lobby.

Lenny appeared and was surprised to see us. Once he looked us over, his expression showed he had been hit with a ton of bricks. He motioned me to the corner of the lobby.

"What in the world is wrong with you coming down here looking like this, Denise?" he whispered. "Why is Noelle barefoot? Are you crazy coming on my job looking this way? You are embarrassing me."

"I want the money back you took out of our account."

"Don't you start any mess down here, woman, I mean it. You'd better get out of here. We'll talk about this when I get home."

I marched past him and the receptionist, heading for the cubicles. He followed me and Noelle trailed behind, trying to keep up with us. I stopped at the first cubicle where a woman was sitting with a lot of papers.

With a gleaming smile I said, "Hi, I'm Denise Garner, Lenny's wife. It is a pleasure to meet you. Let me introduce you to our daughter, Noelle." I picked up Noelle and told her to say hello to the woman. I extended my hand to shake the woman's hand.

"Hello, Mrs. Garner, it's nice to meet you," She stared strangely at us.

"Well, it's nice to meet you, too, but we can't stay long. We have to meet the rest of my husband's co-workers. I just like getting to know everyone since we're always talking when I call. I'd like to put a face with the voices. You have a nice day," I had already forgotten her name.

I quickly moved on to the next cubicle and introduced myself to another woman. We exchanged pleasantries as Lenny watched in amazement. Before I could move on to the next person, Lenny grabbed me by the hand. He led me back out to the lobby and marched me in a corner away from the receptionist. He retrieved his wallet from his pocket and handed me his paycheck, "Take this damn money and do whatever you want with it, but do not, under any circumstances, come here again."

I sashayed out of the office. He followed me to my car and growled, "I'll talk to you when I get home!"

I went straight to the bank and deposited it into our account and rushed home.

When Lenny got home, I lied to him and said that I had viewed the surveillance tapes and knew that he was taking money out of the account in the middle of the night. He denied it was him and planned to go to the bank and sue them.

The next day he stayed home from work. I decided to use another tactic with him. I told him I thought everything over and maybe using drugs wasn't such a bad thing.

"You know, Lenny, maybe I've been too rough on you."

His eyes lit up in surprise as he sat across the kitchen table from me. I continued on. "You've always been so in control of it all. Maybe you can handle it. You do get up and go to work every day. You've held on to your job. Maybe you can do this. It does give you pleasure. Maybe I should try it. Maybe we could get high together and then you'd be home more."

Lenny was blown away and interested, but was looking a little suspicious. I could tell he did not know what to make of the conversation. A puzzled look remained on his face. "*You*—getting high?"

"Yeah, I could try it out. I might like it. And, I'm really good at arranging things. I could organize the whole thing."

Bewildered, he stammered, *"Organize?"*

"Yeah—we'll make a plan. We really don't need all these material things. I have always been so hung up on material things. Jesus! I guess I have driven you to drugs. I always have to have *this* and have *that.* We don't need to have so much stuff. Look at all these things. This nice kitchen set—nearly a thousand dollars just to sit down and have a meal. And a *trash compactor?* Who the hell needs a *trash compactor?* We don't have any friends **who have one. What about that fancy microwave that rotates? I can heat** stuff up in the oven."

I noticed Lenny was silent and his eyes shifted back and forth. I kept babbling on. "We could even save money on the electric bill, too. Let's sell *all* this shit. We're probably going to lose it anyway if we both start getting high, but what the hell. We'll be happy. So, let's start losing the stuff right away. Just get rid of it. I can call some people and have most of the shit gone today. Then we can use that money to start getting high. Eventually, we can damn near empty the kitchen. Then we can move on to the dining room. We don't need that seven thousand dollar dining room table. You always said I shouldn't have bought it."

Lenny was still speechless, but looked a little scared. I got up from the table and started walking around, pointing at objects and yelling out numbers. Then I said, "Okay—this is brilliant—I'm down. Let me get my phone book and call some people. I'll get a pencil and paper and make a list. It'll be like a flea market inside the house. You may even know some people on your job that might want some of this shit. I'm tired of being so responsible, I want to kick back. Yeah, that might be nice for me. Let's lose all this shit and we'll start today. My cousin Junior is a derelict and doesn't have a damn thing—but he is happy. He drinks 24/7 and hasn't worked in seventeen years. He even gets a welfare check. He talks to me all the time about how everyone he knows who has anything is miserable. Junior says having stuff is a serious problem. You know how smart he is. Everybody in my family helps him out. He lives home with my aunt and uncle rent free. Once we get really down and out, my Dad will put us in one of his places. Shit—he owns a lot of real estate. It'll be in the ghetto, but so what. He won't charge us rent because of Noelle. I was raised up down there and I know everybody."

By that time Lenny had come into the living room, observing me examine a brass magazine rack, he said, "Look, I don't want to do this. You are going crazy. We can't sell our stuff."

"Why?"

"Look. You are going overboard just like you always do. I don't want to *not* have *anything*." That's crazy. I just wanted to get high a little bit. I'm not looking to lose everything I've got."

I looked him in the eye and studied him. I growled, "Well, goddammit, motherfucker, you make up your mind *what* you want. Drugs or a nice house and a family. You pick one or the other. You tell me *now*! I am with you either way. What's the deal?"

"I'm going to straighten up. I'll stop getting high." He sat down on the couch.

"And, how will you do that?"

"I'll just stop."

"What's the plan?"

"The plan is I'll stop. Period."

"It has to be organized."

"Nothing has to be *organized*. I'll just leave the shit alone. That's that."

"Oh no buddy, *this* is the way it will be. You get *no* ATM card. You get *no* lunch money. You do not drive the car to the train station or to work. You bring your ass *straight* home from work. *I* shop at the market. *I* buy TV dinners for you to take to work or you take leftovers or sandwiches. You take sodas and juice to work. You get a bus pass from me each month. I control every fucking dime that comes in this house. You get cigarettes by the carton when I shop. You do not hang out with your friends. You take Noelle to the *Please Touch Museum* or the zoo on the weekends and I'll drop you guys off and pick you up. The party is over—you got that?"

He protested and we started to argue all over again. I was being too rough on him. "Oh, no,—you aren't having that much control over me. You're trying to turn me into a punk. I'm doing it my way!" He shouted.

I walked over to the phone and dialed a number. "May I have the personnel department for the Department of Licenses and Inspections?"

Lenny pushed the button down on the phone, disconnecting the call. "What are you doing?" he asked.

"I am reporting your ass to your employer. I am telling them you have a drug problem. I am going to see if they can have you placed in an in-patient rehab or maybe confirm for me that it's okay for people to be on drugs and work for the City of Philadelphia. You are a drug addict. You need help. I am going to get you some help."

"Pleeze—do not call my job. Okay. Okay—I will do what you want."

Lenny cooperated with my demands for about five weeks and then went back to getting high. I left him for a week. I hid our second car and left him with Noelle and a refrigerator full of food. I'd decided that during my week away, I'd have some fun visiting my girlfriends. I packed two outfits in my backpack and went to a different girlfriend's house each night. They were thrilled to see me. It was perfect and this way no one would get tired of me. I took my address books so Lenny wouldn't be able to find me while I was away. I called everyone to see if they were keeping Noelle for him after school and came up with nothing. I called his job each day from a different place and hung up when he answered. I laughed. I contacted Noelle's school and spoke with the secretary whom I knew very well. I arranged with her to speak to Noelle at lunch time each day while I was out of town. Noelle gave me the lowdown that Daddy was taking her to school on the trolley each day and he was getting all mixed up with the lunch he had to pack. She said he hadn't had any company at the house. Each night, I drove by the house to check to see if they were at home, and they were. I knew this would wear him down.

At the end of the week, I returned home, but informed Lenny that I'd come for the weekend and would be leaving again on Sunday night. He decided to give being sober another try. The house was a wreck.

A month passed and he was back to his old ways. One morning, I was vacuuming and found a small plastic bag that had contained a white powder. When he got home at five o'clock in the morning from work and hanging out, I'd had enough.

I did laundry to stay up until he came in. I had been crying. The clothes were folded on the dining room table. When he came in I asked, "Can I talk to you? I'm upset."

He looked at me and rolled his eyes, walking past me into the kitchen. "Leave me alone, bitch," he snarled.

"Don't call me that."

"I'll call you anything I damn well please, *bitch*."

"Listen, Lenny, I can't take much more of us. Everything is all messed up all the time. You need to leave."

"I plan on going nowhere, B*itch*."

"Listen—it's bad with me Lenny. I'm on medication, my nerves are shot, my health is at stake and I have Noelle to raise. This just won't work. You need to go."

He continued to ignore me and heated up the dinner I had cooked.

I sat at the kitchen table and tears streamed down my face. "Okay, if you won't move out, why don't you leave for a few days—just give me some space. I've washed up all the clothes." I headed into the dining room to gather some of his things, went back into the kitchen, and meekly handed them to him. "Take these things and wherever you spend most of your time—go there for a few days." His eyes pierced mine.

"*Bitch*, didn't I tell you not to ever touch my clothes?" He then grabbed me and punched me in the face. He dragged me into the dining room and pointed to the clothes, saying, "Do not ever touch my clothes."

"Let me go!" I screamed. He yanked me down to the floor and we wrestled with each other until we were under the dining room table. He was choking me with one hand and hitting me in the head with the other. I screamed and cried, but could not defend myself. When he was through, he stood up and headed to the basement. He strutted away very confidently.

I laid there for a few moments, sobbing, but grateful we had not awakened Noelle. I got up and stared at the fireplace. It contained a revolver that I had purchased a year ago. I was often at home alone and bought it to protect Noelle and me. I reached into the fireplace and retrieved the gun. I crept down the stairs and walked over to Lenny who was flipping the channels with the remote control. When he saw the gun, he bolted for the laundry room. He struggled to slam the door shut, but there were clothes on the floor preventing it. I fired three times at the door, not knowing where the bullets went. There was silence. I went into the laundry room and Lenny was against the wall shaking and scared. He showed me that he was bleeding from the wrist and the foot. I stood over him and said, "Do you want to fight now, motherfucker? Get up and fight like a man! Do you need some Band Aids, the cops, or the hospital? Want me to take you to the hospital?" He was scared to death.

"I *said* do you want some *Band Aids?*" I shouted.

"No," he said.

I held the gun on him and ordered him to come out. Once he was in our lovely basement, I said, "You are going to listen to me. Do not say a word until I am finished." Then I proceeded to tell him for fifteen minutes all the things he had done to me, how he had made me feel. Tears were streaming down my face as I spoke. I told him I had two more bullets in the gun and if he laid a hand on me, I would blow his brains out. Then I told him to get Noelle's uniform and blouse off the hanger in the laundry room. I made him iron it so she could go to school. Lenny was obedient and with the gun pointed on him, I sat on the barstool and watched him iron.

"Do you want me to call the police for you?" I asked.

"No."

"Do you want to go to the hospital for your wounds?"

"No."

"You know, I'll turn myself in for shooting you. You don't have to call them on me."

"I plan to go to work. I just have graze wounds. I'll be okay."

"Lenny, you know I needed to shoot you, right? You know you needed to be shot. It's as simple as that. Do whatever you want to do about it."

"I'm not doing anything about it. I'm going to work."

"Are you moving?"

"Nope."

Lenny dressed and left the house. I dropped Noelle off at school, returned home and got into bed. I called my Dad.

"Hey, it's me.

"Hey, Babe, what going on?"

"Well…I had some trouble here this morning." I went on to explain that I fired three shots at Lenny.

"Sounds like self defense to me."

"Well, in any case, I just want you to be reachable today. Don't go too far without checking in. I left your information at the school in case you have to pick Noelle up. She gets out at 3:00. I could be in jail by then. We don't know what Lenny is going to do. I think you should get some money out of the bank in case you have to bail me out. Can you run to the bank and take about twenty grand out?" My father and his family had money. They owned rental property all over Philly and he could spare the money. My Dad had also done time for killing a man, so I didn't get the lecture of life about the shooting. It was justified. Lenny deserved to be shot. That was that.

"I'll have the money here. Go on and handle your business. I'll check on Noelle at school."

The next call I made was to my doctor. Dr. Zimmerman and I were crazy about each other. He was one of my psychiatrists and had been treating me since 1987. We were great buddies and he knew all my business. We also discussed great vacation spots, parenting, and the best restaurants.

"Hi, Dr. Z, what's up today?"

"Hi, Denise. I'm just getting in. Are you calling to chat a bit or to schedule or cancel an appointment?"

"Well…I'm calling because I shot Lenny today with my .38—you know—the one in the fireplace."

There was silence on the line and then he spoke. "Okay….what happened?"

After he listened to the whole scenario, he asked, "Where's the gun?"

"Oh, it's right here."

"Where, *exactly*?"

"On the nightstand. I have two bullets left."

"Okay…I need you to get the gun out of the house. Okay?"

"Why?"

"Because it should not be there."

"Well, where do you want me to take it."

"I'm thinking. You just stay on the line with me, okay."

Dr. Z spoke too slowly to me and I didn't like that. He was not his chipper self. I felt he was treating me like a crazy person. I wasn't nuts and was becoming irritated, "Dr. Z, why are you talking to me like I am *crazy*. What's wrong with you?"

"Denise, calm down, I am just trying to work some things out quickly. It is important that you get the gun out of the house. Is there someone who can come for it?"

"I can call Nadine. She'll come over or I can take it to her."

He instructed me not to leave the house and that he wanted me to do a few things. I had to immediately call Nadine. If she couldn't come, someone else had to come for the gun. I was to pack some clothes, at least **five outfits. He immediately wanted information from my current health** insurance card.

"I don't have the cards. Lenny has them. I have to call him. What do I need that for?"

"Listen, Denise. It's time. It's time for you to go into the hospital."

"I'm not sick and I'm not crazy, I told you!"

He told me to trust him. I needed to be admitted as soon as possible to a mental facility. It was crucial. He begged me not to give him a hard time and to do what he was asking. Before he hung up, he said his main problem was getting me into a facility that I would like. He could not put me into some dreary hospital. He knew the kind of place I needed to go to. He didn't want me to go into a severe depression because my surroundings weren't right. He knew me. He'd have to work with another doctor to get me into the facility he thought I'd do best at. "Will you cooperate with me, honey?"

I contemplated what he said and how long we had known each other. "Okay. I'll call you back."

I called Nadine and she agreed to come right over. Then I called Lenny.

"Hey, it's me. How are you doing?"

"I'm okay."

"Did you call anybody to tell on me?"

"No."

"I need something from you."

"What?"

"I need the hospital cards. I need you to come home with them."

"Why?"

"I have to go into the hospital."

"What!" he shouted. "Bitch, you shot me and you're going into the hospital. What kind of shit is that?"

I told Lenny to shut up and that I needed the damn cards. "Come straight home from work with them. Can you leave work now and come?"

"No. I'll be straight home after work. This is some shit. I can't believe you!"

"Okay—just be here by six o'clock."

I asked him to give me the numbers off the cards and to also bring them home when he came.

I grabbed my suitcases and got my clothes together. I had some great new outfits and also packed all my sharp shoes and pocketbooks. I looked over at my Bose stereo system and realized I'd need music so I decided that was going, too, along with all my tapes. Then I went through my jewelry. I couldn't decide what to take, so I grabbed the entire box. Next to consider was perfume, bath gels, all my good pajamas and underwear and curling irons. I had a really sharp, short haircut. Next was my make up case, a few decks of cards, and my photo albums. I was ready. The doorbell rang and it was Nadine.

"Hey, Annie Oakley."

"Oh, shut up." I chuckled.

"Where's the gun?"

"Upstairs, come on."

Nadine looked at the gun, then at me and started laughing. "I can't believe you shot the motherfucker. This is really funny. You shot his ass and he is at work. Humph. I guess his nurse will take care of him. I can't believe you shot his ass twice with a 38 and he is walking around! Damn!"

"You know what, Nadine, I swear I believe God was in that basement with us. It was not meant for Lenny to get killed. I think God wanted to do a couple of things. He wanted to stop Lenny from smacking me around and he wanted to get his ass out of here. God was teaching him a lesson and God didn't want me to get into trouble—so it was graze wounds. That's my take on the situation."

"Well, whatever. The gun is missing three bullets. Reload it and I'll take it to my house."

"I looked at the gun. "I can't reload that thing. I am scared of messing with that chamber."

"Well, you shot the damn gun, how can you be afraid of it?"

"Yeah, I shot it and that was not hard for me. But I never put any bullets in it. When I bought it I was scared to handle it. Lenny loaded it."

Nadine filled the chamber and put it in her purse. "Now what?" she asked.

I was all packed, but I had to take a shower and do my hair. Lenny would be home on time. "Since you can't drive, you need to call that boyfriend of yours. We have to hide the other car. I'm not leaving it here with Lenny. I don't know how long I will be in the hospital."

"Isn't he going to have Noelle while you are in the hospital?"

"Yep."

"So, how is he going to get around and how is she going to get to school and to the hospital to see you?"

"I have to figure that out. Maybe you and Craig can help me with that. Don't ask me too many questions right now. My brain is on overload."

The phone rang and it was Dr. Z. "Okay, where are we, Missy?"

I explained everything and gave him the insurance information.

"Okay, good work. I believe I can get you into Friends Hospital. It is beautiful. It's on *forty-seven* acres of land and has cottages. People come there from all over the world. Denise, it's like a resort. It is your kind of place."

✳ ✳ ✳

Lenny walked in the door at twenty minutes to five. "So, you got off early. Thanks," I said. Nadine was lying on the living room couch. He rolled his eyes at her.

He continued into the kitchen. "Where's Noelle?"

"She's at the after school program. You can run over and pick her up."

"He stood in front of me and said, "I went to the D.A.'s office today and they said you cannot touch my clothes and you can't shoot me anymore."

I looked at that idiot like he was crazy, knowing he was lying. I sighed, "May I have the health insurance cards?"

"I'm not giving them to you. I don't think it's fair that you can shoot me twice and I didn't go to the hospital and you're going. There's not a damn thing wrong with you. I'm not giving you the cards."

"Okay, Mister. You wanna start fucking with me all over again? I'm gonna empty the damn gun on you right now." I ran into the living room. He immediately started fumbling for his wallet and threw the cards at me.

"Take them—*go!*"

I sent him to get Noelle and cautioned him to come straight back with my car. I studied my husband from the back as he opened the front door and yelled, "If you don't I'm going to skip the hospital and come to your job tomorrow and act like a fool." He slammed the door.

✳ ✳ ✳

When we drove up to Friends Hospital, I could not believe the enchantment and serenity of the grounds. There were acres and acres of beautiful trees surrounding the cottages and the landscaping was magnificent with a variety of flowers. Winding roads led you to the cottages. There were ponds, brooks, and tennis courts. "This place is nice. When I shoot somebody, I'm going to come here," Nadine said as we searched for the main entrance of the hospital.

"Wow—Dr. Z was right. This place is like a resort and it is absolutely gorgeous. Damn. I thought the Grand Lido in Negril, Jamaica was posh, but this place is something else! It must cost a fortune to stay here. No wonder he wanted that insurance information to check out."

When we walked into the lobby, there were beautiful Oriental rugs on the sparkling, hardwood floors and exquisite antique furniture. A dazzling chandelier accented the high ceiling. The place was breathtaking. We spoke with the receptionist and waited for me to be interviewed by a doctor.

"Welcome Mrs. Garner, can you sit on the table, we'll need to give you a brief physical examination." Dr. Marian Rittenberg looked like she was of mixed decent—Asian and American. She was fairly pretty, but had sad eyes that reminded me of a Bassett Hound puppy. Black long hair fell to the middle of her back, clipped together in a ponytail with a beautiful gold barrette with gem stones in it. Her nose seemed a bit oversized. I guessed she was in her early forties. I walked over to the exam table decked out in a wonderful peacock blue summer knit pantsuit, and my hair and makeup were applied to perfection.

"This place is lovely."

"Yes, we do have a nice hospital and provide excellent care, too. I'm glad you like it."

I took my top off and she checked me out. She noticed marks on my neck where Lenny had tried to strangle me. She took pictures of them. Then she began asking me questions.

156

"So...what happened, Mrs. Garner?"

"I had a panic attack. I have them a lot. My doctor told me I needed to get treatment for them—in the hospital.

Her reaction showed skepticism. Her facial expression and slight friendliness toward me changed to more of a business demeanor. "Well, how did you get these marks on your neck?"

"My husband and I had a fight. Then I had a really bad panic attack."

"Is there anything else you need to tell me?" She asked with a puzzled look on her face.

"No. I just need to rest and get some treatment for the panic disorder. I've never been in the hospital for that. It's time. The attacks are getting worse."

I was afraid to tell her the entire truth about everything and was determined I'd hide it. I had an automobile case pending and I didn't want that insurance company to get their hands on psychiatric records that stated my husband was abusing me. If they had that information, they'd try to blame all my panic attacks on that situation and get out of paying me for the Panic Disorder related to my settlement. I could use this admission in my favor in that claim if my admission was caused by panic attacks in general. I had to keep this thing low key so it wouldn't mess with my pocketbook later on. I may have been through some fucked up shit with Lenny and needed this treatment and a break, but I was a businesswoman first.

Dr. Rittenberg studied me. Finally she said, "Mrs. Garner, do you want to talk to me about the *gun?*"

Well Holy smokes! She stunned the hell out of me! I was totally unprepared for that question. *How the fuck did she know about the gun?* Dr. Z didn't tell me he was going to tell anyone about the damn gun. Shit!

I was silent. I put my head down, thinking. I didn't want to talk about the shooting. She was waiting.

I sweetly said, "Dr. Rittenberg, you know this has been a tough and long day for me. I really would appreciate if you would get me checked in to my room. I'll get some rest and, tomorrow, you and I could meet. I've really been through a lot today, and it's getting late."

She wasn't buying that shit and sternly replied, "I'd like to know *now*. Your explanation of the events that led you here are part of your admission evaluation. This will also be addressed when you are in therapy here. Can you talk about it?" I didn't feel like fighting. I had been arguing and talking all damn day. I shook my head and told her exactly what happened between Lenny and I earlier that day and all about that gun.

As I was escorted to my private room, I passed by many women sitting in the living area. They looked *normal*—not crazy. None were African American. They were conversing, reading, and seemed content and relaxed. They even looked *happy*. My clothing and belongings had been unpacked in the main lobby and were wheeled in on a large silver luggage carrier. My garments were on hangers and other belongings were at the base of the carrier. As I walked through, the women glanced at the new kid on the block. When we got to my room, the attendant helped me put everything away. The room was sunny, modern, and immaculate. I had a spectacular view of the grounds. There were no bars on the windows and I was grateful for that. There was, however, a lock on the door so I could be locked in. There was a twin bed and a chest of drawers, a matching nightstand with a cute lamp on it. It was very unique. The base of it was circular and the stem was aligned with stars all in a row. The shade resembled a large funnel and the bulb was inside. I loved it! I started thinking, "Reach for the Stars." I felt like the attendant was a bellman and I almost tipped him. After I unpacked, I ventured around, checking the place out. It was indeed lovely and I was so impressed with it. We had a full kitchen on the wing, a baby grand piano, a TV room, and a lounge. There was a bulletin board with a schedule of all the events such as board games, card games, painting classes and discussion topics. I noticed a room with an office that had a huge glass window in front of a desk. I couldn't figure that one out. I didn't start any conversations up with anyone. I was just doing my own thing. I had missed dinner because I'd gotten there late and they arranged for a tray. I was tired and dined alone in my room. The meal, roast beef, asparagus and a baked potato, was scrumptious. Dessert was cherry cobbler. At 10:00 p.m., an announcement came on the PA system. Everyone had to report to the medication window. I came out of my room searching for it. A line formed in front of the room I had seen earlier. I joined the line and was given two medications that I had to swallow right there at the window. The nurse explained I could not walk away with it. Mechanically, I went back to my room and could not remember falling asleep.

The next morning, I had an individual therapy session with a psychologist and visits with two other doctors. One was an internest and the other was a psychiatrist who went over my medications with me. I spent the rest of the day making calls to check on Noelle and my friends. I also called Dr. Z to let him know how pleased I was with the hospital. During some free time, I participated in a bingo game and got a chance to observe more of the facility. It was huge. The hours passed by too quickly to notice. After the medication line, I was off to sleep again.

The third day, I was walking through my unit and noticed about five women in the TV room. I went in and sat down.

"What's your name? A woman asked.

"Denise Garner."

"Are you a celebrity? We saw you coming in the other day and you are stunning. We thought you might be celebrity. I'm Rita." She was a heavy set redhead and I sized her up to be about a size eighteen. She reminded me of Winona Judd. She had a winning smile and perfect teeth.

I smiled back. "I'm no celebrity." All the women had their eyes glued to me and Rita.

"You're pretty and dress really nice," another patient said.

"Thank you."

"There doesn't seem to be anything wrong with you. We can't figure you out," another commented.

"What do you mean?" I asked.

"Well, we all have problems. You don't seem to have one?" I was silent.

"Denise, I'm Mavis. I'm from London. I'm in here because my son died and I've been depressed and going crazy. That's why I got shipped here. I was crying all the time."

I looked at the sixtyish looking redhead and felt sorry for her. "I'm sorry about your son, Mavis. How did he die?"

"It was a boating accident. He drowned." What are you in for?"

"I shot my husband."

"What!" Rita exclaimed.

"No way!" another gasped. They were all looking at me in horror.

"Yep, I shot him."

"Why did you do it?" Mavis asked. I told them the whole story from beginning to end.

"Where is the bastard now?" Mavis asked.

"Downtown at work."

"Let's get together and go kick his ass. Listen, Denise, you know we are on the mildly depressed unit. That means we get passes to go out. We are allowed to go to the mall and stuff like that. We don't have to be supervised. We can go down there and kick his ass. I cannot believe that asshole did all that stuff to you! Know what gang, we need to go and rough that guy up."

I looked around at all the gals and liked their company. "Now ladies, we don't want to get into trouble, do we?"

After that they calmed down and shared their stories. One had been abused by her stepfather, another had three miscarriages and was sad about that. Rita had a work related problem with a supervisor, which put her in depression after four years of being chastised for every little thing. After sitting together for two hours, we formed a bond. That evening at 9:45, I went around to everyone's room calling out to them "come on, let's get our drugs." As we were in line, I was telling jokes. We were having fun. The next morning, I brought my stereo out into the lobby, put James Brown on and began giving dancing lessons. They loved it. In the days that followed, I arranged poker games and gave astrology readings. We all went out bowling on the seventh day and had a great time. Upon my return, there was a message for me that Dr. Z was arranging a meeting at the hospital that would require Lenny's presence. My psychiatrist felt it **would be detrimental to my health and well-being if I continued to stay** with Lenny. He knew the stressful situations my husband placed me in. I had shared everything with Dr. Z and he cared about me. From all my sessions with him, he knew I couldn't continue on this course. Somebody would eventually get killed.

All of my doctors planned to attend the meeting along with my best friend, Nadine. It would be focused on my discharge. Lenny refused to come at first, but Dr. Z got him to agree. At the meeting, the doctors explained that I was ready to be discharged. However, they preferred that Lenny move out of our house because of the violence and the shooting. He refused to leave. When they could not persuade him, Dr. Z explained that if he did not leave I would be in the facility *indefinitely* and that he would be totally responsible for Noelle. I'd left Lenny with no car, so he was using public transportation to get to and from work and to the market. Nadine's boyfriend was taking Noelle to school, but Lenny had to pick her up. Lenny thought it over and finally agreed to move. He did not indicate where.

Two days later, seven year old Noelle called me at the hospital. She said, "Daddy is packing his stuff up and putting it in a car."

"Whose car, baby, I asked."

"I don't know."

"What color is it?"

"Brown."

"Noelle, get a pencil and a piece of paper out of your school bag. Go out there and look at the license plate number on the back of the car. I want you to very carefully write down the letters and numbers on the license plate. You do know what a license plate is, right?"

"Yes, I know."

"Okay. Do that for Mommy and don't let Daddy see you. Just stand around outside and when he goes back into the house for something, write it down. Then come back to the phone."

"Okay, I'll do it."

"Has anybody been to the house today?"

"No."

"Okay, if he takes you in the car with his stuff and you know the house where he goes or the people that live there, you write it down and tell me the next time I call you. Okay?"

"Okay—you hold on Mommy. I'm going out there now and try to write the number down that's on the car."

The license tag number turned out to be a car registered to Carolyn Monroe and Lenny moved in with her. The following day, I was told I was being released from the hospital immediately and discharge papers were being written. I told all my friends on the wing. They were sad I was leaving them and would miss me. Mavis came to my room later crying and begged me to stay one more night—just for her. I could not leave her like that, so I arranged to stay another night. We were able to sit up and talk all night because we faked taking our meds at the window, holding the pills under our tongues. She invited me to come to London when she got out and I promised to visit her until she was discharged.

I received a few letters from other patients after I got back home. They thought the world of me. Noelle and I started a new life without Lenny. It took Lenny a year and a half, but he came by my house one night and apologized for being such a rotten husband and agreed I should have shot him.

It's a poor soul who does not have a dream. Other than those glitter ceilings, my husband, Lenny, never once in our relationship expressed to me that he actually *wanted* anything other than good times in the streets. He never even came in the house excited about wanting anything. Not a leather jacket he happened to see at a shop, not a piece of furniture, not a luxurious vacation that he came across on a travel brochure in our home, not a mansion he saw on television, not even a car—nothing. I never once heard him say, "Before I die I've got to get me a so and so. Or even, "No matter how long it takes me, I am getting me a whatever." There were no dreams—no fantasies—none at all. He had no passion. I don't believe the man even dreamed when he went to sleep. Damn shame.

My failed marriage to Lenny Garner taught me that a person who wanted nothing for himself, couldn't *possibly* want anything for me or anyone else for that matter. Dale had a vision and, because of that, I would always appreciate my time with him. Many men didn't have enough brains or even common sense to know what they had in a woman. Dale Elliott had big dreams for himself *and* for us and the smarts to know what he had when I came along. And God knows he was swift in capitalizing on his find.

CHAPTER 9

༄

Devastation

After my separation from Lenny, Noelle and I remained at our house in Philadelphia for the next three and a half years. I was now a single mother operating without much assistance from her father. He was indeed living with Carolyn Monroe. Other than child support, I wasn't receiving anything from him. In the beginning of our separation, he would visit Noelle and sometimes send her a greeting card with a few dollars in it. He never took her on weekends to his home.

Even though Noelle did not have a father present and on the scene, I compensated for it. She was in an elite private school making friends and involved in numerous activities. She was on the soccer team, in the band playing the flute, and in an after school workshop. Yes, money was scarce and Noelle missed her Dad, but on weekends I kept a house full of her friends, taking them skating, organizing card games, movies and she attended sleepovers. I didn't know how I did it all and kept a refrigerator stocked because things were tough and I was not working. I was surviving on twenty-five hundred dollars a month from disability due to an automobile accident I had in 1990. However, I knew how to stretch that money and the four hundred dollars from child support went toward Noelle's social life. I'd make agreements with utility companies and always ended up paying the minimal amount of the bill. Noelle's private school also offered financial assistance for tuition and let me pay monthly on the balance. My life was a hustle, scrambling to keep everything together. Men were the farthest thing from my mind, or so I thought.

One spring afternoon in 1995, I was in the post office preparing bills for mailing. I was sighing, disgusted about having to pay out so much of my money. I started complaining out loud, "Damn, I am sick of this shit."

A voice said back, "You and me both. Seems like I am in here every day."

"Ain't it a trip?" I answered.

A tall man, his skin the color of caramel, flashed a bright smile.

We began chatting, "I'm going on vacation next month to Disney World and I'm just trying to get this crap under control and out of the way."

"Oh yeah," he said, "I've got to do that, too. I want to take my nephew down there. He's ten years old."

"Really? Listen, I'm an expert on Disney World. I also have a ten year old daughter. I've been down there four times. I have a travel agent's license. Take my card and call me when you're ready.

"Okay. I'll do that. My name is Jimmy. I'll call you."

He called me the following day and we talked for a long time. He had been a correctional officer for the past ten years and lived not far from me. He asked if he could come by and I agreed. We set the time for 2:00 p.m. on the following Saturday—two days away. I called Nadine and had her come over at 1:00 p.m. so I wouldn't be alone in case he was a maniac.

Jimmy was a tall hunk of a man, in great shape, and a pretty boy. Light brown skinned with short curly black hair. He wore glasses which made him look quite distinguished. He arrived in loose fitting jeans and a white tee shirt. He had beautiful teeth and a winning smile. Jimmy looked good to me. I was alive again. We headed for my kitchen and he and Noelle hit it off instantly, talking a mile a minute. He had a gorgeous black Mercedes and let us know he adored a Benz and wouldn't ever drive anything else. He was forty-seven and told us all about his family. His Mom had passed away three years ago. He was very close to his younger sister, who was divorced with two children. Her kids were like his own. He'd been divorced for ten years and never had any kids. Jimmy was an honest Sagittarian, told us funny stories, and had us all cracking up. I trusted him. He seemed normal. I made dinner for all of us and, sitting around the table, he already felt like part of the family.

He called me back the next day and we made a date to go out to lunch and to the mall. Noelle had been very excited that he was coming. We had a lot of fun and he bought Noelle a couple of books. When we got back to my house, I tucked Noelle into bed and then sat down to talk with Jimmy in the kitchen.

"Listen, I like you. I think you're sweet. Tell me something—where's Noelle's Dad?"

"In Deadbeat City living in sin with his girlfriend. We rarely see him. We've been separated for three years."

"That's a shame. She's a wonderful girl. Humph," he said, shaking his head. You're not seeing anyone?'

"Nah. I've been too busy playing Mommy and keeping the utilities on."

"Wanna hang out with me for a bit and see what happens? I'm not seeing anyone and I love kids."

I looked into his eyes and was definitely interested. Everything about him said "yes." I smiled, "I think I'll take you up on that."

"Listen, I have to tell you something," he said.

I was thinking, "Oh shit, here comes something to turn me off." I was expecting him to say he was an ex-con or used to be a drug addict, had some crazy roommate, or was about to lose his house or something. Maybe he had AIDS. I put my head on the kitchen table. "What's the deal? How bad is it?"

He chuckled. "I had a bad fall at work on some ice about a year and a half ago. I really have a bad back."

I lifted my head up and gave him the funny look. "A bad back—is that all? Damn, so what. Even I've got a bad back."

He lowered his eyes for a moment. "Well, I am on medication…it keeps me calm, but it effects me sexually. I'm able to please you, but only orally. I don't get much pleasure.

I refused to change my expression. I didn't want to hurt his feelings, but my brain was sending *"UH OH"* signals. I didn't really understand. *Not ever any erection?* UMM This was new to me. Scared the shit out of me. "Look, let's not get into all that—okay. Just relax. Just shut the hell up. Shit. I'm not ready for all this."

He put both his arms up in the air and said, "Whatever. I'm game."

We began doing a lot of threesome dating during the days and on weekends. He never left Noelle out. She was loving him. She'd get all dressed up when she knew he was coming. I realized then how much she really missed having a dad around. Sometimes, he'd come by and she and I would be fighting for his attention. Noelle would sometimes say, "He came to see me!"

We finally had sex one night and he must have gone off that medication or something because he had no problem getting it up. He wore my ass out that first time and, when we were done, and I was hanging off the bed lifelessly. He said, "You better go to the gym and get in shape, baby."

We were seeing each other every day and he started to pick Noelle up from school. Finally, school was out and we were on our way to go to Disney World. Noelle and I flew away for ten days and we missed Jimmy terribly. We talked to each other every day while we were apart. He was glad when we returned home and Noelle was happy to be back with him. He'd take her to the park, and when he was not working, he would pick her up from summer day camp. Often his nephew would come along on his outings with Noelle, and I'd stay behind. She'd pretend that he was her brother.

The sex was beginning to be a problem and I demanded that he stop taking the medication. He agreed, but his personality changed and he became irritable off the meds. One night, he started screaming at me. "I need my medicine!" He wore a mean look on his face. I knew then that whatever that shit was, he needed to be back on it. I opted to go without the erection. "Fuck it," I said and accepted the oral sex. He happened to be excellent at that, too.

In late June of 1995, I got hit by a car outside my house. I almost lost my left foot. I had surgery and was in a cast from foot to thigh. I was wheelchair bound and Jimmy and Lenny came running to my hospital bed. I don't know how Lenny found out about my accident. It could have been a neighbor who informed him because loads of people were outside my house when it happened. Lenny was surprised I had a man. I did wonder if he was jealous, but I really didn't give a shit. In any case, Lenny was actually pretty nice to Jimmy as each one of them sat on different sides of my bed. They got along well. Noelle wasn't there at the time—she was being watched at a girlfriend's house. Jimmy took over. He got a leave of absence from his job for six weeks and took care of me. That brought the three of us even closer together—just like family.

Three months into my rehabilitation, Jimmy sat me down and talked to me. He explained that his feelings had changed for me. He wasn't interested in us being lovers at all. At first, I was sad and embarrassed. My ego was crushed, for I had grown to love him. But after careful consideration of the facts and because we all got along so well otherwise, I cheered up and accepted it. We decided to switch to being platonic and Jimmy became Noelle's godfather. The transition was smooth and it turned out to be a wonderful relationship. Jimmy and I were like divorced parents who got along famously. Noelle was very attached to him and he was a tremendous help to us both. She filled a void in his life and Jimmy certainly did take the place of her absent father. He attended all her school activities and she didn't have to be embarrassed not having a father. As for her real father, I wrote letters to Lenny, faxing them to his job almost begging him not to completely abandon Noelle. He would go months at a time without seeing her and I would hear stories from friends of ours that he was always in the bars partying. No matter what I said to him, I couldn't persuade him to give Noelle much attention.

Later that year, I settled both my automobile accident claims and walked away with $240,000. I used the proceeds to purchase a home in the suburb of Elkins Park. Noelle and I moved into our new place in February of 1996. That settlement money also allowed me to be a stay at home mom. My days consisted of driving Noelle to and from school and attending programs there. She was now in private school and was enjoying it. I also filled my days decorating my new home. I loved the suburban life, the quietness and beauty of it all, and Jimmy was right there helping me and Noelle every step of the way. He was an amazing dad and I was thankful for him. He loved dogs and got Noelle a Golden Retriever. We named him Casey. He helped her to train him and bought her books all about them. He attended every school function and was with her every holiday. He never missed a beat. We were in perfect unison and he spent quite a bit of time at our house—but never nights. That didn't matter to me. I loved him for what he was to both of us.

Our first Christmas at our new home was approaching. Things couldn't have been better in my life. We were all definitely in the holiday spirit, and Noelle was particularly looking forward to attending her first Bar Mitzvah. I had started shopping early for the holidays. The first week of December, Noelle began complaining of a stomach ache. I gave her over the counter medications, and none of them helped. After two days of that, we headed to the pediatrician.

"It hurts around my navel," Noelle illustrated to Dr. Alsman who had been her doctor since infancy.

Attentively, I watched him examine her and he explained it was probably a stomach virus. "Keep her on flat coke and ginger ale and she can have Jell-O. I'm sure she'll be okay in a couple of days."

I was a person who always had a *Plan B*. If she didn't feel better in forty-eight hours, we would go to the hospital. Noelle was doubled over in pain in the car and said, "Mommy, do you think that my stomach will be better in time for Dean's Bar Mitzvah? That's the 14th. Nine more days. I don't want to miss that. All the kids at school are going."

I knew that party meant a lot to her. "I promise you, we'll be there."

Three days later, we were in the emergency room at Children's Hospital of Philadelphia because Noelle wasn't able to sleep due to the pain. She'd had a bad case of diarrhea. I'd found her at night balled up in the fetal position and crying and I knew we'd both had enough. The hospital suggested I give her Mylanta and Tylenol. That worked for a short period of time, but the symptoms returned. She made it through the Bar Mitzvah only because I gave her a couple of doses of Naprosen and it arrested the pain. I kept her on the Naprosen so she could enjoy the holidays pain free. At the end of December, we were back at CHOP.

Nothing they suggested helped and she was in constant pain. I called Lenny about it and he suggested she had gastritis and said it would probably go away.

The doctors kept giving me the same story. They felt her problem would eventually go away, but I became suspicious and frantic, demanding further diagnostic and blood testing. I was advised to consult a gastroenterologist who gave Noelle an evaluation of home-positive diarrhea.

Noelle had been healthy prior to the onset of this trauma of abdominal pain and diarrhea. Other than an appendectomy in 1992, she had never really been sick. She explained to the doctors that she was having intermittent episodes of crampy stomach pain around the navel as well as loose stools one to two times per day with no evidence of mucus or blood. The pain tended to improve with the passage of a bowel movement. Three days prior to that visit, I did notice a few spots of red blood on the outer surface of a formed stool during a stool collection. I was examining the stool myself, sifting through it with Popsicle sticks. In addition, Noelle had intermittent fevers of 100 degrees. Noelle had lost six pounds in three weeks.

By now, she had been evaluated twice in the Children's Hospital Emergency Room and they thought I was an overprotective Mommy. She was so embarrassed and frightened at having to go through a rectal examination that we had to have *therapy* before she would let them do it. They found blood. The blood wasn't always present, but when it was, Noelle would freak out and scream.

Noelle had been on various medications in an effort to manage her pain symptoms, including Motrin, Naproxen, Tylenol, and Maalox. None of them helped her condition or relieved the pain. More physical examinations and tests revealed Noelle had a small, non-inflamed skin tag in her rectum, a fistula. The doctor felt it was more than likely that Noelle had infectious enteritis, which was improving, as opposed to early inflammatory bowel disease. The doctor gave me containers for a routine stool cultures. If these stool studies resulted negative and Noelle's symptoms of diarrhea continued, the doctor would then consider more invasive evaluations to rule out inflammatory bowel disease. This gastroenterologist felt that she would continue to improve over the next several weeks, but I was terrified.

After a tough day for Noelle, I sat at the edge of her bed to offer comfort.

"Mommy, I am so scared. They have to do so many things to me. They're always looking at my body and up my butt. Those doctors ask so many questions. I am tired of hurting so much. I'm always either sitting on the toilet or looking in the toilet. I'm sick of farting and stinking up my room."

My heart went out to her. She so did not deserve this. I was angry with everyone—including God. I was pissed with Lenny who was never around to help. "I know, baby. We have got to be strong. You just be brave and try to get through this. It'll get fixed. I fart all the time—everybody does. Who cares about that? I love you whether you are stinky or not. Get your stinky butt up and let's go to Barnes and Noble. Get the air freshener."

Unfortunately her condition continued to worsen. The doctor performed an upper endoscopy and colonoscopy with biopsies on Noelle on April 9th. The gross findings of the colonoscopy revealed Crohn's disease. The news not only devastated us, but broke three hearts—Noelle's, Jimmy's and mine.

The doctor started Noelle on a new medication, a dosage of 500mg of Azulfidine a day, which she would increase slowly to minimize some of the side effects. When we returned to the doctor on the 18th to discuss Noelle's diagnosis, as well as the general course of the disease and treatment modalities, she had not much improved. The doctor planned to start Noelle on prednisone at this visit, 20mg per day, to be tapered down over the next several months. We prayed that she would improve dramatically with the institution of steroid therapy. If Noelle reacted well over the next two weeks, her doctor visits would decrease to monthly visits.

I was experiencing a variety of emotions from day to day. Noelle's illness weighed heavily on my mind. I contemplated the events that lead to her diagnosis at age twelve and how petrified she was. We both had to be brave and strong, but I was devastated. I had never even heard of this incurable disease that changed our lives forever. I demanded that the doctor write a report for me. I needed time to study it and to learn everything about it—and I did. I even learned that popcorn, corn and corn products, and seeds were not good for the digestive tract. Those foods could get lodged in the intestines and create pain, infection, and problems.

Crohn's disease caused inflammation in the small intestine. The disease usually occurred in the lower part of the small intestine, called the ileum, but it could affect any part of the digestive tract, from the mouth to the anus. The inflammation extended deep into the lining of the affected organ and could cause pain and make the intestines empty frequently, resulting in diarrhea. It was an inflammatory bowel disease (IBD), the general name for diseases that caused inflammation in the intestines. Crohn's disease could be difficult to diagnose because its symptoms were similar to other intestinal disorders such as irritable bowel syndrome and to another type of IBD called ulcerative colitis causing inflammation and ulcers in the top layer of the lining of the large intestine.

Jimmy helped out a great deal with Noelle's care. Thank God he jumped in taking her to doctors' appointments, running errands to pharmacies, babysitting, and also picking up her homework assignments. By this time, I was working full-time and running this disease. Lenny was absolutely no help and totally absent. He never came to one doctor's appointment. I had been through the ringer, but I never broke down and I refused to shed a tear. I kept my head up. I had to be strong because if *I* didn't make it—*she* wouldn't make it.

Due to her problems of gassiness, I began keeping air freshener in the car and took it to doctors' offices. Our lives became a whirlwind of appointments. Noelle was having a terrible time. The disease affected her social life because she was so gassy, and those farts stunk horribly. She wasn't embarrassed with me and Jimmy. We were able to joke about that part of the disease, but Noelle was afraid to go to sleepovers with her friends, terrified of stinking up their bathrooms when she had bowel movements. We had a five bathroom house, so it was better for them to come to her. Her friends really rallied around her and visited, bringing presents and sleeping over when they could. She also battled the side effects of the medication, undergoing five eye operations to remove painful sties.

Often, I didn't know whether to cook a meal or not. Many times, I'd make a meal and she would be too sick and lifeless to eat it. The nausea and vomiting prevented her from eating much of the time. She was in and out of the hospital and when she had to be admitted, Mommy packed up, too. Jimmy and I did shifts staying at the hospital with her so she never would spend a night alone. Each admission dug a deeper hole of fear inside me. Noelle was sick of the admissions and the needle sticks, and, sometimes, I wasn't sure how much longer she could take it.

Early one afternoon, she was very ill. She hadn't had a meal in three days. I called the hospital and her doctor told me she had to be admitted immediately. I broke the news to Noelle.

"I'm tired. I am not going!" she shouted at me.

I was standing in front of my bed and began to lecture her. She was in the bed balled up, not even looking at me. I had to get control and was entering battle with the defiant Leo the Lion. "You are dehydrated and need to be on fluids," I growled. She put her head under the covers. I moved closer to her, lifting the covers off her to see her face.

"Noelle, you're going to get sicker if you stay here. Come on, get up. We've got to go."

She was adamant that she was staying at home. She started screaming, crying, rocking, and complaining about her life. She never made eye contact with me. She was lying on her side. "I don't care anymore! Leave me alone! I'll just die. I have no life anyway!"

Tears rolled down my face. I knew I was asking too much of her at this time. I felt I had no right. How could I convince her to do this and why should I? Was it fair today? She was in pain in her stomach, up her ass, sick of needle sticks, vomiting her guts up, and crapping her brains out. This girl had a right to give up. I kissed her on the forehead and lifted her face up. I pushed the bangs off her face. A new set of tears welled up in my eyes and escaped. I began to whisper, then talking slowly and gently. I was appealing to her compassion, and this was real—no act, psychology, or trickery on my part. No Plan B, just genuine words. "Please, baby, do it for me. It's not about you—it's about me. I am being selfish. I am a damn selfish person. Noelle, Baby, I cannot *breathe* without you. I need you. Live for me—please," I pleaded.

She pulled my head into her chest and the water from my eyes wet her pajama top. "Come on, mom. Stop crying. We're fighters. Let's go."

She got up and we headed for Abington Memorial Hospital instead of way across town to Children's Hospital. We were there in ten minutes. The nurses got her situated in an Emergency Room bed and were preparing to start the I.V. Noelle just sat there despondent. As soon as the nurse **approached with the needle, she started screaming and jumped off the bed.** "I cannot do it!" I just cannot take it any more." Tears flooded her eyes.

I looked at her and said, "Let's go. Fuck it. Get your shoes on. Let's get out of here, Noelle."

She hobbled out and we got in the car. Still crying she said, "I'm sorry Mommy. I've really had it."

And I knew she had. She was at the end of her rope. "I know, baby. It's okay. I have another plan." She looked at me in bewilderment. I didn't say a word. Ten minutes later, I parked in the lot of Crown Pizza and Sub Shop in Willow Grove. This was a greasy spoon dirty place, but I loved their pizza and often went there if I was shopping at the mall. Noelle had never been there. It was my little secret place and I didn't want anyone to know I'd go to such a dingy place. As we entered, she scanned the room observing the booths, the cheap wooden chairs and tables, and the ugly plaid plastic tablecloths. I watched her looking around in amazement. She eyed the gray cement floor, then nudged me. "You're getting something from here?"

"Yep. This is the other side of fine dining, sweetie. It's my little hideaway." I smiled at the clerk and ordered two pizzas. Then, we found a booth.

"Now, Noelle, you are going to eat this pizza and then die. After you're dead, I'll be in trouble with Jimmy, all the doctors, and the police department. So to avoid all the paperwork and going to court and all, I'll put your dead body in the car, go home, and kill myself. Then we'll be in heaven together and all those fucking doctors won't be able to have us running all over the place."

She laughed hysterically and said, "Mommy, you are so crazy. You're wild! Let's do it."

She ate one and so did I. Afterward, I waited so she would vomit the shit up. I didn't care. Lo and behold it stayed down. I couldn't believe it! I waited another ten minutes to be sure and she was fine. Her stomach wasn't even hurting. We were laughing our asses off. I got home and called the doctor at Children's Hospital of Philadelphia.

"Listen, Dr. Brown. Noelle is fine. We went to Abington Hospital and she refused to stay. She's not vomiting anymore. She just ate a greasy cheese pizza an hour ago. I believe her stomach was missing what it has been used to. My plan is to keep giving her things she's been accustomed to. You know, I believe her digestive system went into shock when it didn't get any greasy junk. You know what I mean? I'll keep you posted and call you if I need you. See ya!" I hung up before he could say a word. Noelle and I were still in stitches.

In the months to come, she still experienced a lot of pain and, at times, I watched my child crawl on the floor trying to make it to the bathroom. Since the pizza worked, I tried to think of more *creative* ways of helping Noelle. I was determined to do *anything* to help her. Since she suffered with depression and was in pain I resorted to herbs. Jimmy always took herbs and raved about them. I sent him out to find me some marijuana. Once I got my hands on it, I headed for Noelle's bedroom. I sat on her bed and said, "Listen, we're gonna try something new. Now you know I don't use drugs, but this is different."

She looked up at me in disbelief. I showed her the brown envelope. "You are losing your mind. I'm not taking any real drugs."

"Oh, shut up. I know what I'm doing. Aunt Eula is 74 years old and we got her some of this pot for her glaucoma. She loved it and it helped her. It's better than all that stuff they give you in the hospital. This is an *herb*. Grown from *natural* stuff. God's green stuff and His dirt. It may help calm your tummy down."

She eyed me suspiciously. "You always told me never to do drugs. I'm telling Jimmy. He is gonna kill you."

I smirked, "He bought the damn shit, Noelle."

She had a bewildered look on her face. I knew she was considering my proposal.

"Okay, baby. Let me just roll one up and see what happens."

"Oh, you know how to roll it up? So, you have used drugs. You've been a pothead. Humph," she said.

"I was never a pothead, but when I was around nineteen, I tried it out. You know—when I used to hang out with Blue Magic. I couldn't handle it, so I stopped. I think I remember how to roll it up. Let's see, here's the rolling paper."

Noelle sat up watching me fumble around with the paper and fill it with the marijuana. I licked it to seal it. It was a raggedy joint, but I had it secure. "Okay Noelle, this is how you do it. I will light it up, then I want you to put it in your mouth and suck on it. Let it go down your throat. Make a sound like "zahh" while you inhale. Let it go in your nose, too."

"I'm not doing it."

"It's okay. I think it will change everything for you."

"Nope," she said, shaking her head. I'm telling Dr. Brown on you."

"Look, Noelle, I'll call him myself. If he says okay, will you do it?"

"Maybe. Call him."

I got Dr. Brown on the phone and explained the plan. He was about thirty-four years old and was always telling me about new developments that were coming out to help Crohn's disease patients. He'd also shared his beliefs that unconventional methods of treatment could help patients. Once he even explained to me that he was researching the use of worm guts to help victims of Crohn's Disease. I had a great rapport with him. After listening to me discuss the marijuana, he paused and said, "Denise, do what you want but I never heard this conversation, okay?" I knew what that meant and he was just covering his ass in case somebody found out about it. "Thanks Dr. Brown, I'll try it."

Noelle was staring at me in shock. "He said its okay?"

"Yep. Let's light up."

"Mom, you do it once to show me."

"I can't. I'll get high and I can't handle this shit. Last time I did it, I started a fire in the trash can and the fire department had to come. That's why Lenny Sawyer stopped getting high with me way back when. I'm scared to do it."

Reluctantly she let me light it while it was in her mouth. She followed my instruction and smoked half the joint. She sat and waited for something to happen or for it to help her.

"This stuff doesn't work. I don't feel a thing. Get that stuff away from me."

"Maybe you need to smoke the whole thing. I wonder if maybe you didn't do enough," I said in bewilderment.

"Mom, get that stuff out of here before we get put in jail."

I gathered the paper and bag together and picked up the matches off her bed. I went for my handbag and was about to walk out of the room when Noelle started to babble and giggle. She was getting high. Then she started to sing some Broadway tunes, interrupting herself to point out that things were moving on the wall.

I was praying it would have a positive affect on the Crohn's and asked, "Is your stomach getting better? Does it hurt?"

"I don't know. I feel funny all over—kinda weird. I don't feel bad. I don't know what's going on. Are there any turkey burgers? I'm hungry."

In the weeks to come, life was getting a little easier. I stopped doing every damn thing those doctors told me. I'd gage treatment on how Noelle felt and let her make some decisions. We used up the dime bag of marijuana, but decided not to continue doing that because the pain always returned and I couldn't have the kid stoned 24/7. After that, we went to a hypnotist, but that didn't work. That was two hundred bucks down the drain. We had been through the fire, but, in some respects, Noelle was doing much better since she started the Prednisone. There was much less diarrhea and the severe pain around her navel was intermittent. But it was still an up and down battle. At one point, Noelle was talking about twenty-three pills per day.She was experiencing headaches and joint pain in the shoulders, hips and legs. Her legs began swelling.

One evening when I was sorting clothes in the basement, I heard Noelle scream for me. When I reached her room, she was hysterical, "Mommy, look at my legs and feet! I look like a circus person. What is going on now," she cried. "I'm scared and I feel heavy. It's hard for me to walk!"

Panic engulfed my system again, right along with my child. *Damn, what the shit was going on now?* I immediately phoned her doctor. He advised me to give her less salt in her diet and to give her Motrin for pain or Bufferin. Sometimes, she awakened and the swelling was gone. Her legs, thighs, and her face compounded by pain in the joints. I was confused about giving her Motrin or Bufferin because I was under the impression that aspirin related drugs would irritate her stomach. I was constantly calling and faxing doctors and keeping daily journals on her condition.

I got a referral for a nutritionist to help me with her diet. We cut out salt entirely and I purchased "Morton's Salt Substitute." Noelle consulted a psychologist for her depression. She had become quite upset about her **condition, the changes in her body, and the side effects of the medication**s. She had crying spells due to the puffiness in her face and the unwanted weight gain as a result of the prednisone.

She developed a hearty appetite due to the drug. She looked better with the weight gain, healthier, but didn't like having to eat in fear of getting fatter. She ate, I believed, only because the drug would not allow her not to. She ate me out of house and home. We were charging food on Jimmy's

American Express card, and Noelle would call in orders to the grocery market when we were working. I'd come home and find boxes of food. I believed that once she was off Prednisone, she would become anorexic or bulimic because she already felt that she was too fat. She started to talk to me about an episode of the Jerry Springer Show of a man they had to cut out of his house because he was too big to get out otherwise. I contacted the Crohn's and Colitis Foundation of America and arranged for Noelle and me to attend support meetings. By then, I was at my wits end trying to run everything. I was handling too many things, running around all over the place, at any given time, juggling finances, medications, stool cultures and was bombarded with appointments with doctors and teachers. I was on the verge of spinning out of control, so I called Dr. Ross who not only wanted to put me on a low dose of valium, but wanted to see me once a week.

Things were so overwhelming despite everything I was accomplishing. I realized Jimmy and I couldn't do it all ourselves. I requested information regarding my medical plan to get a caretaker to help me out with Noelle during the day. I had to work full-time and she wasn't old enough to remain in my home while I worked, be responsible for taking her meds, and getting her meals. I contacted a couple of private organizations. Since I was a single parent receiving child support only from Lenny, I requested an emergency hearing in the hopes that the Court would assist me in obtaining additional funds in case my health plan would not cover Noelle's care. The school system provided a homebound teacher twice a week for two and a half hours. As soon as Noelle was feeling better and the side effects lessened, I planned to send her back to school, starting half days.

We forged on, minus Lenny, with treatment, routine exams, weight, blood and stool monitoring, and vitamin intake. We were swamped with responsibilities and appointments. Noelle was losing energy and was placed on vitamin B12. On top of everything that she was going through, excruciating menstrual cramps took over once a month. She was on so many different medications that I was constantly consulting with doctors about drug interactions. I had to watch everything.

Things were sometimes so spontaneous with this disease that Noelle and I could be lying down watching a movie and everything was going well. Then, two hours later, we'd be in the emergency room and she'd be in pain, crapping her brains out, and vomiting—requiring an admission.

The symptoms were so disruptive, sudden, that if Jimmy called us and we didn't answer the phone, and there was no scheduled doctor's appointment, he'd give us three hours to surface and, after that, he would just go to the hospital. He never made a trip and didn't find us there.

Lenny showed up when I hauled his ass into court and stated that he could not afford to help me pay for a caretaker. He came armed with rent receipts from his *landlady*, Carolyn Monroe. The court said they could not make him visit with Noelle or provide funds for babysitters or nurses. I wanted to kill him! I'd had to quit my full-time job at the radio station and was waitressing at night in order to be at all the doctor appointments and collect Noelle's school work. She missed her friends and cried a lot about that. I was paying a student nurse to keep Noelle while I worked at night. Jimmy was still hanging tough with us and thank God his shift was 2:00 p.m. until 10:00 p.m. Often, he would take Noelle to her doctor's appointments, food shop, and deliver her stool samples to the laboratories. He was a great God-Daddy and just crazy about her.

Ten months later after three hospitalizations, Noelle had felt better one particular day and went to a classmate's home for a party. It was Valentine's Day. Before she left, she gave me a card and a gift. After reading it, I was reminded of how much I loved this child. I was saddened that she was saddled with this debilitating disease. My heart ached for her.

During the years between 1998 and 2006, Noelle was an inpatient forty-one times and critical on three occasions. In the year 2000, Jimmy and I had a gigantic falling out over Noelle during her terrible teenage years. She was his princess and he didn't want Mommy disciplining her. He eventually moved from Philadelphia to Florida and ended his relationship with us. Noelle graduated valedictorian of her high school class and in 2002 entered the University of Maryland at College Park. Every eight weeks an infusion of a new drug called Remicade helped a lot in keeping her in remission.

During the span of those eight years, Lenny visited Noelle four times in the hospital and waited patiently through one of eight surgeries. He never attended any graduation exercises. In view of all this, I had reconciled the fact that he would be totally estranged from our child for the rest of her life. It broke my heart and little did I know that his absence would indeed become permanent.

CHAPTER 10

༄

The Decision

Lenny was now dead for six days. Chief Register of Wills, Mr. Bell, of Delaware County still needed to make a decision as to who the legal wife was. I lay in bed not believing this was all happening this way. Lenny had actually become a bigamist. He must have been under a tremendous amount of pressure or crazy on booze, pot, and cocaine to do such a thing. I was certain that he was not the brains of the operation. He simply was not that clever. I knew who the mastermind was. Lenny and I had spoken for a long time on the phone in 2003. We were actually discussing my plan to get a will done because I had a live-in boyfriend, Nate. If something had happened to me, I was afraid the kids, Natasha and Noelle, would kick him out of my house. That would not have been fair, so I was going to do a will to protect him. I wanted the kids to make sure they gave him ample time to find a place or let him stay at the house.

Lenny told me in that conversation, "If you want those kids to have anything, you'd better divorce me. I mean that. You have been too good to all those girls and they never appreciated it. I mean *all* of them, Tara, Natasha and Noelle. If you die, I am taking *everything*—book money, house, cars, anything in the bank, the furniture—*all of it*. I have never taken a dime from you and you *know* it, but I promise you, if I'm still your husband when you die, they ain't getting shit. So, you'd better do what you've got to do."

Lenny never mentioned Nate. I believe he would have let him stay at the house if I passed. He just wasn't going to let the kids have what I had scuffled to get. After that call, I didn't bother to call my estate attorney back on the will. Lenny made me tired just listening to his threats, and I believed what he said.

In 2005, Nate and I split up and Lenny and I were back on the phone. I was melancholy, mixed up, and going through my shit because of the breakup.

"Let me tell you something. You are the smartest person I know. I am so proud of you! You've written two damn books, bought a house in the fucking suburbs, and taken excellent care of the kids—gave them *everything*. And another thing, I have *never* gotten over you. I swear I haven't. I just did something else. Don't you sit there and feel sorry for yourself because something didn't work out with a motherfucker who probably wasn't good enough for you anyway. If he knew like I *should* have known, he would have kept his ass there and tried to make you happy no matter how much of a pain in the fucking ass you probably were—a dumb motherfucker. You beat *death*! This shit ought to be a piece of cake—a fucking *breakup*? Shut up! Tell *everybody* to kiss your ass! Guess what I'm dealing with? Carolyn's sister stole my fucking camera. I am pissed. Ain't that some shit? Don't tell Zena because she'll tell Aunt Claudia, then my whole family will know and there will be some shit said. I *know* the bitch did it. Your insurance cards are here. I'll mail them or bring them to you or something. Call me when you stop acting like a punk." Then he hung up. I was flattered that he really was proud of my books.

After I thought about that conversation with Lenny, I decided to send the Chief Register of Wills a fax.

November 28, 2006

Dear Mr. Bell, Chief Register of Wills – Delaware County

Carolyn Monroe is something else. This is the same woman who, while I was on my death bed in 2001 (severe pneumonia) on a ventilator in a coma, came to the hospital taking my vital signs and adjusting tubes. She is a registered **nurse and wasn't even employed at the hospital I was in. I was livid about that** *when I finally regained consciousness and people told me she'd been there.*

As per Detective Thomas Glennor of your office, I took his advice and I retained an attorney in Philadelphia County to help me with this case against Carolyn Monroe.

Denise Garner

I kept thinking and plotting. I had to come up with something to impress this Chief, something vitally important to make him know that I was really legally married to Lenny. It had to be something to impeach Carolyn's credibility totally. I pondered. Then I had it! Bingo!

I called the City of Philadelphia. I remembered she had sued me back in the day. I couldn't remember the exact year. I spoke to a clerk at City Hall and explained it to her. I gave her me and Carolyn's names and told her I was the defendant and the case was in the 90's. She pulled up the complaint and I asked her to fax it to the Chief Register of Wills.

The very next day, I got a call to pick up my husband's body. I guess the Chief wondered how a person who claimed to not know another person could sue them fourteen years ago and serve the person at her marital residence. Checkmate!

As soon as I got the news, I was overjoyed. No matter what Lenny and I had gone through and how much of a shit he had been, he did not deserve to be in that damn morgue another day. I called Zena to tell her the news.

"Hey, Girl. It's me. Listen, I got the damn body! Carolyn got bumped."

Zena was silent for a moment. She started stroking me with her words, "That's good. Okay now, you've gotten what you wanted. You've won. You know how you are, you've just got the need to defeat in your blood. So, since you've accomplished that, you have to give that body to Theresa and let his family handle the funeral. You should not be handling the funeral."

Blood ran to my head. Was Zena crazy? I didn't waste a minute saying to her, "I'm not giving Theresa shit!"

Zena got mad at me. "Look, the right thing to do is to let his family plan his funeral. Hell, you just wanted to prove you could beat Carolyn and you did. He has a family—loads of relatives down south. You two were not together and you should not be planning his funeral."

"He's my damn husband! Mine! It's my damn body. I'm doing the damn funeral myself. What the hell are you doing—getting on those two bitches' side?"

She shot back, "Look, I'm just trying to tell you the *right* thing to do. If you do the funeral, none of them are coming. You know what, I'm sick of all this shit. I'm going out of town. I'm not coming. I've had it!"

This was not like Zena. She was usually passive and never got excited. "I need to know how far you are going to go with this thing, Zena. Are you and I going to fall out and lose our friendship if I take over the funeral?"

There was silence on the phone and she finally said, "I don't know."

We both hung up mad at each other. I was worried and shocked that she was contemplating ending her friendship with me. I analyzed what she said. She had me scared to damn death. Zena and I were as tight as sisters and I did not want to lose her. She meant more to me than Lenny's dead body.

I called Theresa, but she abruptly told me that she had nothing to say about anything concerning Lenny. She hung up. She was in a bad mood about something and I figured I was the cause. I waited a few minutes and called her back. We both calmed down and discussed having a funeral. We decided to do it on December 9th to give people time to get to Philly from Myrtle Beach. I had to find a funeral home. I had never done this stuff before in my life. I had the yellow pages out on my bed and began calling funeral homes. I ran around the corner to a fancy funeral parlor in Jenkintown. It was beautiful, but very small and would only hold sixty people. The director talked to me about Lenny. He had not been embalmed since being in the morgue and would have to have a closed casket due to deterioration of the body.

I called Theresa and she suggested we call Julian Hawkins back, the funeral director whom I had initially ordered to leave Lenny's body alone. **We hooked up a conference call and explained the situation and he said that** he could do an open casket. Strangely enough, Theresa and I were working together! I told Zena and Aunt Claudia and everybody was happy again. As soon as the funeral director called to tell me he actually had Lenny's body, I went directly there. He was all wrapped up in plastic and ice. I took a long look at him and felt sorry for him. I wanted to put a blanket around him. He looked good, not what I had imagined. His complexion was the same—as pretty as it had always been, coffee colored with a lot of cream in it. I did not shed a tear. I looked into his eyes and said, "Lenny, I told you this shit would happen. You just had to keep on drinking and smoking and running the streets. Now look what the fuck has happened. I am so sick of your hard headed ass! And…that bitch Carolyn. Didn't I tell you this shit would happen? Don't you say one fucking word while I'm cursing you the hell out. Didn't I tell you there would be a fight about your body? Didn't Zena and your family warn you about this shit years ago? You get on my fucking nerves! Damn, you have been missing in action all your damn life. I had to track your dead ass down just to get you buried! Well, you're not getting buried now. You're getting cremated just like me and Noelle planned for ourselves. That damn Carolyn. I'll fix her fucking ass for lying to those damn morgue people! You know I'll get the bitch. And I better not find out that she did anything wrong and caused your ass to die. I smell a rat already. And…my money…I'm spending a ton of money for this shit. I am sick of you. I had to take a bunch of money out of my account to do this shit! I used Noelle's tuition money. But that's okay, I'll get it back in the life insurance policy. I can't get over your being dead! Humph. Me and Theresa made up. I'm going by Tedd's store to get you some sharp clothes to wear for your celebration. I'm sorry you are dead, but you must have wanted it this way. You wouldn't go somewhere and sit your ass down and leave all that shit alone. See ya, I have things to take care of." I had been babbling on a mile a minute as if I expected Lenny to interrupt me. When I was done cursing him out, the undertaker and his assistant, who had overheard me, came out looking at me like I was crazy. I said to Mr. Hawkins, "This is how I grieve!"

The services were scheduled at Julian Hawkins Funeral Home on Saturday, December 9, 2006, viewing 12-1 p.m. and funeral 1-2 p.m. The repast would be held at The Draught Horse, a nice restaurant and bar. I went shopping for Lenny's attire and ordered flowers. I also wrote a hilarious poem to recite at the funeral. However, I ended up not reading it because of Aunt Claudia,.

His family was happy with my arrangements. I felt good about doing it. They had no money to bury him and I knew I did the right thing. I was frantic running around trying to take care of everything. Noelle was unable to assist in anything because she was sick with a flare-up of her Crohn's Disease.

I was spending *boo-coo* amounts of cash for Lenny's funeral. It was crucial that I got my ass over to the City of Philadelphia, Department of Life Benefits. I wanted to get the life insurance policy stuff straight so I would be able to pay for the funeral. I had already spoken with the benefits coordinator, Nancy Tucker, who had also spoken with Julian Hawkins guaranteeing payment. When I arrived at her office, she apologized and said there was a problem. She had received a call from Carolyn Monroe. She asked me to sit down.

"Mrs. Garner. Are you *sure* you are married to Lenny Garner?"

In amazement, my expression went from controlled and in charge to anger and exhaustion. "Yes, I am. I have my marriage license and the death certificate."

"Well, there are two problems. Carolyn Monroe has told me that she never knew anything about you or your daughter until after Mr. Garner's death. She said she's never heard of you and has been living with her husband for seventeen years. She never heard of you until he died. Now, Mrs. Garner, I have to ask you again, is Mr. Garner *really* your husband?"

Livid, I was going to put an end to this charade. I took a deep breath and said, "Mrs. Tucker, what is your fax number?"

I took out my cell phone and called my cousin Lynne. "Lynne, would you please fax that document that you have to a place for me?" In five minutes, Nancy Tucker was reading a copy of the Complaint filed by Carolyn Monroe suing *Denise Greene Garner* in 1993 serving me at the house Lenny and I had purchased together—our marital residence. Mrs. Tucker was stunned and sat shaking her head.

"Wow. Okay, Mrs. Garner. I have to also let you know that we have **found a change of Beneficiary Form. Your husband signed this, changing** the beneficiary from you to Carolyn Monroe. We just came across it. I apologize. This form is signed and dated by your husband on November 8, 2004 This states he changed the beneficiary to *Carolyn Monroe, wife.* We cannot pay the policy to you until this is investigated. I don't believe you will have the funds to bury your husband from this policy by Saturday.

"Well, she's not his w*ife*."

"Okay, let's get started. I'll need you to write a letter to explain all the facts, and that letter will be sent to Prudential Insurance Company. They pay our life insurance claims. They will make the decision. I do want you to know that if you have to go to court and need a witness, I will testify for you."

I wrote the letter, thanked her, and left. The next day, I withdrew six thousand dollars to bury Lenny from my savings account. I ran around like a bat out of hell trying to prepare the funeral. He was a veteran, so I had to pick up his flag from Veteran's Administration. I wanted him laid out sharp as a tack so it was a five hundred dollar *Lubiam* suit. He was going to look like he belonged to Denise and Noelle Garner—the suburban Black American Princesses that made it on the *Oprah Show* in April of 2005 and sat across from the *Kennedys*. Yep, Oprah had flown our butts out there *after* the TV crew had come to our house and spent seven hours in Elkins Park filming all the things I had provided Noelle with, even if I had stayed in the red most of the time because of it. Lenny Garner was going out in style even if I ended up in hock for this. Presentation was *everything*.

I forged on with the funeral plans. I wanted balloons released after the ceremony, so that was another hundred thirty five dollars. With the twelve hundred dollar restaurant bill and the undertaker's bill, I'd spent close to six thousand dollars. It was out of pocket because that damn Prudential Insurance Company didn't know which wife to pay the six thousand dollar insurance policy to. Miss Carolyn had her memorial at a church on Friday December 1st, a week before mine—*without* his body. Her memorial service program featured photographs of her and Lenny's *family*—and their wedding picture. Lenny was in a tuxedo and Carolyn in white wedding gown and veil that shocked his entire family. His relatives in Myrtle Beach opted not to come. They didn't want to travel all the way to Philadelphia to attend a funeral without a body. She and her friends celebrated after the affair at a local VFW post—chicken dinners, I heard. Humph.

Theresa and I were becoming real sisters–in-law and friends. We were sharing all kinds of information with each other. We were both thrilled to be back together and she was extremely grateful to me for rescuing Lenny from the morgue.

By this time, Carolyn had probably obtained my address. That crazy bitch could have ordered a hit on me. For that reason, I wanted to bust this whole case out in the open. I didn't trust her and didn't know just how crazy she was. If I choked on a piece of chicken, I wanted people to know that she could have shoved it down my throat. I knew that bitch was hot with me.

My new buddy Theresa told me that Carolyn's original plan had been to get Lenny's body quickly, have the funeral, keep it quiet, and not let me or Noelle know Lenny had died. It backfired when Theresa called Zena in D.C. and told her to find me so that I could let her niece know her Dad had died. Carolyn demanded to know who in the family had "leaked" the information to his cousin Zena and Carolyn was furious with Theresa.

Lenny's funeral was held on December 9, 2006. It turned out to be quite an affair. We had about eighty people. The weather between Lenny's sister Janete and her immediate family was chilly toward me because Janete was tight with Carolyn. But I got through it. It was wonderful to see so many people that I hadn't seen in years. I hadn't seen Lenny's baby sister, Rhonda, in fifteen years and a lot had changed. She'd had a brain aneurysm in 2001 and developed pneumonia on top of that. Rhonda nearly died that year. I'd heard about it from Lenny who had helped out with her care. She did not recognize me when she first looked at me in the funeral parlor, but after I talked to her, she remembered me. She reminded me of a retarded child. I was saddened to see her so different from the night I met her at that club. She had remarried since her first husband, Chuck, had died of liver cancer in the year 2000. Her new husband Barry seemed to be a great guy and very attentive to her. It was like a party for me and I was happy I had done the funeral. Lenny's first wife, Frances, had helped me out with a lot of the arrangements, as well as my friends. Everyone was asking about Noelle, as her picture was in Lenny's casket beside him. Unfortunately, she **was in the hospital and could not attend. We called her from the podium** so she could listen to the services. She was hysterically crying throughout the entire funeral, but refused to hang up. The repast was also an elaborate affair. We gathered and played music in tribute to Lenny. It turned out to be Lenny's favorite thing—a party.

The day after the funeral, my right foot was extremely swollen and painful. I ended up in the emergency room a couple of days after that. To top it off, I had a bad feeling about cremating Lenny. Something was gnawing at me. I had mixed feelings about it. Noelle and I had decided long ago that we both would be cremated, so I had made the decision to do it with Lenny. However, my gut was telling me not to do it. I called my godmother Marian in South Carolina to discuss it. I told her I wanted an autopsy. She listened, then told me that he had suffered enough and that I shouldn't let him get cut up. Let him rest, she said, he'd been through enough. She had convinced me to go on with the cremation and I agreed.

Ten days later, still with a sore and swollen right foot, I kept my scheduled visit with my physic, Mr. Dee. He read tarot cards and had a crystal ball. I usually went to him twice a year and had been going to him periodically since 1991. He'd predicted a lot of shit over the years that had come true or happened prior to my reading with him. Lenny's dead ass took over my tarot card and crystal ball reading that day. Mr. Dee said, "The Leo that has left you forever, don't you be so sure that what's on his death certificate is the truth. A full investigation needs to be done." Then he went on and on. The next day, I called the medical examiner's office demanding a toxicology/autopsy report. My antennas were definitely up. I regretted having cremated him.

I had been so busy over the last month with Lenny's death that Christmas had crept upon me. This was the first year that I had done no shopping. Noelle was out of the hospital and with her boyfriend Vincent. I hadn't seen her since she'd been discharged. I'd planned a trip to Greenville South Carolina to visit my godparents. My foot was still a mess and I had scheduled an MRI for December 23rd, before I left town. I was having a nice visit with them, but it was abbreviated because my doctors got the MRI results back and discovered that the foot was fractured, possibly infected, and the doctors had to rule out Osteomylitis. They called me in Greenville and insisted I fly back immediately to the emergency room. On December 28th , I was admitted to the hospital for six days and then transferred to a skilled nursing facility in Willow Grove, Pennsylvania on January 4, 2007. While there, I was watching *Good Morning America* on a

Saturday morning. There was a headlining story about a woman accused of killing her husband for a boob job.

The murder trial was about a young mother accused of using arsenic to kill her Marine husband. The murder mystery had gripped San Diego and a Marine Corps Air Station. The woman was accused of poisoning her husband with arsenic for financial gain so she could afford plastic surgery and a shopping spree. She was also accused of murdering her husband to collect his $250,000 life insurance policy. Prosecutors said that soon after he died, she spent $5,400 on breast implants and hosted boisterous parties at her home on the base. They recounted what she had said when medics removed his body and the fact that his parents confirmed he had been complaining of stomach pains prior to his death.

It was like a bolt of lightening hit me. That murder made me remember one of my discussions after the funeral with Theresa. She told me that Lenny had stomach pains on Thanksgiving Day. She had gotten that information from her brother Marvin who had spoken to Lenny the day he died. Quickly, I got on the computer and e-mailed my attorney, Tony Marino. On Monday, I called the Philadelphia Police Department to discuss the similarities of both cases. My gut was telling me that Carolyn had something to do with Lenny's death. I set up a meeting for Tony to come to the nursing facility to talk to me privately about this case. I also called the medical examiner. Dr. Relman of the Delaware County Medical Examiners office was very interested and was going to order further testing, specifically a heavy metals test that would show if there was poison in Lenny's tissue and blood. He had not known about the stomach pains when Lenny was at the morgue. Dr. Relman hadn't been the one who examined Lenny's body, but would get in touch with that medical examiner with this news. I wondered if that information about the stomach pains was in the Emergency Room or paramedic record. One question I had for sure was **did Carolyn withhold that information from medical personnel. Detective** Adam Hartman of Central Philadelphia Detectives had been assigned to talk to me. He'd been a homicide detective for many years and therefore well seasoned in criminology. He was also interested in my findings and planned for us to have a meeting when I was discharged. I got busy trying to get my foot better in rehabilitation and was determined to find out if there was foul play.

Things were heating up. I wanted all the facts straight from the horse's mouth. I called my brother-in-law, Marvin Garner, in Tucson, Arizona.

Sixty-eight year old Marvin answered the phone sounding like he was a bit tipsy. He was notorious for having diarrhea of the mouth. I didn't have the time or patience to spend two hours on the phone with him, so I cut right to the chase. "Hey, Marvin, it's Denise. I'm up to my ears in bullshit about Lenny's death. I need you to clarify some things for me."

"Hi, Denise. Well, this is a mess. Stomach pains don't go with a heart attack. I know that. I've been checking with people out here."

"Yeah, Marv, I heard. Listen. What time did you talk to Lenny on Thanksgiving Day and who called who?"

"I talked to him around...well...two twenty in the afternoon. I called him."

"So, you have phone records—you know—your phone bill?"

"Well....I called him from my cell phone."

"Do you have that bill in your papers? I need a copy of the time of the call and how long it lasted."

"You can go to the Internet for it and pull it up. I'll give you the information to do that."

"I don't want any Internet number. I need you to get it for me. Can you do that and mail it to me. I have to have proof of the call."

"Okay, I'll do it."

I slowly recited my mailing information. "Okay Marv, now I need you to tell me what Lenny said on the phone to you. Do you remember exactly?"

"Yeah, I do. He said he had the worst stomach pains he's ever had in his life."

"Okay, what else did you two talk about? Was Carolyn home?"

"All we talked about was him being sick. Yeah, Carolyn was home. Lenny told me that."

"Did you talk to her?"

"No. I let him go because he was so sick. I was concerned, but I figured since Carolyn was at home with him, and she was a registered nurse, he would be okay. She would know what to do."

Listening to Marvin, I was imagining Lenny doubled over in pain. I had a vision of Carolyn watching a movie or doing a crossword puzzle while waiting for Lenny to kick the bucket. "Okay, Marvin, say hi to Ellen for me and I'll send you an affidavit in a few days. I want you to call me when you get it. We'll get on the phone together and I'll be at my computer. We'll go over it and edit it together to get all the facts correct. After that, I'll mail it to you. I want you to sign it in front of a notary public and mail it back to me. I'll need it for court."

"You're going to court? You're really going after her?"

"Damn straight. Can I count on you to back me up?"

"Of course. Like I said, stomach pains don't go with a heart attack. Lenny also told Ellen that day how bad he was feeling."

"Oh yeah? Well now, we'll need two Affidavits. Give me your address and all your numbers."

"Okay, I'm on it."

"Marv—how'd you find out he died?"

"Theresa called me four hours after I talked to Lenny. She said he had a massive heart attack. Denise, did you know I was in Philly in June of 2002?"

"No, what were you doing here?" For a moment, I thought he might have come for Lenny and Carolyn's wedding and kept it quiet.

"I came for a visit and stayed with Carolyn and Lenny from June 15th to June 20th. Funny, they never mentioned getting married and I didn't see any wedding stuff around."

"Marvin, I've gotta run, baby. Get your work done for me and expect mail soon from here."

Finally, Friday had come and I had a lot to discuss with Tony. Before getting to the Lenny stuff, we discussed a few personal injury cases he was thinking of handling for me. Tony would represent me if I had any legal problems or claims for accidents. After that, I told him the story about Lenny and explained about the Change of Beneficiary Form. He was attentive, never taking his eyes off of me. I found myself gazing back at him. Tony Marino was a very good friend of mine. He was Italian, dark complected with a beautiful set of aquamarine blue eyes. He was six feet two inches tall and weighed two hundred twenty pounds. Tony ate the right foods and worked out. He had a shaven head and a gleaming smile—perfect teeth. As usual, he was dressed to kill that day. For a moment, I thought about the night we met. He had interviewed me for a position at his firm. We hit it off from jumpstreet and I worked for him for about a year. We parted company because we had depended too much on each other and fought like a married couple. But we remained friends and both knew one thing—we were a lot alike, type A personalities, crazy, super intelligent, hard working, and super suspicious. As a team, Tony and I were aggressive and we always got the job done. We always protected and looked out for each other. Together, we were unbeatable. After I left his employment, I would help him out occasionally on files or come into his office to work if he had turnover problems. He could go through some secretaries because he was so demanding.

He was taking it all in while I was talking. When I was finished, he said, "Do you have the Change of Beneficiary Form?" I reached into a bunch of papers I had brought to the hospital with me and handed it over. He studied it. "How do you know he signed this? Does this look like his signature to you?"

I was surprised he'd asked that. I responded, "I never thought he hadn't signed it. Yep, Lenny probably signed the thing. I don't know. I've been concentrating on so many other things. I was more concerned about the *wife* thing at the top—see up top where he indicated she was his wife? I thought that was my case against Prudential, the life insurance carrier. Lenny probably signed it, but she's not his *wife*."

"Well, you don't know for sure if he signed this thing," Tony said suspiciously.

We adjourned our meeting. I was pumped up again because he was suspicious. And if Tony felt it was fishy—something was probably up. I got back into my hospital bed and searched through my documents. I came up with Lenny and Carolyn's marriage license application from 2002. I compared it with the Change of Beneficiary Form and his signature did not match. Then I thought it might be my imagination and let my roommate take a look at the signatures. She didn't think they were the same either. So I got the number of Prudential Insurance Company and faxed the documents to them with a note to Karen Bearden, the claims examiner. That aspect of the case created a flurry of activity. The signature had never been questioned. We had always focused on who the legal wife was and never considered that the form could have had a bogus signature.

I was on to something and I wanted some media coverage. I hooked up with Chris Brazzi, a crime reporter for a major newspaper. I also retained Angela O'Neill Pelham, Esquire, an estate attorney, and filed a complaint with the Pennsylvania Insurance Commission. I called the Commission in because, at one point, Prudential was threatening to pay the proceeds of the six thousand dollar life insurance policy to Carolyn. I wasn't going for that shit.

I was on a roll, gathering and piecing together information. I believed that my findings would ultimately pave the way for additional claims against Carolyn. I turned out to be quite a little bloodhound and a toxicology report was mailed to my home while I was in the rehabilitation center. It prompted a new investigation and more testing. Chief Medical Examiner Dr. Relman now stated that Lenny's death was not due to a heart attack. The death certificate was amended. Dr. Relman said Lenny died of an adverse reaction to a drug or medication and that cocaine was present in his system. The number two factor and cause of death was listed as hypertension. The medical examiner planned to continue with a more intense investigation. This news prompted me to make a claim against Carolyn's homeowner's insurance carrier regarding his death. I wondered if I could be successful in a wrongful death claim. Carolyn Monroe owned that property and my husband died as a result of being in that property. Lenny was not listed on the deed or the loan to buy it. What a dummy—she thought she was screwing him over by keeping his name off the deed but in the end it was going to benefit me. Thanks Carolyn. Checkmate!

Detective Adam Hartman was hanging tough with me. We were on the phone daily swapping information. I had been advised by Detective Hartman to report to the D.A.'s office to file a criminal complaint against Carolyn Monroe for cashing Lenny's pension check after he died. She signed her name to the $1600 check and deposited it into a joint account she shared with him. I was elated that she was as greedy as she was. This was a criminal offense and certainly a notch against her credibility. I was praying they would put the bitch in jail. So, while the Chief Register of Wills was trying to determine who the legal wife was, the *illegal* wife was running around cashing his checks. Just the thought of them showing up on her job to arrest her or dragging her out of her house cuffed was equivalent to an orgasm to me. And to boot, Lenny's pension account was overdrawn as a result of this. Before I could establish my right to the pension, I had to pay funds to the pension board to cover the overdraft. That was another $542.00 out of my pocket.

I was discovering all kinds of information through repeated calls to the pension board and keeping up with Detective Hartman. Hartman made an appearance at the pension board and was told that Lenny had not gotten a "DROP" lump sum of $131K as I had suspected. Detective Hartman shared that he had actually received 53K in November of 2004. I was sure that all that money was totally gone over the two year period.

Theresa had become a great ally and was supplying me with loads of information and gossip. Miss Carolyn was hitting Lenny up from all sides. She had taken out a life insurance policy on Lenny's life for 10K through her job at Pennsylvania Hospital. It was not going to fly for her because I made sure to alert the benefits administrator at her job. Anne-Marie Kidston of Pennsylvania Hospital informed me that the hospital and/or their insurance carrier wouldn't pay that policy unless Carolyn came up with a death certificate that stated she was his wife. I believed she had other policies on him that had come in the junk mail. I remember Lenny telling a Court officer years ago while we were in support court for child support that he had an "accident" policy on his life. I was sure Carolyn had received it in the mail, filled it out and sent it back. Any reputable insurance company would require a medical examination of him to issue a life policy. There was no way she could have gotten one like that. It would be denied. He used cocaine, and that's why the two of them got along well—they both liked the drug.

Massive amounts of information and advice were coming in from all over the place. I'd been to Voter's Registration regarding Lenny's change form. It was now time to let Karen Bearden know the deal. On January 29, 2007, I wrote to her at Prudential Insurance Company

Dear Ms. Bearden:

As per our most recent telephone conversation, I have obtained current handwriting samples of my husband, Lenny Garner. These samples came from the Pennsylvania Voting Bureau in Philadelphia. Detective Adam Hartman of Central Detectives of Philadelphia (215-555-3041) has examined them today and shared with me that it is his opinion that the signature on the Change of Beneficiary Form and the current samples from Voter's Registration are not a match. I have samples of the years 2004, 2005 and 2006. They are on the way to you.

Noelle was now missing in action, as her dad had been many times. She never showed up at the rehabilitation facility to see me. She'd called to say she was coming, but we'd end up fighting about something and hang up mad. She was irritable. She didn't want to talk to anyone in the family because she was stressed out. Noelle insisted she just needed a break from everything and everybody. She continued to stay with Vincent. Everybody in the family was inquiring about her. We'd call and she wouldn't answer her cell phone. The first week of February she was admitted to a hospital near Vincent's apartment. I found out when our health insurance carrier called needing an additional payment or her admission wouldn't be covered. I immediately called the hospital, but they wouldn't give me any information on her due to the HIPPA LAW. I called both her and Vincent's cell numbers for three days and got no return calls. I planned to kill both of them. I decided, however, to leave that shit alone and concentrate on Carolyn. I was sure the hospital would take care of Noelle.

Lo and behold, bad news was coming down the pike. When I called Dr. Relman on February 10th, he confirmed that the heavy metals tests conducted in search of poisons in Lenny's body had shown up negative. I **was not expecting to hear that, for it was contrary to everything I believed**. As a result, there would be no additional change in the cause of death, which had been deemed an adverse reaction to a drug and the presence of cocaine in his system. I was hoping for a change in the death certificate to indicate a homicide. The bottom line was Lenny did not die of a heart attack and that was a victory in itself.

As we went on to talk he said, "Mrs. Garner, if you desire any additional testing, due to my massive caseload and problems with funding, I suggest you hire a private forensic toxicologist and pay him. That toxicologist would know what additional tests to order in a search to find out if your husband was administered any medication which may have led to his death. However, that testing may or may not be able to be done if he did not have adequate fluids left over from his previous testing."

Now I was livid with him and suspicious. They should have had money to conduct this shit on their own. "Dr. Relman, my husband's medical records for his emergency care at Mercy Fitzgerald Hospital on Thanksgiving Day were faxed to me. I examined them closely. Lenny was alive when he arrived at Mercy Fitzgerald at 5:39 p.m." I had thought Lenny was dead when the paramedics retrieved him from Carolyn's house. Dr. Relman had some additional explaining to do. What was this new shit? I continued on, not allowing him to respond. "My in-laws told me that Carolyn claims to have been with him for a week prior to his becoming ill. That time frame covered the trip down to Myrtle Beach and back and the few days leading to Thanksgiving at home. The records I received indicate that at 5:53 p.m., Lenny was pronounced dead at Mercy Fitzgerald." *What the hell was going on?* I imagined the doctor's ass sitting with all those dead bodies, and most of them had probably received much better care than Lenny. Lenny died on a fucking holiday and his staff was probably happy and bullshitted around when his dead body arrived. Maybe they were pissed they had to work and never followed proper procedures. Now their claim was that they had no more money to spend on his ass and they were bogged down with work.

When I got done talking, suddenly he was very busy and had too much work to do. "I'll call you regarding those samples after I check them."

I didn't trust any of their asses at this point and, after we hung up, I reexamined the hospital records. I noticed something interesting. Carolyn Monroe was present when my husband arrived at the emergency room and, in fact, had called paramedics to her home. She signed authorizing his treatment. I was certain that all the information the hospital received regarding Lenny, such as insurance information, had been provided by her to the triage nurse. The records indicated that Lenny had no known allergies to any drugs and was on no medications. On page 13 of the medical record, the question asked: *List below all of the patient's medications taken/prescribed prior to admission including over the counter, herbal, street or illicit drugs.* That page is marked unknown. In a more extensive review of the records, page 11 noted that Lenny's abdomen was distended. I had no doubt that Carolyn was with my husband from the time he arrived at the hospital until the time he was pronounced dead because she refused on page 14 of the medical record to donate his organs. This was at 6:20 p.m. on Thanksgiving Day.

The pieces of the puzzle were coming together. I now had to wait for the Emergency Medical Services record from the paramedics. It was my feeling that Carolyn had opportunities during the day to seek medical treatment for Lenny. Being a trained professional and a registered nurse, she could have also assisted him. From what Detective Hartman explained to me, Carolyn had more medical training than those paramedics. If Lenny was complaining at 2:30 in the afternoon of intense pain in the abdomen, then Lenny must have had those symptoms prior to speaking with his brother Marvin. Family members were given little or no information by Carolyn about the events of the day before Lenny fell ill. She explained that when she realized he had pain, she "massaged his groin" and "fed him his Thanksgiving dinner while he lay in bed in pain." Relatives, who had arrived at her home, listened to her account of what happened and noticed an uncut, cooked turkey on the stove and pots containing vegetables. It appeared the food had never been touched. None of them had been called to come to the hospital after he died. Family members were told different stories such as "he died at home," "died at the hospital," "vomited at home during the day." They really didn't know what happened and Carolyn had the nerve to tell them that she could not answer any questions.

My antennas were perked because I had heard more information from Theresa. Lenny had been evaluated and admitted to Pennsylvania Hospital, **Intensive Care Unit on February 10, 2005 where Carolyn Monroe worked** in skilled nursing. Why didn't she inform paramedics or the emergency room physicians of that?

Prudential was moving too slowly on the matter of the life insurance proceeds. I called Karen Bearden and told her plainly that I was disgusted. She had everything she needed since the beginning of February, Carolyn and Lenny's bogus marriage license, the City of Philadelphia Benefit Change Form signed in November of 2004, and Lenny's voter's registration samples. Even though Prudential had their own fraud unit equipped with a handwriting analyst, her company was unable to conclude that it was indeed Lenny's signature on that Change of Beneficiary form. In order to resolve the matter, it was my obligation to furnish Prudential with more current samples of Lenny's handwriting in the form of signatures from Voter's Registration. I supplied those samples to her on February 6th, which included samples of 2004, 2005, and 2006 signatures. Why was she giving me the run around?

It was eight o'clock in the morning as I held the phone to my ear, waiting for witch Karen to answer. She picked up on the third ring. I was glad I didn't get a voicemail. "Karen, it's Denise Garner and we're approaching the end of February with things still up in the air. I'll hold on if you need to get a cup of coffee. You'll need to be alert and we'll be a while."

I could feel her seething with anger. I sat at my computer tapping a pen on my workstation, knowing she could hear it. I was thinking of that Chinese water treatment dripping thing that drove people crazy. I continued on with the noise and sighed as I waited for her to respond. I wanted her to start her day off right, with my foot up her ass.

"Look, I have no more information. Nothing is going on. My analyst, after reviewing the samples from the Voter's Bureau, is still unable to determine that Mr. Garner signed the Change of Beneficiary Form allowing Carolyn Monroe to be the beneficiary of his life policy with the City of Philadelphia."

"Oh yeah? Well, he must not be competent. Do I need to get an expert of my own—it seems I have to do everything else for Prudential?" I said sarcastically.

She started in on me. "Mr. Garner had the right to designate his life policy to anyone he pleased. Seems to me he wanted Ms. Monroe."

"Don't rush to judgment, *hon.*" I purposely call her h*on* because I knew that irritated women. "I am aware of your position and the fact that *my husband* could designate anyone he wished to be the beneficiary. However, its *my position* that his signature would be necessary in order to effectuate any transfer or change of beneficiary."

"Well, we can't figure it out right now and need more time. It'll stay in pending until we get to it. I'll send you an update in a month or so. You have a nice day."

I wanted to come through the phone and strangle that bitch. "Not so fast, I'm not done. I know that the City of Philadelphia Life Benefits Department forwards blank Change of Beneficiary forms to the residences of City employees by mail. Since this is a procedure, Carolyn Monroe, residing with my husband at 8319 Union Avenue at the time this form was allegedly signed by him, would have had access to the mail. So, she would have had the opportunity to handle this form and return it back by mail to the City of Philadelphia Life Insurance Benefits Department. Also, the form did not require a *notarized* signature. Thus, she or anyone in the household could have gained access to the form, signed and returned it to the City of Philadelphia Life Benefits Department changing the beneficiary of Lenny's policy."

She didn't utter a word, so I continued that my take on the situation was that, as a result of Carolyn Monroe's past history of lying on marriage applications, lying to personnel in the Delaware County Medical Examiner's office in an attempt to obtain Lenny's dead body, cashing my husband's checks, and lying to City officials in the Life Benefits office about not knowing he ever had any other wives (and she was indeed aware of his two marriages, and I could prove it), I had to question whether or not the change form was indeed signed by my husband. Was I the only one with a fucking brain to watch over these imbeciles? That lazy bitch better find my fucking money.

"Look, Karen, on or around February 20, 2007, you promised to inform me of the disposition of the matter and indicated a decision would be made whether or not your company would pay Carolyn Monroe or myself the proceeds of this life policy. What's so complicated about this thing?"

"We have a backlog—other cases. You're not the only person with a dead husband."

"Okay, let's start getting me some documents. I want a copy of Lenny's life insurance policy, the curriculum vitae of Prudential's handwriting analyst who examined all of my husband's signatures, and copies of their notes and or reports concerning this investigation."

I listened to her exhale and she said, "The only thing I can do is pass all this information on. I'm not in charge. I'll see what I can do."

I wouldn't let up and would ride her ass until I got satisfaction. I sternly advised, "If you refuse to voluntarily convey those documents to me, I'll subpoena *all* records. I'm suggesting you forward information to me as to *who* at Prudential should receive the subpoena. And another thing, I have opened an estate regarding my husband's death."

In a smart allecky manner, she said, "That's your prerogative and a normal practice when someone dies."

Karen was pushing every button to provoke me and it was working. I sat there in contemplation. I wanted to have her taken off the case and wondered if I should request another claims examiner to keep from going to jail for murder. "Look, Missy, if it is your intention to pay Carolyn Monroe the proceeds of Lenny's policy, I would appreciate your advising me immediately and before you make payment to her. And by the way, I also confirmed that my husband's death has been ruled accidental due to an adverse reaction to a drug by the medical examiner of Delaware County. That means double indemnity to the tune of 12K. I also know that Nancy Tucker of the City of Philadelphia Life Benefits Department has filed that claim with your company and you received a copy of the amended Death Certificate."

Letting me know she wasn't impressed, she sighed nonchalantly. "Yeah, okay. We have to wrap up, it's my break time."

I was boiling! I hammered on that I had telephoned her on the afternoon of February 15, 2007 to advise that I had received a copy of a letter dated January 24, 2007 to Carolyn Monroe from the City of Philadelphia Board of Pensions. In that letter, the Pension Board was requesting repayment from Carolyn Monroe regarding an overpayment of my husband's pension fund which occurred as a result of her cashing his pension check that was payable to him and mailed to her home after his death.

Her reply to that information was, "Whatever the Pension Board has or whatever happened over there is none of Prudential's business. You need not forward a copy of their letter to me," she curtly said.

"Oh shit! This is *IT*," I screamed and slammed the phone down. Karen had fired me up and sent me into orbit. Steam was coming out of my ears. I said out loud, "Do I kill this bitch *now* or in fifteen minutes after I *think* about it first!"

I started typing. I wanted to document that conversation and sent copies of it to all attorneys involved, Chris Brazzi at the Philadelphia Daily News, Detective Adam Hartman, The City of Philadelphia Pension Board, The City of Philadelphia Life Benefits Department and the Pennsylvania Insurance Commission. All this shit would be on paper. In the event I took their asses to court, I'd have names, dates, times, and places. That would make me look smart, efficient, and organized. They wouldn't be able to trip me up. I was covering all bases, my ass, and letting everybody know Carolyn Monroe was a crook and that Prudential Insurance Company was dragging their feet in this case.

The Philadelphia Daily News continued to stay in touch with me and Chris Brazzi got back to me regarding one of his interviews. He had interviewed Theresa and one jarring detail stood out: Carolyn's thuggish friend threatened Theresa to keep her "damn mouth shut" when she started asking some innocent questions after Lenny died. Theresa said that when she told Carolyn about the threat, Carolyn giggled. Brazzi thought it sure sounded sinister. Just the thought of that bitch laughing about Lenny being dead sent a rage through me. Her actions made me feel that there was something peculiar about her personality. I looked at it as an ingredient in her recipe of murder and conspiracy.

I knew I could find out a lot about Lenny and Carolyn's lives through their bank records. I'd be able to determine how they lived—their lifestyle, where they shopped, and what assets they had. Plus, I simply wanted to know where the hell his money went and how much he had. I had a feeling Carolyn's ass was desperate for money. I got a hold of some bank statements and they reflected Lenny and Carolyn's joint bank account was now overdrawn a little over $500.00. I added up their monthly income for the past two years and, after taxes, both of them cleared about $6700 monthly together. Their mortgage was around $860.00 a month. Based on the overdrafts, they were always broke. Theresa told me Lenny was also working under the table laying carpeting when he died. I didn't even count that money into my calculation. That $6700 included Carolyn's monthly take home, plus Lenny's pension and social security checks. From my review of the statements, they had been living from hand to mouth every month. Utilities were about to be turned off, or minimal amounts were paid on them. Checks bounced all over the place. They were so broke just before Lenny died that they had to borrow money from his sister Janete to stay at a hotel while in Myrtle Beach to bury Lenny's brother Dennis. Then Carolyn came home after that funeral and on November 27, four days after Lenny's death, she was on a shopping spree? And she was still buying crap based on the automated system records I checked at the bank for transactions. She also took a trip to Florida after her memorial service for Lenny. Either she was holding out on the money when she went to Myrtle Beach for Dennis's funeral or she had some money stashed. Either way—I was going to find out. She wasn't fooling me.

Anything I couldn't find out on my own, Theresa was supplying. One Sunday I got some additional information from her and quickly sent Tony an e-mail.

To: Tony Marino

From: Denise Garner

Today is Sunday. Just heard that Lenny was involved in an automobile accident in 2006. Carolyn was the driver. Lenny was a passenger. The passenger can never be at fault, darling. They better show me the money. I do not know the exact date of accident, but I'll find out—I betcha that. There was rear end damage to the car Carolyn was driving. I have no idea if Lenny had a claim with her company or with another company. His sister believes the accident occurred somewhere around 7/4/06. Let's see if Lenny or Carolyn were collecting anything on that or if an attorney was involved in that claim. Lenny was working at a company laying carpeting through a friend. Could have gotten lost wages and was being treated. I am not sure. I'll be on this in the morning.

Denise

After a more thorough check of the bank statements and cancelled checks, which I had received as a result of rerouting Lenny's mail to my house, I was able to determine the name of the car insurance company and policy number. I was one smart cookie. I started snooping around on the phone and got a clerk in the automobile claims department. I got all the information I needed and called Carolyn's car insurance company to put in a claim as Mrs. Lenny Garner. I was on a roll. I waited a couple of days, then called them back. An adjuster on the phone listened intently to the entire situation. I spilled the beans telling him that Carolyn had a second car on the policy, which was her granddaughter's car. Since Charmaine Johnson was only twenty–two years old, I advised him that if she had not been listed as a driver, she was definitely driving the car. Lenny had provided the funds to purchase the car for her graduation. I advised him that maybe her rates should be increased since Charmaine was under twenty-five. Lenny hadn't had a driver's license for over thirty years because he'd had a judgment against him for running into someone and never paid it. I suggested he check his records to see if Lenny was listed as Carolyn's husband. I knew if you were married, you got a better rate. With all that information, including the juicy gossip of the two wives deal, that white man was floored. He'd certainly gotten an earful of our dirty laundry. I didn't give a shit—I was out to burn the witch. He said he couldn't talk to me until he had Lenny's death certificate, my Short Certificate, and my marriage license. I'd promptly fax the documents to him. I wondered if that slick ass Carolyn had settled that case after Lenny's death and collected the money. I couldn't put anything past that slick ass bitch. Now, I had to admit that I did like a bitch, but not this type. She wasn't my kind. I had no respect for her. She was ruthless, mean, and dirty, a far cry from Karen Bearden.

Lenny always kept a chick on the side, and I knew he had one. Her name was Debbie. I was going to find her. I was sure she had some information I could use. She probably knew his habits from hanging out with him and would know a lot of his business. If I played my cards right, she would give me stories about him and Carolyn that I could use against Carolyn. Later I called Detective Hartman and Chris at the newspaper to let them know I was looking for my husband's chick on the side.

I was exhausted after all that Columbo stuff and being mean to every damn body. It was a responsibility to be on guard all the fucking time. The shit was worse than a real job. I laid in bed and thought it all over. Regarding Prudential Insurance Company, I'd originally decided not to fight them if they gave Carolyn that $6,000 life policy. I didn't want to go that far because I would have to pay Tony 2K to go after 6K. I was thinking differently now. It was a pot of 12K now and I could afford to pay Tony's legal fees to go after that. If I won, Carolyn or Prudential would have to pay my legal fees. I wanted to fight.

My plan would be to wait until Prudential officially told me that they would pay Carolyn. Wait until I was kicked out. If that happened, I'd file papers to refrain them. At the present time, Prudential was just getting the signatures they requested from Voter's Registration. Yep, I'd wait to see if they would knock me out. If they did, I'd go after them and hold everything up.

CHAPTER 11

∾

Two Smart Bitches

I had a list of things I needed to do. A priority was finding Lenny's chick on the side. She would be important to this case. Theresa had told me a little about her. Lenny introduced Debbie to Theresa in 2003 when they were all at a bar called Cookum's located at 15th and Arch in Philadelphia. It was across the street from Lenny's job. Lenny and Debbie were actively dating prior to and in the year 2003, and their relationship continued well into 2006 until his death. On February 6, 2007, I finally tracked her down. I'd gone through Lenny's cell phone bills and found a number he frequently called. I called it and a woman answered. I asked to speak to Debbie and she said that she was Debbie. Then I told her I had the wrong number, excused myself, and hung up. I simply got cold feet not knowing how to approach her. I didn't want to scare her off.

I phoned her department again in a couple of days. A woman answered the phone. In a friendly voice, I asked if she was Debbie. The woman replied, "No, Debbie is upstairs working."

I lied, "I'm doing the flyers for the trip. She wanted one. What's her last name? I'm sending it down for her."

The woman answered, "Randall."

I called back at the end of the day and got Debbie on the phone. I explained who I was and made her comfortable. I knew she had been introduced to his family members. I let her know that I was not in disapproval of her relationship with Lenny and had named her "Lenny's chick on the side." She was flattered and relaxed after that. I began to question her. She had talked to Lenny on Monday the 20th of November, the day he got back from Myrtle Beach, but never heard from him again. She had not seen him during the week he died. She was shocked when she heard the news of his death. She told me he'd sounded fine when she talked to him. They usually talked every day, but during this period he hadn't called her after Monday. I figured she was telling the truth because Carolyn had told Theresa that she and Lenny had been together all week, up until the evening he died. Debbie was employed by the City of Philadelphia, Water Revenue Bureau located in the same building that Lenny worked in. I found out that Lenny and Debbie had been dating for five years. Debbie had also met Lenny's Aunt Claudia and had been to her house many times. She'd also met my brother-in-law Barry. Debbie had held her own memorial service for Lenny after he died. I'd heard about that from another City employee.

There was a thirst in me to nail Carolyn on every possible count, to get her in trouble for anything and everything she *ever* did. I had an *"Attack Carolyn To Do List"* taped to the wall of my bedroom. I reviewed it daily and each night before I went to bed. I thought I'd be able to dream up some shit if it was fresh in my mind when I closed my eyes to rest. Each time I would think of some way to harass her, I'd add it to the list. The things I would accomplish, I'd check off. This case was the first thing on my mind in the morning and the last thing at night. I was relentless.

I uncovered more medical information that would prove that she had been aware that Lenny had health problems and had been on medication.

As it turned out, Lenny definitely had an allergic reaction to a drug in early February of 2005. I got all the information by calling his former doctor who went over Lenny's treatment with me. Lenny had been treated in Pennsylvania Hospital. Now I knew for sure that Miss Carolyn knew he had an allergy to something. Funny she didn't tell the emergency room staff at Mercy Fitzgerald about that when she signed him in the hospital the day he died. She had the triage nurse thinking Lenny was Ward Cleaver of *Leave It To Beaver* and all he did was drink milk and help wifey-poo June Cleaver dry the dishes. Bullshit. Lenny was Jesse James.

When Lenny was admitted to the E.R. at Pennsylvania Hospital, he was unable to breathe. From what I understand, he drove himself to the hospital. Carolyn was not around. I did some more checking and obtained those records from Pennsylvania. His face, lips, and tongue were swollen. His airways were blocked. As I combed through the records, Lenny admitted he was an alcoholic and had been on blood pressure medication for over fifteen years. He'd been kept in the Intensive Care Unit for two days and been given Benadryl. He was discharged on Atenolol, a blood pressure medication and beta blocker. Carolyn's signature was on some of the admission papers and she was listed as his wife. Apparently she was working that day. Dammit, I had concrete proof now in black and white that she had lied about his health.

* * *

By the end of February, I was bushed. It was nine thirty in the evening. I had one hell of a week and it was only Wednesday. I had been fighting with Karen Bearden of Prudential since what seemed like forever. Things had been boiling between us—two witches, since the end of November, brewing for nearly three months.

Apparently, all my letters and phone calls did not impress her. She hadn't called me regarding a decision and I began calling her to demand that her company take some action and settle this life insurance matter. She was very curt with me and I was abrasive. We absolutely hated each other. She was withholding information from me and claimed she had no idea when they would make a determination about the signature on the Change of Beneficiary form. I was pissed and kept sending her letters. By this time, I didn't even care if I ever collected the insurance proceeds, I just wanted to make her miserable. And she was truly challenging me and holding her own in this situation. We were two equal bitches, determined and relentless. I must admit, I like a *bitch* that is smart and on the ball. In my own way, I respected and liked Karen even though she was egging me to come to her office and choke her to death. Lately, because of my frustration, I would go to bed at night and lay in bed literally thinking of ways to aggravate her when she got to work the following morning. We had a lot in common and I realized that. The bad situation between us was continuing to escalate and I faxed a letter.

Dear Ms Bearden:

With regard to our telephone conversation of February 20, 2007, I am requesting that your company supply me with the documents I have requested in my letter to you dated February 16, 2007.

In our conversation of February 20, 2007, you advised that your company had no documents regarding this claim. It is my understanding after speaking with the City of Philadelphia Life Insurance Benefits Department that they do not have a copy of the life policy. I am sure that your company has that and I would appreciate your forwarding it to me.

You also stated that you could not provide me with the name of the attorney handling this matter for your company and that he was away in California fighting a case for Prudential. You said you were not sure when he or anyone from your company would be in touch with me regarding my husband's life policy with Prudential.

Also, you informed me that you had no information as to who reviewed and examined my husband's writing samples which you had requested I obtain and forward to you from Voter's Registration.

I have enclosed another copy of my February 16, 2007 letter and I am requesting you forward information to me requested in that letter. I am also enclosing a copy of a subpoena and a short certificate. I would appreciate your relinquishing the requested documents to me, or I will have the subpoena completed and served.

Also, to date I have not received an additional status letter from your company. You indicated in our conversation that you forwarded same to me on February 20, 2007.

Thank you for your attention to this matter.
DENISE GARNER

I was holding my ground and sniffing into everything, not leaving a stone unturned. On Monday, February 26, I presented myself to Citizens Bank in Elkins Park Pennsylvania to arrest the joint account of Lenny and Carolyn. I was armed with my short certificate and a subpoena. After a conference with Assistant Manager Daniel Bishop, I filled out the subpoena they required. I sat in front of Daniel and carefully prepared a rough draft of the subpoena. I was being careful, they cost ten dollars each. I instructed him to call his legal department to go over it with them. It had to be in compliance with the requirements of that department in order to release all bank statements and copies of cancelled checks to me. As I sat there, I became engrossed in Daniel's family pictures. He had the cutest nephew in the world sitting in a frame on his ledge. That picture reminded me so much of my own daughter and her relationship with her Dad long ago. It felt like a lifetime ago. But as I sat in this chair and he hung up from the call, I was pulled from my thoughts. There had been no happily ever after. We chatted about his family and I let him know how important it was to stay close with relatives. All of a sudden, I found myself melancholy and continued to discuss personal matters simply for comfort. We then traded information on our hopes and dreams and I shared with him that I was a writer. Daniel was impressed. His side thing was being a member of a band. He played guitar.

After that, we discussed Carolyn's bank account. I found out there were actually *two* accounts. Carolyn and Lenny had closed one account in November 2004 and opened another in December 2004. I surmised that when Lenny received his lump sum retirement check, they opened the new account. I ordered statements going back three years on both accounts on the subpoena. I instructed Daniel that if he had any problems with the legal department releasing the information that he should call my home and leave a message.

I left the bank in route to meet with the paramedic department that went to Carolyn's home on Thanksgiving. I had arranged to pick up their records and to go over them with Mr. George Rawlings with whom I had been conversing by phone since Thursday of last week. He was in charge of records. It was crucial to have those records, but it was a pain in the ass and a driving nightmare for me. The Eastwick section of Philly was far away from Jenkintown and I still had my driving phobia. I got lost twice, but finally found the place behind a strip mall. He checked my documents and identification and then Mr. Rawlings provided me with the records.

I could barely let out a thank you before I was headed to the leather couch in the lobby. He followed me and sat on the other end of the sofa. **I carefully went over the records and asked questions about the time of** arrival to the house and the hospital. George explained military time to me. He was quite helpful. We also discussed the response time from the moment they got the distress call to the time they arrived. Five minutes. I asked if I would be able to interview the paramedics who arrived on the scene. Mr. Rawlings agreed and I would have to get in touch with the two men and schedule interviews. I couldn't locate one of the workers and the other one did not return my calls. I decided to nix them for a while. I could always get them subpoenaed for a trial or deposition.

I still needed more answers. Lenny's family basically knew nothing other than the fact that he had died and, prior to his death, Carolyn massaged his groin and fed him his Thanksgiving dinner. They had no idea of Lenny's movements from the time of his return from South Carolina on Monday November 20, 2006. Carolyn was withholding information and details from them. Theresa and Barry had prepared affidavits and had them notarized weeks ago for this case. They had been given to Tony Marino for him to examine in relation to a possible wrongful death action and the likelihood of Carolyn's negligence. If we had a case of this nature, a claim would be brought against her homeowners' insurance carrier. Those notarized affidavits stated that both Theresa and Barry had observed Carolyn snorting cocaine at their homes on many occasions. Carolyn was chastised at Theresa's house for coming out of her bathroom with a white powdery substance coming from her nostrils. Barry's affidavit indicated that he had never seen anyone in the health profession snort as much cocaine as Carolyn did on his kitchen counter and living room coffee table. He felt sorry for the patients at Pennsylvania Hospital. Three days after Lenny's death, Theresa's affidavit also stated that she had asked Carolyn about the events of the days leading to Lenny's death and the day of his death. Carolyn was evasive. Approximately a week after that interrogation, Theresa had received a call from Carolyn's friend, Daisy Brown. Daisy said to her, "Theresa, you need to stay off the phone. Stop asking so many fucking questions. You know all you need to know—and that's where you are going to be on Friday December 1, 2006. You are going to be at Carolyn's. Eleven o'clock. And from there, you are getting in a limousine—there is a seat in there for you. You put your butt in there and, other than that, I don't want to hear nothing else and no more questions." Daisy slammed the phone down.

Theresa was livid with Carolyn. She called me one night after midnight to express how it was all driving her crazy. It bothered her that her questions went unanswered. She wanted to know if her brother was upstairs or downstairs when paramedics arrived and how long had he been sick before Carolyn called 911. She wanted to know where he had gone the night before. Carolyn said they were at home together. She'd asked if he had been drinking or snorting cocaine. Carolyn said he hadn't had a thing.

All Carolyn knew was that Theresa's brother died, she massaged his groin during the day because he was in pain and fed him Thanksgiving dinner while he lay in bed too ill to have dinner at the table.

After that conversation, I jotted down a note to myself to have Carolyn's employment records subpoenaed to see if she had reported to work at any time during the week of November 20, 2006. Carolyn had been in Myrtle Beach with Lenny to bury his brother Dennis. If she was not at work after their return from the funeral, maybe she was with him all week and was not lying about that.

On Thursday March 1, 2007, my home office was open for business at seven o'clock in the morning. I had brushed my teeth, washed my face and my butt, turned on *Good Morning America,* and sat down at my computer. In two hours, Pennsylvania Hospital in Philadelphia had a fax from me. I wanted to make sure the Human Resources Manager had something to read while she sipped her morning coffee.

Dear Ms. Helfman:

Please be advised that I am the Administratrix/Executor of the Estate of Lenny Garner, Deceased and also his wife. My husband passed away on November 23, 2006 while living at the residence of Carolyn Monroe who is employed at your hospital. An investigation concerning his death is being conducted. Ms. Monroe was with my husband prior to and subsequent to him becoming ill on November 23, 2006 I have been instructed by the Register of Wills of Philadelphia County that my enclosed Short Certificate and Subpoena should be honored in order for me to gather records. I am requesting employment records regarding Ms. Monroe, more specifically the following:

a)Dates of absences including sick time, leaves of absences, vacation, personal days, family emergencies, and bereavement from 1991 through **the present date;**

b)Any complaints, reprimands or warnings from you as employer to Carolyn Monroe from 1991 through the present date;

c)An outline of Ms. Monroe's current job description and duties as well as her initial application for employment with your hospital including test scores, background checks and full information regarding the interview process prior to her being hired.

d) Copies of records relating to promotions, including reviews of her position and/or employment;

e) Copies of any and all insurance policies Ms. Monroe has on the life of a spouse or any other person describing the coverage and indicating the effective dates of said policies and how premiums are paid. This information should also include the name of the company, and policy number;

f) Verification of Ms. Monroe's salary and increases from 1991 through the present date;

g) Your opinion of her capabilities as a skilled health care professional and her ability to act in emergency situations;

h) The results of any drug testing performed by your company, more specifically cocaine and marijuana;

i) Information relating to any ongoing educational program that Ms. Monroe enrolled or participated in from 1991 to the present date. Please indicate the name of the educational institution, address, curriculum and dates of enrollment from 1991 through the present date.

Kindly telephone me at 215-555-0558 to discuss this matter.

Thank you for your attention and cooperation in this matter.

Very truly yours,
DENISE GARNER

Cc: Angela O'Neill Pelham, Esquire

I waited an hour and by nine fifteen I called the hospital to speak to Ms. Helfman. I wanted to verify the receipt of the fax. She had received it. I was going to find out every time that bitch Carolyn farted from the time she started working at that hospital. I'd already contacted Human Resources and advised them that I had signed affidavits that that bitch was on coke and that I was telling the newspapers everything. I told them that if they didn't believe me, they should have her damn hair tested for cocaine.

I put a load of laundry in the washing machine, made my bed, and did some other housework. I planned to cook some lunch in two hours and go to Mr. Dee's office to give him a $40 deposit for Theresa's upcoming reading. He charged $140 for the combo—crystal ball and tarot cards, and Theresa wanted the entire package.

The following night, I was calling Theresa, complaining and needing to vent. I was flabbergasted regarding Lenny's organs. Whatever organs he had in good health, I would have liked to donate them. That thieving wench Carolyn was something else! How could she not let his organs be donated? She signed off on that at the hospital, and I'm the wife. Noelle and I were organ donors. Carolyn wouldn't let him live and then she decided not to let anyone else live when he died. Humph. I vowed to nail that bitch no matter what! I'd be worse than Columbo on her trail. All I needed was a trench coat!

That damn Noelle! I could not keep up with her. She'd gotten out of the hospital and called me a few times. Each time we talked, she'd find a way to start a fight. She'd hang up midway through the fight and then refuse to answer when I'd call back. She was back to work full-time. If I'd call Vincent, he wouldn't call me back. Finally I'd had enough and left her a message. "Noelle, you know how psychic I am. You'd better call me. Something is going to happen. It's going to be a tragedy."

That evening she called, "What's going on?"

I was so glad to hear her voice. I was missing her and had been worried. "Listen, let's take our time and not get into an argument. You need to know a few things and I'm your mother and I love you. You know that. Now here is the deal. Something is going to happen to separate us permanently. I don't know if it will be me going away or you. But it is going to happen. God is getting tired of it, Noelle. He is about to intervene with you in some way, shape or form. He's putting a stop to the nonsense."

Noelle was silent. I had her full attention. She was interested. She knew how much shit I had predicted in the past. I heard her whimpering. "Noelle, stop crying and listen to me. This is important. You may be able to fix this."

"Mom…Mom, everything is so messed up. How can I fix anything?"

"Well, what's messed up with you? I don't know a damn thing. You don't call me. The whole family is worried. Why are you hiding? What have you done?"

"I am stressed out. I hate the job. I get sick so much. I'm always broke because I have my car note and insurance, daddy is dead, and I don't understand that whole thing. I'm mad at him. I want to go back to college to get my degree. But most of all, I hate that job, talking to all those people who call me for advice on their medications. They call in from all over the world complaining."

I felt sorry for Noelle. She began to cry hysterically. "Look, baby, pull yourself together and listen to me. The first thing you have to do is pray to God and ask him to straighten this mess out. Apologize to Him. You owe him an apology for all the rotten things you said to me and how you treated me. He knows you were wrong and does not like it. Until you apologize, shit ain't gonna turn around. Next thing to do is get yourself *organized*. Have a *plan*. Everybody needs a plan. Work from the list. Prioritize. Make a list of what you need to do. The first thing is to get your health together. Get your meds straight and keep your doctors' appointments. Get strong."

"I have a new doctor I've been going to. Why do I have to apologize to God? I didn't do anything. I go to church. I'm not apologizing because he's not mad at me."

"Okay, have it your way, but I'll tell you this: What goes around comes around. You haven't been right with me. You owe me, so that means you owe God. Do what you want, but bad luck is headed your way if you don't humble yourself. And…remember…when bad luck comes you do not know which way it flows. You pocketbook may get stolen or your car breaks down. You may get caught in the rain or you may get cancer. Maybe it'll be a robbery or a heart attack, but baby, it's coming. If you can afford to owe God and not pay up, you keep right on doing your thing. But I will tell you this—he's about to intervene and make you appreciate some things. It's coming. You are hurting yourself, me, and your family. Keep on. You'll be sorry."

She had been silent as I spoke. After that, she cried and I comforted her. I told her to stop blaming everyone for her troubles, to take a trip to Children's Hospital to see the babies with cancer if she thought she had troubles or to Walter Reed Hospital and look at the amputees if she thought her life was so bad.

"Mommy, I'm sorry. I love you. I'm coming over to spend the night on Sunday. Call my brother Lamont and have him over there, too. I'll do better."

"That's my girl! Blow your nose and I'll see you Sunday. I love you."

I was happy I was getting through to my child, but it was now back to business with my husband's aborted life. I placed a call to the 12th District Police Station in Philadelphia, which was the closest police station to Carolyn's house. I wanted my husband's shit out of that bitch's house. The officer instructed me to park my car in front of her house and call them. Then they would escort me inside. I suggested he call ahead to Carolyn, making an appointment for me to come there, but he declined reiterating I could go whenever I wanted without giving her notice. I was disappointed because I didn't know her work schedule and didn't want to drive all the way out there not knowing if we could get inside. I added that to my *To Do* list. I knew that hussy would be shocked and fuming as she watched me haul Lenny's belongings out of there.

Theresa had been so sad, distraught, and angry that I was truly worried about her. She had Lupus, worked a full-time job and was aching for her brother. She was determined to find out what happened. She swore Carolyn did *something*. Theresa was very thankful that I was so smart and so persistent. She nicknamed herself Barney Fife, my deputy. I admired Theresa's courage. She was fearless. She was seventy-two years old and ready for a war. She was not afraid to send her affidavit to Carolyn's job and was ready to testify in court. Even though she admitted that, in many ways, her brother was a shit, he did not deserve what he had gotten in the end, to be left lying in pain for three damn hours while Carolyn did nothing when doctors could have saved him. Many in her family simply wanted her to calm down and realize that Lenny was gone. Her children would tell her to let go, but she refused to give up and was totally dependent on me to come up with the answers. She said her brother was coming to her in her dreams and appearing in her kitchen pleading, "Listen to me, Theresa. Listen to me, Theresa."

When I would give her copies of documents for her records, she organized them and read through them so she would understand. She was smart and understood medical terms. She was actually a help to me. It made her feel important that she was my right hand woman in this investigation. I was her only link to her finding out what happened to Lenny because I had the power—a marriage license and short certificates. We decided to hold off from getting Lenny's belongings from the house.

We'd save that for much later and if the bitch had gotten rid of them—I'd sue her for that too.

A marriage certificate was a piece of paper that held a lot of weight. I had learned long ago to be smart and decent enough not to date a married man. Carolyn's situation taught me that a married man was ultimately worthless to the live-in in the end if death occurred—will or no will. And in Carolyn's case, I believed God was upset with her about Lenny's kids and the way she *assisted* him in alienating them from their father.

Stepmothers could truly be *The Wicked Stepmother*, excluding the husband's other children and estranging them from their fathers. Those evil witches had baseline characteristics of insecurity, jealousy, and selfishness. That was definitely the case with Carolyn. I couldn't stand that kind of shit. It fired me up royally because it was so unfair.

In Noelle's case, this kid was truly sick—with an incurable disease. She'd had forty-one hospitalizations over ten years. She saw her Dad one Christmas morning over fourteen years. Carolyn never invited Lenny's child for a holiday or a birthday. Not a birthday card came her way. Not a graduation did he attend in fourteen years, and the kid, despite her hardships, graduated valedictorian of her high school class. Had I been in Carolyn's situation, I would not have shoved my granddaughter Charmaine down the throats of Lenny and his family, my in-laws. This young lady happened to be the same age as Noelle. I would not have bragged to his family about all of the presents and attention the two of them gave Charmaine, including a car for her college graduation. Carolyn told friends and my in-laws that Lenny had purchased the car. Lenny's older daughter Tara, whom I had gone to get from New York when we first hooked up, was the same age as Carolyn's only daughter Caroline. Lenny was *Daddy* to Caroline. Tara felt like shit and used to cry about it. I was positive God was not happy with Lenny nor Carolyn.

There were times during our separation when Lenny did make attempts to be a better father to Noelle and he would visit us. Many times, the guilt was so thick inside him that he would be silent and simply let the tears stream down his face. But he was never there long because his beeper or cell phone would go off. Carolyn needed him to come wherever she was for one reason or another, interrupting his time with Noelle. Once I'd *had it* with Noelle in her teenage years and sent her over to their house. Noelle claimed she had overhead Carolyn in a rage screaming at Lenny. "I told you I did not want to be bothered with Noelle and Denise. I told you that when we hooked back up!" Theresa told me after Lenny's death that when I was in a coma with pneumonia and expected to die in 2001, Carolyn came to her house complaining and said, "I cannot get stuck with Noelle." Theresa had offered to take Noelle and raise her if I did not make it. I know Lenny, weak ass Lenny was truly at fault, but God was going to hold them both accountable. If Lenny did buy Charmaine that brand new car after he retired, I hoped he hadn't paid cash for it. It would serve her right to end up with two car notes. I checked it out and it was registered in her name like the house and everything else. Ms. Carolyn wouldn't have the monthly income she was used to collecting from my husband. I'd let her anguish over how she'd pay two car notes. I had been religiously checking on the joint bank account, and it had been overdrawn since December 2006, a month after Lenny died.

My brother-in-law, Barry Conrad, was truly irate with Carolyn and determined to get to the bottom of this caper about Lenny's death. He was crazy about *Lenny Garner*. Barry telephoned me after Lenny died and went on and on. He was adamant that Carolyn Monroe had either caused Lenny's death by giving him a medication or something in the *cut* of cocaine he had ingested. Cocaine stayed in a person's hair up to six months or even longer. Since Lenny was cremated On December 11, 2006, his hair had not been tested for the drug. His body fluids and blood, frozen by the medical examiner, were tested in January of 2007. If he had died from the coke, it would have been *recent* coke because it only stays three days in the fluids. We were certain Lenny had gotten that coke during the days after his return to Philly from Myrtle Beach. Since Carolyn was swearing to his family that they had been together all that time, she must have been with him the last time he snorted some coke.

I received word from Citizens Bank the morning on the 26th of February that everything was fine with the subpoena. I knew it would only be a matter of time when I would be examining every banking transaction Lenny and Carolyn made for the past three years. I'd also requested copies of all cancelled checks, which would enable me to track down her insurance policies on the house and determine whether she had been paying on any other life policies on Lenny. The bank records that I already had in my possession consisted of merely one statement that came to my house when I had Lenny's mail rerouted after his death. In a minute, I'd have everything.

Karen Bearden and I were still driving each other crazy. I felt Prudential wouldn't work on my claim unless I kept a fire under their asses. So, I remained relentless with my letters, memos, and phone calls and Karen stayed sick of me. On February 27 and 28, I had sent additional letters out to Karen by facsimile and also copied her legal department which was in Newark, New Jersey.

Miss Karen had insisted I could not serve Prudential with a subpoena at their Dresher Pennsylvania office fifteen minutes from my home. Their legal department was in Newark and I would have to go there to serve it. She gave me an address and no one's name who would see me or take care of the matter. She had no telephone number for her company in Newark and suggested I call directory assistance. She had no fax number—nothing. I was mad as a hornet and kept arguing, insisting she had more information until she finally came up with a telephone number. By the end of that call, I was panting like a dog after a fight.

I went though a few people at the Newark office and was finally informed that Christine Mancini handled subpoenas. I immediately faxed her copies of my prior letters to Karen along with my short certificate and a blank subpoena. I requested her review of everything and to expect my call. It was my plan to get Karen's ass in trouble. That afternoon we connected and Mancini advised me I had been given the wrong information from Karen. I could *not* serve a Pennsylvania subpoena in New Jersey. Her instructions were to contact Terri Sharp in Prudential's Dresher office when I got there with the subpoena.

Christine and I got along well and I planned to capitalize on that conquest. I felt confident and when I called Karen I'd gloat and acknowledge that she had made a mistake. I picked up my phone the very next day and we fought.

"Karen—it's Denise Garner. Why did you give me the wrong information about serving the subpoena?"

"I wasn't aware of all the facts."

"That seems to be the story of your life. I want this thing *handled* and I want it done efficiently. You've been on break since *November*."

"Don't order me around this morning. I apologize for giving you the wrong information."

"Just don't ever try to send me on any wild goose chases again."

She had schemed to purposely screw me all up and have me going all the way to Newark for nothing.

"What's going on with the *accidental* death claim due to the amended death certificate and adverse drug reaction which occurred with Lenny?"

"Your husband was sick long before his death. I have to examine his medical records."

"That's baloney about Lenny being sick. Even if he did take some illegal drugs, he damn sure didn't mean to kill himself. That was *definitely* an accident. He hadn't committed suicide and if the medical examiner ruled his death an accident, then Prudential has to pay double to the tune of twelve thousand dollars."

"I beg to differ. Hypertension was also on the new death certificate."

"The heart attack is *gone*. Don't you forget that because I won't. Let's move on to the next issue."

"And what would that be?" She said sarcastically.

"*Who* at your location was handling the file? *Who* examined the signatures from Voter's Registration and all other documents. *Who* is in charge?" I said *who* so many times in the conversation I knew I was starting to sound like an owl.

"I can't release the person's name."

I tried to negotiate down to a phone number and was unsuccessful. She remained rigid and I was so angry and exhausted from listening to her gibberish for nearly three months. Karen was worse than the CIA and getting things from her was like trying to break into Fort Knox. When I **continued to badger her and threatened to subpoena the phone number**, she got tired and succumbed, telling me to hold on.

"His name is Maurice Dean. He's at the Livingston New Jersey office where I am. He's my supervisor."

Now I was armed with a phone number. Checkmate!

Mr. Dean admitted to me that he was unable to make a decision as to whether or not Lenny had signed that Change of Beneficiary form from the City of Philadelphia. He needed *original* signatures, but I had none. Then he suggested we get the original change form from the City of Philadelphia Life Benefits Department. Damn if I was going to wait for them to write a letter or depend on Prudential to make a phone call for me. I could not deal with the Livingston New Jersey office that had ignored me since the end of November again. God had already done me a favor with Christine Mancini's office. I didn't want to get on God's nerves.

I put Mr. Dean on hold while I three-wayed the call to Nancy Tucker of the City of Philadelphia Life Benefits Department. After listening to Dean's plight, Mrs. Tucker agreed to forward the original change form to him by mail. Dean promised to return it to her after he examined it. I made up my mind to give him six business days, three for the mail and three to check it with a magnifying glass. Then I would call him back for an answer.

After that conversation was over, I went outside to check my mail. There was a letter in it from Karen. She had sent me information describing Lenny's life insurance coverage. She had *cut* and *pasted* information from her actual policy and sent it to me in a letter. I immediately called her back and wanted the *entire policy*. She said the entire policy had been sent to me by mail and to expect it soon. I went over her correspondence with her. She requested a toxicology report and a signed medical authorization. She stated in her letter that it would take a long time if she had to go through the medical examiner for the report. I felt her trying to cooperate for the first time. I liked that. I responded with a letter.

Dear Ms Bearden:

I am in receipt of your correspondence to me dated February 23, 2007, a copy of which is enclosed. I am also enclosing a copy of the requested Toxicology Report of December 23, 2006. I have also completed the Authorization for Release of my husband's medical records in case you need any additional information along those lines.

Thank you for your attention and cooperation in this matter.

Very truly yours,

DENISE GARNER

DG
Enclosures
Cc: Nancy Tucker, City of Philadelphia Life Benefits Department
  George Donyan, Pennsylvania Insurance Commission
  Detective Adam Hartman, Central Philadelphia Detectives
  Chris Brazzi, Crime Reporter, Philadelphia Daily News
  Angela O'Neill Pelham, Esquire
  Christine Mancini-Prudential Financial Legal Department/Subpoenas

I made sure she could see on the carbon copies that I was keeping everybody in the loop, including Christine Mancini in Newark. After I sent that letter, I thought about her getting to work every morning and having to put up with me. I began melting. I wondered if Karen had children and a family. I imagined her going home nights exhausted from fighting with me and other claimants. It had to be stressful. Even though she played a large part in my attitude, provoking me by calling me at seven thirty and eight o'clock in the morning with her abrupt commanding tone, I didn't want Karen to have a heart attack over people like me. She was a person and I was beginning to feel guilty for being such a bitch. I believed I was right in being aggressive and handling my business, but I decided on a surprise peace offering by sharing with her other medical records I had gathered.

I dialed her number. When she heard my voice, she fell silent. I could tell she was thinking, "What hell is she going to start up with me now?" I put on a cheerful voice said and told her I knew she needed my husband's medical records regarding his treatment rendered at Mercy Fitzgerald Hospital on the day of his death. I told her that I would fax them along with the Philadelphia Fire Department Record. I offered that paramedics responded to my husband at 8319 Union Avenue, Philadelphia, Pennsylvania on **November 23, 2007 and then took him to Mercy Fitzgerald Hospital**. If those records were not satisfactory and she would rather have them mailed to her directly from Mercy Fitzgerald, I would personally make a call to the Administrator of the hospital to ensure that her request was effectuated in a timely manner.

She eased up. "You have *all that* stuff?" Her voice was soft, minimally friendly and non abrasive. It was a refreshing and a welcomed change. I was tired of fighting and being mean. I could also sense she was impressed with me for having those documents. Little did she know, I had two accordion files that contained seventy-two sub files of information I had collected. That information consisted of medical records, notes, documents, photographs, e-mails, funeral programs, and newspaper articles. I was ready for Freddy.

I told her I had to run out to a meeting and she should check her faxes and to call me back after she reviewed the records. When I got home, there was a nice message from her indicating that she had the fax, but the hospital records were pretty hard to read. I expected that because my attorney and I had a time reading them, too. Without delay, I got on the phone with her and agreed they were blurry and that the nurse's handwriting was atrocious. She offered to give them to her clinician to decipher. I said to her, "I like our tone with each other now." She agreed and we both relaxed.

We had a long talk and I went on to explain why I had such determination in the claim. I smelled a rat with Carolyn Monroe from the beginning. I explained all the circumstances, sharing with her what my in-laws and family had been through having no real closure. I had a meeting scheduled with Mercy Fitzgerald Hospital on March 13 at 11:00 a.m. I planned to interview the nursing administrator and hopefully the triage nurse who had taken care of Lenny in the Emergency Room on Thanksgiving Day. The records sent me were illegible and I had questions. We then joked about Britney Spears being crazy. Karen was taking a few days off, returning on Tuesday of the next week. She was hoping her clinician would be able to read the records. I told her to also take a look at the paramedics report in detail and that it was typed and legible. Softening up was the best thing I could have done. We would have to work together and we couldn't accomplish much of anything by acting like bitches and uncivilized toward each other. The last thing I wanted to tell her was that Lenny had been riding around with me for the past four weeks while I collected records—his ashes in a box in my trunk. But I decided to keep that information. She may have thought I was crazy.

* * *

Luckily, I got Theresa in to see my psychic, Mr. Dee. It was a good reading and in the question and answer phase, Theresa had questions about Lenny's death. The cards showed that Carolyn would not get away with what she had done. Theresa was relieved. Now she wanted to see Sylvia, the psychic that came on the Montel Williams show all the time. Sylvia talked to the dead. She was hell bent on finding her. Theresa needed help—I was convinced of that. I talked to her about grief counseling and therapy. I was seriously trying to keep her calm. I didn't want her to have a heart attack or a Lupus flare-up. Every bit of information I collected, I shared with Theresa and let her make copies of a lot of my records. She was keeping a file and said if anything happened to me, she was going after Carolyn.

During that week, I also wrote a long letter to Lenny's brother Marvin and my sister-in-law, Ellen, in Tucson Arizona. They were the last family members to speak to him alive. I brought them up to speed on what was going on. I sent them two of my books, autographed so they could show off, along with copies of his toxicology report and paramedic report.

The Philadelphia Daily News Crime Reporter Chris Brazzi spoke to me during that week, too. I called him with an update. Instead of running the story soon, we decided to hold off because an abundance of information was being gathered. We both agreed that we had an intriguing and powerful story and it was surely heating up. We wanted to wait until we had all Lenny's records and I got through the meetings I had scheduled. All our ducks had to be in a row, and then I'd strike.

CHAPTER 12

❦

Relentless

I also planned to attack Ms. Carolyn down the road in Small Claims Court. If Tony Marino could get her on a Wrongful Death claim for not performing her *nursely* duties while my husband was dying on Thanksgiving Day, her homeowner's insurance policy would surely come into play because Lenny didn't *own* the house. His name wasn't on anything. He died in *her* house. If we could prove negligence on her part, that would be an additional blow to nursey pie's head. To boot, her insurance premiums would go up sky high if her carrier didn't cancel her thieving ass who'd stolen families and lives. The way I figured, she'd be out at the next renewal of the policy. She was probably carrying at least a hundred grand in coverage on that property. I could live with that. As it turned out, the tryst Lenny had back in the day with a co-worker produced a son, Lamont. Those funds I would obtain from the wench's homeowner's company would certainly put fifteen-year old Lamont and twenty-two year old Noelle in college for a couple of years. The rest could be split up between me and the other kids Lenny fathered.

Carolyn never gave a shit about those kids—she didn't even know Lamont's *name*. She had him listed as *Winton* on the funeral/memorial program she had put together after Lenny died, the memorial with *no* body. She was such a jerk. I figured that the Judge from Small Claims Court would grant me my five hundred forty one bucks back, if nothing else. If the bitch couldn't pay up, my intention was to obtain a judgment against her and put a lien on her house. I remembered the words of my girl Ivana Trump. "Don't get mad, get everything."

On February 28, 2007 I sent a letter to the Pension Board. Carolyn owed them $541.31 for cashing Lenny's pension check after he died. They had already sent her a letter in January to this effect, but I didn't want them to forget about her.

As the real Mrs. Lenny Garner, I let the Board Administrator know that I had received my first pension check on February 16, 2007 in the amount of $2591.27, covering the months of December 2006 and January 2007.

I wondered if Carolyn had responded to the Pension Board's letter to date. Since I was the Administratrix and Executor of Lenny's Estate, I wanted documents and information confirming the exact amount of money Lenny had received in the lump sum payment from the *DROP program*. In my last conversations with the pension administrator, Mrs. Katherine Young, she was going to contact their legal department to determine if I would need to subpoena the information. They had been so cooperative with me in the past and I had a good rapport with them. I was requesting *all* sorts of records relating to Lenny's pension account including contributions, withdrawals, and disbursements. I didn't want to go too *legal* with them by threatening them.

My take was that Carolyn had been desperate, broke, and tired. I strongly suspected she had either given Lenny medication for blood pressure or a medication that could have caused him to become ill and die. I just could not figure it out nor prove it, so I decided to write an additional letter to Pennsylvania Hospital requesting more information. To single her out, I had to rule out that our insurance plan was paying for medication or paying doctors' bills for Lenny, and that no health official was monitoring him for the medications other than Carolyn. I sent letters to both companies.

The more I thought about the possibility of Carolyn supplying Lenny with medication for his high blood pressure, the more I figured it out. She actually took the meds out of the hospital where she worked or had him on her health plan through her employer. For the past twenty-two months from February of 2005 through November of 2006, no pharmacies had issued any medications to Lenny. I had not checked them all, but Rite Aid hadn't filled a prescription for him since February of 2005. Lenny was a creature of habit and went to Rite Aid for years for his medications. To be thorough, however, I planned to call other chains. I kept in mind that even if I did make the calls, pharmacies filled by prescriptions *only* for blood pressure medications.

I ran a check with Aetna. Lenny, Noelle, and I had our prescription plan with them. So far, they had no record of any medications they paid for him since February of 2005 when he was admitted to Pennsylvania Hospital for that allergic reaction. That was the last time they filled anything or had any claim for his treatment. I sent Aetna a subpoena and my short certificate, as well as a completed form for their legal department. I wanted them to go back five years to search all his claims and let me know when and whom they paid for his medications and treatment.

Pennsylvania Hospital got subpoenaed for information on life benefits under Carolyn's policy to check if she had made any claims for death benefits. I also subpoenaed her health insurance plan to find out if Lenny was insured under her health policy and if he got meds for high blood pressure through her prescription plan. Lenny should have been dead of a heart attack or a stroke *long* ago if he had gone off blood pressure meds for twenty-two months prior to his death. That bitch lied when she told hospital and paramedics on the day he died that she knew nothing of him taking any medications. I detested her, just plain could not stand her ass and was obsessed with nailing her.

The Human Resources Department at Pennsylvania Hospital got a subpoena from me requesting records on Carolyn. I wanted MEGA information. During Carolyn Monroe's employment with their hospital, had they had any knowledge of anyone employed at Pennsylvania Hospital who was assigned to monitor, distribute, and/or handle the accounting of drugs and/or medication in the areas of the hospital on the dates and during the shifts when Carolyn was assigned to care for patients? Had the Skilled Care Facility ever been informed, notified, or advised by telephone, verbally (face to face), e-mail or by formal written report or handwritten note that any drugs and/or medications were unaccounted for, missing, lost, stolen and/or if any shortages of drugs and/or medications occurred or were reported, during or after any her shifts? If they came across anything, I wanted the dates, times, nurse's stations or places, and, more importantly, the names of the drugs and any documentation relating them.

Also to discredit her regarding the Complaint she filed against me in 1993, I was on the hunt for a security guard. Carolyn alleged in that Complaint he was on duty when I showed up there, and he had to restrain me. This never happened. I believed she paid him to give a report so she would have more muscle to win that suit against me. Pennsylvania Hospital would now have to provide me with information regarding Cornelius Hector, the Director of Security named in the Complaint. I wanted his dates of employment and current job classification. If he no longer worked for them, I wanted information to contact him by mail and phone. I planned to have his ass deposed by Tony and scare the shit out of him. I believed he lied for Carolyn and if I could prove it, that would make her look even worse. I'd let everyone know. My uncovering her in *any* way would be marks against her character.

The plan was I would wait until AETNA, the health carrier got back to me on the claims made for treatment of Lenny, then I'd try to track down some more pharmacies. Lenny had to be getting medication from somewhere.

To impeach Carolyn's credibility, I needed to prove she was a liar. She'd been lying all her fucking life. If this woman swore she knew nothing about him being on any meds, I had better not find through a pharmacy search that she had ever gone to pick up meds for him at a pharmacy. People sent a family member to pick up their prescriptions all the time. I was determined to find out if she had done that.

I had to be careful. If I wanted to go after the wrongful death claim, I had to be sure she was negligent in their eyes and didn't mean to cause his death. I was playing both sides. Deceit and lying would get me the policy for the life insurance and negligence would get me the100K on the wrongful death claim against her homeowners' insurance carrier. Conspiracy would get Carolyn's ass in jail for me, my kids, and my in-laws. On the back burner, I had a pot brewing to try to retain a powerful domestic relations attorney who specialized in family law. I'd have that attorney file a civil action against her for home wrecking—down and out destroying my marriage. I'd be crying my eyes out when they deposed me and snot would be running out of my nose like water. I'd make sure I had pretty handkerchiefs and not tissues. I'd have Noelle and Theresa there weeping with me along with Lenny's sister Rhonda who had brain damage. She'd be babbling away not knowing what the hell happened or what was going on. All she'd know was that she was looking for her brother who used to take care of her. I'd explain to the court how I almost lost my life in 2001 and my damn house in 2006. Once I got a judgment against that bitch, I'd make sure I took *her* house.

I'd already started preparing for cases down the road and had a list of Interrogatories that I planned to serve up. Then I'd move on to having her deposed. She'd think 59 times before fucking with somebody else's husband.

So far, everyone was being very cooperative with me in accepting the Short Certificates and Subpoenas.

Apparently a little sugar and bonding with Karen Bearden from Prudential worked. I sent an e-mail to Tony Marino, copying Angela, the Estate lawyer, and Philadelphia Daily News Crime Reporter Chris Brazzi.

TO: Tony Marino
From: Denise Garner
Cc: Chris Brazzi
  Angela O'Neill Pelam, Esquire
  Hi Tony:

  Victory at Prudential.
  Today is Saturday, March 10, 2007. I got a call from Karen TODAY. On damn Saturday! She was at work working on this thing. She said it is going to Court. They cannot figure out which person to pay the policy to—Carolyn or me so a judge will decide. The handwriting samples aren't helping them— though they thought they would. She said I will be hearing from her counsel on this. I told her Thank You and this is a good thing for me.
  Now, I am hoping your mean smart ass will take over this part. You can burn Carolyn's ass and I know it. I want her credibility impeached. I don't even give a damn about the $ any more. She was responsible for his death one way or the other. Either negligence in calling the Paramedics too late OR she got him

with some medication or drugs. She did something or DID NOT do something that helped his ass to die. I want to burn her ass!

Now I want us to make a firm decision as to who will go into Court on this and run things. If you don't do it—I want to go in Pro Se. Nobody can handle this better than you and/or I. Nobody is as mean as us. If I have to go in—you have to guide me. Also I'll have to get permission from the Court to go Pro Se. I have done this only once in my life for my brother. I won. The judge thought I was awesome.

Once we get a Court Term and number, we can serve that bitch with ROGS—detailed INTERROGATORIES. I already started them a month ago. Angela and I had talked about this when she first decided to do the Estate thing.

This Prudential case has nothing to do with the action you may be able to bring against her homeowner's carrier, right? That I believe is entirely separate—another case against her and another pot of money for me.

Nancy Tucker, Philly Life Benefits—Yep—Testifying for US. Remember Carolyn told her a bunch of lies and got caught.

Pension Board is on board with me. Director of Pension Board (the big cheese) sent me a letter I got today. They reiterated they are going after her for the check she cashed and they said for me to get my subpoena ready for them. They will give me all info on the lump sum retirement $ Lenny got in 2004.

I am still waiting for the bank statements on the joint account of Lenny and Carolyn. That's 3 years of statements from Citizens Bank. They have my subpoena.

Still waiting for Pennsylvania Hospital to give up their records on Carolyn's health insurance and employment records. Last I talked to Pennsylvania's counsel, he thought he could give me health and life insurance info on Carolyn to help determine if Lenny was on her health coverage. Regarding the employment stuff, her employer does not have to give employment records under the Register of Wills case. Their subpoena I got from Register of Wills. PA Hospital said we **have to have another case to get those records.**

Angela: You told me to research the "Good Samaritan Law" to find out if it exists in Pennsylvania. The answer is YES. So, I guess under that law we may be able to go after Carolyn for not being a Good Samaritan and getting his ass to the hospital when he was dying. We'll play that card if we have to.

Still waiting for Aetna (Lenny and my health carrier) to send me info regarding all his claims for treatment over last five years.

Tony: You wanted to make sure I was the valid/legal wife. The answer is YES. There is no problem with that whatsoever. Pension checks are now coming and there is NO question whatsoever with that. Lenny was living with her still married to me the whole time. The marriage between them is not valid.

As soon as I get the correspondence concerning Prudential putting this in Court—I will make sure you and Angela have copies of everything.

Chris Brazzi-Philly Daily News: Just hold tight Mister. This thing is heating up.
See ya!
Denise

I decide to let my girl Liz know what was going on. I was so excited and couldn't sleep. I gave her a call. The phone rang six times.

"Get up. I know its four thirty in the morning but I can't sleep."

"I know you are crazy calling me this time of morning. I have to get up in three hours for work. Go away. I was on line until one thirty this morning."

"I've got news. Come on. Get alert."

Liz started muttering and sighing. "What…what is it?"

I told her all the dirt and my plans for destroying Carolyn. She started lapping it all up. After fifteen minutes, I finally shut up.

Liz was howling laughing. "Girl, I just love you. You told that Daily News guy to just hold tight, Mister. I love it! I know he has never dealt with the likes of someone like you. Girl, you don't need to work for anybody else as a private eye. You need to open your own agency and have people working for you. I would love to test read this case because I feel so connected to it. Hell, I'm not doing much court work anyway and my days are numbered there. You just wore that insurance woman down. I know you drove her crazy, but I bet you one thing, she has a whole lot of respect for you. I'm glad things are falling into place. Maybe you ought to go to law school. Hell, you make your lawyers' jobs easy."

* * *

I did some more detective work. My findings totally convinced me that Carolyn was giving Lenny medication. She could have even caused the allergic reaction that he suffered when he was admitted to the hospital on February 10, 2005. If it was the doctor who had fucked up and given him the wrong medication, causing that problem, why didn't Lenny mention that when he got sick? When his doctor was prescribing medications all along, Lenny had no problems. He'd never been admitted for anything! I had researched this thoroughly. I found out that Lenny was NOT on Carolyn Monroe's prescription plan through Pennsylvania Hospital. She got her prescriptions filled at Pennsylvania Hospital's Out Patient Pharmacy. She was insured with Pharmacare and they paid her claims for her prescriptions. Once the Pennsylvania Hospital's Out Patient Department verified that Lenny had never received any prescriptions from them, I started schmoozing with the rep and I got more information. By the time I was done playing girlfriend with her and listening to her problems, she had given me Carolyn's Social Security number and told me what medications she was on and when *her* last prescription was filled. This shit was scary in another way, as I realized that people could find out anything they wanted about another person. There was little privacy in the world today. After I got Pharmacare's direct number from her, I called them.

Lenny was not on their plan or in their system at all. I made them check all records. No prescriptions for Lenny Garner were found and he was not listed as Carolyn's husband. Aetna, my carrier was giving me the same story. However, I was waiting for the arrival of the official records. If both prescription companies confirmed no blood pressure medication since February of 2005, I knew we couldn't prove it. That bitch Carolyn, however, had to be bringing that shit out of the hospital. I didn't know when she started doing it, but I did know this—he was admitted to the ICU in February of 2005 for an allergic reaction to a medication and very sick. If she was giving him meds prior to that admission, she could have caused that shit. In the Pennsylvania Hospital records, Lenny told doctors he was on blood pressure med for a number of years, at least 15 years as per the records. Where the fuck was he getting that stuff after 2005? Mexico? I think *NOT.*

I also realized that the reason Carolyn and Lenny did not share health insurance plans was because the bitch knew she wasn't really married to him and that I was alive and still in touch with members of his family. She didn't want to risk me finding out that he had gotten sick. She knew I'd appear and start interrogating doctors, just like he did when I had pneumonia and when I got in an accident. But what got me was the nerve of them two standing up in a church all dressed up and lying their asses off. I'd be scared to mess with God like that. If I had been monitoring Lenny and his money, calling all the time for something and asking questions about why he was broke and where all his money was going, she would never have been able to pull this shit off. I was glad that back in the day, in 1991 when Lenny and I were dipping and dabbing with each other and decided on getting back together that I had made his ass stay there with that hussy until Valentines Day. I told him I didn't want his ass back home with me until Valentines Day evening. That bitch had a crying fit when he came home to her after work that day and immediately packed his shit while she was standing there with cards and gifts for him. He simply walked in and announced that he was going home to his wife and daughter. She had a fucking fit and threatened to kill herself. I wish she had. He told me she had climbed up onto a chest of drawers and dove off into a wall. When he got to our house, I was waiting for him in a red nightie. I fucked his brains out and laughed at the bitch while I was doing it. She called Theresa that night crying and said she was through with him.

* * *

It was now time to follow up with Mercy Fitzgerald regarding the records that were illegible. I was sharp as a tack when I showed up at the hospital for my meeting to decipher the records on March 13th. I planned on taking very detailed notes and would make them go through every procedure with me.

I met with Dr. Alexandria Sheridan and a nurse to discuss the medical records, ask questions, and figure out the triage nurse's handwriting. We went through each page of the record. The triage nurse's handwriting was indeed atrocious. I listened to them and took notes.

"Mrs. Garner, your husband was agonol upon Emergency Medical Services' arrival at Carolyn Monroe's home," the doctor said.

I was never ashamed to ask a question and said, "What does *agonal* mean?"

She smiled. "It means he had limited respiration, his breathing was very limited."

I jotted that down on my legal pad. She continued, "Upon arrival, he was pulseless and asystolic."

More comfortable because she was friendly, I said "What's the meaning of asystolic?"

"Oh, that's real simple. It just means he had no pulse. These records also indicate that paramedics tried to resuscitate him before he got here. They assessed him and he was in cardiac arrest. Your husband's pupils were also non-reactive."

I continued to write as fast as I could and tried to listen and understand at the same time. "His history was given by paramedics and the initial complaint was that he collapsed. There was no bystander CPR, meaning no one gave him CPR at Carolyn's house before paramedics arrived. Paramedics did the CPR."

Anger infused me. I understood at that moment that the bitch, the ICU skilled nurse who loved him, didn't even bother to try to revive Lenny. I shook my head in disgust. I was dying to get Tony on a speakerphone and let him listen to this shit.

The doctor noticed I was upset and offered to give me a break, but I declined. She resumed. "Mrs. Garner, the treatment your husband received before he got to Mercy Fitzgerald was oxygen with a mask and he was intubated with the breathing tube. This intubation was done by **paramedics before he arrived here. He also received medication prior to his** arrival."

I wanted to know every detail. "What medications did he get?"

"He got Epinephrine, which is adrenalin. This was a resuscitation medication to get his heart restarted. He was also given Atropine which is also a resuscitation drug to get his heart to pump. Regarding his past medical history, Mercy Fitzgerald personnel was told he had hypertension. The doctor was unclear as to whether he had that illness. That information came from paramedics. So I suspect Carolyn Monroe told Paramedics that when they got to her house, they passed that on to our personnel. Regarding his initial exam, there was no evidence of trauma. Breath sounds were equal with the breathing tube. This means the breathing tube was working and doing its job. This does *not* mean that Mr. Garner was breathing. He still had no pulse at that point."

"Well, since he wasn't dead, what did you guys do for him when he got here?"

"CPR was performed at that point. A central line was placed. This is a *big* IV used to give medication. We couldn't save him, so the Medical Examiner was called."

The staff in the emergency room did not question Carolyn. Hands on personnel didn't even know if Carolyn was there. They never spoke to her. They never asked questions about the medication Lenny was taking. Mercy Fitzgerald dealt with and relied on the information they got from the paramedics. Paramedics got their information from Carolyn when they arrived at her house and from the information they received on the phone when she called for a rescue squad.

I sat with my face in my hands. "*Wow,*" I said out loud. I had a question. "If he had been given CPR earlier or if Carolyn Monroe had called ahead to the paramedics or here at the hospital and advised that he had cocaine in his system, would you guys have been able to save his life. I mean if he'd gotten some Benadryl or something, could my husband have been saved?"

The doctor was reluctant to answer, but I would not take my eyes off her. I knew she was smelling a lawsuit. "Listen, I'm, not going after you guys. You did what you could with what you had to work with. Carolyn Monroe is an ICU nurse. That's who I'm after. Trust me. Now, please, answer my question."

"She looked in my eyes and, lowering her voice, said, "It's quite possible he would have made it if we had more information before he got here."

We made it through to the end of the records. I became riled up again when I saw that an organization called Gift of Life was assigned to get organs. In Lenny's records a check mark indicated the family refused organ donation. Carolyn had apparently refused to give his organs. I was seething. The Patient Registration Form indicated no telephone number. Mercy Fitzgerald wasn't sure how they got any information, but I figured it came from Lenny's wallet or belongings. They were not sure either if Carolyn had provided any information for this form. At the meeting, we also chatted about whether Lenny had been a prior patient at the hospital, which would perhaps explain where they got insurance information to bill Aetna. It was unclear. What the heck would Lenny be doing with a wallet if he went to hospital in his underwear and a robe?

Another thing the records confirmed was that Lenny and I were on the same card and listed me as spouse. Regarding the Consent For Hospital Treatment, Carolyn signed for treatment. According to procedure, the Insurance Department at Mercy Fitzgerald signed Lenny in, and later a representative from that department came and found Carolyn for insurance information. I wanted to find out who this person was because they'd know what Carolyn's demeanor had been and if she'd had that actual insurance card. I wondered if they had copied it. After adjourning our meeting, I called Detective Adam Hartman to give him the information. This would help to build his case against Carolyn.

The next day, I went on a hunt to find the paramedics. One of the workers was teaching at the Academy and was not available, and no one knew the whereabouts of the other one, so they told me. My plan was to subpoena the two men for a statement if necessary. I would be unstoppable.

After staying on top of Geico for the following two days with phone calls, I finally received a call on Friday, March 16th from Henrietta Faulkner. She was brand new on the matter and had reopened the case. She needed a lot of information from me. That White woman was astonished to hear my story about the two wives. I made sure she understood who the real wifey-poo was. They had some problems about liability, like whose fault the accident was. Both cars involved in the accident were insured by her company. I put in my two cents and helped her to understand that either Carolyn or the other driver was at fault, and I really didn't care about that. I knew who *wasn't* at fault because *he* was a *passenger* being driven around by *Ms. Carolyn Monroe*. It didn't matter to me that they insured both cars involved in the accident. There was damage to the car my husband was in and there was a police report *documenting* his injuries. She would not give me any personal information on the policy claims history of their insured, Carolyn Monroe, or the Declaration Sheet for either policy. I backed off on that and was sweet. I knew if push came to shove, I could subpoena *all* the damn files. Ms. Faulkner promised to call me back in two days to discuss settlement. Good work Deputy Fife for hipping me to the fact that there had been an accident. Checkmate!

CHAPTER 13

〜

The Mean Green

The possible Wrongful Death claim was still in the works. I wasn't going to miss a beat in any attempt to hang Carolyn's ass. Every time I thought about those three hours Lenny spent in her fucking house needing medical assistance on Thanksgiving Day, I got a surge of energy and a shot of adrenaline. I was fired up. As I sifted through the bank statements and cancelled checks, I came across a cancelled check for Carolyn's mortgage payment. I decided to give the mortgage company a call. I wanted records and information on the loan, specifically information received by her company regarding the funds paid to purchase the property. Were any funds paid by my husband? I pointed out to the clerk on the phone that I did understand that my husband's name wasn't on the loan itself and asked her to forward copies of any and all cancelled checks which Ms. Monroe had provided as down payments and/or settlement fees, appraisal costs, application fees. Information regarding the name, address, policy number of all homeowner's companies, which insured the property throughout the inception of the loan, were requested along with a copy of the current policy and the policy in effect at the time of my husband's death. Lastly, I asked for a copy of the loan payment history and wanted her to find out if the homeowner's insurance payment was incorporated in the loan payment. After we hung up, I immediately faxed her a copy of a completed subpoena, my marriage certificate, a short certificate and Lenny's death certificate. No stone was left unturned.

∗ ∗ ∗

On March 14th, I received a call from Katherine Young of the Pension Board. She explained they had tried to fax me on March 13th. My subpoena would be delivered directly to Regina Murdock, Senior Legal Assistant, who would contact me to schedule a meeting during the week of March 19th to pick up the documents pertaining to Lenny's DROP money. They would continue to pursue recovery of the payment made to Carolyn Monroe. I scheduled an appointment to meet with Regina on the 21st of March. Those records would indeed solve the mystery as to exactly how much money Lenny received when he retired. I could not wait for our meeting.

I got an e-mail from the Pension Board. Carolyn had made a payment to me through them. I was shocked. It was $50.00 toward the overpayment she caused in my pension account when she cashed that last check after Lenny's death. That hussy was just trying to cover her ass in case we ended up in court. She wanted the judge to see she was *trying*. I thought about all those checks she wrote from his pension and Lenny not being able to breathe on Thanksgiving Day. I made myself a note to be sure I made it down to file the claim against her in Small Claims for that $541.31. Fuck her!

Noelle was being a good girl for Mommy and very supportive. She wasn't helping me with the case against Carolyn, but she continued to work full-time while looking for another position. She had enrolled in college and was to start back to school early in the summer. She'd paid for her classes herself. She was trying to become more independent, she said. That was my girl!

It was a busy week! I received a call from Citizens Bank for me to come to the bank to pick up additional documents regarding the joint account Lenny and Carolyn had. They had already supplied me with over a hundred pages of documents the week before. When I examined them, I was stunned! I typed up a report for Tony and the police department. My intention was to discuss it with the police to see if I could have them build a case against Carolyn. These were cancelled checks from of December 2004. Even the bank manager was alarmed that twenty checks were written between December 17, 2004 and February 14, 2005, nearly exhausting Lenny's pension! She had purchased everything from pizza to fake hair. There were also ATM withdrawals ranging from five hundred to fifteen hundred dollars per day.

I was floored! Two damn cars and sixty-five dollars worth of pizza, among other things. In a twenty-four hour period of time, that bitch had spent $27,460.68 and continued to go strong after that! I went straight from the bank to Barry's job with those checks. Between December 17, 2004 and February 14, 2005, she had gone through $36,100.31. This occurred in less than two months! Barry was absolutely livid and wanted to go to the police station. Instead, I went home and he called Theresa. I thought she was going to have a heart attack when she called me. There was no doubt that Lenny's drugged up stupid ass had been under Carolyn's *complete* control. This made me think of the O'Jays' song. I couldn't get that song out of my mind.

> *Money money money money, MONEY*
> *Some people got to have it*
> *Hey, Hey, Hey – some people really need it*
> *Hey, listen to me, y'all do thangs, do thangs, do thangs – bad thangs with it*
> *Well, you wanna do thangs, do thangs, do thangs – good thangs with it – yeah*
> *Un Huh, talkin' bout cash money, money*
> *Talkin' bout cash money – dollar bills y'all – come on, now*
> *For the love of money*
> *People will steal from their mother*
> *For the love of money*
> *People will rob their own brother*
> *For the love of money*
> *People can't even walk the streets*
> *Because they'll never know who in the world they're gonna beat*
> *For that mean, oh mean, mean green*

Since I was aware that he was using and abusing drugs and alcohol, it would be the understatement of the year to say she was able to manipulate him. I had been contemplating *everything*, especially since I'd been reading the book *Addiction* in which Professor Anna Rose Childress supplied research and findings on people who abused drugs and alcohol. One passage remained in my mind. *"When the primary focus of someone's life is getting and using a substance that alters their way of thinking, everything else eventually falls by the wayside. Personal relationships are strained, education is interrupted or ended, and bills go unpaid. Drug addiction is especially insidious because it affects the very brain areas that people need to "think straight," apply good judgment and make good decisions for their lives. Eventually the drive to seek and use the drug is all that matters despite devastating consequences. Control and choice and everything that once held value in a person's life, such as family, job, community, are lost to the disease of addiction."*

I had learned through reading his book that addiction was a sickness, like diabetes or Crohn's. It was an honest to God *illness* and affected the brain. Lenny had been using for at least thirty years. I looked over the bank statements and, between Carolyn and Lenny, they substantiated ATM withdrawals three to seven times a day and sometimes to the limit of five hundred dollars a day. Of course, Lenny was at fault also, but his main problem was that he was with an extremely clever woman from jumpstreet—since *way* back in the day. He was totally out of his league with Carolyn. His situation was even more serious, his well-being *detrimental* under her influence. That combined with being unfocused made a grave situation turn deadly. Unfortunately, Lenny was not in the arms or bedded down with a person truly concerned about his future, security, or his health. That certainly compounded his problems. He paid for it in the end, reaping what he sowed. He stepped on a lot of people whether his brain was operating correctly or not. Carolyn hit the jackpot with Lenny Garner.

That Change of Beneficiary form was supposedly signed by him in November of 2004. Since I had examined the first set of bank records, I knew they were in deep financial shit in 2006 prior to his death. In November of 2006, they were basically broke. They required financial assistance from family members and were borrowing money from them. That lump sum DROP payment came in December of 2004 and in March of 2005, Lenny had to drain a City Savings Fund program account of $4,800.

My theory was that Carolyn was really sick of Lenny. She saw a way out with insurance proceeds, pension, and social security benefits. I believed she had him pay her car off when he received his DROP money, got her house fixed up, purchased a car for her granddaughter, and, bought furniture for her home, was all ready to get herself *set up*. He lay in her house on

Thanksgiving Day for three hours and she didn't call paramedics or take his vital signs because he was better off to her being dead. Carolyn Monroe never called one family member to let them know paramedics were on the way to her house or that Lenny was fighting for his life in the hospital. She did not notify any family members until she returned home from the emergency room and he was dead and gone.

I was building an air-tight case against Carolyn. I also obtained a sworn affidavit from my buddy Liz Edwards. Liz confirmed in the affidavit that on Saturday, December 9, 2007, she attended Lenny's funeral at Julian Hawkins Funeral Home in Philadelphia. She was at the funeral from 12:15 p.m. until approximately 2:15 p.m. She didn't attend the repast. Instead, she had a meeting to attend with the Parents Association of her daughter's school. After that, on her way to Springfield, Pennsylvania, she stopped at the B.B's Que Shot Lounge located at 527 Baltimore Pike, East Lansdowne, Pennsylvania to catch up with a good friend of hers, Sophia, one of the barmaids working that day. Sophia used to be the manager of Leroy's Showcase at 4912 Baltimore Avenue in Philadelphia, a place that Lenny and Carolyn frequented. Sophia's work schedule prevented her from attending the funeral, so Liz wanted to show her the funeral program. While in this establishment, Liz countered Daisy Brown. She had known Daisy for a number of years, but wasn't aware of her relationship to Carolyn Monroe. Daisy asked to see the funeral program.

I learned that on the night of Lenny's death, Daisy received a call from a hysterical Carolyn. "Something was wrong with Lenny; she thought he was dead and needed her to come there." Daisy was on the road and could not get back over there to her house and Daisy proceeded to call another friend to go to Carolyn's assistance. It was Liz's impression that Daisy had been at Carolyn's and Lenny's house earlier that day. Ms. Brown also stated to Liz that, as his wife, Carolyn already had a Memorial Service **for Lenny and that she (Daisy) had played an integral part in the planning** of the service. Liz wasn't shocked that a Memorial service was planned and an invitation was not extended to me, but wondered how they could plan a memorial service and not extend an invitation to his daughter, Noelle. Daisy Brown had taken over the planning of the service because Carolyn was in no shape to do so. She made some type of statement that

Carolyn didn't know Lenny had not been divorced. This struck Liz as odd simply because when you applied for a marriage license, you usually applied as a *couple* and was asked if any of the partners had ever been married. If so, a copy of the certified divorce decree had to be submitted. Liz told Ms. Brown that she was a friend of Lenny's wife, *Denise*, and that because I was the legal wife, I would probably reap the benefits of his life insurance from the city and his pension. Liz also added that if Lenny was in the DROP and/or Deferred Compensation program for city employees that it was possible that *Denise Garner*, his legal wife, would also be entitled to that.

Daisy stated something to the effect that Carolyn was *not worried about money*, that she would be alright, that she got *hers* or words to that effect. Daisy didn't go into specific details of what Carolyn meant by those words.

$$* * *$$

I believed Carolyn kept him drugged up and drunk, and that was a way of controlling him. I was still waiting for *more* bank records, but continued to study what I had in a feverish manner. I noticed that her granddaughter Charmaine's college tuition was paid for at Delaware State University, including her apartment rental of $560.00 a month. Everything Carolyn had on paper, the house and cars, were all in her name only. Lenny had nothing he could recover from Carolyn Monroe if they split up. She had personally seen to that. The mistake Carolyn made was that she underestimated his *wife*. Because his *wife* was absent and wasn't keeping tabs on him and nickel and diming him, she thought she could get away with her plan.

I had a long conversation with Detective Adam Hartman of Philadelphia Central Detectives. I enjoyed talking to him about this. The handsome Caucasian detective had dark brown hair and brown eyes. He was about six feet tall and had a little pouchy tummy. He wasn't a flamboyant dresser, but neatly dressed. He wore a regular suit, not designer. It was a surprise to me when I found out he was *White* because he talked—*sounded*—just like a brother. When I met him, I was truly shocked. He was very informative.

We had been sharing information on the telephone for two months and always listened to each other's theories.

"You know, Denise, I've checked Carolyn Monroe out. Even though she has a clean police record, I know she's dirty."

"Well, I do believe she's a witch and has been up to something all along, but what's on your mind. Anything new," I asked.

"The first marriage is kind of a mystery. She was married to a man prior to hooking up with Lenny, but we could not locate any information on him. We suspected she had killed him, too."

My eyes lit up. My thought was *"Whoa*—the shit was getting deep for real if Hartman truly suspected that. I'd also found out about her previous marriage when I reviewed the application for marriage she completed when she married Lenny. She indicated no name or city for the other husband and kept her maiden name—Monroe.

Detective Hartman and Chris Brazzi toyed with the possibility that she was a Black Widow. Chris Brazzi tried to track the other husband down in Atlanta and couldn't come up with a thing on him. He then got busy with other homicides in Philly and had to get off my case, but Detective Hartman was relentless. If Lenny had not died in Delaware County, Philly would have had jurisdiction on the case. Detective Hartman could have opened up an investigation and blew it out. Carolyn would have had a better shot at digging up Johnnie Cochran and bringing him back to life to defend her than getting Detective Adam Hartman off her ass. He was thoroughly convinced she caused Lenny's death.

Detective Hartman taught me how to go through cell phone bills and watch patterns of numbers. I learned that there are books, phone books detectives use that give you all types of information on cross-referencing cell and home numbers and addresses of people. I spent time with him at the precinct and he assisted me by going through all my documents. Insofar as the cocaine being in his system, Lenny had done coke for years and Detective Hartman explained that Lenny's body had built up a tolerance for the coke and alcohol.

"Denise when your husband died, tests showed he had a minimal coke in his system. That little bit of coke did not kill him."

He had my full attention, but I needed to jump in. "Listen, the bank statements were very interesting, too. They have me going. Of all the checks written, he signed very few, less than ten checks. From looking at them my guess is he would write a check and then wait for her to come to sign it. This was a joint account. She must have told him that he could write checks, but she'd have to okay them."

"I'll buy that," he answered. "And, look, let me tell you something about poisoning a person. It can be done over a period of time in small dosages and placed in a person's food."

I was drinking this knowledge. I'd never known this stuff and it was fascinating.

Lenny's sister Theresa informed me that she had met with Lenny on many occasions on a weekly basis during 2006. He was contemplating leaving Carolyn and was not happy with her. They had talked about him *"making a change."* And then there was *Debbie.* He had introduced her to Theresa and other members of his family. She was a major player—she'd been seeing him for five years. Maybe Carolyn knew about her. I know from examining the cell phone bills that Lenny was definitely *missing* a lot and Carolyn was trying to find him on her cell. I studied those bills like I was preparing for a college exam.

Lenny may have been planning to make a move in 2006. I wonder if that's what he wanted to talk to me about in August of 2006. I left messages for him on his home phone in late September 2006 that simply said, "Call me. I got your message from Noelle." Carolyn could have thought he was seeing me, too. Little did I know that those messages coming in on Noelle's cell number were from my old boyfriend Lenny *Sawyer.* I didn't find out the truth until December when Sawyer e-mailed me to curse me out because "he'd left messages on Noelle's phone and didn't like the idea that I wouldn't return his calls." I realized that I was responding to the wrong *Lenny.* Noelle hadn't told me *"Daddy"* called. She said *"Lenny"* called. I assumed that because she wasn't speaking to her Dad, she was calling him *"Lenny."*

I kept wondering throughout this investigation what my husband had wanted to talk to me about in August of 2006 when I didn't show up at Zena's father-in-law's house. But I did know one thing—I was not in love

with him and I would never have taken him back. I would have helped
him—rehab, support system—anything else. I would have seen that he
went to the doctor and monitored his care. But I had moved on. We didn't
have much in common. I wasn't friendly with alcohol. I was merely an
acquaintance that allowed it to show up in my life temporarily, maybe
numerous times within a year for amusement purposes. I valued my safety
and there were only certain classes of people that I liked, I had my own
standards—so I wouldn't frequent any hole in the wall bars that attracted
the riff raff. As for drugs, I detested them. I didn't even socialize with people
that used. A few lines of coke to snort and some joints were fine way back
in the day. I loved it. But after Richard Prior set his ass on fire, me and the
blow had a big falling out and never made up.

Detective Hartman smelled a giant rat when Carolyn failed to inform
paramedics or hospital personnel at Mercy Fitzgerald that Lenny had
been in the hospital before at Pennsylvania Hospital ICU for an adverse
reaction to a drug or medication and that he used drugs and alcohol.
She clearly withheld facts that could have helped him. She also waited
three or four hours to call paramedics knowing he was ill at her home?
Nah….shaky territory. This was a skilled registered nurse with twenty-
two years experience. Something was *wrong*—it just didn't add up. There
were too many questions, but he was definitely certain her motive was
money.

On March 14, 2007, at the request of Detective Adam Hartman, I
placed a call to Sebastian Lehrman, M.D. who was a well-renowned forensic
pathologist in New York. Detective Hartman felt Dr. Lehrman might be
interested in this case. We had some samples left over of Lenny's fluids that
were with Dr. Relman at the Delaware County Medical Examiner's office.

Dr. Lehrman performed autopsies and was affiliated with the HBO
show *Autopsy.* I tracked him down and left a message. On the following day,
his secretary telephoned me. I explained the case. We wanted to determine
if Lenny had been poisoned or if he'd been given a medication to cause his
death. I told her that Lenny had been cremated, but she said they could
still work with the case. They would need records, but preferred going
through my attorney. To review the case, Dr. Lehrman required a $7,500
retainer fee. I told her I'd be back to her.

That night I re-thought it all. I decided I was too far into this and could not afford it. The retainer fee was just too much. I had responsibilities and bills and I had to pay Noelle's college and her health insurance. On top of everything, I needed to move because my landlords were pissed with me for going after their homeowner's insurance to get my expenses paid after a gas leak. They ordered me out my house on April 8th, and that was less than a month away. I decided I couldn't deal with them and I'd just have to stay there until things calmed down and my brain was in order to relocate. I'd get a lawyer. I was used to it by now. It would take them at least ninety days and a court hearing to get me out. I'd simply put their rent money in escrow so I'd have it when I went to Court, I'd been so busy with all the Lenny stuff and my follow up doctor appointments that I hadn't put much time into finding a new home. Dammit, everything in the world was upside down and here I was trying to rescue the dead pain in the ass, Lenny. I was livid with him! Documents, correspondence, folders, files, to do lists, E-mails, memos and papers were in every room of my house. The entire house had become my office. Cracking this case had become a full-time job. The constant ringing of the phones, making calls, faxing shit, composing letters, having copies made, I was sick of his dead ass! Shit!

He hadn't helped me with Noelle's college and had abandoned us in exchange for a bitch that ended up causing him to die. I was exhausted with the whole thing. I decided not to spend the money on the forensic doctor. Theresa offered to pay for him by taking a loan out on her house. I contemplated her gesture. She was seventy-two years old and still working every day. I didn't want my sister-in-law to have to go into hock and have a mortgage at this stage of the game. This was *her* time. It should be all about *her* now. She was supposed to be shopping and taking trips and going to restaurants. It was time for her to kick back. I told Theresa to forget taking out any loans.

But for some reason, I just could not stop. I couldn't leave this thing alone. I was truly obsessed with the caper aspect of it and I loved being a private investigator and digging around. It was because of this case, at the suggestion of Tony Marino, I applied for my license to be a private investigator. I got a charge out of snooping around and it was equivalent to having an orgasm when I'd uncover something. I had a way with people and

I was definitely a *people person*. I was able to *listen* and could feel a person out through their voice and know how to come on to them. My being very articulate was an asset. People knew I was no ghetto bunny. I found it incredibly easy to obtain information. People would give up everything if I approached them in the right way. Also, these clerks really didn't want to be bothered. This could work either way when I was investigating. Either they were going to give me what I needed in order to get rid of me, or flat out refused. When they seemed frustrated with the situation, I would change the subject and start talking about how much I hated my job and my company didn't appreciate me. I'd start explaining how I needed a vacation and sometimes I'd ask if they could get me an application to apply where they were. After all that, I'd establish a little *relationship* and a *rapport* with the person on the phone. I'd be in like Flint and could walk away with the goods. The generosity of today's workers in many places in America put us all at risk for identity theft. This really was something to think about.

I had other special techniques, too, that always bore fruit for me. I enjoyed organizing the facts, lining all my ducks up in a row and planning the plot. I would often get lost in this work and lose track of time at my home office. I kept impeccable records. I labeled things and put them in folders. I wrote every damn thing down. Frequently, I'd have to *make* myself stop for a meal, and, often, that would take place after being on the case straight for twelve hours. And I never underestimated Carolyn. She was ruthless and I knew it. I went to the police stations in Philly and in Jenkintown. I talked with the officers and told them what I was working on. I copied my files for them and I had disks made. I e-mailed my friends so they had copies of my stuff. If that bitch tried to off me or paid someone else to do it, she'd be looking the cops in the face. I didn't want to die—no way was I ready to go, but I wasn't going to let that hussy scare me into letting Lenny's death be swept under the rug. I may not have been willing to pay Dr. Lehrman eight grand, but I could fuck with enough companies and government agencies to keep her tensed up. I was marinating her ass for the kill and I planned to be the biggest pain in the ass that scank had ever experienced.

If I could remember correctly she was about five feet tall, black as coal, small built and, as Lenny told me years ago, *"she looks like a black monkey."*

Jesus Christ—let us pray. When they first hooked up, one of my play aunts called me and said, "Denise, my man Kitten ran into Lenny and his girlfriend at a bar tonight. Kitten said she was the ugliest woman he had ever seen in his life! The first thing he said to me when he walked in was, 'Is Lenny crazy?' Then, he went on to tell me about the girl." I *hollered* as I listened to Aunt Vera.

I remembered the time I went to Carolyn's apartment and kicked the door in. When I was out there carrying on, her downstairs neighbor came out. She asked me why I was doing that. I responded that I was trying to talk to my husband and he wouldn't come out. I told her the baby was sick. She said, "*That's your husband* that lives up *there?*"

"Yes, Ma'am, it is."

"I knew it!" she exclaimed. "I knew that good looking man didn't belong to *that* ugly woman!" The neighbor closed her door. I noticed a five gallon drum of paint in the hallway. I proceeded to pour paint everywhere. Damn if I knew who was planning to paint, but I painted for them, pouring white paint all over the chocolate covered rugs, up the stairs. Then I laid the drum down on its side in front of Carolyn's apartment door. They lived on the second floor. I let the rest of the paint seep under the door and into the apartment. I could hear them all inside yelling as I did it. The drum was now empty and I went down the stairs heading to my cousin Lynne's car. She had driven me out there to "bring my damn husband back home." Lynne started to drive off. I put my hand in the pocket of my black leather jacket and realized the keys to my apartment were not there.

"Lynne, I must have left my keys out there. They had to have fallen out of my pocket! We have to go back. I won't be able to get in the house or drive my car anywhere."

"Oh no, we're not going back there. You fucked up everything. I had no idea you were gonna go completely crazy out there. We're gonna get in trouble."

"You need to shut up. You started all this mess! I wasn't even going to come out here and you made me do it! You better turn this car around."

When Lynne parked, I ran into the duplex searching for the keys. They were nowhere in sight. Then I spotted the drum. I reached inside and the keys were there. I snatched them out and ran back downstairs to the car.

I noticed a police car and sped up my step. I didn't want to run and draw attention to myself. Before I could get to Lynne, the police officer exited his patrol car. He called me over to him.

"What are you doing out here, Miss?"

"I came to see my husband."

He was African American and fine, about five foot eleven and skinny. He had alluring eyes and looked damn good in that uniform. He took a long look at me, gazed back to the duplex with the door kicked in and said, "Does your husband live over there, where the door is lying?"

"Yes."

"And exactly what were you here about?"

"Well, the baby is sick. I came out here to talk to him, but he wouldn't come out."

He looked suspiciously at me. "Let me get him for you. You stay here."

By this time, Carolyn was looking out of the same front window that she had taunted me from when I had first arrived and asked nicely that Lenny come out to talk to me. The officer told her to get Lenny. Lenny came to the window and told the officer he was not coming out. The officer walked me over to his patrol car and we both leaned against it. It was after midnight.

"Do you know anything about all this damage out here?"

"No, sir. I just came to talk to my husband."

He was silent, still looking at me. "Do you love your husband?"

"Yes."

"And you know nothing about all this paint?"

"No, sir. I don't know what happened with the paint." I flat out lied.

He eyed me again, dropped his head a bit towards the ground and shook his head. He looked back up into my eyes. "Baby, you're full of paint. You've even got paint in your hair." He touched my long wavy hair. It was a five hundred dollar weave that nobody would suspect was not my own lovely locks.

I hadn't had a chance to look at myself. I had no idea I had paint on me. He showed me the paint on my slick black leather jacket. I put my head down. I knew my ass was going to the slammer. Damn!

Instead, to my surprise, he said shaking his head, "Look, you're too pretty for me to take to jail. Get your butt in that car and go home."

The way I heard it much later from Theresa was that Lenny was holding Carolyn and her friends off from coming out to jump me. The next day, Lenny came to my Mom's house and got me. I was hiding out there in case I was going to get arrested. Lenny joked with me about what I had done and decided to take me on a vacation to Myrtle Beach. I agreed to go for a variety of reasons. It would piss Carolyn off; I absolutely loved Myrtle Beach. I wouldn't be around to get into trouble if the police changed their mind about locking me up, and I'd have a lot of sex. We left the next day.

On the way, he fulfilled one of my fantasies. I had always wanted to go to a cheap motel. I was such a Black American Princess and I was a Hyatt, Loews, top of the line girl. But my true fantasy was to go to a sleazy place and go with my *husband*. As we drove, we found one of those spots you pull off from the highway. No real lobby or anything. We went into the room and it had an ugly cheap flowered bedspread on the bed. The room smelled musty and could stand a strong deodorizer. It had a brown and rust color long shag rug on the floor. The bed squeaked and the mattress was flimsy. It had a small beat up television set and awful plaid curtains. The lights from a neon sign flickered on and off advertising the place to highway drivers. I couldn't even remember the name of it, but it should have been called *Pay Less for Sex* or something like that. The shower curtain had brown rust spots on it and it hung in front of a beige tub that needed caulking. It and a *"regular"* rubber stopper. The place was my dream and it was twenty- two dollars a night. We made noise all night in that creaky old bed. Lenny swore we were both going to end up with the crabs or lice or some awful disease. We had a great time that September of 1991. In Myrtle Beach, I reverted back to my normal self, and we checked into one of my BAP spots. That was a condo on the beach. He moved out of Carolyn's when we got back to Philly. He told me he had to pay her for the damages to the place and she was pissed. Checkmate!

CHAPTER 14

❧

The Big Payback

It was painstaking for me to make a thorough reevaluation of the trauma of my life. Realizing my words were true in August of 2005 in my letter to Lenny that I would never see him alive again hit hard. Working on my new novel made me relive some of our happier times and I was feeling pretty low. I felt bad for both Lenny and Noelle and was angry that he had basically ignored his child throughout her life threatening illness. I could count the times on one hand that he actually showed up at the hospital to see her. I was so ashamed of him. She could have really used her Dad during those horrific times. When I would start to hate him and back out, the book titled *Addiction* would be staring me in the face and I accepted that Noelle was not the only one afflicted with an illness. Her father was as well. God was also breathing down my neck, concentrating on me, testing me to see if I'd do the right thing—*anyway*.

After I had spoken to some friends about the whole thing with Dr. Lehrman, I decided I would go ahead with him anyway. What was done was done. I was still going to help Lenny and I had forgiven him. I called Dr. Relman at the medical examiner's office in Delaware County and told him that we would need the last sample he had to be tested by Lehrman. I vowed I'd find the damn money. This thing was now equivalent to a poker game. In poker, scared money did not win. I wasn't about to fold my hand. I **was going to get that** bitch Carolyn! She did **not know who she was fucking with.**

On Saturday, March 17, for the first time, I completely broke down and screamed and cried. I was hysterical. I'd been sitting at the computer working and began to think about when Noelle was born. Lenny had been so excited when he picked her up from the hospital. They had been such a pair when she was a toddler. I contemplated what he could have been and I imagined him just before he died. I wailed inside my bathroom and prayed to God to help me.

That weekend the east coast had experienced a severe ice storm. I was stuck in the house and both my cars were iced in on my small street. The wireless mouse of my computer was not operating correctly because it needed new batteries. I had none and was going crazy trying to get work done on the computer. I'd been removing and replacing batteries from other things in the house trying to rectify the problem. It was still a pain in the ass. On Sunday morning at around seven twenty, I left my house and walked to a convenience store five blocks away.

I loved Jenkintown. This morning it was extremely cold, but the quietness, lack of traffic and people, was absorbing me with tranquility. I looked at all the shops in this quaint town and hoped that I'd find a nice place to move in this same community. It was my definition of a tiny paradise. I felt so safe there and loved being able to walk a block and be in the heart of this town. Residents could leave things in their cars and on their porches and nobody ever touched them. I wasn't living among thieves. I was able to relax. The trash was picked up twice a week, unlike in the city. Strangers said hello to you when you walked by. The police station was two blocks away from my house and the post office was around the corner. Jenkintown had a vacuum cleaner fix it shop, an old fashioned movie house that didn't have a zillion movies playing at once, and thrift shops with great clothing, jewelry and shoes. It also boasted two small bars that were friendly, safe, and sold good food at very reasonable prices. There was also an array of elegant restaurants offering outside dining and all types of ethnic foods. The best mechanic in the land was across the street from my house and his shop also sold used cars and offered services like car inspections and oil changes. There was even a store that taught astrology, tarot card readings, and sold essential oils. I liked that kind of stuff.

I finally made it to the convenience market and, while walking back, I noticed that Dream Girls was playing at the old movies. I had seen it while in Greenville visiting my Godparents over the Christmas holidays. I loved that movie and I had purchased the sound track and listened to tunes many days to soothe me while driving. As soon as I saw the title flash on the marquee, I immediately started singing one of my favorite tunes. Then I started doing a little dance in front of the movie house while singing Eddie's Murphy's *Jimmy Got Soul*. That damn Eddie Murphy was a trip in that movie! He made me crazy about him. Being sponged in peace and quiet on this Sunday morning made me happy. It was a pleasure to be momentarily away from collecting documents, faxing things, and dealing with reality.

On Monday morning it was back to work for me. It was time to let Carolyn know the *news*. This would be the first time she heard from me *directly* since the day after Lenny died. I sent her a letter by FedEx, Certified Mail Return Receipt Requested, and regular mail. I wanted to make sure the bitch had it and could not tell any authorities she hadn't received it.

Dear Ms. Monroe:

I have been advised that the Philadelphia Board of Pensions and Retirement forwarded my late husband's monthly pension check in the amount of $1,653.82 to your residence subsequent to his death of November 23, 2006. This check was payable to my late husband and deposited into your bank account at Citizens Bank, specifically into account number 8114711409. It is also my understanding that my late husband was a joint owner on your account. As a result of your depositing this check, it created an overdraft in the pension account, which is now owned by me. The overdraft amount, which I satisfied, was in the amount of $541.31. I have been advised that you made a partial payment in the amount of $50.00 with a promise to pay the remaining balance biweekly in $50.00 installments. That payment was received by the Pension Board and your terms of repayment are unacceptable to me.

I was advised today after an investigation and a conference at Small Claims Court that you are liable for the entire amount of the funds deposited into your account concerning the November 30, 2006 pension check. Thus, payment should be made in the amount of $1653.82 minus your $50.00 payment.

I am hereby requesting that you make payment to me via Brianna Jasper in the amount of $1603.82 no later than 14 days of the receipt of this letter, that date being April 8, 2007. If Mrs. Jasper has not received the funds on or before that date, I shall file a Petition against you in Court to recover the funds. Should you fail to make payment, I shall also seek repayment of my attorney fees and the costs incurred by me which shall also include court processing, filing and servicing fees in connection with this matter.

Very truly yours,
DENISE GARNER

CC: *Angela O'Neill Pelham, Esquire*
  Anthony J. Marino, Esquire
  Detective Adam Hartman, Central Philadelphia Detectives
  Karen Bearden, Prudential Insurance Company
  Brianna Jasper, Philadelphia Board of Pensions and Retirement
  John J. Glanzmann, Supervisor, First Filing Unit, First Judicial
  District Court, Philadelphia Municipal Court-Small Claims
  Allen S. Valentine, Chief of Police, Department of Police, Jenkintown, PA.
  Paul Corbett, Esquire, Prudential Insurance Company
  Nancy Tucker, City of Philadelphia – Life Benefits Department
  Steve Sirantos, City of Philadelphia Treasurer's Office
  Noelle Garner

I purposely made sure I copied everyone so she would know I was *lawyered up and* was spreading the word to everyone else. I knew this letter would make her nervous, confused, and just plain crazy.

I got all dressed up and headed downtown to meet with the Pension Board. I had been excited for days about my meeting to collect the records regarding the *DROP* money Lenny received when he retired.

Lenny got 120K. I was given all the papers related to his pension. When I got home, I called my estate attorney, Angela Pelham. I needed her now. I had questions and wanted to know if by being the legal wife, I was entitled to half the pension. The money went into Lenny and Carolyn's joint account. Since I got nothing, could I go after Carolyn for at least half of the 120K that I should have gotten? If I was able to do that, couldn't I take her to Court and put a lien on her house for at least 60K? Angela said that Lenny should have had a spousal waiver signed by me in order to get that money. I never signed any spousal waiver. She wondered if Carolyn had signed it so they could get the money. If she did, whose name did she sign—hers or mine? If she signed her own name as Lenny's wife, then the Pension Board was off the hook. If she forged my name, I could bring charges against her. And if no spousal waiver was given by the Pension Board for them to sign, I should be able to go after the Pension Board for my part of the money. I was on a mission. I had snooped around and found out that if I was disabled at the time Lenny got that money, since I had no income, he could have had to share it with me for that reason. At present, we needed to find out if I would have been entitled to half the pension because of my disability. If the funds went into her account and I *was* entitled, I could go after her for one-half of the DROP lump sum payment, Lenny's share in their joint account. I called Angela back. I was not currently working due to an illness and I had not worked one year prior to that. I was disabled from December 2004 through August 2006. I had a few surgeries during that time. One was to my wrist and two eye surgeries. Angela requested all the records for examination and would review them and get back to me.

Tony had to be kept abreast on major issues of the case, so I called him.

"I spoke to the attorney for Prudential regarding the Interpleader. He was very nice and he is going to explain some things to me and try to give me a time frame as to when we will go to court to decide who gets the life insurance money from that City policy."

"Okay, Columbo. When you get that, call me immediately. I'll have to clear the date on my schedule. I'm busy. I've got to hang up."

Later that day, the mailman delivered a letter from the attorney for Pennsylvania Hospital where Carolyn worked. He gave me the name of the insurance company that issued the life policies. I could speak directly with them to determine if Carolyn actually made a claim on that 10K policy on Lenny's life. They were only supposed to pay the wife.

There was also a letter from Citizens Bank informing me of the arrival of more statements. I decided to call Carolyn's bank in the morning to pick up those records. I wanted to see where that 120K went.

I was continuing on my roll to take Carolyn Monroe completely down. Through the bank statements and cancelled checks I discovered that Carolyn Monroe's home was insured with Lloyd's of London. I got the policy number, telephone number, address of the company, and amounts of coverage. She had coverages of $80K on Dwelling, $100K on Liability; 40K on Contents, and a $500 Deductible.

After chatting with a clerk, I was told to contact the company directly that handled their claims, Moraski and Moraski. I had other fires to fight, and I'd get to them later.

On March 22, I delivered the pension records to Angela.

I plopped an accordion file down on Angela's desk. "Regina Murdock, Senior Legal Assistant at the Pension Board, and I were on the phone a couple of days ago, too. She prepared all this and told me they don't require a spousal waiver. The *DROP* and Pension Fund are two different things. I had no rights to that *DROP* money."

A frustrated Angela looked up at me and said, "She's an idiot if she told you that. They had to have a spousal waiver. If they don't have one in this pile of documents, I'm going after them. You're legally married to him and would have had to sign something waiving your rights to part of that money. That's Federal law in pensions."

I was sick of all this *he said she said* shit. Angela was a qualified attorney and I knew that. I trusted her, but the whole fucking case was getting on my nerves. I wanted it over. "Angela—look, Katherine Young is the Executive Director of the Pension Board and Lauren was her assistant. Both have been helpful to me in this process. I had a lot of trouble getting things done and Lauren and Katherine Young were of great assistance. Give them a call and you'll get the correct information and all your questions answered. Just avoid Brianna Jasper because she'll be of no assistance to you. She's not only a trainee counselor—but also an idiot. She's the dummy who approved that last pension check that Carolyn ended up with."

"Okay. I'll get on it in a few days. Anything else you need to tell me?"

I leaned back in the chair and let my head drop back. I took a deep breath and exhaled. I was staring at the ceiling trying to concentrate, gathering my thoughts. "Listen, in my review of the records from them, Lenny chose Choice 2 for the DROP (Deferred Retirement Option Plan) to get paid directly, less 20% for Federal Income Tax. He signed this on 11/8/04 and his amount payable was calculated at $53,658.25. Where'd the other 65K go? On April 15, 2002, he signed a form choosing Option 4 and indicating wife as Carolyn E. Monroe. He also indicated on this date that he wished to enter the program starting July 8, 2002. This could explain the need for the June 22, 2002 marriage of Lenny and Carolyn. He also signed an Affidavit of Pension Eligibility. You need to review that stuff. I'm worried they could take the pension away from me entirely due to any of the clauses. There's a fraud clause in there on one of those forms. He did lie, saying Carolyn was his wife. I want to know if I'll be jeopardized by bringing an action against the Board."

Angela was taking notes while I was talking.

"I found nothing where *Carolyn Monroe* signed a spousal waiver. I did see a form that Lenny signed making her beneficiary of the pension. However he didn't date the form. No date makes that invalid—just in case we have to move and try to get them on *technicalities*. This was a Change of Beneficiary Form that was not honored because the Pension Board had a rule—you had to be married 10 years to collect an employee's pension. The dumb bitch probably didn't know that, but I bet Lenny did," I chuckled.

Now Angela was sick of all this mumbo jumbo. "Alright Denise, I'll go through everything with a fine tooth comb and work through Director Young. I'll talk to you next week."

Once I got home, I started going through everything again and noted in my files that for Lenny's Retirement he chose Option 4, meaning that the surviving widow or dependent children would receive 50% survivorship benefit. This was signed on April 15, 2002 when he signed up for the *DROP program.*

Regina Murdock called. She had made a mistake in telling me Lenny got 120K as a lump payment. Damn, everybody over at the pension board was crazy and mixed up except Lauren and Katherine. Regina said that 120K was a *projection* figure. If he had stayed in the program and not retired early, he would have gotten that amount. Because he left early, he got $53K.

I was told to call the Treasurer's Department to get a copy of the actual **cancelled check in the amount of $53,555.04. It was issued on December** 10, 2004. I made sure that was on the way.

Now it was time to notify the investigative company, Moraski and Moraski, who worked for Carolyn's homeowner's insurance company, that nursey pie did not do her *nursely* duties on November 23, 2006 and wifey-poo was disgruntled about that. After quickly explaining my situation and position, I immediately faxed Moraski a *kit* on Lenny which was comprised of all my administrative documents and his death certificates. Later in the day, I sent them a letter revealing that Ms. Monroe was a registered nurse with twenty-two years experience and employed in the Skilled Care Unit of Pennsylvania Hospital. I explained Lenny's cause of death and that he was in the care of Carolyn at her residence when he became acutely ill. Instead of obtaining the medical care he so urgently needed, Carolyn assumed responsibility for his care. That mistake proved fatal, as her delay of four hours or so in getting him emergency treatment greatly increased the risk of death, which he later found at Mercy Fitzgerald Hospital in Darby, Pennsylvania.

I informed them I was still investigating whether or not Carolyn Monroe was responsible for negligently administering the drug to which he had an adverse reaction. Initially, it was suspected that Lenny had died of natural causes, more specifically a heart attack, but after further investigation of this matter, his death certificate was amended. A change of a death certificate was a big deal. Tony had told me that I had really scored in getting that done.

This was a damn tough week. On top of everything else, I still had to make appearances as an author. Being Columbo was costing me. If it wasn't high gas prices, it was train fares, copying fees, and paying for subpoenas and short certificates. I was dead tired from lecturing last night at Rosemont College to students in a class on marketing, editing, and publishing. That had been a three-hour discussion with me doing most of the talking. I loved it. Thursday, March 29, 2007 was a busy day of doctor's appointments, errands, and banking. Around nine-thirty that night, someone was banging on my door and I couldn't imagine who it could be. It turned out to be a process server hired by Prudential's attorney, Corbett. I was served at my home with an Interpleader Complaint regarding Prudential's $6K Policy on Lenny's life. I had spoken with Corbett a couple of weeks before and had been advised this would happen, but I thought it would be done during normal business hours. He told me that we'd be in court about ninety days after Carolyn and I were served.

My plan was to get through the weekend and get that hundred thirty-one page document copied and in Tony Marino's office so he could Answer the Complaint. When Carolyn got that pleading, she was going to shit a brick. That bitch would have to spend some money on an attorney now. I knew she was sick of me *and* Lenny. I wrote a letter to Prudential's attorney advising I had been served with the Interpleader Complaint, which I would shortly answer.

I asked him to drop two defendants, Hawkins Funeral Home and Ford Acceptance Corporation as monies owed to these defendants, for Lenny's funeral had been paid directly by me.

Now I had to organize *this* whole thing. Another fucking project! Damn! My in-laws and other family members wanted to attend the court proceeding. I'd have to find out if this would be allowed. As soon as we had a definite court date, Lenny's relatives in other states had to make travel arrangements and request time off from work. I also had to inform all counsel that Nancy Tucker of City of Philadelphia Department of Life Benefits would be a witness for me. God knew I needed her.

I wrote a letter to Corbett, Prudential's attorney, and copied Tony, Nancy Tucker, Hawkins Funeral Home, and *Carolyn*. I was glad to copy that bitch on this letter so she would know I wanted to fight and was bringing Lenny's family with me to help me kick her ass in court *and* give the hussy some dirty looks in the waiting areas.

* * *

I had a million things to do over the next few days. The published author, Denise Garner, had snagged a promotion to do for nine hours with Fashion Fair Cosmetics Company. I had been working like a Trojan all week on that project.

MACY'S AND FASHION FAIR PRESENTS
AUTHOR DENISE GARNER

Fashion Fair, the nations leading cosmetics, specializing in women of color and Denise Garner, the published author of Penguin NAL's hot seller Heartburn and its sequel Afterglow have teamed up together!

Yes, the dynamic Denise Garner writes multicultural fiction at its best and has received stellar reviews. To her credit are appearances on The Tom

Joyner Morning Show Fantastic Voyages, The Jerry Mondesire Show, nationwide book signings, radio commentaries, and numerous magazine and newspaper articles praising her work. She was also chosen to make a special appearance on the **Oprah Show** after **Oprah** sent a TV crew to her home to film Denise and her daughter Noelle in 2005. Yes, **Denise** and her daughter Noelle were invited to discuss mother and daughter relationships in the company of the **Kennedys**, namely **Maria Shriver** and **Eunice Kennedy Shriver.**

Those who would like to meet Denise Garner, a resident of Jenkintown, PA will have an opportunity to do so at the Fashion Fair Counter of Macy's, Willow Grove at Willow Grove Mall between the hours of 2:00 p.m. and nine o'clock p.m. on Friday, March 30, 2007. This will be the first stop of a series of events Fashion Fair is hosting for Ms. Garner.

In this promotion with a $50 purchase of Fashion Fair Cosmetics including fragrances, you can purchase the novel at a substantial discount of $8.00, meet the gregarious Denise Garner and...of course, she's going to autograph your copy of her book!

In addition to autographing her books, she will also preside over a blind raffle open to any patrons who purchase $50 of Fashion Fair products. All raffle prizes will be associated with characters and/or situations depicted in her novels.

Take a look at what **Frank Quattrone** of the **Montgomery Times Chronicle** newspaper has to say about **Ms. Garner:**

By Frank D. Quattrone

Ticket Editor

"Somewhat in the manner of William Faulkner in "As I Lay Dying," Garner opens each chapter with the name of a key character and propels the narrative forward through each character's unique vision and point of view. Pretty bold stuff from an author who's never gone to college but whose street smarts clearly equal, or surpass, her book smarts. Not bad for this passionate earth mother who swears, "These stories come right through my brain to my hands onto the computer screen." The more you listen to, the more you watch, local novelist Denise Garner, the more you realize that she is so much more than a mere storyteller. A hard-working single mother who tends to her two

daughters as lovingly as she infuses fire into her words, Garner comes off as an earth goddess, a phenomenon of nature, and a force to be reckoned with."
Don't miss this event!!

Theresa made sure my flyers were posted and distributed at Pennsylvania Hospital to make sure Carolyn was embarrassed and jealous that Denise was a celebrity.

The Friday before I left to do the Fashion Fair gig, I quickly gave a call to Moraski and Moraski, the investigative company for Carolyn's homeowner's carrier. I knew they had gotten my notice of the claim letter regarding the homeowner's insurance policy. I spoke to a clerk and requested the name of the adjuster assigned to handle the matter and a gentleman got on the line.

"I have received your letter. Can you tell me what your husband was doing at Carolyn Monroe's house on Thanksgiving Day?"

I knew I had some explaining to do and, by this time, I was damn sick of telling the story. His tone wasn't friendly and I had run out of patience. I quickly remembered from Tony's training to simply answer the question and shut up. "He lived there."

"How long had he lived there?"

"Fourteen years."

"You two never divorced?"

"I'm still married to my husband."

"You've been estranged from him for fourteen years?"

"Separated."

"Well, let me offer my condolences. This is a very complicated case. We have to order a lot of records. We are sending a letter out to you acknowledging the claim. That should come soon. It will take us at least four weeks to get all the records and investigate this matter."

"**That's fine. You'll be handling the matter?**"

"Yes."

"And, what's your name?"

"Ken."

"*Ken*, may I have your last name?"

"Moraski."

"Mr. Moraski, may I have the claim number."

"Yes, its GB20678"

"Thank you, I will wait for your initial letter and then expect to hear from you in four weeks." When we hung up, I wondered why the hell it would take him four weeks to talk to Carolyn. Hell, all he had to do was call her ass up or meet with her. They were representing her and knew how to get their hands on her.

Little did *Ken* know that I had eighty-two sub files of information and he wouldn't even be able to read the Mercy Fitzgerald records without my deciphering them. My case was padded with five signed and notarized affidavits from people stating that his insured was a liar and a coke head. My trump card was Restatement (Second) of Torts Section 324A. I was saving all that for dessert. Section 324A provides in essence that *one who undertakes for consideration to render services to another which he should recognize as necessary for the protection of a third person is subject to liability to the third person for physical harm.* I knew I had this bitch. I had her on the Good Samaritan law—good samaritans give assistance to people in need—and I had her ass on Section 324A. She'd be damned if I chose to go after her on either law. I chose both.

I imagined her kitchen table being covered in paperwork in the last seven days. First the Small Claims Court shit, then the Pension Board, the Interpleader Complaint, and now this. I was teaching her well and she was learning her lessons about fucking my husband. Checkmate!

Lo and behold, Nursey Pie must have been catching hell because she went crying to the Pension Board in order to keep the arrangement to pay fifty dollars bi-weekly regarding her cashing Lenny's pension check. I had definitely turned the heat up on Carolyn Monroe's ass. I received a letter in the mail on March 31, 2007, which sounded as if they were going to accept her arrangements. When I was informed that the pension was legally mine, they offered me no payment arrangement to pay the overdraft that Carolyn left me. In fact, they said the pension could not be set up and no pension checks would come to me until I paid it in full. I wasn't about to let them protect that trollop. I shot back by calling Suzanne Ridges, a counselor at the pension board. I told her it had been explained to me by the court system that Carolyn had to pay the full amount of Lenny's pension check, which she cashed after his death. Although I was aware of the partial payment she had mailed to the Board, I reiterated, however, that if I did not receive the full amount of the check cashed by Carolyn by April 8, 2007, I would proceed is Small Claims Court against her. I also reminded Suzanne that in her last letter to me she had not specified when she would forward the $50 payment accepted by her to me.

After that conversation, I backed it up with an e-mail and I copied every damn body again—including Suzanne Ridges' boss—the director of the pension board. Nobody was going to forget I was working on this case. It would not be swept under the rug. It was my intention to stay on top of everybody.

I heard back from Mr. Corbett at Prudential. He let me know the Answer to the Interpleader Complaint was due in twenty days and that it was required both Carolyn and myself to submit a letter stating why we felt we were entitled to the insurance proceeds. If a party did not answer the pleading and/or show up at the hearing, they would be out due to a default judgment. I e-mailed Tony, who was on vacation, and let him know that information. Then I began working on my letter and gathering exhibits to give Tony a head start.

The following afternoon I telephoned the Pension Board to follow up with them on the money Carolyn owed me. I left voicemails for Jasper and Ridges advising them to check for my faxes and reiterated my position. I then placed a call to Executive Director Katherine Young. She wasn't in, so I explained to her assistant, Lauren, what was going on. Lauren agreed I should not get the money piecemeal and said I should receive the fifty dollar payment Carolyn made in my April pension check. Slick, I took the opportunity to ask her to explain a spousal waiver to me. She was surprised I had not been notified by the pension board when Lenny received that DROP lump sum payment in 2004. We both agreed that there was going to be some mess. Lauren assured me that they would look into everything and get back to me. I ended the call by letting her know I had an attorney working on the DROP money.

Next, I called Carolyn's homeowner's investigative department. I left a message for Ken, the adjuster, that I had received his initial letter and that he should call me. He'd told me in a prior conversation that his letter to me would state that they would need to gather records and investigate. How in the world would they get records without my signing for them? We did have a HIPPA Law. Also, he wouldn't be able to read a damn thing he got from Mercy Fitzgerald. I didn't want this thing held up and wanted him on the phone. If he needed signed authorizations from me, he should send them out now. His insured, Carolyn, had better not sign a damn thing to get records. I'm the wifey-poo and they had better not forget that. If they wanted records from me—they should send me a check for the copying fees, too.

It was only one o'clock in the afternoon and I was pooped. I'd been up since six a.m. trying to make things happen. I'd been to the supermarket, post office, Tony's office, UPS copying service, and the Social Security office. It was time for a nap. Tonight would be another evening of filing papers away and cleaning up the house. I had to be ready for the IRS in the morning. I decided to subpoena nursey-pie's tax records from 2001 through 2006. If she truly believed she was his wife, I wanted to know if she filed joint income tax returns with *her husband.*

I called Frances Garner, Lenny's first wife. I left a message that I would need a signed and notarized affidavit from her concerning her first encounter with Carolyn. Since Carolyn claimed she never knew Lenny had ever been married, how the fuck did she know Frances way back in the day? When I get done snooping around and gathering more evidence, this wench's credibility would be zilch.

As I lay down waiting to drift off to sleep, I laughed out loud. That damn Merritt Crew, my buddy, just started dating a wonderful new guy that she was loving to death. He just happened to be the Mayor of Jenkintown. His best friend is the Chief of Police and Merritt had dinner with both of them last week. I hoped the Chief didn't have so much fun that he misplaced that disk and letter I left for him almost two weeks ago. He'll know everything and everybody involved in this case once he inserted that disk in his computer. Small world.

When I woke up from my nap, Suzanne Ridges of the pension board, called me. She wanted to plead with me to let Carolyn make $50.00 per month payments to me.

"Mrs. Garner, you need to understand that Carolyn Monroe is *trying.* I want you to be a better person."

I was on to Carolyn, but apparently Suzanne Ridges wasn't. Without a moment's hesitation I said, "I appreciate your *opinion,* however, if I do not have my money by the 8th of April, on the 9th I'll be at Small Claims Court. Maybe if you had a kid who'd been hospitalized forty-one times and a wench who had hidden your husband's body, maybe you'd feel differently. It's my opinion that Carolyn Monroe is wretched."

"You're being wretched, too. Why not think this over?"

"Thanks for calling me. I'll get a judgment and put a lien on Carolyn's house."

"Now, now, Mrs. Garner. Hold on a moment. Let's talk a bit more. Maybe we can come up with something."

All I could think of was that bitch Carolyn signing her name to Lenny's check and the damn pension board sending it out to her *after* I asked them not to. I had sat in that damn office with that fucking trainee three days before the check was mailed out. I asked that woman not to mail it. Now her boss was telling me I was wretched.

"I have a suggestion. Tell the Board they should forward a check to me. This check should cover the amount of the November 2006 payment due to me plus any monies I paid to settle the overdraft in my husband's pension account. If this request can be granted, I won't pursue this matter in Small Claims Court. Also, any funds you guys receive from Carolyn Monroe regarding her payment plan arrangement, the Pension Board should keep. How about that?"

Suzanne Ridges sighed. I knew she was sick of me. "I'll look into it and discuss it with Director Young. I'll call you back."

"Well, all you guys have a Happy Easter, and if we can't do it that way, then I want a letter going out to Carolyn Monroe on your letterhead from the pension board director's office stating that Monroe is responsible for the full amount of the check and the overflow payment I made. I insist that **letter to go out before April 9th, 2007, and a copy to me. I will need to take** it to Small Claims Court if this was not settled. Good bye."

It was my desire to see Carolyn squirm. Tony was a great trial attorney. Seeing him in action was like going to the theater. I couldn't wait for tickets to the showdown at Court, so I decided I would have Tony take her deposition in his office. In this way, he could get a lot of information out of her ahead of time that I could use in all my cases against her. I wanted it scheduled as soon as possible. Luckily, Liz, the court reporter would provide services for free.

On April 3, 2007, Tony and I were trading e-mails while he was on vacation until April 9, 2007.

Denise:

> *Sure we can do a dep of her. Great that you'll get the service for free.*
> *I will cap my fee at 2K and bill $200 per hour (re: Interpleader case).*
> *Tony*

I responded as follows:

> *Hey Tony:*
> *Okay—Yep—Let's do the dep. I was on the phone with Liz when this E-mail came in from you. Count her in. I'll let Paul Corbett know this is happening in case he wants to come to the dep. I'll give him a heads up with no date and check his schedule with him so you have some dates to choose from in case he wants to participate. Keep in mind that if Carolyn does not file an Answer to the Interpleader Complaint—she may be out of the Prudential thing and I'll win. Even if that happens, I'll still want to try to get that dep in case we want to use it in the Wrongful Death thing. I can be at the dep—right? Pleeze? We've gotta make sure we serve Carolyn the Notice of Dep by regular, cert and FedEx because she will swear she never got the thing and won't appear.*
> *Fine with the fee arrangement with you.*
> *Guess what? Lenny's sister Theresa called tonight. She is going crazy about her brother's death. She is going to her credit union tomorrow. Putting in for an 8K loan right away. It's to pay Dr. Sebastian Lehrman. She told me to get things together as far as the sample fluids and medical reports and have everything in place. You know Lehrman said he'll only deal with an attorney. I am going to give him a call to try to do some of this myself. I have most of the records he'd need. Gotta watch Boston Legal.*
> *Bye.*
> *Columbo*

* * *

It was April 4, and I was trying to track down Dr. Phillip Hennen of the City of Philadelphia Medical Examiner's office. He was the medical examiner who first got Lenny's body. He worked with the Chief, Dr. Relman. Hennen was away on vacation and due back on Monday. I faxed information and requested it be placed in his mailbox. I'd never spoken with Hennen, so I let him know who I was and what the deal was. He would know that I had been dealing with Detective David Hartman along with Chief Relman who suggested I get in touch with him. Additional tests which would be paid for by me, needed to be performed on Lenny's fluids. We expected foul play in Lenny's death and it could be a homicide. We'd be using forensic pathologist Dr. Sebastian Lehrman to examine them. To facilitate this, Relman wanted a call from him and I was waiting in line for one, too.

* * *

I felt I had to stay on top of Carolyn's Homeowner's investigative company. They were doing some investigating and would be back to me, but I wondered how they could investigate without records. It was now the first week in April and I wanted to know what the hell was going on. I faxed Moraski and Moraski a copy of the report deciphering the Mercy Fitzgerald records, but I didn't send the records. They would have to work for them. Two days later, I received a letter from them denying the claim. They had interviewed Carolyn and felt she was not negligent. That didn't bother me. I'd just sue the bastards.

Theresa and I had been having some conversations. She was still upset and anxious for answers. She got that 8K and had already mailed it to **Tony**.

* * *

On the 11th of April, I finally got around to some things that were on my *To Do List*. I had one running precisely for hanging that bitch. It was time to start dealing with the Internal Revenue Service, to get copies of Carolyn's Federal Income Tax Returns. Since I was attempting to impeach her credibility, the returns would be crucial. She felt she was legally married to Lenny. My thought was did she file taxes with her *husband* during the years 2002 through 2005? After all, she was living with him and that's what *wives* do when they are living with their *husbands*. If she had filed with him, it would turn out to be an innocent mistake, and if she had not, it would prove that she knew better to fuck around with the government. I called the IRS and went from department to department with my same crazy story. At last I got a clerk who handled decedents. Ms. Nagle explained that I would have to submit documents and Lenny's returns would be sent to me. I decided that would be good enough because they would show whether or not he filed with her. I was already in possession of some of the paperwork required and could go on the IRS website to retrieve an additional form. I quickly faxed a letter to the IRS telling them the scoop and giving them verifications for everything. I requested Lenny's 2002 through 2005 Federal Income Tax returns and I gave them the required Form 2848 to get them.

Once that was done, I decided I would have a Plan "B" in case the Feds took too long getting to my request. I would need those records for the settlement conference for the Prudential life policy, which would probably take place in a month. I knew this letter would scare the shit out of Nursey Pie and made sure I kept referring to Lenny as *my husband,* knowing those words would stab her every time she read them—the jealous bitch. Not a person in America ever wanted to have to gather tax returns or have the IRS snooping around. I sent this letter by Federal Express, Certified Mail Return Receipt Requested and Regular Mail.

RE: Estate of Lenny Garner
   File No: A2412-2007

Dear Ms. Monroe:
   Please be advised that I am the legal spouse, Executor and Administratrix of the Estate of Lenny Garner, Deceased. Enclosed please find a Short Certificate as well as a subpoena. I have been instructed by the Register of Wills of Philadelphia

County that this Short Certificate and subpoena should be honored in order for me to gather records.

It is my understanding that my husband was a joint owner on two Citizens Bank checking accounts with you. Those account numbers are 811495-370-9 and 620964-141-9. At your earliest convenience kindly supply my estate attorney, Angela O'Neill Pelham with copies of your tax returns for the years 2002, 2003, 2004 and 2005. We are also requesting the names, addresses of all banks and account numbers other than above mentioned at Citizens Bank which you and/or you and Lenny Garner deposited and withdrew funds, wrote checks against and withdrew cash from ATM machines from 1992 through 2006. These records and all requested information should be forwarded directly to Ms. Pelham at the following address:

Angela O'Neill Pelham, Esquire
Suite 1519
Land Title Building
100 South Broad Street
Philadelphia, PA 19110

Should you have any questions regarding the contents of this letter, please do not hesitate to contact Ms. Pelham or have your attorney contact her at 215-555-1730 or fax her at 215-555-1833.

Thank you for your prompt attention to this matter.

Very truly yours,
DENISE GARNER

The week of April 9, 2007 was another rough one for me in my attempts to keep up with everything in this case and to relocate due to my landlord problems. Following up on everything as well as keeping my **doctors' appointments was exasperating and I was going out of my mind.** I still had a mountain of papers and files. I had placed repeated calls to Medical Examiner Dr. Phillip Hennen from April 9th and by the 11th I was frantic not hearing back from him. Theresa was a nervous wreck, calling constantly and she, too, swore that Carolyn had caused Lenny's death and was searching for information to prove it. Then she'd get melancholy and began telling me stories of how she had taken care of Lenny and her younger siblings being the oldest of six children. Those kids were like her own. She reminisced about how she would get pears off the tree in Myrtle Beach for them and how she used to brush Lenny's hair and get him ready for church.

By Wednesday, I left a pleading message to Dr. Hennen. My phone rang on the morning of April 12th. I could hear it ringing, but could not find it. Both my phones were cordless, and they were ringing and missing. When I finally found a phone, I saw I had missed Dr. Hennen's call! I was pissed! He left a message that he would call me back. I telephoned him back right away. We played phone tag the entire day due to the errands I had to run. The last message I got from him was that he would be in Delaware County with Dr. Relman the following day and I could call him there. The good thing was he still had fluid and sample tissue.

I was going to battle for a dead husband when my life was falling apart. I had to stop worrying about everyone else's ass and literally deal with my own. My butt was sore in the rectal area. I had been having problems with fissures and blood in my stool off and on since December. I had an appointment with a gastroenterologist the next day at 1:00 p.m. and a psychiatry appointment at 9:00 a.m. because everything was driving me crazy. Two damn doctors' appointments in a span of four hours! Whew! I also needed to meet with my real estate attorney at some point because I was due in Court on Monday the 16th regarding my eviction notice. My aunt Betsy, Lynne's Mom had passed away on Tuesday and I had to get ready for the funeral. I was grieving and had to write a poem for my sweet aunt and read it at the funeral. I didn't know what the hell I was going to wear and I had to get a spectacular arrangement of flowers to the Church by 8:00 o'clock Saturday morning. My hair was a wreck.

I had a tough time sleeping and woke up on Friday morning at 4:00. My mind was racing. Something told me to get all Lenny and Carolyn's bank statements and cancelled checks out to carefully review them. Even though monthly checking account deposits were between five thousand and seven thousand dollars, I noticed that between November 2004 and the month of Lenny's death their account was overdrawn on a monthly basis to the tune of 9 to 22 times at $38 a pop. Sometimes overdraft fees were as much as $836.00 in a single month! I made notes of everything and attached my findings on separate sheets of paper to each statement. It included columns of total number of deposits, withdrawals, ATM withdrawals, service charges, number of overdrafts and any deposits that I could not connect to a Social Security check, payroll check of Carolyn, or pension check. I made notes to investigate any deposits I did not understand. Carolyn might have also been providing people she knew with medication by stealing it from the hospital, and those customers, in turn, gave her a few bucks. I didn't put anything past Nursey Pie. My plan was to have the bank send me the front and backs of all those deposits. I was hoping her "customers" paid her by check and not cash.

At 1:30 in the afternoon, I was sitting on the gastroenterologist's table about to let him look inside my butt when my cell phone rang. It was Dr. Phillip Hennen—thank God. However, it was a bittersweet conversation that stunned and left me in tears. He informed me that they had found arsenic in Lenny's system after examining the fluids.

There it was, in my face—what I'd suspected all along. Arsenic. Humph. "Damn," I said. "The bitch really did it!" Even though I was hell bent on proving Carolyn the devil did something, I didn't want her to have done anything as deliberate and cold blooded as this. I cried on the examination table. The doctor had left the room to give me some privacy when I got the call. I got myself together and called Tony. He told me to keep a lid on it. I knew he didn't mean not to tell Angela, so I called her. She was shocked and said to me, "Be careful. Carolyn Monroe is crazy. Watch yourself."

I summoned my doctor back to the exam room, was examined, and received a prescription and a referral to a surgeon.

As soon as I got home, I sent a fax to Dr. Hennen to request a phone consultation next week with him. He'd be held up in Court for a few days and I wanted him to schedule me in on one of the days he was free. A face to face with him was what I wanted.

Once I got a few more calls in and checked on Noelle, I sent Dr. Hennen an e-mail.

TO: Dr. Phillip Hennen

FROM: DENISE GARNER
RE: LENNY GARNER
Dear Dr. Hennen:

Regarding your finding of arsenic, I'd also like to take some notes and I am wondering when you will have the test results back which show the level of arsenic in Lenny's system.

He called me in two hours and I spilled my guts telling him everything, *including the fact that* Carolyn had a husband prior to marrying Lenny and we could not seem to find him. Was he dead or alive? A couple of other people died while living with her, too, prior to Lenny dying. Something was definitely going on.

* * *

I waited four days and called Tony to bring him up to speed.

"I'm still at it. I talked again to Dr. Hennen and at first he said he felt no reason to have police investigate or even question Carolyn because there was such a low level of arsenic. I heard him out and then I spoke my mind. I also sent him a copy of my Court Letter which tells everything in more detail."

"Okay, after you ordered him around and drove him crazy, what did he decide to do?"

"Discuss it with his boss—the Chief in Delaware County, Relman. I also questioned why on Friday I was just hearing about arsenic. It seems they found it *weeks ago.*

"I swear," Tony sighed. "Maybe you *are* going nuts with this thing. You need to put this damn file down. Can't it be that perhaps you hate the woman so much you can't concentrate on anything else? She probably didn't kill him. There's arsenic in cigarettes. Shit."

"Yeah, yeah, yeah. What are you doing, moving over to her side?"

"Don't try to start a fight with me. I'm just giving you something to consider."

"Well, I don't want to hear it. Mr. Dee the Psychic said something is wrong."

"Here we go again with the Mr. Dee shit."

"Don't start knocking him. Guess whose one of his clients?"

"Who?"

"The fucking medical examiner—Hennen."

"You're lying," Tony said as he howled laughing.

"No I'm not. He's been going to him for years. He goes once a year and said Mr. Dee is usually on point."

Tony was silent. I knew he was reconsidering the fact that I was going off on a limb trying to get Carolyn for murder. Tony would handle things with Dr. Sebastian Lehrman.

A letter needed to be sent out to Dr. Lehrman along with a phone call to him because we were ready to proceed and wanted to send his retainer fee. I wanted Tony to contact Drs. Hennen and Relman to let them know he was on this. They would be swifter knowing he was around. Theresa was prepared to withdraw another 20K to retain an attorney to file suit against Delaware County Medical Examiner's office for not coming up with results sooner or something like that. She'd FREAKED OUT ON ME TODAY because she felt medical examiners had screwed up this thing from the beginning and were still farting around now. I had managed to calm her down, but a lot was going on.

"I'm on my way to the hospital to see your Dad. I've got to make sure the personnel at that facility isn't fucking up." Tony's Dad had recently had a stroke.

"Yeah, I heard you called up there four times yesterday interrogating two nurses and called the Administrator because they weren't picking up the phones fast enough. I've got work to do. Go to the hospital."

I liked Tony's dad a lot and was worried about him, too. The senior Marino was a hell of an attorney himself, filthy rich, was actively practicing, and drove a red Jaguar. He and Tony shared a suburban mansion that was their offices. They both also had their own homes in the affluent suburbs of Richboro and Huntingdon Valley.

* * *

Bright and early the next day, I called Hennen. "My sister in law Theresa does not want the samples wasted or even touched again by the Delaware Valley Medical Examiners office. She made me call your boss, Dr. Relman to explain that since we have so very little of the sample left over, we don't want to jeopardize having enough for Dr. Lehrman. I'm supposed to call Dr. Relman back once I reported to you and to keep you abreast of things because he is so busy."

I could tell he was sick of me. He very curtly said, "I understand."

"Okay, I'd better hang up and call him back. Have a nice day. We'll get this case straightened out. I'll get to the bottom of it," I sweetly said.

Dr. Relman listened patiently as I informed him that Carolyn Monroe stood to gain a total of $978K with Lenny's death and that figure included what she had already received since he retired. We had acquired so much more evidence. My family really wanted Dr. Lehrman on the case. We were certain Lenny did not die of an overdose of cocaine. Even if it was just a *bit of arsenic,* it was *there.* Carolyn was with him every day from the week before he died up until the death. She had taken a leave from work and told family members they were together uninterrupted during that seven day period. She had enough time to kill.

On Friday, April 20, I decided to send Tony an E-mail. I had just hung up from speaking with Dr. Lehman's assistant. I had called for instructions and to get the procedures down pat.

Hey Tony:

I called Dr. Lehrman to let him know we are working on this. I was told they DO NOT need any samples. What they need is ALL medical records to evaluate. He won't ever need the samples. Samples should not be destroyed in any case just in case he comes up with something and we go to trial. His $7500 fee is to review those records and make a determination as to what killed Lenny.

I notified Dr. Relman asking him for all records in his possession. Lehrman gave me a list of what he wants. Genevieve at Lehrman's office said you should call her next week when you are ready and she will explain the entire procedure to you and answer any questions you may have. I will copy the records. Relman is sending me everything. See you on Monday.

P.S.: I am working on the Writ of Seizure for Philly County to get Carolyn's computers to a forensic Computer Expert. Angela, my Estate attorney will handle that. Carolyn's Bank is cooperating and the Prothonotary's office is guiding me. I just have to get a Summons done and take that with me to

Prothy's office Monday a.m. with the Writ and Order. I'm okay with this other than the Summons. I'll buy one from you. Do you have any? If you do, I'll be up there for it today. Just E-mail me back if you have it. I have to be at the bank to pick up a letter from them about Carolyn having the on line banking.

Denise

I gave a quick call to Angela and explained that things were heating up and what was going on with Tony. Detective Hartman told me today to seize Carolyn's computers. Because she did online banking, we were allowed to have the actual computers and go into hard drive. Daniel Bishop, the manager Citizens Bank was preparing a letter confirming her use of online banking. Good old Daniel, the guitar man—I sure was glad we had bonded together that day at the bank when I went with that subpoena. I'd spoken to the head clerk in charge of filing documents at Philly City Hall Room 280 and given the necessary information to get a writ and seize the computers. I also had to file a suit by Summons at City Hall, which I would do on Monday. I already had a forensic computer expert lined up to actually take the computers away from her house. Detective Hartman has set that up and they were **MILES COMPUTER FORENSICS** A Division of Miles Technologies, Inc. **Corporate Offices** 300 West Route 38 Moorestown, NJ 08057. Phone: (800) 496-8001 Fax: (856) 439-9910 Email: forensics@milescomputerforensics.com.

The rule was I could not have the computers in my possession. Chain of Command thing. Carolyn could allege that I tampered with them. The fee for the computer forensic people would cost me three grand.

Since the arsenic thing came about, Detective Hartman said looking in her hard drive would tell us a lot about what Carolyn was up to.

I left Dr. Relman a voice mail. He had my permission to release to me all medical reports and results of testing of tissue and fluids in his possession relating to Lenny's death. Any tissue samples or fluids he had stored should remain preserved, as I expected we would need them at a later date. I asked him to send everything to my home address as soon as possible. Overnight if it was within his *budget*.

I waited a week and got nothing. I left another message and got no return call. Then I finally found him in his office on a Sunday, the 29th. After that phone conversation, I was very suspicious as to whether they performed all the necessary tests on Lenny's body from the onset. It was alarming to me that he was making excuses about everything and contradicting everything I said. He was abrupt with me. He was too busy to talk to me and he said I was taking up too much of his time. I called Tony at home. He could call me crazy or whatever, but there was some kind of cover up or something going on in Delaware County. I never got the medical reports Relman had promised. Even though Tony, Theresa, and I decided not to use forensic expert Lehrman because he was charging $7,500.00 just to *look* at records and NOT examine tissue and fluids, I still wanted all the reports. I never told Dr. Relman we'd changed our minds about Lehrman and I wasn't gonna tell him now. I had also requested all his correspondence in the case.

Relman was a nervous wreck during our conversation. That was interesting and aroused my suspicions of conspiracy within their department. Relman said he had to talk to the City Solicitor in Delaware County and that's why I had no reports. He needed a higher up's approval. He needs approval mainly to release our *correspondence? Correspondence* between *him and me?—Bullshit.*

Relman went on to tell me that on Friday he called Detective Adam Hartman of Central Detectives in Philly. I had been *BEGGING* him since January to call Detective. Hartman. Relman wasn't interested. Now all of a sudden he was calling him? When I questioned Dr. Relman about that call, he said "He just decided to call him"—*Bullshit.*

At one point Dr. Relman asked me, *"Why the urgency* of getting the records? That we had a two-year Statute of Limitations." Where did that come from? Why was he talking to me about statutes within their department? Relman was supposed to be responding to my request for records. On the 20th of April, all I needed to do was send an authorization and he'd get records together for Lehrman and mail them to me. Now, he was having problems with doing that. Something was just not right.

I shared with Tony a point Detective Hartman had made. If Lenny hadn't been an African American and was someone else with money, that investigation would have been done differently. Detective Hartman swore I ought to sue the medical examiner's office for mental anguish. He felt they were negligent. I was too swamped to even get to thinking like that. He said with all this bigamy, arsenic, pension, hiding bodies thing, Carolyn the nurse would have been brought in for questioning if Lenny were White. This was indeed interesting. I ended the conversation telling Tony that my antennas were up for real.

After we hung up I sent Dr. Relman a stern memo documenting our conversation and copied Tony.

April 29, 2007
Dear Dr. Relman:

This memorandum is to document our telephone conversation of April 29, 2007. It is my understanding that you will instruct Marybeth of your office to forward to me all information pertaining to tests results and blood work of my husband including toxicology report and heavy metals testing. Any reports available regarding examination of my husband, I would also appreciate. I will reiterate if it is not in your budget to overnight these reports to me, please let me know and I will either pick up that expense on my end or come to your facility for the requested information.

*Also, with regard to the chain of command at your facility, during the early morning hours of Saturday, November 25, 2006, I had a couple of conversations with Erin of your office. Prior to finding Erin, I had been searching for my husband's body from five o'clock in the afternoon. All communications took place from my hotel room at the Hyatt Hotel in New Brunswick, New Jersey. I have kept a detailed log of all events regarding Lenny's death and can supply you with notes and information regarding all of my discussions with Erin and **other members of your staff.***

Insofar as the correspondence between you which I forwarded to you over the last five months, you plan to discuss with the city solicitor the release of that information. Please also keep in mind that I did advise that I have subpoenas from the Philadelphia County Register of Wills to request records and information should you require one.

Also, I'd like to confirm with you that I was not advised until April of 2007 that there was any level of arsenic in my husband's system. I received that information from Dr. Phillip Hennen and was extremely surprised with the result of the heavy metals test which was performed in January of 2007. Why were these results kept from me?

I was also surprised to find that you have conferred on Friday April 27, 2007 with Detective Adam Hartman. I have mentioned Detective Hartman to you many times since January of 2007 and you'd never followed up with him or called him. I really had given up on your ever discussing this case with him, but am glad you two have talked. I share with Detective Hartman as well as Crime Reporter Chris Brazzi their opinions that the amount of cocaine in my husband's body could not have killed him.

At your suggestion in March of 2007, I did follow up contacting the Darby Police Department in an effort to open a homicide case regarding my husband's death, or at least have them question Carolyn Monroe. As you know, the detective there indicated there was no need for that and, if so, maybe another police department in Delaware County should be handling the case. He suggested I have you call him, which I did by speaking directly with you and leaving a phone message. I discussed that phone conversation with you. I had faxed the police department in Darby information relevant to my suspicions of foul play.

I'd also like to confirm with you at this time your explanation to me many times that your office had "no budget" financially to pursue any further testing of my husband's specimens. Also as I have informed you, prior to my cremating my husband's body, Erin of your office explained to me in December that there was no need for an autopsy. That discussion took place on the day your office was preparing to release the body to my funeral director.

I have listened to you today explain to me that Erin had no authority to advise me on certain things as she is not a medical examiner and I should have requested to speak with one immediately after Lenny's death. However, please understand that I have never been in a situation such as this and when I finally reached Erin on Friday, November 25, 2006, I was under the impression that she was in charge. I'd only been through thirteen people before I got to her.

I am a lay person is this respect. Erin never offered or directed me to a medical examiner. She was there with the body and very familiar with the case.

Erin and I had many conversations between November 25, 2006 and April of 2007 and she never told me about any arsenic.

I noticed on the toxicology report and medical records that my husband's stomach was distended. As his brother informed me, Lenny had violent stomach pains four hours prior to his death. I have a sworn Affidavit by Marvin Garner and his wife Ellen Garner who talked to my husband around 2:30 p.m. on November 23, 2007. Ms. Monroe was with my husband at that time. I also have phone records which prove the conversation took place.

I am not requesting any further testing by your office as I understand the financial burden you are experiencing. As per your suggestion, I have no problem paying for any further testing with a private forensic pathologist.

Insofar as your suggestion that my requests are "urgent" and there is a "two year statute of limitations," I feel after five months since his death and there are still questions being raised, my request for medical records being sent immediately is not unreasonable.

Thank you for your cooperation in this matter and I assure you we'll get to the bottom of this.

Denise Garner

Cc: *Anthony J. Marino, Esquire*
Detective Adam Hartman
Chris Brazzi, Crime Reporter, Philadelphia Daily News

Dr. Relman was flabbergasted and ran crying to Tony. His office would mail the documents to me by overnight mail and I was to stop all communication with them. He only wanted to deal with Tony. I knew then I had their asses, too. Checkmate!

Several days later, at a meeting with Tony concerning the Interpleader Complaint, I was informed that Carolyn had an attorney. I really was shocked that this lying wench was actually going to go through with this and show up in Court and try to get some more of Lenny's money. Apparently she was broke and had gone to Community Legal Services in Philadelphia to obtain free counsel to represent her. My antennas immediately went up. I wondered how in the world she could get free legal services making the amount of money she made as a registered nurse. After three days of stewing over the matter, I decided to give them a call.

"Good morning, Community Legal Services, Rachael speaking."

"Good morning, Rachael, I'd like to apply for legal services. I want to know if I qualify and what the procedure is. I'm afraid I may make too much money. I make sixty thousand dollars a year. Is that too much?"

"Ma'am there are a lot of different things we consider. You must come in to the office and complete the application."

"Where are you located?"

"Well, we have a few locations."

"I'd like to come to the office located at 3638 North Broad Street in Philadelphia. Can I apply there?" I had remembered seeing the address of the office on the letter Tony had at our meeting. I hadn't asked him for a copy of the letter because I knew he wouldn't give it to for fear I'd start corresponding and calling them up.

Rachael answered, "Certainly. We take applications on a walk-in basis on Mondays, Wednesdays and Fridays between nine and twelve noon. Bring two picture I.D.'s with you, proof of residence, proof of income, and your Social Security Card."

"Okay, I'll come in one day next week."

In forty five minutes, I called the clerk back. "Hi Rachael, my name is Denise Garner. We spoke earlier and I was afraid I made too much money to apply. Do you remember me?"

"Yes...Ms. Garner, I remember you. What can I help you with?"

"Well...I am in a pretty tough situation and I want to be honest with you. I didn't tell you everything when I first called. Do you have time to talk to me or shall I call back."

"I can talk to you, but I may have to put you on hold a lot. These phones are very busy and will interrupt us. This is the intake line and I'm the only one working it."

"I don't mind being on hold."

"Okay, let's begin."

"Well, I have this situation. My husband died and the woman he had been running around with and living with is a defendant in a matter. She's trying to collect all of his money and jip me and my daughter out of his pension and life insurance policy. We have a case and I heard that she has free attorney. She makes a lot of money and is a registered nurse. I have a sick kid with an incurable disease. I want to know how in the world this woman can get free legal services and I had to pay an attorney. Her name is Carolyn Monroe. Can you look her up in the system and tell me who is assigned to the case? I want to take a look at her application. I believe she lied about her income. She's lied about everything else and even lied to City officials. She's got a lot of phony documents, too, including a marriage license saying she is married to my husband."

Rachael was loving this juicy gossip, but her phone was ringing. "Hold on, Ma'am." I waited almost five minutes and she picked back up. "Okay—where were we?" she asked.

"Rachael, can you look Carolyn Monroe up in the system and fax me a copy of her application?" I'm not just Denise Garner, I'm *Denise Garner* the *author* of *Heartburn* and *Afterglow*—two hot novels. I've been on Oprah. I write novels. This is going to be a big case. The police department is involved, too."

"You write novels! I read all the time. Jesus—you've been on Oprah? Wow! I have never spoken to a real author before. It's like—you're famous! Whoa."

"My books are in Barnes and Noble and Borders. Now listen, I cannot let this woman get away with anything. Can you help?"

"What's her name again?"

"Carolyn Monroe. She lives at 8319 Union Avenue in Philly."

Rachael's phone rang again and I was annoyed when she told me to hold on. In a few minutes, she was back again.

"Okay, let's see—Carolyn Monroe.....yep, she is here, but the attorney's name is not listed. I'll have to have it researched to find the file. Give me your information and I'll have someone call you back."

In three hours, I got a return call from a manager. If an applicant was at least sixty-two years of age, they automatically qualified for free legal services in Pennsylvania. The manager could not discuss the details of the case with me due to attorney/client privilege. I told her I would subpoena the file anyway and politely thanked her.

* * *

A couple of months later, I called Angela, my estate attorney, with more news regarding a recent meeting with Tony Marino on the Prudential case.

"Angela, Carolyn is definitely going Pro Se representing herself in this action to collect Lenny's life insurance. Tony found out that the attorney she had gotten is not going to represent her. We are still scheduled for Court in Newark on August 29, 2007 on this case."

"She probably doesn't have any money for an attorney. She's blown it all."

"You're probably right. She never answered that huge Interpleader Complaint wherein she and I are both defendants. She merely sent a letter in to the Court claiming everybody was lying about everything—including the City official that told us Carolyn stated she never knew me or Noelle existed. Nancy Tucker was the City official and had the letter that Carolyn had sent in to the Court. Ms. Tucker is outdone and anxious to testify."

"Carolyn Monroe is going to mess around and end up in jail. Denise, this woman is deranged."

"I have a copy of the letter. I'll read it to you."

"Where'd you get that?"

"I called a Court Clerk in New Jersey who handled dockets. I made sure to do it when Tony was out of his office. He'd have a fit if he knew I went over his head directly to the Court. I posed as a Charita Sloane, a paralegal in the matter, working from home for Mr. Marino due to an emergency. He agreed to fax the letter to me."

"I can't wait to hear it. Tony is gonna strangle you."

"I know. Listen up, Girl. I'm reading it just like she sent it. Full of mistakes and typos.

UNITED STATES DISTRICT COURT
District of New Jersey
Summons in Civil Action
Case No: 07-CV-01321 (DRD)

Carolyn E. Monroe
8319 Union Avenue
Philadelphia, PA 19153
April 24, 2007

The Prudential Insurance Company of America,
Plaintiff,
Vs.
Denise Garner, Carolyn E. Monroe, Julian Hawkins
Funeral Home and Ford Acceptance Corporation,
Defendants.

Re: Exhibit C

To Whom It May Concern:

Enclosed you will find a letter which will address the authenticity of Lenny Garner's signature on his retirement papers. I have also enclosed several documents that have his signature on them.

Re: Exhibit D
There is a death certificate on file with the city of Philadelphia which does not reflect the findings of the death certificate presented to the Prudential Insurance Company by Denise Greene Garner. I have brought this to the attention of the Attorney General's Office of Pa. Enclosed is a copy of the letter I sent to the Attorney General's Office on April 20th, 2007. I have also enclosed the original copy of the death certificate that I requested thirty days after Lenny's death. There is also enclosed a copy of a death certificate Denise sent o the Internal revenue Service. The IRS sent a letter to my home @ 8319 Union Avenue **Philadelphia, PA. 19153. Denise supplied the IRS with a death certificate** *that did not reflect the findings of the death certificate she gave Prudential Insurance Company of America. I have enclosed the letter sent to my home for Mr. Lenny Garner from the IRS. The original death certificate has information that Denise Garner gave the coroner's office which is also incorrect. The mailing*

address listed on the original death certificate, which is the one I received thirty days after Lenny's death has 410 Wheatsheaf St. Jenkintown, Pa.19046. This is incorrect; Lenny's mailing address has been 8319 Union Avenue Philadelphia, Pa. 19153 since January 7, 1995. However, on the death certificate that I believe has been tampered with, has the address listed 8319 Union Avenue Philadelphia Pa. 19153; this death certificate has a negative cause of death. Could this be the reason Denise chose to place the correct mailing adders on his death certificate? Denise has given death certificates to the Prudential Insurance Company of America, The City of Philadelphia, and The Internal Revenue Service. The death certificate which she has given to Prudential appears to be the same as the one sent to me thirty days after Lenny's death, even though the mailing address is not correct. But the death certificates Denise has sent to the City of Philadelphia and The IRS have different information.

Re: Exhibit E

At the time of Lenny's death I did indeed inform the city that I was his wife. I never implied that I was unaware of his former marriages. That statement is a blatant deliberate lie. After information came forth which indicated that Lenny had not completed divorce proceedings against Denise Greene Garner, the only conversation I remember having with Ms. Tucker was one which informed me that I would be entitled to insurance benefits, because I had been named as beneficiary of his life insurance policy. I would not be entitled to pension because it had been decided that proper divorce papers had not been filed by Lenny, and therefore Denise would be entitled to the pension only. This is the only conversation that I recall having with anyone connected with the City of Philadelphia's benefits department. Also Lenny led me to believe that he was going to retain a City of Philadelphia attorney to handle his divorce matters.

I never stated to anyone that Lenny had never been married. I was not asked when we applied for our marriage license if Lenny was married or if he had ever been married. I was only asked about my marital status, which I answered and provided divorce papers as well. Lenny answered the questions which were addressed to him; and I believed at the time that the papers he provided were his divorce papers. I must admit I am only guilty of trusting Lenny. It was very easy for me to trust Lenny, he was the most loving, kind, gentle, considerate, and thoughtful person I ever know, bar none. I have never indicated that I doubted the marriage of Lenny to Denise; I only stated that I was not aware that Lenny had not completed his divorce proceedings. Therefore a calculated deliberate lie by Denise has been told concerning my knowledge of her marriage to Lenny Garner, as well as my knowledge o her existence. As I previously stated I have always been well aware of Denise's connection to Lenny Garner.

Re: Item #1 of Exhibit E

The complaint in civil action No. 5913 was the result of another deliberate lie that Denise brought forth that spoke to my credibility relative to my career. I in turn filed a civil action against her, which is correct. I am not denying knowledge of Denise Green Garner, she is again attempting to discredit me, and cast doubt on my integrity as a person, and as a professional.

Re: Item #2

I really do not understand this ridiculous lie. Denise has never lived with Lenny and I at any time during the yeas of my relationship with Lenny. I am really perplexed as to why this statement was made. She is well aware that it can be proven that she never ever lived anywhere with Lenny and I. Denise's address has never been the same as my address. There was on several occasions when letters from Aetna Insurance Company would come to my address at 8319 Union Ave. Philadelphia, Pa. 19153, when Lenny was alive. I would bring those letters to Lenny's attention, and ask him to take care of it, and stop her from having the insurance company send information concerning her to my address. Lenny always stated he would, and he would attempt to reassure me by telling me not to worry about them. This worked; I did not worry about those letters after that conversation with Lenny. However, after Lenny died, I began to return those letters to sender stating that Denise did not live @8319 Union Avenue Address. Also after Lenny's death I began to go through his personal papers, and I came across many faxed documents that Denise had faxed him over the years to his job that I was not aware of; he brought all these papers home after he retired, but I never bothered to go through his personal things until his death. The following are examples of several faxes which will show **that Denise did not live with us at any time**.

Re: Item #2, 2nd paragraph of Exhibit F.

At the risk of redundancy, again I never stated that I did not know Lenny have been previously married at any time. My only statement to all concern parties was, I thought he had completed his divorce proceedings.

Re: Memorial Service of Exhibit E

Yes, Denise is absolutely correct. I had a memorial service for the man I loved and believed to be my legal husband. The coroner would not release the body to me or Denise, because of the discrepancy concerning who was legally married to Lenny. I had to do something, there were too many people who loved Lenny including me, and needed some sort of closure from this very painful sudden death. There were over 300 people at the memorial service.
RE: Exhibit E continue

Noelle Garner, Lenny's and Denise's daughter did live with me and her father while her mother was in the hospital. What is the point, has anyone denied that fact? Is this another devious tactic brought by Denise in order to cause one to doubt by credibility?

As she stated previously in 1991 I had to bring civil action against Denise Greene Garner. She went to Lenny's job on a Saturday, and told security she was his wife; security allowed her to enter the building (Lenny often worked overtime on Sat.). Lenny had left for the day, (this is what Lenny told me had happened). She pushed redial on his desk phone and discovered he had spoken to me last. She trashed his office, found a bottle of tetracycline, which is an antibiotic I believed I had lost; I had visited Lenny on his job the day before. I dropped the pills, and Lenny put them in his desk drawer.

I brought charges against Denise because she contacted my employer with bogus accusations relative to my professional integrity, after she fond the pills. I have been employed at Pennsylvania Hospital 8th & Spruce Street Philadelphia, Pa. 10107 as a registered nurse since November 15, 1982. I am a preceptor, this involves training registered nurses who are newly hired at Pennsylvania Hospital. I am a member o the Governance Committee; this committee looks at ways in which to improve the everyday operations of your unit. I also met the 1st Tuesday of the month with the Vice President of the hospital, along with eight other registered nurses, to discuss how to improve overall hospital operations. I was the representative sent from my unit to meet with a think tank that Pennsylvania Hospital hired in order to find ways in which to develop better interpersonal relationships among our hospital employees. I am also attending Lasalle University; maintaining a 3.67 GPA. I will have a Masters in Nursing in 2008. Pennsylvania Hospital is paying my full tuition. My credibility with my employer has not been tarnished by Denise's accusations.

In following the order of Denise's accusations, I find myself being redundant; please forgive me, but I must categorically deny that I ever insisted that I had "no knowledge" of Denise Greene Garner. I only stated that I was not aware of incomplete divorce proceedings.

As far as the issue of my wedding being a secret, the only thing I will say is a wedding is a most private affair, and that is at the discretion of the bride and groom as to who will attend. In addition Lenny asked me to keep it a secret from his family only; so I did. We had a wedding ad a reception, 80 people attended.

I did tell Lenny's sister Theresa I could not find the divorce papers; I do not remember telling her Lenny had lost the divorce papers. During the time of Lenny's death I felt that I was going to die also, and this same sister Theresa told me on the third day after his death, when I and two of my girlfriends went to her home to get her input for the program for the memorial service, that I had to move on and stop crying all the time.

Denise has recently attempted to file insurance claims against my car insurance company, and my homeowners insurance on behalf of Lenny. She contacted my car insurance company in March 2007, and was denied. There is a taped deposition on record with my car insurance. Then she attempted the same tactic with my homeowners insurance, there is also a taped deposition I gave to my homeowners insurance. The insurance adjuster for my homeowners insurance informed me that they were going to deny Denise based on the information they had obtained. Enclosed you will find a letter sent to me by my homeowners insurance regarding this matter

Enclosed you will find a copy of a letter I sent to Paul Corbett, Esq., and Wilbur Elsmann.

Sincerely
Carolyn E. Monroe

Angela was hysterical laughing. "I told you that woman is crazy. She is a freaking piece of work."

I planned to burn her and she just provided me with some lighter fluid. After reading this letter, I had mixed emotions—I stopped laughing. Carolyn Monroe was going to succeed at one thing—convincing all that read it that she was not only a complete idiot, but she was also illiterate and a liar. I was embarrassed that she was a *woman* and that she was *African American*. Reading it reminded me of occasions when we view people on televised news reports. The media would always find the most ignorant

person to interview at a crime or incident scene. The ones with no teeth in their mouth, not properly dressed and groomed, and always using incorrect English. They were the "Know it Alls" of the neighborhood and if they were of our race, we were always embarrassed. Her letter had a zillion typos in it and the stupid wench sent it in to the United States District Court! The dummy with the 3.67 grade point average that was going for her master's degree had definitely flunked the English language. She also shot herself in the foot not only by admitting to accusations of home wrecking, but listing and literally bragging about her great nursing skills. Unfortunately, even with her abundance of experience, training, nursing skills and teaching abilities, she didn't have enough sense to call paramedics in time to save Lenny—or do anything herself to help his condition. I want this simple bitch to keep right on talking so I'll win every case against her. She's definitely assisting Denise Greene Garner and I'm preparing to subpoena some more records and start deposing folks at all her insurance companies and that job of hers.

"Denise, this is really a caper. I cannot believe your life is so eventful. I hate to leave you, but I've got a ton of work to do." Angela said.

"You can't leave me just yet—I've got more stuff to discuss with you. Give me another fifteen minutes. Charge me. Send me a bill."

"Come on Denise, what's next. What else did you uncover?"

"Last Thursday, the attorney for the insurance company, Mr. Corbett, told Tony he was going to file pleadings to get a default judgment and kick Carolyn out for not answering the Interpleader Complaint. This would mean there would be no trial or settlement conference if his Petition is granted. I'm waiting to hear back on what happens with that."

Angela's voice perked up. "Well, it would be good if that would happen. It would avoid a lot of work for all of us and you'd get the money. I hope it happens."

"Angela, Tony has an Estate question. There is a possibility that we will want to sue Carolyn's homeowner's carrier because Lenny died in her home as a result of her negligence. If I were the plaintiff or beneficiary, the 100K should go to me, but what did I lose with Lenny dying is one question. I got the pension. So Tony wants to know if the Estate could be the recipient/plaintiff in a lawsuit like this. I may have it phrased wrong, but can you figure this out for us? You know what we are trying to determine. Can an Estate go after a defendant in a Wrongful Death Claim? Do we need an Estates Litigation attorney to sue the Homeowner's Company? What's your take on this? Also, I want to let you know that the Pension Board made good and paid me all the money that Carolyn had spent from Lenny's pension check. I received that check a couple of weeks ago. They are proceeding against her for the return of their money. I received about $2200. I've also found out that if I die, the pension rolls over to Noelle and she collects it for the rest of her life. She qualifies because she has an incurable disease. That's really good news."

Angela's daughter and Noelle were the same age. Angela hade known Noelle since she was eleven years old and watched her fight Crohn's Disease. She'd hauled Lenny into court on many occasions and often represented me for little or no money. "That's great news! You're really making some headway kid. You deserve it. You've been through the ringer with those two for years."

"Thanks, Angela. You've hung with me for a long time. We're getting there. I have another question, too. If the Pension Board was sending Lenny $2400 a month for pension checks prior to his death—and he took an option that if he dies that his spouse gets fifty percent of his regular monthly pension check - what happens to the other half of the monthly pension. Does anyone get it? Does the Pension Board just get to keep all that money? We can't figure it out. If you know, tell me. I do plan to ask the question at the Pension Board, too."

I finally shut up and Angela was ready. "Okay, Denise, jot this stuff down for Tony. Here is some information which should help you guys:

1. Pension—No one gets the other half. It's just a designated benefit **that continues that is set at one-half of the original payment. Lenny's** original payment was $2400 and you the spouse get half of that. This is what he elected when he got into the *DROP program*. Spouse gets half, Denise—that's it. He signed a contract.

2. Wrongful Death—The Estate can bring a wrongful death and/or a survivor's action. Wrongful death recovery is not subject to Inheritance tax, survivor recovery is. The beneficiaries of a wrongful death action are

the intestate heirs, the beneficiary of a survivorship action is the Estate, and whoever is named in the will. Since Lenny had no will, in this case the beneficiaries are one and the same, that is, you and Lenny's children. If Lenny has other children other than Noelle (and my recollection is that you told me that he did) then you get one-half and all the children divide the other one-half. If Noelle is the only child your share is $40,000 plus one-third, she gets the rest. The proper person to bring either legal action is the Estate administrator (you) and generally these are done by personal injury lawyers, not estates lawyers, as the action is brought in Civil Court not Orphans Court."

"You are so smart and helpful. I love you."

"You're welcome, Denise."

"Okay Angela. Thanks. I gotta run. I will fax you right now a copy of my response to Carolyn Monroe's letter to the Court.

I couldn't take it any longer. I had to mail the dumb bitch Carolyn a letter and I couldn't wait until Tony got hold of her ass in Court. *Pro Se*—he would eat her alive. Even though I really did not give a damn about the insurance money—I knew I'd end up with it anyway. I had the baddest, smartest, and meanest trial attorney on the East Coast representing me. I surmised her lawyer at Community Legal Services either dropped the case because of all of the lies her client had told or because the insurance company had jurisdiction in New Jersey. Carolyn was a Pennsylvania resident. She would have had to apply to Community Legal Services in New Jersey and would be ineligible because she was not a resident of New Jersey. In any case, this was another feather in my cap. Checkmate!

June 15, 2007

Carolyn E. Monroe
8319 Union Avenue
Philadelphia, PA 19153

RE: *Prudential v. Denise Garner, Carolyn Monroe, et al*

U.S. District Court – District of New Jersey – Newark Vicinage
Civil Action No: 07-1321 (CRD)

Dear Ms. Monroe:

I am in receipt of your letter dated April 24, 2007 to the Court regarding the above captioned matter. Since you seem to be a bit mixed up with the facts, I will clarify them for you as follows:

(1) When you refer to "Item 2" on page 4 of your letter, you seem to be under the impression that I indicated to Prudential and/or the Court that I once resided with you and my husband. This is not so. If you examine the facts in my letter and the exhibits, you should see that I was addressing the Complaint in Civil Action which you filed against me. The Title Report I referred to in my letter states that I was served with the Complaint at my marital residence. My marital residence was 7415 North 20th Street in Philadelphia, Pennsylvania, 19138. This is the same residence that I shared with my husband and the same address you used to serve me. That's what that means. It does not mean that the three of us—(you, me and my husband) lived together at that residence or any other residence. The attachment (the Title Report) I provided with my letter to Prudential Insurance Company dated December 5, 2006 explains, verifies and confirms that and confirms that you knew of my existence and my marriage to Lenny Garner. This became an issue because I was informed by Nancy Tucker and the Medical Examiner's office that you informed both those parties that you "knew of no other wife." I am certain if and when the Attorney General's Office or the IRS contacts me, I shall be able to explain the facts. If you remain perplexed, please refer to my letter of December 5, 2006 and perhaps you'll be enlightened. If that does not work, you should retain an attorney and provide that person with the legal pleadings and letters to assist you.

*(2) Insofar as my "tampering with Death Certificates," at all times I **supplied correct information to all parties involved as soon as I received same**. It was me who noticed a mistake in one certificate regarding my husband's address at the time of his death. I requested a change to indicate your Union Avenue address. With regard to any information being changed relevant to my husband's cause of death, those issues were addressed by the Medical Examiner after a full investigation of his death was ordered by me. All Death Certificates were forwarded to Prudential Insurance Company. For your information, it*

does not matter which Death Certificate the Internal Revenue received at the onset of my requesting my husband's tax returns. The point being—he is dead, I am his wife and the Executor of his Estate. I am entitled to examine his tax returns. If the IRS has questions for me regarding his cause of death or residence at the time of his death, I have no problem clarifying the situation and/or cooperating should they request additional information along those lines.

(3) In your reference to Noelle Garner residing at your home in 2001, the "point" is that I addressed it because you had claimed (as per information given to me) that you did not know us. That's the "point" I addressed. I was proving you indeed knew of me and who my children were.

(4) The medication I found in my home that my husband told me you had provided him with in the 1990's, was indeed found in my home and not at his office. Yes, I did trash his work area, kick up quite a fuss and reported it to your workplace, however, this medication was not in a container labeled or prescribed to you. I won't say more about the incidences of medication at this time as they will be addressed in the future.

(5) You and I both know exactly why none of my in-laws or my children knew you and Lenny had married or were invited to the wedding. Ms. Monroe, I know the procedures that take place when a couple makes application for a marriage license. I know the questions that are asked of both parties and that both parties apply together and are able to listen to each other's answers to questions asked on the application. How could you think my husband had a batch of divorce papers at the Marriage License Bureau on June 3, 2002 to present to them when he had checked off while he was there that he had never been married—that his marriage to you was his first marriage?

(6) With regard to documents which were requested of you by subpoena from me which include bank statements and IRS records, I shall follow up with the Register of Wills and the Courts to advise that you have not adhered to the subpoena. As you know, the two of us (you and I) have a lot of issues to resolve regarding my husband's death. As soon as this life insurance issue is settled, I shall resume or have my attorneys address all other matters. My husband is dead—died on your watch—and nobody, no company or any agency is off the hook without a fight from his wife. Please rest assured that it does not matter to me how much time and money I have to expend to get to the bottom of this investigation.

(7) In my opinion, my husband would be alive today had he not been associated with you. We also know that he may have resided with you and carried on an affair with you for many years, but he always protected me. He did so by making sure I was covered with his medical insurance and in the end, he made sure I'd have his pension and life insurance benefits. Believe me, there was a reason he neglected to divorce me. Lenny and I were on very good terms prior to his death and long before his death, which will be proven at trials and will probably surprise you. I know a lot more than you think I do about events which occurred on Union Avenue, at family gatherings, in public places and at the homes of my in-laws, contrary to the happy and blissful relationship you describe. My husband not only had high blood pressure, but additionally on many occasions he had diarrhea of the mouth that went untreated. It is my job and my focus at this point to protect my husband. Ms. Monroe, let me reiterate that I assure you not a stone will be left unturned and everything will come out in the wash.

Sincerely,
DENISE GARNER

P.S.: For your information, I did not give a "deposition" to any of your companies (Homeowners, Car Insurance, etc). I provided recorded statements to those companies. There is a difference between the two procedures. A deposition takes place in a forum where a person (deponent) is asked a series of oral questions by an attorney and a court reporter is present.

CHAPTER 15

∽

Room Service

Lo and behold, I did get evicted from my house in Jenkintown on May 14, 2007 even though I had hired a Real Estate attorney. Tony came to my rescue and sent a scathing letter to my attorney, Thomas Merkin, who had caused all kinds of problems for me. That man might as well have been working for the landlords.

I was put out of the house by a Constable and I had been promised by Merkin that this would not occur. I had given Merkin a retainer in the amount of $250 for his services and I did not get the benefit of any legal services. I suffered substantial loss. Given the abruptness of the Constable's actions, I was caused to leave behind furniture and other belongings in the value of approximately $2500. I also lost my security deposit in the amount of $500. Tony calculated my total financial losses alone exceeded $4,000.

Tony described me as a long-time friend in the letter and explained to Merkin that he didn't want to accuse another attorney of committing malpractice. Tony was sure that, at all times, Merkin's intentions were to best serve me, but for whatever reason, his execution was not sufficient to save his friend all those losses.

Merkin's malpractice insurance had a certain deductible and that $4,000 was surely an amount that fell within his deductible. Tony wanted to avoid the necessity of Merkin having to report to his carrier any potential claim of negligence, so he'd appreciate Merkin giving him a call to discuss how, in any way, they could make *his friend* and Merkin's former client, Denise Garner, whole.

In ten days, my remaining belongings were delivered to my beautiful new home located in the affluent suburb of Lafayette Hill, Pennsylvania, and a check in the amount of $6,000 was mailed to me by Tony. Checkmate!

Prudential Insurance Company was still trying to get out of paying double indemnity on the policy. Tony got on the phone with the Appeals Committee and conferenced me in. He warned me not to say a damn word or even breathe loudly or he would kill me. The gentleman handling the file picked up.

"Good morning Mr. Boyer. I have your letter denying Denise Garner's claim for accidental death benefits with regard to the late Lenny Garner, her husband."

"Oh yes, Mr. Marino, I know that file. I have it out. Our policy precludes coverage under the accidental death benefit if it results from sickness, whether the loss results directly or indirectly from the sickness. Her husband had been sick a long time before he died."

Tony was in no mood to listen to this mumbo jumbo bullshit. He shot back telling Boyer that in his denial letter, he accurately pointed out that on Lenny's death certificate the immediate cause of death was "adverse drug reaction" with a significant condition contributing to death as "hypertension." In that letter "sickness" was defined in the policy as "any disorder of the body or mind of a covered person." Tony informed him that the word "disorder" was not defined."

We could hear rumbling on the other end of the receiver as Boyer flipped through pages. I had a copy of the policy in front of me and was at page 65 where the definition was found. Tony had the shit in front of him, too. We waited in silence.

"Umm....okay – I have it here. You're right, Mr. Marino. It could use some clarification."

"Look, Mr. Boyer, we need to examine this thing so you understand. It is clear that my client's husband died as a result of an accidental death. He suffered an adverse reaction to the ingestion of cocaine."

"Yes, I am aware of his drug use. I've read the file."

Tony asked him to consider the fact that the toxicology analysis revealed the presence of cocaine and that no other drugs had been found. The emergency response team's report contained no indication that Lenny had been under any medication for any hypertensive problem. With regard to medications that he had been taking, it indicated "unknown." When Lenny was treated at Mercy Fitzgerald Hospital, it was clear that there was no indication of a prior cardiac history nor was there any indication that he had been on any medications.

Boyer listened carefully and admitted he saw Tony's point and would reconsider. The records were not all examined—or certain facts weren't noted properly.

Tony breathed a sigh of relief and continued. "In short, there is no evidence in the medical records upon which Prudential may rely to suggest that a "sickness" indirectly resulted in his death. Further, it is questionable as to whether hypertension in and of itself can act as a "disorder" since "disorder" is not defined in the policy."

That pretty much ended the conversation and Boyer said he would be back in touch.

* * *

It was August 29, 2007, Tony and I walked into the Courthouse together. We both carried briefcases. He went to sign in with the clerk and I sat on the hallway bench. I noticed Carolyn sitting alone. It was the first time I had seen her in fourteen years. As I stared at her, all the events of the elapsed months were running through my mind. I was fascinated that she'd become such an intricate part of my life. She truly was ugly—there was no doubt about that. The stories I'd heard in the past were definitely true. She reminded me of an old African woman. She was little. She couldn't have been more than five feet tall, about a size eight. She was wearing a black skirt that fell to her knees and a fuchsia cheap knit top. A thick leather belt with a large brass buckle was around her waist. She wore black leather high heel mules and was in desperate need of a pedicure. I could not believe she was carrying a shiny gold clutch handbag. The hair—oh my God the hair! Fake braids were pulled back off her face, a black and gold headband holding them in place. For jewelry, she wore large hoop earrings and a charm bracelet. My husband *had to be* on something to have that.

We sat there gritting on each other and I was the one who started that. She was defiant, staring right back at me. I was all dressed up in a two hundred fifty dollar green polyester and spandex skirt and top. The skirt was long, hanging just above my ankle. It flared out so when I walked, the bottom moved with me. It made me feel very lady-like. When I first tried it on at the boutique, a customer stopped dead in her tracks and noticed me in front of the mirror checking myself out. She immediately said to Tedd, "I want just what she has on—jewelry, shoes and all. She looks fabulous! The lovely set of jewelry was a matching necklace, earrings and bracelet. The stones were cream colored with hints of shades of light and deep gray. I had on green patent leather sling back heels, a very sexy shoe with the toe out from Nine West. The handbag, from the same designer, matched perfectly. My outfit had been put together by a friend of mine who'd been dressing women for over thirty years. Noelle was also his client and he'd put together an outfit for her to wear to Court. She was as sharp as a tack. He had a swank and upscale boutique in Philadelphia called Babe. I met him the same night I met Lenny. At that time, he also had an additional store in the Cedarbrook Mall, above the bar l worked at. Tedd carried very unique items and also sold men's clothing. I purchased the suit Lenny wore for his funeral from him. Tedd Wynton was a very talented African American buyer. When you got an outfit from him, people raved about it. So, I put him in charge of my size fourteen ass for the trial. I'd gotten a deep colonic the day before to ensure my tummy would be as flat as a pancake.

My hair had been done earlier that day at the classiest shop in Philly, Panache Hair Salon. My stylist, Frank, had opened the shop at seven in the morning just to get me and Noelle's hair done. He was an Italian magician and I'd been going to him for twenty years along with Noelle, a customer since she was twelve.

I noticed a bunch of people coming toward the hallway. The Garners had arrived full force. Leading the mob was Theresa, the matriarch of the family, flanked by Lamont, Lenny's youngest son from that brief encounter he had with a co-worker during one of our separations. Lamont was now sixteen years old. Theresa was all decked out, too. She was wearing a **navy and beige summer knit suit. It was gorgeous. Perfect for court.** As I watched my in-laws approach, they were all dressed appropriately for the occasion. I was proud of all of them. Theresa hugged me. "You look amazing!" We all began hugging and greeting each other and people sat or stood where they could. My brother-in-law Barry marched his ass over to Carolyn's side and sat next to her. We all watched him face her and give her a contemptuous look. I called his name out to distract him and motioned him to come to me. I patted the bench. Noelle got up and let him sit next to me. Carolyn gave us the finger and continued to study us. Finally, Tony approached and alongside him was a woman who continued over to Carolyn. She was carrying a briefcase. Family members surrounded Tony to greet him. Twenty minutes later, our case was called and we entered the courtroom.

I was confident sitting next to Tony. He was as dressed to kill as usual and I knew I was in the best of hands.

Sitting strong behind us were thirty-seven members of Lenny's family. Theresa, Noelle, and Barry were seated together holding hands. As we waited for the trial to begin, Tony concentrated on the letter I had sent to the Court. Carolyn was seated across from us with her new attorney. She was a pretty woman, tall, about five feet ten inches. She was Caucasian and had long blonde hair that parted on the right side with minimal bangs covering the left side of her face. She had beautiful blue eyes and her makeup was light and perfect. She was a knockout. Dressed in an expensive red suit with tan accessories, the woman had class. She looked to be in her early thirties. There was a Coach handbag on the table that looked authentic, so I knew it didn't belong to Nursey Pie. I noticed she was wearing a wedding band. I wondered where the hell Carolyn had found her.

I got a tap on my back. When I turned around, Theresa handed me a pink sealed envelope. She didn't say a word. She simply smiled. I immediately opened it.

Dear Denise:

No matter what goes down in here today, whether we win or lose this case, I am a better off. I have my family back—meaning you and Noelle. I want you to know how much I appreciate your taking charge, working diligently to get to the bottom of this—and for the justice you are seeking regarding my brother's death. I want to thank you for pulling me out of a dark hole of grief about Lenny's death. You are so refreshing, full of energy and such a beam of light in my life. I am so sorry we missed so many years together not allowing ourselves to love each other. I am sorry I got on the bandwagon with others in my family mistreating, ignoring and hating you for no reason. I apologize. You are such a treat to my life and a boost to my well being. I am so sorry Lenny was not a better husband and father. Please my love—keep me. Keep me smiling and keep me not only as your family—but always as your friend. I promise to take better care of you this time. Thank you for listening to me so many days and nights. I am so glad you took charge, as you always have in your life. I am very proud of your becoming a published author. I am eternally grateful that you were generous enough to take me into your arms. I can feel the love you have for me and Lenny. We would not be here today collecting justice had it not been for you—Wifey Poo. You are a powerful woman and an asset to us all. You make things happen, baby. My niece is gorgeous—looks just like Rhonda and talks just like me—that's something I can brag about while I continue to adore her. I'm looking forward to Noelle and I having a lot of fun together and learning one another.

Theresa

Tears streamed down my face. I looked over and gave Theresa thumbs up. Tony was still reading my letter to the Court.

The Court Crier said, "All rise as the Honorable Deron Clancy enters the courtroom. This is a trial to determine who should receive the life insurance policy on the life of Lenny Garner in the amount of $6,000 and double indemnity due to accidental death."

Judge Clancy said, "Counsel Marino, are you ready to begin the questioning of your client, defendant Denise Greene Garner?"

"Good morning, Your Honor, and yes I'm ready to begin. I'd like to call Denise Greene Garner to the witness stand."

I approached the stand and placed my hand on the bible, I took the oath. I could feel everyone's eyes on me. My mind was telling me to stay relaxed and try to exhibit self -confidence and control. I was seated and family members were smiling at me. Carolyn had a blank expression.

"Please state your full name," Tony said, giving me a wink and a smile.

"Denise Greene Garner."

"Ms. Garner, when did you first meet additional defendant, Carolyn Monroe?"

"I have never been formally introduced to Ms. Monroe."

"Do you remember the first time you ever *saw or* spoke to her?"

"In approximately 1981 or 1982 on the telephone."

"How did that occur?"

Before I answered the question, I relived for a moment that afternoon twenty- five years ago. I glanced over at Carolyn in dismay, knowing that this had been the very beginning of her scheme to demolish my relationship with Lenny. I responded to Tony. "She called my apartment. Lenny and I were unmarried and living together at that time."

"What did she want?'

"She wanted Lenny to come to Georgia and assist her in moving back to Philadelphia."

"Did your husband go?"

"No. He explained to her that he could not do that."

Tony asked me how I felt after the conversation ended. I remember Lenny's explanation that she was a long time platonic friend and had attended nursing school in Atlanta. There was no reason not to believe my husband, I explained, as he had many platonic relationships with women. The call had not bothered me.

"Did you ever hear from Carolyn Monroe again?"

"Yes. She continued to call him throughout the years."

"The calls continued after you and your husband married?'

"Yes."

"Did you and your husband have a wedding?'

"Yes, we had a lavish wedding in 1986."

"Were any of his platonic friends invited?"

"Yes, many."

"Was Carolyn Monroe invited?"

"No."

"Do you know why she was not invited?"

"No. Lenny had his own guest list and she was not on it. We were trying to keep the list at 200, so I figured he left her out because she wasn't very important. The next time I spoke to her was the Monday after our wedding when she called our house to speak to Lenny. That call was unusual to me because I remember saying to her that I would get my *husband*. At that point, she questioned why I was referring to Lenny as my *husband*. I informed her that we had just gotten married on Saturday."

I watched as Carolyn tensed up. She seemed angry and surprised, her body language accusing me of lying. I anticipated her fake display of emotion, but I remained focused, my eyes on Tony.

"How did that make you feel?"

"My antennas went up and I wondered why she was upset. I called my husband to the phone and I overheard him answering *yes* and *no* to questions. Then I heard him confirm that we had gotten married on Saturday.

"What happened after the call was over?"

"I cursed my husband out and accused him of having an affair with her."

"And what was his reaction?"

"He denied it and told me not to worry about her. He said she wasn't his type and that I should see her. He said she was a little short black monkey that I should not worry about."

Carolyn's facial expression showed I had humiliated her. The sounds from the courtroom were mixtures of gasps and laughter.

"Mrs. Garner, have you ever assaulted Carolyn Monroe?"

"I never *actually* assaulted her, but I lunged at her and I kicked her car when I caught her in the early 1990's at a bar around the corner from our house. She was having drinks with my husband. Another incident occurred in 1992 when I went to her apartment for my husband and I kicked the door in and I threw paint. The paint was in her hallway in a five gallon drum. I was angry and poured paint on the rugs throughout the hallway, up the stairs, and under the doorsill of her apartment. Subsequent to that incident, I went to her job and had a talk with some supervisor because she was giving my husband medication unprescribed out of the hospital where she worked. I'd found the medication in our house and my husband said she had given it to him and told him to take it. I also told the people at her job that my husband claimed she provided him with cocaine. Other than sending her letters about this case, I had no other altercations with her."

"Did you call her apartment or her house subsequent to going to the hospital to report her?"

"Yes. I called to check on our daughter, Noelle, when she went to live there or when she went to visit. And I called periodically to talk to my husband about our medical insurance once we separated. Sometimes, I would just call to chat with Lenny and I called Carolyn Monroe's house when I got the news that my husband had passed away. Oh, I forgot.... I also had the hospital call there for me one time when I was in the emergency room one night about three years ago for insurance information."

"Why? Didn't you have your own health insurance cards?"

"Yes, I did, but often they would mail my cards there to Carolyn's house. They had me listed as living there. Lenny would see that I got my cards, but sometimes we didn't hook up for me to get them."

"So.....your mail went to Carolyn Monroe's house?"

"Yes, it did."

"If your husband was living with Carolyn Monroe, why didn't you divorce him?"

My facial expression took a drastic change as if Tony was asking me a stupid or ridiculous question. I gasped. "Oh, I couldn't do *that*. I had to have my medical insurance. I couldn't work all the time and he said he didn't want to have to *marry* her. I had the house and *this* and *that*. We just decided not to divorce. It was too much trouble."

"But there were two divorce complaints filed, one by you and one by your husband. Can you explain that?"

"Oh, yes—*that*. See, sometimes we would get into arguments. So we were mad twice and filed. Both times, we made up and decided to let them go." I said with a wave of my hand.

"How often did you see your husband?"

"Several times a year. He'd sometimes come by the house or I would meet him in town or stop by his job and we'd go to lunch. But if something happened, like a problem, we'd get on the phone and decide what to do."

"When was the last time you talked to him?"

"In August of 2006. He wanted to hook up with me. He came to meet me, but I had something to do."

"Were you two sleeping together?"

"No."

"When was the last time you had sex with your husband?"

"1994 at our house in Philadelphia."

"That's two years after the two of you separated?"

"Yes."

"Does your husband have any other children?"

"Yes."

"When did you learn your husband had married Carolyn Monroe?"

I gave Carolyn a loathing look, pausing before I answered. I was still hot with her for hiding his body. Without taking my eyes off her I said, "On Monday, November 27, 2006, I found out about the marriage. I learned it from a clerk at the Medical Examiner's office when I was trying to claim his body and prepare his funeral. After that telephone conversation I went to City Hall and got a copy of the marriage certificate. It stated they got married in June of 2002 and that my husband had never been married. I was shocked."

I continued to tell Tony that I knew his first wife, Francis Garner, and she had a son. He was now in his forties. My husband adopted him when he and Frances got married. My husband also had a daughter and two sons from previous relationships. I knew for sure that my husband divorced Frances Garner before marrying me because I was working at a law firm and one of the practicing attorneys in our suite handled my husband's divorce. Lenny divorced Frances in 1984. Tony announced he had no further questions.

He gave me another wink and a happy look. I could tell I'd done fine. He headed for our table. As I sat there, I knew the beauty queen sitting next to Carolyn was coming to cut my throat.

"We'll now have Cross Examination by Giana Santiago, attorney for defendant Carolyn Monroe. Ms. Santiago, you may begin," Judge Clancy said.

She strolled over thanking the judge and bid me a good morning.

"Good Morning, Ms. Santiago," I said, looking at her wedding band. **I knew her husband was Latino or something because she was definitely of** all white blood.

"So….You're quite something else." Sarcasm filled her voice. She paused, then continued, "You attempted to attack Carolyn Monroe and I also hear you shot your husband twice. Is this all true?"

"Yes."

"And where did you come across this *gun*?"

"My husband took me to purchase it after we were married."

"Why?"

"I wanted it for protection in our home."

"Why did you shoot him?"

With nonchalance, I answered "He needed to be shot."

She looked at me in amazement. She was speechless for a few seconds. I could hear faint laughter in the courtroom. I saw Tony's head sink. I didn't know if he was laughing or crying. Carolyn was smiling in triumph. I figured they would at least know I was honest. I didn't care if Tony was pissed off.

The judge banged his gavel several times and ordered Ms. Santiago to continue with her questioning.

"Why did he need to be shot, Mrs. Garner?"

"Because he had been abusing me. He would hit me and one night he strangled me. So I shot him."

"What happened after that?"

"He went to work and I went to a mental facility."

"So, you admit you have mental problems?"

"I guess I did, or I do. I have Panic Disorder."

"So, when did this shooting occur?"

"In 1992."

"So, your husband left you after you shot him."

"No, my husband went to *work* after I shot him. He had graze wounds and he refused to leave me after I shot him."

"So, you are telling me that after you tried to kill him, he wanted to stay with you?"

"Yes."

"So why did he leave?"

"My doctors refused to let me leave the facility unless he left the residence."

"I imagine you are quite jealous of Carolyn Monroe—you know, her taking your husband from you?"

"No. I'm not jealous of her. I just hate her."

"Why do you hate her?"

I looked directly at Carolyn. She was still smiling and confident. She was happy as hell that I was stone fucking this all up for myself. I looked at Santiago and said, "I hate her because she came between my husband and his children and she went to my daughter Noelle's college and upset her when I was out of the country in 2003. Also, she provided an abundance of alcohol and drugs to my husband. She's a liar on top of all that. That's *precisely* why I hate her."

Santiago then asked me if I thought Lenny intended for her to have this life insurance policy. "My husband was sick and confused and full of alcohol and drugs. I honestly don't know what he intended." She had no further questions and I was excused. When I returned to the table Tony whispered, "You are a piece of work. You should get the Academy Award for best actress in the category of airing your dirty laundry."

"Shut up counselor, they're changing the channel. Here comes scene two."

"We'll now have questioning of additional defendant Carolyn Monroe by counsel Santiago," Judge Clancy announced.

Carolyn stood up from her seat and her demeanor was very composed. However, I could tell she was having a time navigating in those heels. I was hoping she would trip. All eyes were fixed on her. She took her seat and was sworn in. When she put her hand on that bible, I thought about her getting married and lying in church that day with Lenny. I had absolutely no respect for her.

"Good morning, Ms. Monroe," Santiago sweetly said.

Carolyn indeed was very relaxed and she answered with a smile. "Good morning, Ms. Santiago."

"Can you tell me when you met Lenny Garner?"

"I met him in the late sixties."

"Where did you meet him?"

"In a bar in Philadelphia."

When she answered that question, I imagined the scene and how young and gorgeous Lenny was. I wondered again how the hell he had ever said anything to her. He'd always been a vain person and had a true dislike for ugly people. Seeing her so close up, I was definitely confused about how she pulled him that first day they met.

"Was he with anyone at the time you met him."

"He was with a male friend. A roommate or something like that"

"When did you begin having an affair with Lenny?"

She answered, "In 1982."

Studying her and listening carefully to her answer, I ran through the year 1982 to remember all the events of that year. I pictured the two-bedroom apartment Lenny and I had lived in with the girls and how strapped we had been for cash that year.

"Did he ever indicate that he was married?"

"No."

"Did he ever mention his prior wives, Frances Garner or Denise Garner?"

"Well, he mentioned in 1982 that he was living with a girl named Denise."

"What happened between the late sixties and 1982? Why hadn't you dated him before that?"

"I don't know. We were friends meeting up at bars sometimes and then I went away to nursing school. It was platonic."

"So you did begin to date him while he was living with Denise?"

She looked right at me and responded proudly, "Yes." My eyes were locked onto her and every family member was quiet. Tony was taking notes beside me.

"Well, how is it that you informed Nancy Tucker, Administrator of the City of Philadelphia Life Benefits after his death that you had never known of Denise Garner or her daughter Noelle?"

She repositioned herself, started moving her hands and replied, "I didn't tell her that. I told her that I didn't know that Lenny was still married to Denise. Lenny had told me that he'd divorced Denise. Ms. Tucker misunderstood me."

Nancy Tucker was seated in the courtroom. We glanced at each other for a second. She showed no emotion. She didn't make a sound. I thought, "Good work, NT." I had come to like her very much through our conversations since Lenny's death.

"Did you ever furnish Lenny with medication or drugs?"

"Never. He had prescriptions from his doctors. That's how he got his medication."

"What were the events of the day he died?"

When that question was asked I looked away. I had to look over at Theresa and Barry. I was expecting trouble to come shortly in the form of an outburst. I was worried. This is a subject we had talked so much about since he died. It always struck a nerve. They were both leaning in as far as they could, concentrating on her every word. Both of them had smirks on their faces.

"He was feeling fine most of the day. In the afternoon, he said his stomach was hurting. After our family—all of us—had had Thanksgiving dinner, he went up to the bathroom and called for me. When I got up there, he had collapsed."

Barry shouted out—"The turkey was never cut!" The Judge shut him up and Tony gave him "The Look." Santiago continued on.

"Did you call paramedics right away?"

"Immediately." Theresa's head went down when Carolyn said that.

"Then what did you do?"

I was very upset and I answered all their questions on the phone and upon their arrival. Then I followed the ambulance to the hospital. I waited around and he died. Then I came home and called his family."

"Who, specifically, in his family did you call?"

"I called his brother-in-law Barry and he came to my house. Then Lenny's niece and nephew came over. I also called a girlfriend of mine."

"Did you call Denise or Noelle?"

"No, I just figured his family would do that. Denise and I didn't get along."

I wanted to smack the bitch. I knew she had no plans of telling us anything.

"Was Lenny on any medications at the time of his death or prior to?"

"Not that I know of."

"Did you know about him using any street drugs around the time of **his death**?"

"**If he was doing street drugs, I knew nothing about it. I worked most of the time and he was retired and home during the day. I can't say for sure what he did when I wasn't with him.**"

"What about in your thirty-seven year association with him—did you ever observe him using any street drugs?"

"Yes."

"In your opinion, do you believe he had a problem?"

"No, I believe it was recreational. He got high on the weekends."

"What about alcohol—do you think that was excessive?"

"No. I believe he was a moderate drinker, a drink or two a few times a week."

"Have you made claim for any other life insurance polices regarding his death—I mean other than this six thousand dollar policy?"

"No."

"How did you feel about Lenny, Carolyn?"

"I love him. I have loved him for many years. We had a wonderful relationship. We were very good to each other. I am devastated that he is gone."

"This Change of Beneficiary form—did you sign it?"

Carolyn took a look at it. She was completely calm and said, "No, I didn't. Lenny had that form. He said he was filling it out to make sure I had money to pay bills in case anything happened to him."

"Do you know if he brought the form home with him from work or if it was mailed to your house?"

"No. I don't know where it came from. But he had it at home."

"I have no further questions, Carolyn."

Judge Clancy motioned to Tony. "Mr. Marino you may now cross-examine the witness."

With a pleasant smile, Tony approached the witness stand. My thoughts were, "Oh shit—the piranha now has the guppy. It's show time."

"Good morning, Ms. Monroe."

"Good morning."

"So, you met Lenny Garner in the late sixties in a bar while he was out with a male friend that he lived with?"

"Yes."

"Do you remember that friend's name?"

"No, I can't remember. It was a long time ago."

Tony asked her if the name Cedric Barnes rang a bell. He described him as being about 6'4," medium brown. He lived in Washington, Pennsylvania and was an old Army buddy of Lenny's. Tony asked if she had called him when Lenny died to invite him to the memorial service she was planning and if *that* had been the friend Lenny was with the night she met him? Carolyn was stunned and had to take a breath. She shook her head. "Oh—yes—that's him. Yes."

"And the name of the bar was Ted Knight's Showcase and that was at 48th and Chestnut Streets in Philadelphia where you met Lenny? Correct?"

"Yes—I think that was the bar."

Tony then paused to address the Court and asked permission to move from that line of questioning temporarily, as Cedric Barnes would be arriving as a witness. He'd been held up and Tony expected him within forty-five minutes. Tony wanted to cover other points in the meantime. "Would Your Honor and Ms. Santiago agree to this?" Carolyn immediately got a forlorn look on her face.

"What does the testimony of Mr. Barnes have to do with the Change of Beneficiary form? It's not relevant," Santiago snapped.

At that point, Tony directed his gaze at the judge, and then looked over at Santiago. Carolyn seemed to relax more as if she anticipated that questioning was over. She exhaled with relief and smiled at her attorney.

Tony said, "*Character*. Mr. Barnes knows both defendants. *Credibility*. Mr. Barnes can testify that Carolyn Monroe knew Lenny Garner was married when she met him. As you know, the marriage application of Carolyn Monroe and Lenny Garner indicated Lenny Garner had never been married. Defendant Monroe completed it with Lenny Garner and attested to that." Lenny's family members started grinning and giving the "thumbs up" in approval of Tony's statement.

"I'll allow it," Judge Clancy said. Theresa blurted out, "Thank God," and Lenny's fifty-six year old brain damaged baby sister Rhonda said in her childlike voice, "Cedric's coming? I haven't seen him in a long time. This is nice." Carolyn repositioned herself in her seat.

Tony continued on. "So, Ms. Monroe, you were not aware that Lenny used cocaine?"

"No."

"Have you ever used the drug?"

"No."

"Do you know why Lenny's family members suggest you do, and filed Affidavits with the Court alleging that?"

Carolyn glanced over at Theresa and Barry with a look of betrayal and answered, "There are two sides here. They wanted to be on Denise's side because she ended up with the body and because she has Noelle. I believe they went against me because of that. They lied. Barry and Theresa lied. Plus, they got mad because I didn't call them right away when he was on his way to the hospital. So they hate me for that and sided with Denise."

Theresa and Barry shook their heads in disgust. I, having been trained by Tony and thoroughly prepped for this trial, knew never to show any emotion no matter what. But I was thinking about the times Lenny would come home from being with her and had those little plastic coke bags with leftover residue in them. Wow what a lying bitch she was.

"Can you tell me why you and Lenny kept your marriage a secret from the entire Garner family for four years?"

"Lenny made that decision. He said he had to in order to keep Denise on his medical insurance. Denise was always getting sick and she wouldn't work. Also because Noelle had Crohn's Disease and Denise was handling all that. He said Denise would get stressed out having no health insurance for herself and may not be able to take proper care of Noelle. So, we kept it a secret. He said if his Aunt Claudia got wind of our marriage that she would tell his cousin Zena and Zena would tell Denise."

"Were you friendly or did you know most of his family members?"

"Yes. I knew everyone and had no problems with them."

"And Lenny between both sides had one hundred ninety-seven people in his family at the time you two got married?"

"I don't know the exact number of his relatives."

Tony walked back over to the table and sifted through some documents. He got what he wanted and returned to her. "Well, I do. Here's a list of them. Even his Dad was alive then, your father-in law-Clyde Garner. Take a look at this list—do you recognize these names?"

Carolyn glanced at the paper, spotted a few names and admitted, "Yes, I know them?"

So, out of one hundred ninety-seven people, you could not invite one person to your wedding? And you had a very nice wedding, I hear—about eighty people at a church and a reception—dinner and all?" he said sarcastically. You couldn't trust one person out of all these relatives to know you were marrying the man you loved and had been with so many years?"

"No. I wanted Lenny to be happy on his wedding day and he didn't want them there."

"Did Lenny smoke cigarettes?" She looked surprised at that question.

"He used to. He stopped in 2005."

"That's a good thing. What prompted him to stop?"

"I came down with an illness one year and had to be hospitalized. It was very serious. Doctors said if I smoked I would die. So, to help me out, he stopped smoking." Tony snidely remarked, "That was pretty noble of him."

"Do you know what medications Lenny had been on for high blood pressure?"

"Atenolol."

"Do you know anything about the drug Atenolol?"

"Yes, a little."

"You're a Registered Nurse?"

"Yes."

"How much experience do you have?"

"Twenty-two years." She proudly said, looking at me. I knew she probably thought I was a dummy because I had no college degree.

"And you work in an ICU unit?"

"Yes."

"Well, let me fill you in on Atenolol because pharmacists have provided me with a lot of information on it. Atenolol is a beta blocker prescribed for hypertension. It is true that Cocaine usage reduces the effectiveness of Atenolol. Atenolol has a side effect which is impotence. The use of cocaine can cause sexual dysfunction, too. And by the way, if you stop smoking cigarettes, the Atenolol dosage has to be reduced because your liver will break down the drug more slowly.

"I know nothing about that. I'm no *expert* on medications," she shot back, showing she was irritated.

Tony kept his pace. "I've done a little investigating and I have checked with Lenny's health insurance carrier, Aetna, your health insurance carrier, Pharmacare, and his primary physicians. For the last three years, Lenny had no prescriptions filled by either carrier and did not see a doctor subsequent to February of 2005, after his discharge from Pennsylvania Hospital, ICU. You stated to the emergency room physicians at Mercy Fitzgerald Hospital on the date of his death that Lenny had not been under the care of a physician for two years. Do you have any idea where he was getting his medication for hypertension, you know—the Atenolol?"

"No."

"And you lived consistently with him for the past fourteen years?"

"Yes."

At this point, I was ecstatic with joy. Tony was on top of his game and getting prepared to clobber her.

"Did you two ever separate or talk of separating over those fourteen years?"

"We were very happy. We loved each other. We never wanted to leave each other."

"But weren't you concerned about his health?" I mean didn't you give him a hard time about not going to the doctor or taking his medication?"

"If I would question him, he would get irritated, so I left that subject alone."

"Okay. Let's move on to money. We all like money, don't we Ms. Monroe?" He sarcastically said. Tony neglected to wait for her answer and rapidly walked back to our table sifting through papers. Carolyn had a frantic look on her face. Tony winked at me when he got found what he wanted.

"You two had two joint accounts. Did he handle the bank statements?"

"No, I took care of that. I usually paid the household bills."

"Well, if you examined monthly statements, did you notice that he was taking money, sometimes a thousand dollars a day from the ATM machines?"

"Yes."

"Didn't that alarm you?"

"Yes. I was unhappy with that, but it was his money. What could I say?"

"What did you think he was doing with all that money on a daily basis?"

She shrugged, "Just *regular* partying—drinking."

"Were you having sexual relations with Lenny?"

"Yes. Quite often."

"So, you really were happy with him?"

"Very happy, Mr. Marino." She looked dead at me in conquest.

"Well, can you explain why you left him for four days—moved out of your house and he was planning to relocate while you were staying at your girlfriend's house in 2005?" She fell silent. She seemed keyed up. I could see one of her knees moving up and down.

"We had a spat, that's all."

"What happened? What caused such a problem that you left him?"

"He made me mad in a bar."

"What did he do?"

"He was drunk and he disrespected me."

"How so?"

"He called me a name and I didn't like it?"

"Was it a Black Monkey?" She gasped and family members chuckled.

Carolyn was silent. She looked as if she was in a daze, then seemed embarrassed. She began to cry. Just as she was crying, Cedric Barnes walked into the courtroom. She looked at him and really began sobbing. Cedric took a seat.

Tony politely excused himself from Carolyn, went over to Barnes and shook his hand. Then he addressed Judge Clancy. Family members were whispering to each other and waving hello to Barnes. Carolyn requested a glass of water. Rhonda blurted out—"Hi Cedric."

Tony said, "Your Honor and Counsel Santiago. I'd like to reserve the right to complete my questioning of Ms. Monroe when she has regained her composure. At this time, I would like to call Cedric Barnes to the stand."

Judge Clancy dismissed Carolyn and she walked away shaking, carrying the cup of water. I could tell she was no longer relaxed.

Cedric was sworn in and Tony addressed him. "Good morning, Mr. Barnes. Will you tell the Court about your association with Lenny Garner starting with the time you met him?"

I listened to Cedric tell the Court that he and Lenny met at Fort Bragg in boot camp in 1965. They became best friends and Lenny subsequently became engaged to his cousin Vernetta while they were in the service. They didn't get married because she did not want to move to Philadelphia and Lenny didn't want to move to Washington, Pennsylvania, where Vernetta and Barnes lived. A few months after their discharge in 1968, Barnes moved from Washington to Philadelphia. He moved in with Lenny and his wife, Frances Garner.

"So when you met Carolyn Monroe at the bar in 1968, Lenny was married to Frances."

"Yes."

"Was Carolyn aware of that?" All eyes were on Cedric Barnes.

"Yes. I overheard him tell her when they met that he was married." Sounds of sighs and huffs exploded from the courtroom. Santiago looked over at Carolyn and whispered something in her ear. Carolyn put her hand on her forehead and leaned on her elbow to hold her head up.

"Did you see Carolyn Monroe any time after that first meeting?"

Barnes answered that he and Lenny sometimes stopped over her house. They would all go out together drinking and sometimes they'd arrange to meet at bars. They just partied together. Lenny wasn't seeing Carolyn. He was still having an affair with his cousin—even after he married Frances.

"In your opinion, was Lenny attracted to Carolyn when you guys first met?"

"No. He just liked partying with her and she was into the drug scene. He liked drugs. He said he'd never hook up with her because of her looks. He had a pet name he called her and it was *Monkey.*"

Carolyn shot Barnes a mean look. Barnes went on to say that Lenny said she looked like a chimpanzee. Later, after he moved back to Washington, he often came back to Philly to visit. He was surprised Lenny had left Denise and was living with "Monkey."

"Why?" Tony asked.

"Because Lenny always liked pretty women. My cousin was a knockout and Denise was ten years younger than all of us and really pretty, too."

I smiled at Cedric, thanking him for the compliment.

"When did Lenny and Carolyn begin having an affair?"

I noticed everyone hanging on to Barnes' every word. He said it was around 1982 after Lenny and I hooked up, but before we got married. The last time he spoke to Carolyn Monroe was when she called him right after Lenny died. She wanted him to come to the Memorial Service she had been planning.

I watched Carolyn immediately take a sip of her water. I knew she was too through with the Garner family, Tony Marino, and Cedric Barnes. I was loving Tony's performance and thought Cedric was doing a superb job, too.

"Did you attend?"

"No. I decided against going to either service because I wasn't sure who to support. I didn't actually know who the legal wife was."

"Have you ever seen Carolyn Monroe or Lenny do drugs?"

"Yes, many times when we were out together. It would be cocaine, monster, and marijuana. We all got high together."

Well, it was evident that nobody prepped Santiago not to show her emotions because she looked over at Carolyn and shot her a dirty look and whispered something else in her ear. She slammed her ink pen down onto her legal pad. I could tell she was absolutely livid! "Thank you God," I thought.

Tony forged on with his questioning. "When was the last time you saw Lenny?"

"He came to Washington in late 2005. He spent two days with my cousin Vernetta. He also came to see Vernetta in June of 1995, but had to leave suddenly because Denise had gotten hit by a car in Philadelphia."

Tony placed both his hands up in the air in bewilderment. I loved it when he resorted to theatrics. He started shaking his head slowly back and forth as if he was trying to figure something out. He was very confused. He said, "Let me get this right. In *1995* Lenny was *separated* from

Denise. Are you saying he *still abruptly left* another woman to go to see about *her*?"

"Yes."

"Wow! He must have had some really genuine and serious feelings for the real *Mrs. Lenny Garner*. I have no further questions. Thank you, Mr. Barnes."

As Tony walked away smiling, Noelle was chanting, "Go Tony, Go Tony." The courtroom was buzzing with light chatter. All the Garners were delighted, smiling, and giving thumbs ups. Santiago had her eyes glued to the courtroom window ignoring her client who was seated beside her looking aimlessly up at the ceiling.

In a stern voice, Judge Clancy said, "Counsel Santiago, you may cross-examine Mr. Barnes at this time."

She shifted her eyes from the window. "No questions, Your Honor." I could tell she was fuming. Carolyn had lied to her.

With the victory of Santiago's refusal to question her client, Tony's eyebrows raised and he gave a quick smile to twenty-two year old beautiful Noelle whom he'd known since she was fourteen years old. He smacked his lips together, indicating he was sending her a kiss.

Judge Clancy said, "Let's bring Ms. Monroe back for questioning by counsel Marino and then we'll take a fifteen minute recess."

Tony waited until Carolyn was seated, then approached her. "Okay Ms. Monroe. Lenny Garner had hypertension for years and was on medication from his doctors until 2005. So, in February of 2005 no more medication and no more doctors' visits. He's functioning *off* medication for nearly 20 months and feeling just fine—well, I mean *after* he was admitted to your ICU Unit in 2005 for an adverse reaction to a drug or a medication. Is that correct?" Tony asked.

"Yes," Carolyn answered. She appeared distraught, restless, and petrified.

"You must have been a bit peeved with Lenny with everything he was doing. I mean he had other women, screwed up money, and called you names. Are you sure you were happy with him or is that a lie—like the other lies you told this morning and since he died?"

I listened intently to her explain to Tony that she didn't care about any of that. It didn't bother her. He wanted to know if it bothered her that he was sexually inadequate and broke most of the time in 2006. Her bills were in arrearages and her bank accounts overdrawn as many as seventeen times a month, with service charges totaling thousands of dollars in 2006. That had to be depleting her funds—the money she was placing in that joint account from her own salary as well as the thirty eight hundred dollars a month Lenny was kicking in from his pension check and his Social Security benefit. She admitted it was stressful at times but they made out okay and he wasn't sexually dysfunctional. I observed Carolyn. She seemed to be pleading with her eyes for Tony to have mercy on her and shut up.

He hammered on. "You made out *okay*? Well were you *okay* when his brother Dennis died in November of 2006 and you two had to share the cost with the other siblings of having him buried? From what I understand, both of you had to borrow money to make it to the funeral in Myrtle Beach, South Carolina, and you couldn't pay your part of the funeral bill. Don't you still owe Theresa Roglich your share of the bill? And also, didn't Lenny's sister Janete have to pay your hotel bill on that trip?"

"Yes, Janete helped out and Lenny hadn't paid Theresa back."

"And weren't you also strapped with college and apartment bills for your granddaughter, Charmaine, whose Mom, your daughter, is addicted to crack cocaine?"

I noticed her getting testy. She showed her embarrassment and rolled her eyes at Tony. She replied, "Yes."

"And your mortgage payments were in arrears and you were making arrangements with the utility companies to keep your services on?"

She stammered, "Yes, I admitted we had some financial problems."

Tony held both his hands up in the air briefly and then placed them on his hips. He froze for a moment in front of her and said, "All this was going on and Lenny wouldn't go to the doctor and you needed him alive, didn't you—because you *loved* him. And nearly seven thousand dollars a month was going into the bank accounts."

"Yes. I loved him"

"And, your mortgage payments were $854.79 a month?

She seemed dumbfounded that he had that information. "Yes."

Tony suggested that maybe Lenny wouldn't take the medicine because it hampered his sexual ability and asked what her thoughts were about that. She reiterated that they'd had a decent sex life and she didn't have any complaints. He asked her if she had been supplying him with Viagra or if he'd been buying it on the street. She said she wasn't getting it for him and had no idea if Lenny had been getting it elsewhere. Then, Tony straight up asked if Lenny had been having any erection problems and she said she didn't know. Judge Clancy then interjected warning Tony to move on, so he withdrew the question.

"So, you had access to the medications that he needed to stay alive. Did you try to keep him alive, Carolyn? You loved him! Did you try to keep him *alive?* Didn't you bring his medication home from your hospital and give it to him? Isn't *that* how he stayed alive and well for twenty months from February 2005 through November 2006? Isn't that what happened?" Tony shouted. The courtroom was silent and Tony's eyes were piercing Carolyn's.

"I didn't do that!" she screamed.

"How much does that medication cost—Atenolol—if you purchase it directly from a pharmacy?"

"I don't know. I don't know." she cried.

"Well, *I* know. It's thirty four dollars a month—a mere thirty four dollars. Do you think he was paying for some pills? Did you see any debit withdrawals or checks paid to Rite Aid or any other pharmacy for thirty four dollars for medication? You said you handled the bills?" Tony was relentless and kept banging on her with his words.

"I cannot remember!" she wailed at him hysterically. By this time, she had both her hands in her hair, running her fingers through the extensions of that cheap weave. Her head was shaking back and forth. Santiago had a look of captivation on her face. Tony raced over to our table and grabbed some papers. All I could say in shock was "Damn." There was a flurry of anticipation in the courtroom. Tony was doing his thing—big time, and Carolyn was on overtime with it all. I thought she was going to have a breakdown right on that stand.

"Well here is Exhibit H, which are *bank statements.*" He waved the papers in front of her face holding a pile in each hand. He continued. "There are two hundred thirty-six pages of banking information from the only accounts you two had from December 2004 through November 2006 and he paid for no medication directly. We checked every pharmacy and drug chain in the tri-state area, Ms. Monroe. So, if he didn't buy any medication directly and you didn't get him any—you were helping him to die. Isn't it true you wanted him dead because he was a pain in the ass and strapping you? You were sick of Lenny Garner, weren't you? You believed he was divorced from Denise and you were his *wife,* so you knew you could collect his pension and his Social Security. If he was dead, he couldn't go to the ATM machine all day while you were at work. You'd have been on Easy Street with him dead and gone. And you didn't have to be embarrassed when he called you a little black monkey! So—you decided to let him die. That's exactly what happened, isn't it?" He paused to listen to all the sounds coming from the family and to look at them for a moment.

Carolyn shouted "No! That's a lie! I tried to help him. Stop it! Stop saying that! I gave him forty years of my damn fucking life! I even gave him the meds. Yes, I brought them home and gave them to him! I did it. I gave them to him. I cannot take any more of this shit! I'm tired. I loved him. I did everything to make him happy! I brought the medication home and gave it to him. Please—let this end."

Theresa, Noelle and Barry started screaming. Judge Clancy called for order. I still refused to show an iota of emotion though I wanted to scream, "I know the bitch did it!" I kept hearing Tony's words to me, "I want you reserved at all times." I had promised him I would not get out of control in any way, shape, or form. I would not embarrass my friend and my attorney.

When there was silence in the room, Tony gently took Carolyn's hand and held it. He asked her if she needed another drink of water or some time to compose herself. She just sat with tears streaming down her face. He gave her his handkerchief and quietly said, "Carolyn, you signed that form, didn't you? You signed that Change of Beneficiary form and sent it back to the City Life benefits Department, didn't you. You did that, didn't you?"

She whimpered. "He told me to sign it. He said I could sign it as his wife. I had permission to sign it."

Once Tony had that confession, he turned back into the monster he'd been all along and shouted, "Did you have permission to sign his pension check after he died?" Ten days after he died, you signed your name to his pension check and deposited it into your account and went shopping. Did he tell you to do that!"

She placed her face in her hands and sobbed uncontrollably. She never answered, but he kept going anyway.

"Why, when he was fighting for his life on Thanksgiving Day didn't you tell the paramedics he was on medication?"

"I…I didn't want to get into trouble. I was scared. I was so scared. It all happened so fast." she stammered.

He took her hand gently again. Now, he was back to being the soothing Mister Nice Guy. I knew he was wearing her out because I was worn out from all of it. "So, Carolyn, his death was an *accident*. Lenny nor you knew that taking those meds and the side effects of not smoking cigarettes and using cocaine would kill him." She moaned, "I didn't know all that stuff would happen. I didn't know he would die." "No further questions," Tony announced.

Pandemonium erupted in the courtroom. Some family members were hugging each other and others were crying. People were running over to me congratulating me, but my eyes were fixed on Carolyn as she remained on the stand unable to move. I never flinched. Tony kissed me on the forehead and whispered in my ear, "It's done." I watched Santiago walk up to Tony and hand him a business card. "If you have any openings at your firm, I'd be interested in working for you." She then shook his hand. Chris Brazzi of the Philadelphia Daily News was rapidly taking notes. Santiago just stared once more at Carolyn and left the courtroom. With everything going on, no one other than me seemed to notice Rhonda wander to the witness stand. With a look of disbelief on her face, she began to slowly question Carolyn. "You gave Lenny his pills and he died? He used to take good care of me when I got sick. Why did he have to die?" I tapped Tony on the arm and pointed to Rhonda and he led her back to her seat. The judge ruled in my favor—an accidental death—double indemnity. Checkmate!

The story was to hit the papers and the television news the next day. The headlines would be *The Worst Nurse*. A jubilant Chris Brazzi met with me late that night to review the final draft before it printed. Once I read it, I asked him to hold off and explained I had a plan. I called Carolyn at two thirty in the morning. I was very direct and cut right to the chase. I explained that the story would print in the newspaper and that the case would probably be on the television news. If she didn't want to lose her job, then she should meet me at one o'clock in the afternoon. I gave her the address. She started to tell that me that she was sick of everything and wasn't going anywhere. She hated me and all the Garners. Tony was a maniac. I told her to do whatever she wanted but if I were her, I'd make the meeting. I abruptly hung up.

It was nearly over. Ten months of talking and making deals. I was relaxed on the bed, flipping through my Real Simple Magazine. I was reading an article about using lemons for things other than lemonade. It was very interesting. I jumped from the bed when I heard the pounding on the door.

"It was the best decision you could have made agreeing to this meeting Carolyn." Carolyn had on a sweat suit, a cheap pair of sneakers, and her hair was a wreck. Her eyes were red and swollen. She entered the hotel room. I had booked a room at the Hyatt in downtown Philadelphia just to talk to Carolyn.

"Look, Denise, I just want all of this to end. I've been through hell with it all. I did not mean for Lenny to die. What's this shit have to do with my job? Now what are you trying to do, make me lose that? Why'd you have me come down here? What's this newspaper stuff?"

I was not done with this bitch and wanted her to know it. I needed this one on one with her after all these years. I'd been frustrated with her black ass for what seemed like an eternity. "I've got the media in my pocket. They go the way I flow. I'm making up my mind about that. It depends on what you and I work out today. You have done a lot of shit, Carolyn. My take on the situation is that you merely started out as a home wrecker and in the end you saw dollar signs. You capitalized on the fact that Lenny didn't know what the fuck he was doing. I'm going to make an offer for me to be whole again and you can walk without having to do time. Do you want to hear it?"

Carolyn sighed and sat down at the table. "What's the deal and hurry up?"

"Sadie Watkins."

Shocked and bewildered, she replied, "That's my grandmother. What does she have to do with all of this? She's dead."

"Yes, I know she's been dead since 1997. I know how she died but why don't you tell me your version, sweetie. How did she die Carolyn?"

"My grandmother had a heart attack."

"She was living with you, right?"

"Yeah." She huffed, letting me know she was sick of me already.

Well, my private eye found out that her life insurance policy was made out to you and you were in charge of that Social Security check she was collecting. Is his information correct," I said coyly.

She confirmed that she took care of her grandmother until she died. There was no one else to do it.

I thought about that bitch *taking care* of Lenny on Thanksgiving Day. "Yeah, you took care of your grandmother and that's *why* she died."

She shot back, demanding to know what I was getting at and called me a bitch. I jumped right back at her. I knew Granny had Alzheimer's and was a pain in the ass not knowing one day from the next and having screaming fits. The way I heard it she was always getting lost. She had to be watched almost constantly and Carolyn got real tired of being nursey pie at work and then coming home to see what the hell she'd gotten into. Even though he was living with her, Lenny couldn't help out much with Granny, and I knew that.

"So what does that have to do with her having a heart attack and dying?"

"You sedated her one Sunday afternoon and you tied her ass up in a chair. Then you and Lenny went to Aunt Claudia's bar and partied about three hours. Then you guys made your rounds to all the other bars and got home around midnight. Granny was dead. You and

Lenny untied and removed her from the chair and put her in the bed, then you called 911 explaining that you came home and found her dead."

Carolyn was stunned to hear those words. She gasped. Her face sank. She looked in my eyes. "You don't have a damn bit of proof that I did that. That's a lie."

"Carolyn, take a look at this." I handed her a letter.

June 5, 2007

Hey sister-in-law. Do you think you can have Carolyn's Grandmother, Sadie Watkins' body exhumed? It'll help the case. You're the wife and I can't have it done. I have the money to put up to do it if your cash flow is light. Remember I told you that Lenny got drunk here at my house back in the day and told me that Carolyn tied her Granny up and came back and found her dead. Both of them had been partying all day that day and I was with them. We were all at Aunt Claudia's bar. I can testify to it. I was working the bar serving her and Lenny. It was on Janete's birthday. We were celebrating at the bar.

Theresa

Carolyn sat and shook her head and began to cry. "Denise, what do you want? I have lost everything, including Lenny. I have nothing left. I just want to be left alone. You've gotten the pension and the life insurance. Because I paid for the cars with his *DROP* money going into my account, I had to turn them over to you. My homeowner's company dropped me after they paid you $100,000 on your Wrongful Death Claim. All I have left is the house and you're trying to put a lien against *that*. How the hell you managed to get my car insurance company to pay you twenty grand for him being in that car with me in July of 2006, I'll never know. Now **you want me in jail for murder. I'm damn near suicidal and about to file** bankruptcy. Why can't you just leave me the fuck alone? Lenny wanted to be with me. You know he could have left any time and come back to you. Why can't you just let this thing die?"

"Because, *Bitch*, you let my husband die. I'm pissed. And you had the fucking nerve to take your Black ass down to the University of Maryland at College Park and curse Noelle out while I was out of the country doing my book thing."

"I did not curse Noelle out!"

"Look, Carolyn. I made arrangements in 2003 for Lenny to move Noelle from one dorm to the next when school ended. It would have been a time that the two of them could have spent a weekend together. *One damn weekend* between a father and a daughter. But no, you had to take your ass down there with him. The way I heard it, you got pissed off because she had too much stuff to move. You were irritated because you needed her to hurry up because you and Lenny had to go to another part of Maryland to visit your daughter and your sister. You yelled at my baby, telling her that her shit should have been packed and ready to go. When my ship docked in St. Thomas, I called Noelle and she was crying. You guys were gone. And I believe you also brought your ass up to that hospital when I was almost dead to finish me off!"

"I did not curse Noelle out and I was trying to help you—that's why I went to the hospital. I went to make sure they were doing things correctly."

I was so sick of this lying woman and so intent on teaching her a few lessons. I told her to shut the fuck up and listen to me. "I know you have two life policies for accidental death on Lenny and they are worth $500,000. I know you are sitting on them because the heat is on. You are being monitored and investigated by everyone. I know you closed both your checking accounts so I can't watch you and I know they have stayed overdrawn. You have been living from hand to mouth since he died— well, *after* you went on that shopping spree after he died, spending his last pension check."

She started screaming, rocking, and moaning. Then she paced the hotel room.

"Do you want me to order you a drink to calm you down? Or do you prefer some blow? Do you want me to give Reno a call—you know—your granddaughter's boyfriend—the one who Lenny was buying his drugs from?"

Now, she was shocked again. Carolyn regained her composure and growled, "What's the deal, bitch?"

"I have a question."

"What?"

"On those policies, are you listed as spouse and beneficiary, or is it just spouse and no name? Did you simply check off a box or something on the application? I know they came in the junk mail and I know you have them because my husband told me a long time ago while we were in support Court. He had to tell the support officer whether he had life insurance. He said he had accident policies. So, what's the deal? Did you sign them as spouse?"

"Yeah, I just checked the box and Lenny signed the forms."

I was relieved and knew it would be no problem with her making the insurance company pay. I continued on questioning her. "And aren't there two regular policies on his life and one accidental policy?"

I could tell it was starting all over again for her and I was now picking up where Tony Marino left off. She was definitely getting ruffled under questioning. I loved it. She said, "Yeah. Listen, I want you to order me a drink." Carolyn was running her hands through her nappy hair and I was calling room service.

"What do you drink?"

"Gin and grapefruit juice."

Room service arrived in 10 minutes with a bottle of Tanqueray Gin, a bucket of ice, four empty glasses and four large grapefruit juices. Carolyn immediately made herself a big drink and gulped half of it down. I stared at her loathing her ghetto ass and those cheap horrible braids in her nappy head. I was certain she didn't have an iota of class. I shifted my gaze to my calculator and paper and said, "Okay—back to business, I want the policies. Let's go over how much they are worth. Talk to me."

Carolyn paced while drinking. "I have one policy for two hundred fifty thousand on accidental death and two one hundred fifty thousand dollar policies on straight life insurance."

"Okay, then the accidental death will pay just the two hundred fifty thousand and the life policies probably pay double indemnity. That'll be another three hundred grand. So…. we have five hundred fifty grand." I calculated.

I asked her if she had ever made a claim on any of these policies and she told me that she had not. I was relieved, but not entirely satisfied. So I was more specific with the question and asked if she had called any company at all. "No," she said again. She had gotten worried when all the shit started going down with the pension board and the IRS wanting records. She needed a Death Certificate and my name was on that. Carolyn knew they would question her about that and didn't want to get into trouble and have Charmaine be left alone. Charmaine's Mom, couldn't take care of her, she was a misfit. Carolyn had to keep the girl and Lenny, too. That's why he helped with her college.

That last statement sent me into orbit. I knew I was going to go for the jugular vein with my plan. The nerve of her! "Yeah, right," I snapped. I was seething with anger and had no sympathy for her or Charmaine and didn't want to hear that bullshit, especially with Noelle having Crohn's Disease. "The money for the premiums on the insurance—did it come out of that joint account you had with Lenny?"

Carolyn was nervous and sweating from the interrogation and took a long swig of her drink. She answered, "For a while. In the beginning, they came out of my regular account. Then we got the DROP retirement money, the fifty three grand in 2004, and I made payments from there."

"Okay nursey pie, here's the deal. You get me those policies by nine o'clock tonight. You bring them here to the hotel and leave them in an envelope at the desk for me. You follow my instructions and I will not turn you in about your grandmother. I'll send in the death certificate and make a claim for the policies. I'll contact the companies myself. You stay out of it. You do what I tell you and I get that money. Then I'll leave you alone about Granny and I'll hold the newspaper off—and the television station." I grabbed my handbag and snatched a fifty dollar bill out and threw it on the table. "Take a cab—don't drive drunk."

Carolyn made another drink, gulped down another half a glass, and stared at me. She said nothing.

"Do you have a problem with my instructions because if you do, we can adjourn this meeting and I can head over to the police station? It's not far from here."

"I...uh... have a question," she stammered.

"Shoot."

"Are you planning to give me any of that money? I am going along with you."

Now *I* was shocked. One thing I could say about her was she had a lot of nerve. "Are you planning to give me my husband back?" I snapped as I got up from the table. Carolyn looked confused. I refreshed Carolyn's glass with gin, added ice, and handed it to her.

I bent down and looked into her eyes. "Let me tell you one fucking thing right now, Carolyn. Listen to me very carefully. If you don't do what the hell I say, *everybody* is going down. That means you, Charmaines's boyfriend, and Charmaine, too, if I can tie her up in this shit for being an accessory with the drugs. I know for a fact that Central Detectives questioned Reno early in the game, back in January they called his house. Reno told the detective he had Lenny's cell phone, which he got from Charmaine. That's how the detectives found Reno—through the cell phone bills that I managed to get. Let's remember, the cell phone bill was in Lenny's name only. So... as his legal wifey-poo and Administratrix of his estate, and having Short Certificates got me all Lenny's bills and access to anything the two of you had together. Want me to get transcripts of the cell phone conversations, too? I can also file a Writ of Seizure and get everybody's damn computer. I'd love to see the e-mails that went back and forth to people and check to see who was researching what on the Internet. Maybe somebody was trying to find out about arsenic or poisons to lace cocaine with. All your asses will be sitting in the slammer together—one big happy family. Fuck with me if you like—I'll win again. Also, in my investigation, I found that there were **magazine subscriptions going to your home in Lenny's name. It certainly** is interesting that he subscribed to *Fast Company* and *Entrepreneur*. Was he going to start his own business—you know, try to get himself together with his DROP money or, were you going to off him and start your own business? The subscriptions began in early 2005—after the DROP money came through."

Carolyn was stunned I had so much information and didn't answer the question.

"Okay, cat got your tongue."

I was now pretending I was Tony. I told her I'd withdraw the question and do without a reply. I revealed that I knew she'd had a lot of fun in Atlantic City on the slots. I had her ID number with her play time and points. I commented she hadn't had much luck down there either. "Lenny was last down to play on November 11th—twelve days before he died. He was at the Showboat. Were you with him or did he take *Debbie*? I'll have to remember to ask *Debbie* about that." She was fuming.

It was all coming down on Carolyn and the last thing she wanted to do was turn those policies over to me, but she knew one thing for sure, a detective had called Reno and he was scared shitless when it happened. That was it. She'd had it. I'd gone too far.

She stood up and shouted, "Let me tell *you* something, *Bitch*." Her lips curled when she said the word *Bitch* and I was taken aback. "I am sick the fuck of you and have been for damn near twenty-four years! I'm sick of your *perfect* world. I had to wait through two fucking wives and a bunch of tramps to have Lenny. I had to listen to everyone brag about you living a first class life. You and your hundred and fifty dollar negligees and trips to the Caribbean staying in those high class resorts. I heard about how the *Mr. and Mrs. Lenny Garner* got on the planes with their family and you brought gourmet fucking lunches on board so the *Garners* would not have to eat airplane food. Ten day stints to Disney World staying in seven hundred dollar a day villas instead of a regular hotel room. Hear me loud and clear—I can't stand that little wench Noelle talking White like that damn White ass Theresa who I never was good enough for! No matter how hard I tried, I couldn't make the grade with Theresa. And every time I turned around you were doing something that grabbed Lenny's attention when we were together. We couldn't have a minute's peace and that's why we got fucked up a lot—to get away from you! You did everything you could to break us up. You either played dead with some illness or had Noelle play dead. You got yourself hit by a fucking car and he had to rush to your side. When the health shit calmed down, you wrote two fucking books and got published—making me look unimportant all over again.

Lenny couldn't shut up about that and he had the nerve to read the damn books in my goddamn house! Then you and that bitch daughter of yours wound up on Oprah and everybody was yakking about that. I had to take shit continuously from you—somebody who shot his ass with a fucking 38—tried to kill him. And what does he do, the dumb motherfucker—he wanted to stay with you anyway. I was sick and tired of him protecting you. He owed me goddammit! How the hell do you think we paid the bills throughout those child support years? He was shelling out eight hundred dollars a month to you and damn near five hundred for that other brat, Lamont or Winton or whatever his name is. I was the fucking laughing stock of all time to my friends. You never loved Lenny. I don't believe you *ever* did. You know what a bastard he was—you lived it—had a front row seat watching him create havoc. And you're a selfish little cunt, too, who has absolutely no manners. You couldn't even calm down and appreciate me when you put that little bitch of yours out of your house when she was driving you crazy when she was sixteen. When we took her and she complained that her room wasn't *adequate,* you tried to send a damn decorator to my house! I cannot stand your uppity ass. You and your white wines, designer clothes, Broadway shows, and fur coats. I deserved to have something so *yes*—I spent his damn retirement money as soon as I could—every dime I could! I got my house fixed up and paid off every bill in sight. And Charmaine deserved something so I bought her a brand new car. I made sure I got mine from his sorry ass because I was *due.* We had a wedding, yep, Cinderella finally went to the ball—whether it was *legal* or not. And, yeah, I let his ass die, *Bitch.* Yes *Mrs. Garner,* your stupid ass whoring ass husband was killing himself for a long time and I let it be the end for him on Thanksgiving Day. You and Lenny can kiss my black monkey ass! I had to work like a fucking slave wiping patients' asses and I was doing it on double shifts while your *husband* partied and fucked up **every dime I couldn't keep my eye on. And you have the nerve to parade** around like you're some saint? You lived with two damn men while you were married to him. You're a fucking whore! I even had to listen to him complain and be hurt about that. You and your suburban life, house on the hill, private schools, baby grand piano and a Russian piano instructor showing up twice a week to teach the Black American Princess, Noelle

Garner, how to play *classical* music. You're so highfalutin you make me want to puke. And I'm embarrassed that I swallowed my pride and begged him to divorce you, and he wouldn't do it. I'm glad his ass is dead. And, by the way, I sold his jewelry in the end to pay for my attorney to go to trial with your ass. So, don't start looking for that stuff. I told you this already and I'll say it again—kiss my ass! And you better not fuck with my granddaughter."

EPILOGUE

He held my hand and kissed it. Then we lifted our glasses to a toast. "To Carolyn Monroe, a squeezing, retching, grasping, scraping, clutching covetous old sinner." We both smiled.

I sighed. "I'm glad it's over. Now I can get on with my life—and I love my new life and my man." He kissed me quickly on my lips. I continued on. "You know, this has really been a caper. I'm glad she's in jail. She deserved it. I even sent her a little present directly to the prison before we left."

"Oh really—and what was that?" He asked amusingly.

"His ashes. You know…I never took them to blow them away. I'd been so busy I never even gotten a chance to put them in an urn. They've been in that box that the funeral director gave me in December after the services. Later I decided that since the bitch wanted him so badly she could have him. So now she's got him. But she's pissed with him for everything, including running his mouth to Theresa. What a shame for her."

He was floored hearing this new information and nearly choked on his champagne. He'd have to get used to it. Denise Garner was always pulling something out of her hat. "Well, everybody pulling together on this thing certainly bore fruit. She *was* dirty. That was horrible—her actually killing the first husband. That Clerk in the Vital Statistics Records office in Atlanta was a gigantic lead. I'm glad we flew down there and hooked up with her. A real Georgia Peach she turned out to be. Humph. Three people living with her dying of heart attacks. Carolyn Monroe—a serial killer. Wow. Lenny made the wrong move when he hooked up with her."

"It's really a shame he was so stupid. He and I could have had it all. But—it just wasn't meant to be," I said sipping my champagne.

He hesitated, his eyes questioning me for a moment. "Don't you feel a little bad about double crossing her? After all, you promised her that if she gave you those policies you'd leave her alone."

"Now, sweetheart, don't you go soft on me in the end," I said, rubbing his thigh. "I told her I wouldn't turn her in on *Granny*. I never mentioned that first husband she had. So, *technically* I didn't double cross her." I ended my sentence by kissing him on the cheek.

"Well, the broad ended up with two consecutive life sentences. Are you satisfied, baby?

"I'm fine." I cooed seductively.

He put his hand in mine and squeezed it. "Are you sure you don't want to marry me, Ms. Garner? I'd love to have you legally."

"Nah…I'm a business woman, baby, not that I don't love you to death. I've got a lifetime pension that could be affected if I remarry. I have to check on all that for sure because the pension board sometimes gets things ass backwards. Also, I collect Lenny's Social Security and remarriage could be a problem there, too. I want to relax for a while and quit playing detective. Let's just do a live-in thing and have a big party. Will that work?"

"Tell me more, baby. What's the plan?"

"Well, let's have a fabulous affair called "Guess Who's *NOT* Getting Married" on October 14, 2007? How about you and I shacking up and staying engaged for the rest of our lives? And of course, you'll collect your pension, too, when you retire. Let's spare no expense on our celebration in October and we'll buy a knock down drag out house on Knob Hill. We can afford it."

The hostess approached, distracting us. "Mr. Adam Hartman, your table is ready in the Emerald Room. I'd like to officially welcome you to Maui and wish you a pleasant stay. I understand you'll be with us for two weeks."

Detective Hartman of Central Philadelphia Detectives held his fiancé's hand as we strolled lovingly to our table.

Thank you, author Linda Goodman. I love your books. You are one smart Aries and have taught me so much. I miss you. I know you are giving the Angels astrology readings. It is my pleasure to borrow the following quote from one of my favorites by you—Love Signs.

Adrienne
Libra- 10/14/53

"The older Librans grow, the wiser they become. After playing both judge and jury, and weighing decisions of yes and no, wrong or right, stop or go, thousands of times, a person gradually begins to have confidence in what he (or she) is doing. It takes practice.

Libra men and women (and children) never pretend to know things they don't know, as some of the other Sun Signs tend to do. They ask. They deliberate. They discuss. If they're in doubt, they frankly admit "I'm in doubt." They're obsessed by a moral compulsion to do the fair thing, rather than the unfair thing. To do something that they consider morally wrong, gravely disturbs their consciences. That's why, when a Libra finally does say something, people believe it's trustworthy—and nine times out of ten, it is."

A CONVERSATION WITH
ADRIENNE BELLAMY

Question 1: What inspired you to write The Bitch Tried To Steal My Husband's Body and what questions did you ask yourself when you were working on it?

Answer: The inspiration was my very own eventful life. Things are never normal or run of the mill with me. Murphy's Law—yep—that's Adrienne Bellamy. And, believe me, the truth *is* stranger than fiction. The questions I asked myself while writing it were "Can I get through this thing?" When doing the investigative tasks, it was simply mind blowing receiving the information. I was going from place to place, on the phones and then literally riding in my car to meet people giving me advice and trying to teach me things.

Question 2: Denise is an exceptional character. How was she developed?

Answer: Her character was found and developed actually through the flow of information, research and paperwork regarding an investigation into my own husband's death. The amount of zeal Denise had and her aggressiveness from the onset triggered me. I've written a novel of fiction, and enjoyed developing Denise. She was so passionate and had no boundaries—no limits, not only in finding her husband's body, but never giving up until she proved he had not died of a heart attack.

Question 3: There are many characters in this novel. Who is your favorite character and why?

Answer: I have two. Theresa, Lenny's sister. She is courageous in not backing down. She is humble and loving when she embraces Denise in the end.

This seventy-three year old woman had no fear of Carolyn. Tony Marino, one of Denise's attorneys is a knockout in and out of the courtroom.

Question 4: What was your vision when you began writing The Bitch Tried To Steal My Husband's Body? What helped you get started when you actually began the first paragraph?

Answer: The vision was the face of Dr. Anne Highland, my Psycologist. She passed away in early 2006 due to breast cancer, but she spent a lot of time telling me that events of my life were worth writing about. This was months before my husband's death. When the going got tough—I'd see her face in that office—in her chair—telling me to relax, take a deep breath—and finish the job.

Question 5: What was the hardest scene you had to write in The Bitch Tried to Steal My Husband's Body?

Answer: Scenes of Lenny and Noelle especially when Noelle was a baby and her suffering because of her disease.

Question 6: What were your favorite chapters and scenes in The Bitch Tried To Steal My Husband's Body?

Answer: Well, I'm a Libra and you know we have trouble making up our minds. We'd really rather not have to make a decision. However, I have to come up with three favorites: Hands down—Glitter is hysterical and I love to laugh. Room Service is phenomenal and Two Smart Bitches intrigues me. I love Carolyn in Room Service. She puts it down! Favorite scenes for me—the Courtroom and Noelle and the marijuana.

Question 7: Are there certain times during the day that you write? Do you ever get writer's block?

Answer: I believe I get lazy—not really *writer's block*. You know we Libra's have our *lazy* times. But I guess I have experienced writer's block in my career. Okay, I'll concede to that and admit I believe six weeks was the longest period I ever experienced. I am a writer who will not write if I don't feel I have good material. Many times material would come to me while I was driving. I'd try to retain it by jotting a few words down at a stoplight or often just turning around and going back home to my computer if I was on a personal errand.

Question 8: Are you working on other projects?

Answer: I have completed my third novel, *Arrivals*, a sequel to *Departures* and *Connecting*. Some of the characters from *Departures* and *Connecting* are featured in *Arrivals* and I have introduced new ones who will not only knock your socks off, but cause you to laugh hysterically. My favorite new project is an astrology book. It's gonna be awesome. I do love astrology.

Question 9: At any point in your writing of The Bitch Tried To Steal My Husband's Body did you know how the book would end?

Answer: Yes. Once I learned all about the medications, I knew the ending. I knew exactly what Denise was going to do. When the book was about 50% completed, I wrote the ending and then went back to the middle. Regina Bellamy Johnson, a test reader, made a statement about one of the characters that propelled me to the explosive surprise at the very end of the novel.

Question 10: Can you tell me some of the ways you get material?

Answer: Much of my material I receive in my dreams—while sleeping. I also get a lot of inspiration while I am driving my car. Sometimes a small event will happen to me, a friend, or family member and that will trigger me.

Question 11: Can you share with me some of the compliments you have received from your readers?

Answer: They absolutely loved the title and are intrigued by it. It's a juicy, scandalous title. It makes you want to know the scoop.

Question 12: What chapter or scene in this novel caused the most controversy, discussion or sparked the readers?"

Answer: The Dale chapters: Shaky Ground, Closing the Door and Showing Up. This is absolutely Sizzle City compounded by a marriage and children. Everybody will have an opinion on this part of the novel.

Question 13: Who are your favorite writers?

Answer: R.M. Johnson, Wally Lamb, John Grisham, Vincent Bugliosi, Linda Goodman and Diane McKinney Whetstone.

Question 14: Did you learn something about yourself when writing this book?

Answer: I learned that I am an excellent private investigator. It's like I am a dog with a bone and I want to lick it clean. I love digging around and finding the facts. I get charged up when I am like being challenged. I am relentless, my best attribute. And, I like cops and men. Men will take care of you—if we *let* them.

Question 15: You write a lot about astrology. How do you know so much about it? Have you studied it?

Answer: I am fascinated by Astrology. I don't want to even deal with a person unless I know what sign they are. I have to operate with them based on that. **It's always a plus for me that give me clues on how to handle them and how they will react to situations.** I have read up on astrology for years. I am not an expert. I find it intriguing and I totally believe in it. In all my relationships, (co-workers, bosses, lovers, friends and relatives) I have used the assistance of astrology to guide me in the way I handled those relationships. I have raised and handled my children using astrology. My daughters are Leo and

Aquarius—exact opposites. The Leo I have to handle with kid gloves. I
have to request, ask and be gentle with her if I want something done. She
requires praise. Whenever I would make commands—nothing got done. I
had to realize and understand that lions are king of the jungle and we are
their loyal subjects. We are beneath them. Knowing my astrology and their
personalities, I knew how to approach her. Praise and flattery will always
put you ahead with them. The Aquarian with the bad temper always did
me in. However, I also knew I had the smartest person in the zodiac in
my house. I had to learn to deal with her belligerence, which is part of her
characteristic. You'll always walk on eggshells with an Aquarian female,
even though they are true humanitarians. They will always belong to a
group of something. Maybe it will be a church, cult, sorority, or singing
ensemble. My favorite signs are Sagittarius, Aquarius.

Question 16: What is the most amazing and/or surprising thing that has
ever happened to you?

Answer: My house flooded and my daughter Alia and I were living at the
Hyatt in Philadelphia while our home was being renovated. This was in
October of 2001—post September 11, 2001 terrorist attacks. My birthday
was approaching. I was born on October 14th. I'd heard on the radio that
Sinbad, the comedian, was coming to town. He was my favorite comedian.
I had enjoyed a couple of his concerts in the past. He was expected to be
in downtown Philadelphia on October 18, 2001. I jumped for joy when I
heard he was coming to town. That concert was going to be my birthday
present to myself! The Hyatt Hotel was across the street from where he
would be appearing.

My sixteen year old daughter was in night school at the time. Because
of her illness, she required so many doctor's appointments, we switched
to evening classes in private school. Starving for the concert, I made a
lot of calls trying to get someone to pick Alia up from school at nine in
the evening on the night of the concert. I didn't have much luck and
didn't want to keep her out of school. I remember having a conversation
with Alia in the hotel room about it and then I started stomping

around like a little girl saying "God, I just want to see Sinbad." I pouted a while and just let it go. I was just going to miss that concert. I accepted it.

A day and a half later I was walking a couple of blocks from our hotel. I decided to stop in a favorite restaurant of mine, The Oyster House. I had dinner at this restaurant many times for over 20 years. But this was lunch time and for some reason I decided to go there for lunch that day. I sat down at the counter and ordered. It was around two in the afternoon and I had beat the lunch crowd. There were no other customers at the counter.

After about 10 minutes two gentlemen walked in and sat across from me. I looked directly at them. I was astonished. One of them was Sinbad! Jesus, I was in the Oyster House in Center City Philadelphia and Sinbad had walked in! I could not believe it. I gazed at him. I was surprisingly silent for a few moments. I was trying to get myself together. Finally I said to Sinbad "We have been very sad here in Philadelphia. It is good to see you. You are just what the doctor ordered." He smiled and thanked me. I enjoyed my lunch while lightly conversing with him. I didn't want to be a pain in the butt or act star struck or make him uncomfortable.

When I left the restaurant, I immediately made arrangements to get tickets to go to that show and ordered flowers to take to Sinbad. I was all excited. My daughter insisted that she was going to miss a night of school so that I could attend that concert which was to take place in two days.

Unfortunately when I went to the Academy of Music to pick those tickets up, I was told that the show had been canceled due to a lack of ticket sales. It was explained to me that many people were just not in a comedy mood **because of 911 and the show would not go on**.

I knew then that Sinbad had been placed in that restaurant just for me. I remembered my words in that hotel room "God, I just want to see Sinbad."

Two years later in May of 2003, I was on board a ship. This was the Tom Joyner Fantastic Voyage. I was now a published author promoting my first novel, *Departures*. I was on my way from my cabin to a fire (if the ship sinks) drill, which all passengers were required to attend. I couldn't even figure out how to put the life jacket on. I was hurrying with it in hand trying to get some assistance. I ran into Sinbad and his wife on the elevator. Well, we were all late and missed the drill. We were too busy reminiscing. I reminded him of that day in the Oyster House in Philadelphia and he remembered who I was. We had a great time I also got a chance to tell him how well I did heckling him at the Keswick Theater in Glenside, Pennsylvania ten years ago in 1991. I told him that when I left the Keswick Theater that night after his concert I heard people saying "There she is walking to her car. She works for Sinbad. That's the one that was talking from the audience all that time." He had a gleaming smile listening to me. And, as we stood in that elevator and proceeded onto the deck, the three of us talked all about *Departures* and his wife's plan to write a novel.

Of course, after catching up with Sinbad and his wife, I really did have a Fantastic Voyage. Let this little story remind you that God is always listening and that there is no such thing as a *coincidence*.

Question 17: Let's go inside Adrienne Bellamy. Do you have a humbling and appreciative moment which occurred in your life? If so, did it change you, your behavior, or how you look at things? Share it with us.

Answer: Yes.

THE ANGEL

On March 19, 2005 I was wrapping up a three hour book signing at Barnes and Noble in Jenkintown, Pennsylvania. Managers of book stores looked forward to my appearances because I was gregarious, sweet and was a marvel at hand selling to walk-in customers. I had my own little speech for my customers including a gigantic smile, and they loved me. On this particular night, as I packed my things to leave the signing, a woman walked up to me. She was Caucasian, short with gray hair. "Hello. I really liked your first book. I'm getting the sequel today," she said.

I immediately autographed her book. "Thank you so much," I said with a gleaming smile.

"You're welcome. Listen, I only have one complaint about you." Her face tightened.

I was startled, taken aback and I stood there frozen. I couldn't imagine what kind of complaint she would have because I always put so much into my signings and was used to my public loving me. I was always friendly and made a fuss over everyone. I chit chatted with my customers and fans and I hugged them. They knew I was grateful and gracious. I could captivate a crowd. I also always took the time to answer their questions about publishing and encouraged them to write. I loved playing with their children and letting them know they had special talents.

Unable to figure it out, I finally spoke "I'm sorry," I said to the woman. Have I done something to offend you?"

"No, you haven't offended me. Well, the thing is—I'm not satisfied with you because I don't feel you try hard enough," she said.

At this point I was completely baffled and asked, "Try hard enough at **what**?"

"You don't try with Oprah. You need to try harder to get to her. She would love you. You are so sweet like she is. Why can't you try to get on her show? Why can't you send her your books?"

I thought this woman was sweet. "Ma'am, I did send Oprah my books. My publisher also sent them to her. She never responded. I imagine she is really busy and simply hasn't had time to read my novels. She gets a lot of books, you know. I don't want to worry her to death."

As her face tightened for the second time, I knew she was not happy with my answer. "You see, that's what I'm talking about. You just won't keep trying."

"Well, I don't want to be a nuisance. You know what I mean?"

"No, I don't know what you mean. I want you to try harder. I want you to promise me that you will write Oprah a letter or send her an E-mail. That's it—a letter or an E-mail. Just E-mail her and tell her who you are and get on that show. Can you do that?"

"Well, I guess I can. I'll do it." I answered thinking she could be a little loony or crazy.

"So, you are promising me you'll send her an E-mail. Right?"

"Yes, Ma'am—I'll send it."

"Okay. Try harder. See you. I loved your first book. Can't wait to start this one."

The little old lady who appeared to be in her mid seventies walked out of Barnes and Noble. I was dead tired from all the talking and running around that day and had a book club discussion that started in half an hour.

On Monday night, March 21, 2005, I was laying in bed trying to go to sleep. As I lay there I remembered the little old lady and my promise. I've always been one to get a guilty conscience if I don't keep my word. I always try to keep my word. I was so tired, but got up and went to my computer.

I booted it up and found Oprah's website. I am not totally computer savvy and sometimes have a hard time. I couldn't find a way to simply send a message to Oprah. The more I tried, the more lost I became. As I scrolled down I saw the words "Be on the Show." There were topics listed that you could click on to. I saw five topics I qualified for. One that particularly interested me was called "Have you Spoiled your Daughter?" I knew I had done that. God knows Alia had taken me for a financial ride—limos and all.

I clicked on and typed my story. I wrote about how I delivered hot lunches to her at school from kindergarten through fourth grade each school day. I let them know about her receiving a baby grand piano for her 11th birthday. And, of course, the limousines I hired to cart her and her friends around on her birthdays. I told of all the clothes purchased from Saks Fifth Avenue and Bloomingdales all her life. I couldn't leave out the expensive vacations including cruises. She'd been in private school all of her life and just loved going to Manhattan to see all those Broadway shows. She was the restaurant and hotel queen and to boot—Miss Alia went on a shopping spree with $29,000.00. Yep—she was definitely spoiled. I then answered a few more topics, did an E-mail telling Oprah about my books and called it a night. I hit the sack.

On Tuesday morning, March 22, 2005, I decided I could not make a scheduled doctor's appointment. I was too tired. I wanted to spend the day relaxing. I usually showed up for my therapist, Dr. Anne Highland—but this particular day I called to tell her I couldn't make it. I was supposed to be there at 11:00 a.m. but instead I got back into bed and turned on the television. Around eleven twenty my phone rang. The person on the phone asked for me. "I'm a producer from the Oprah Show," she said.

"This is Adrienne," I calmly answered.

"I'm calling regarding the E-mail you sent to the Oprah Show."

I never flinched or showed any emotion. I was completely calm. The only thing running though my mind was my psychic. Yep. My psychic. I love that stuff and had my cards read about a year and a half prior to this phone call. The Psychic—Mr. Dee had said in the reading that I would get a call—not directly from Oprah—but from her "people." He said it would be regarding an interview. That was all that was registering in my brain—that Mr. Dee had been right again about something else. I'd been going to him off and on since 1991 and many things he predicted have come true. He'd even forecasted the success of my novels. He also told me some details of the affairs that my no good cheating husband had during our marriage. I regained control of my thoughts and answered Oprah's producer's question. "I actually sent five E-mails. Which one are you referring to?" I asked.

"Well, do you have a spoiled daughter?"

"Yes, I do—Alia."

"Well, I'd like to talk to you about her?"

Miranda Creighton and I talked nearly an hour. She grilled me. She had many questions and also asked me if I had pictures of Alia in limos and did I really have a baby grand piano. She wanted to know what I did for a living, if I received child support from my husband and wanted more details about things I did for Alia. I told her how every Christmas I had a budget for Alia—that I'd spend about $1500.00 on her gifts. I explained how one Christmas Alia gave me a list in November of all the things she wanted. I purchased all the stuff. She was about 8 years old at that time. I hid all the stuff and the second week in December Alia presented me with another list. She had changed her mind. I kept all the previous gifts and then went shopping again spending about $1200.00. I explained to her that when Alia began losing her baby teeth, she would put the teeth under her pillow. I would put $10.00 under the pillow for each tooth. I would also alert all my friends and family she lost a tooth. I would have them mail five dollars for each tooth missing from "Tooth Fairy Land." I told her how Alia got a lot of mail for the teeth. I told Miranda about all the giant sleepovers Alia had for her birthdays and the Miss America Pageants we had at the house.

Miranda questioned me about Alia's clothing. I answered all her questions and then she wanted to know where Alia was. I explained that Alia was a student at Temple University in Philadelphia on honors and was at school. I let her know that Alia also worked for the President of Temple University part time as she was a full time student. She then wanted to know where Alia got $29,000 to go shopping. I explained it had been an insurance settlement she received from an automobile accident which occurred in January of 2001. I told her Alia was eighteen and away at college at the University of Maryland when that case settled. Even though I begged our attorney not to send the money directly to her, the law was that it was her money and she was an adult. He had to send it to her. I also explained that I'd done everything I could to persuade Alia to let me put the money away for her, but she refused. I told her Alia spent the entire sum of money between October of 2002 and July of 2003. The producer then wanted to talk to Alia. I gave her the main number to the college as well as Alia's cell phone number. She said she would call me back.

I hung up the phone, turned over, got comfortable and watched TV. I then called a couple of friends to let them know what had happened. I started to think about that little old lady in Barnes and Noble who approached me three days prior to Miranda's telephone call. Many things were going through my mind about the events that transpired between Saturday and Tuesday. I thought about all the sessions I'd had with my Psychic, Mr. Dee over the last few years and how in his office after many meetings he talked to me about Oprah, telling me I'd indeed come in contact with her. My thoughts were interrupted when I received another call from **Miranda Creighton, Oprah's producer. She said she could not locate Alia** and needed to talk to her. Miranda said Alia's cell phone was turned off. She gave me a number to give Alia to call her. I called straight through to the President's office and got Alia. I explained what was going on and told her to call Miranda. In about thirty five minutes I received another call from Miranda. She went over a few more things with me regarding how I had raised Alia and then said "I've talked to Alia. She'll be home early today at 5:00 p.m. We want to set you guys up for an interview."

"Okay—that's fine. We'll talk when she comes home."

Another call came in twenty minutes from Miranda. "Listen, we're preparing for the interview."

"Okay," I said

"Well, we'll need a few things from you for the interview. We need pictures of all the stuff you bought Alia—you know, get those things out. Also, we need pictures of the limousines. Do you have them? If you have videos of the Christmases, we need that stuff, too.

I told her I had many pictures and I offered to send them in.

"Well, you don't have to send them. You see, we're sending a television film crew to your house. You can give the things to them."

"Okay, what day will they come?" I asked.

"Well, they will be there about four o'clock today. They are coming to your house today. They will be there a long time filming you and Alia and her things."

I was stunned. "What?" I screeched. "Today? You mean this interview is not on the phone?" I was dumb struck.

She tried to calm me down. "Listen, you can do this. Just start getting it together. I'll call you back later. The crew will call you. Everything will be fine."

"Oh my God! I look like hell. I don't have any clothes on. I have to wash my hair! I have to find all the stuff! Jesus Christ! Oh shit!" I was screaming and jumping out of the bed.

"Okay, Adrienne. You calm down and get things together. The people coming will have a lot of equipment, too. I'll talk to you soon." She hung up.

I stared around the room. I didn't know what to do first. I'm not normally a neat person, but over the last three weeks I had cleaned and organized my house really well because I was having a party to launch my new novel *Connecting* on April 3rd, 2005. Today was March 22nd. I had put so many things away in the garage and basement because I expected company from out of town for this event. I had cleaned my screened-in porch and washed all the covers for the furniture. The covers were laid out in the living room waiting to be put back on the furniture. I didn't know where a damn thing was as far as all those pictures! Where in the world had I put all those old pictures? What the hell was I going to put on to look pretty? Lord have Mercy!

I walked into my own bedroom. For the last three weeks I'd been lying around in another bedroom so I wouldn't wreck my cleaned up room before the party on April 3rd. I started looking for a nice outfit to wear for the videotaping. My hair was all over my head. I had panties and a tee shirt on. It was 3:15 p.m. Shit.

I ran into the bathroom and plugged the curling irons on to heat up. Then I began making the bed I had been in all morning. I ran to the basement looking for pictures and old videos I had taken of Alia opening her Christmas presents. I started tearing the house up. I ran to the closets hunting for all those expensive dresses that I had bought for Alia. I couldn't find the pictures albums. Shit! I started cursing Oprah and Miranda out as I ran around. I was hysterical!

I went into the living room and grabbed all those sofa and chair covers that belonged on the porch and took them to the basement. I looked in my closet and found some picture albums—none had the limos in them. I was still running around in panties and tee shirt. The doorbell rang. I ran to the door and peeped out. It was a White guy. I knew it had to be the TV man. I yelled through the door asking who he was and that was him alright. I ran up my stairs and grabbed a robe. I was tying the belt as I came down. I completed the tie and let him in. I know I looked like a maniac and I was in a frenzy.

I let him in, he introduced himself and I immediately began apologizing for looking so scary and I was trying to hold the bottom of the robe shut. I was pissing and moaning about not being able to locate all the pictures. I began showing him what I had dug out to see if they would do. He then said "There are two more people coming. We have equipment to install and work to do. You just calm down and get your stuff done."

 I went back to my huge basement and began ripping open boxes searching for pictures and videos. Then I ran to the garage and found some photo albums. I threw them in the living room and headed up the stairs. The two other guys arrived and the crew began setting up poles for lighting, undoing smoke alarms and my burglar alarm system to insure that no beeping from those devices could interfere with the taping of the interview. The phone rang and it was Miranda. "What now?" I thought."

"I'm E-mailing something for the crew. When it comes up, do not read it. Don't even look at it. Just print it out and hand it to them."

"Okay," I said and we hung up. I wanted that call to end quickly because I thought she may ask me to hunt down some more stuff and I didn't want that job.

I jumped into the shower. After I got out I went for the curling irons which were heating up in the other bathroom. I started trying to curl my hair and they broke. They just broke! I moaned in the bathroom. I sat on the toilet and tried to fix them. I was unsuccessful because the piece couldn't be put back on. I looked around for the Crazy Glue and couldn't find that. I was naked. I couldn't go down the steps because the guys were down there.

I started crying and running around looking for a wig. I tore the closet up in my bedroom looking for it. Luckily I found it. I put it on and it didn't look right. Perhaps it was because I had no make-up on—I didn't know. I looked atrocious! I snatched the wig off my head and headed for my other clothes closet for something to wear. Thank God I had gotten all my suits cleaned because of my book signings and the upcoming party. I grabbed a black and red pantsuit that I always received compliments on whenever I wore it. I found some pantyhose and was trying to work my now fat size sixteen butt into them. Now I had to find my black suede pumps. Unfortunately my shoe tree carousels had had collapsed a week ago and I hadn't had time to order new ones. Therefore, I had thrown all of my shoes into two trash bags and placed the bags in the corner of my bedroom. I was now frantically rooting through sixty four shoes trying to come up those pumps. I finally found them. Then I started on my makeup. Just as I began that, I heard Alia come in the door. I raced down the stairs to greet her. She looked like the average college student, exactly like a refugee—beat up jeans and a sweater. Her hair was all over her head. I growled at her "Get upstairs in your room. You'd better be looking like a million dollars in twenty minutes! I can't find the pictures of you in the limo when you were eight years old!"

"I know where they are. I have them on the third floor."

"Well, we need them. My curlers are broken, too. I need help." I then pointed at the crew. "These guys are interviewing us. These are TV people—from Oprah! This place is a wreck because I tore it up! Get up the steps and please—get the curling irons fixed. I'm gonna kill Oprah and Miranda. You know I love Oprah but I'm gonna kill her!

Alia, usually rebellious to taking orders from anyone, knew I was not up for any lip or any mess. "Okay Mom, I'm outta here. Where are the curlers?"

I was relieved she was being cooperative and blurted out "Second floor Frog bathroom. Grab 'em. I have to get my make up on. I'll be in the blue bathroom." Alia and I live in a house with five bathrooms, one of which is decorated with all kinds of frogs—versions of stuffed animals and glass knick knacks.

She repaired the curlers and as soon as I got my make-up and hair done, the crew wanted me. I grabbed the document Miranda sent through the computer and headed down the stairs. The crew and I went outside to film and talk. I showed them Alia's beat up Mitsubishi Mirage. She had purchased that bomb which had only one headlight for $1900 with her insurance money. Then the crew wanted me back in the house after they filmed that. Lights were erected inside my home and they interviewed me privately while we waited for Alia to get ready.

They asked me a zillion questions about my life, Alia and the purchases I had made, spoiling her to death. We talked about her adventures in life, our fights over the way she handled that insurance money and basically how I raised and cared for her. I admitted the mistakes I felt I made in rearing Alia which were the fact that I probably gave her too many things, didn't require her to have chores inside the house. I'd basically spoiled the child rotten. I admitted if I had slowed up on the giving, she would have appreciated the things I had done. We discussed my work and her disease. She was on the third floor getting ready and could not hear our discussion. They had told her to stay upstairs until my interview was over. Then it would be her turn.

Alia finally got down the stairs. She looked pretty. They wanted us to go outside and walk on the grounds of our house. They filmed this and then we returned to the house. I was told to go upstairs and stay in my bedroom until Alia's interview was over. While I was waiting, Miranda called back. "Adrienne, how is it going?" she asked sweetly.

"Well, I gave your E-mail to the crew and I did not look at it. They are downstairs with Alia and I was told to stay in the bedroom. I guess it is going okay. I found the pictures."

I figured the film crew would turn the tape in to Miranda and it would be viewed along with hundreds of tapes they were probably going to get from across the country. Then I assumed there would be a process of elimination and we'd know in a few weeks if they were using our tape. My thoughts were interrupted. "You sound calmer. This will be okay. You're doing great," Miranda said.

"Well, I hope it comes out okay. I'll tell them you called."

"Well, Adrienne, listen, I have something else to tell you. You have to do something else."

I froze. I wondered what the hell else I had to do. I wondered if I was about to go crazy looking for other things. I was scared of what was going to come out of her mouth. I sat silent—waiting.

"Adrienne, you need to pack a bag. We are flying you and Alia out here to Chicago tomorrow."

I was stunned! My mouth flew open and I began rambling on. "What! What! You are kidding. You mean pack bags? Alia can't get packed. She's doing the interview! What the hell will she wear? I may need to go shopping. I can't get to the mall! Oh my God! This is getting real crazy. Come out there for what? The guys—don't they bring you the video and pictures? The house is torn up?"

"You and Alia will be on the Oprah Show and the taping is early Thursday morning. Someone from our staff will call you to go over flight times with

you. Make sure you pack before you go to bed. Stay calm, you can do it."
We hung up.

I screamed. I was grateful, happy, scared to death, and blown away—all at
the same time. I lay down on the bed. I wanted to cry again.

I was trying to think straight. Things were moving entirely too fast for
me. I grabbed my schedule book. I had an important book signing in
Washington, D.C. for Thursday. It has to be cancelled. I immediately
called my publisher. I told them what was going on and told them to cancel
B. Dalton Book Store at Union Square and tell them I had a good excuse
for not coming—Oprah. Believe me, my publisher was happy to make that
call. They were thrilled about this news of Oprah. I cancelled my meeting
for the next day with the caterer for the launch party. I called my buddy
Nigel to be on standby to take me to the airport the next day. I took a few
minutes to think about Mr. Dee and ran to grab all my past readings to go
over them. There it was in black and white. I take notes at every reading.
I was floored and I thought again about the little old lady in Barnes and
Noble—the Angel.

In an hour the TV crew had finished their private interview with Alia and
I was allowed to come down. Alia's clothes and fur jackets were all over
the living room. There were shoes and dresses everywhere. The crew then
announced we were "breaking for dinner." It was about seven o'clock in the
evening. We had been going for three hours.

A gentleman from the crew went to Wawa's for sandwiches and retuned
with dinner for all. As the five of us enjoyed the meal in my breakfast
room, we swapped stories and talked about their relationships with their
own children as well as the wild things I had done when Alia was sixteen
and wanted to date. We discussed my struggle to raise a sick kid with an
incurable disease. We laughed about a lot of things regarding parenting.
We talked about how I always fought with and for my child. We chatted
about my work and the fights Alia and I have had. I showed the crew a
journal entry I had from 1996 when I took my then eleven year old Alia

to Manhattan to see some Broadway shows. While on that trip I took her to have pancakes at the Four Seasons Hotel and we also had dinner there to sampling the crab cakes that Oprah suggested on TV so long ago. I later found out eight years later in 2004 that one of Oprah's favorite restaurants in New York City is Serendipity's. Alia and I discovered that place in 1998 and love it there.

After dinner was over, we resumed taping and acting out things that Alia and I had fought about in the past. She then played the piano for the crew. Alia plays classical piano, taught by a Russian instructor that I hired to come to our home when she was thirteen.

My phone rang again and it was someone from Oprah's staff. This young lady was in charge of booking flight and hotel reservations. Alia and I were booked to leave on American Airlines the next day around noon and we were staying at a familiar place that I loved—The Omni Hotel. Mommy had been to Chicago many times, but this would be Alia's first trip to the windy city. We were thrilled!

I returned to my basement I spotted my luggage in a corner. I grabbed two suitcases and dumped my summer clothes out of them. Then I began hunting around scanning clothing racks for an outfit Alia could wear on TV. I considered things, wondering what would be appropriate for her. I'd received no instructions on attire. Alia and I had both been on television before but those broadcasts were not nationwide TV. Those shows were a far cry from the Oprah Show. I'd heard rumors many times that Oprah was a perfectionist and also, I didn't want her to be embarrassed by us in any way. I wanted her to be proud of us—the suburban BAPS. I'd appeared on a local talk show in Philadelphia for my books in December of 2004 and Alia, because of the severity of her Crohn's Disease had been selected to do medical documentaries twice since her diagnosis. So, we were not strangers to the camera and media. We'd also made the newspapers on several occasions due to my books and Alia's disease. We'd both had some exposure to the spotlights so I knew we'd have no problems along those lines.

At the time this was all going on, I was very focused on my books. I knew that my being on the Oprah Show could be an opportunity for the world to know about my work. I was extremely excited about that. I imagined Oprah mentioning my work and I was so grateful for that. Friends of ours were going crazy as I had taken an opportunity to call a few people to let them know the good news about us going on the show.

We did a little more taping and shortly after 11:00 p.m., the crew packed up and left our house.

I had decided on wearing my navy blue Jones New York pant suit, navy suede shoes. I knew my hair would be fine as long as those curling irons kept working. I had no time to purchase new ones. I'd just had my hair cut and frosted by my magician, Frank, owner of Panache Hair Design in Philadelphia, three days before the Oprah Show made their first call to me. My hair was in great shape. By 3 a.m. we were packed and I hit the sack. The plan was that Alia would go to school for a couple of hours and then meet me at the airport. Before I went to bed, she and I had fought about what she would wear on the show. I suggested a nice pantsuit or some sort of suit. She had great clothes. She fought me on that saying she was wearing jeans. I had a fit! She would not give in. I packed her a suit anyway. I said to her "Don't you piss Oprah off. She may not want you in jeans. I have packed you a nice suit—the one from Cache. What you will do is appear at her studio in jeans. If she gives you a look or tells you she didn't want you in jeans—the suit will be with me and you'll change your clothes. That's the deal."

"Okay Mom—just leave me alone. I'm tired.

The next day was Wednesday, April 23, 2005. I had a lot to do. I put the final touches on the packing, ran some errands, picked up two hundred dollars from the bank and returned home to get dressed to leave. I was worried about what we would eat on the plane. Since Alia had been born and whenever my family traveled, I packed our food. I had no time for this today.

Nigel, a good friend of mine took me to Philly International to catch my flight. As we were leaving my house, I glanced around taking one last look at the living room, dining room and hall. Shit was everywhere. I wondered how I would put the place back together in time for the launch party which was less than two weeks away.

Everything regarding our trip to Chicago had been taken care of by the Oprah Show. My ticket was waiting. The plan was that we would be in Chicago Wednesday and Thursday, then fly back to Philly Thursday afternoon after the taping. A limo would greet us at the airport taking us to the Omni. When Nigel dropped me off, I got in line to check in for my flight. Everything was in order. I received my ticket and boarding pass. I walked to the gate and sat waiting for Alia who shortly showed up. It sure felt good bragging in the airport restaurant about where we were going and my cell phone was going off like crazy with friends being so proud of us.

THE VOUCHERS

We had a wonderful flight until we started arguing about something. Alia always manages to tick me off about something when we are traveling. By the time we landed in Chicago we weren't speaking. I was threatening to get on a plane and go directly back home. We made up in the limo and finally got checked in to the Omni—as proud as we could be being Oprah's guests.

I had packed my tarot card reading to show her—proving this trip was definitely in the works long ago. I also took her autographed copies of my books and another favorite book of mine—"The Million Dollar Divorce" by R.M. Johnson—a Chicago native. That book was hot and a page turner.

It was given to me as a Christmas Gift in December of 2004. I was not only impressed with it, but it had held me hostage the entire Christmas day.

When we arrived in our suite, and unpacked, we noticed some meal vouchers on a table. Oprah was certainly making sure we ate well at the Omni. We decided to go out for dinner and found a place nearby. It didn't matter—we didn't mind paying for dinner. We'd use the vouchers at the hotel before we went home.

Later that evening Alia decided she was ordering from room service at the hotel. She grabbed the meal vouchers and began looking through the menu. She made a selection, called room service, placed the order and informed the clerk that she had meal vouchers compliments of the Oprah Show. Once they told her the total of the bill, Alia began going through the vouchers in preparation for payment. What she ordered came to $17 or so and, she'd of course add on the tip. Alia is really into tipping and gives at least a minimal straight 20%. She and the clerk got into a discussion because she had pulled out a $25 voucher. During this conversation she was informed that no matter what the bill was, there would be no change and no credit voucher issued. So, if her meal cost $9 and the smallest voucher Alia had was for $25—no change. Alia's question was "Do you credit Oprah back for what's left over?" The answer was "no." Alia hung up, declining to order.

As I listened to that conversation, I was surprised because in twenty years of Alia's life she had never watched money and certainly never tried to save me a dime. She'd been in some of the finest hotels and restaurants in and out of the United States. This was truly a Black American Princess. She was used to things. We'd even nicknamed Alia "The BAP"

After Alia hung up—she wanted to talk to me about the situation. "Mom, this is not fair. Look at all these vouchers," she said holding them up. There were vouchers for $50 and $75—a bunch of vouchers. "Mom, I don't like the fact that they are keeping Oprah's money. That's what they're doing—they are keeping her money if I order and tip for less than the voucher amount."

I knew trouble was brewing. One reason everyone in our family insisted Alia become an attorney is because she can usually out talk people. Opponents get tired and give up—just to shut her up. I know I've done it countless times. I'd surrender to her point of view for mere peace and quiet. "Alia, maybe something has been worked out with Oprah and the hotel that you don't know about. Can't you simply order what you want and pay the people or go out again and eat? I'm tired. I feel like I've been up for two days. Come on, don't start with those vouchers."

"It's not fair, and I'm hungry," Alia protested.

I was so tired I turned over and pretended I was falling asleep. That didn't work and she wouldn't shut up so I hit the shower. Fifteen minutes later, here comes a bunch of food. I cannot remember what she ordered but there was a lot of it. The girl made sure she spent $25 and she also tried to eat every morsel of it. She was making damn sure the Omni didn't take a dime of Oprah's money. Alia conked out from eating. Now keep in mind she has Crohn's Disease. The digestive track gets screwed up. These patients get diarrhea and their condition flares if they break the rules. Eating small meals is better for them.

I went to sleep and woke up about two thirty in the morning. I started walking around the room with a lot on my mind. I was restless. I kept thinking about the events of the past two days. There were things on my mind. I wanted to chat with Oprah about my loving to write. I grabbed a pen and some hotel stationary. I threw on some jeans and a top and headed to the hotel bar, which I knew would be closed. Housekeeping was cleaning the beautiful room. "Hi, I couldn't sleep and I have a letter to write. Do you mind if I sit here at the bar and write it? I won't be any trouble and I don't want anything to drink."

March 24, 2005

Dear Oprah

It is now 3:37 a.m. and I am sitting in the Omni Hotel bar. I just woke up, the bar is closed to patrons but that's okay—I don't need a drink. I need quiet to write this letter. First of all—thank you to you and your staff for choosing Alia and I to come on your show. We deserve it—I have truly spoiled my daughter. I am a writer and convinced I could write a hilarious novel telling of the events that landed me on your show. For three years, people have been not only suggested I try in same way to meet you—but many were about to write to you themselves or start a petition to get me on your show.

It's now 4:48 a.m., Thursday morning, March 24, 2005—almost time to get ready to meet you. You've turned my world upside down in two days and I still have to put that house of mine back together since your crew did the home taping. But—I am grateful for wonderful memories.

Adrienne Bellamy

∗ ∗ ∗

At approximately five o'clock in the morning I returned to my room. I found my daughter on the toilet crapping her brains out. Yep—all that food she ordered and ate had indeed caught up with her. She was scared to death she'd crap all over Oprah's studio.

I smiled at her and said, "Well, it's a good thing I brought a change of clothing for you, you know—with your having diarrhea and all." I shook my head and laughed as I walked out of the bathroom.

"Where've you been?" she asked.

"Down at the bar writing a letter to Oprah telling her how crazy she's made me. I'm plugging the curlers in and when you're done I'll get my shower. We have to be down in the lobby for the limo at 6:45. I assume you aren't ordering breakfast." I sarcastically said. She never answered.

WHAT A DIFFRENCE A DAY MAKES

We boarded the hotel elevator at 6:40 a.m. We rode down with two women from an automobile company who were very excited about going to the show. They were thrilled to have received tickets to be part of the studio audience. We proudly let them know that we were guests on the show. When we reached the lobby concierge, we were advised we were on the list for a limo and it should arrive soon. The clerk also informed us that we would be sharing the limo with another family being featured on the show. I wondered what they had done to impress Oprah to make the show. The clerk and I got into a conversation and I mentioned I was from Philadelphia. His eyes lit up and he boasted a gleaming smile. "This is something," he said. I have relatives in Philly, lived there for a spell and I also met and helped another guest of the Oprah Show a while back. She was from Philly, too. She made the best macaroni and cheese in the nation—so Oprah thought."

"Oh, you mean Delilah. She's my friend. We go way back. She has a few restaurants in Philly and my daughter started eating her food when she was three years old. Alia is 20 now. I love Delilah. I'll have to tell her I met you." We then exchanged business cards.

In ten minutes a pretty and well dressed African American woman arrived. We chatted a bit and she explained her daughter was still getting ready for the show and would be down shortly. While waiting, we laughed about the hustle and bustle of the prior day. Her attractive seventeen year-old daughter then appeared and we were whisked into the limo. During the **drive, we continued to share stories about our daughters and our lives**. This family was from Ohio. The girls began telling each other the events of their lives and schooling and laughing about their neurotic mothers. Her mother and I began explaining our occupations. She worked at a television station. I was impressed. I did notice one thing that made me a little uneasy—her daughter was chewing gum. I have this thing in my life—no chewing gum.

I just hate it and since Alia was born she was never allowed to do that. Of course with my good manners I never said a word in that limo but I was praying to God that when we arrived at the studio, the gum would go. Not only did I hate it, but I knew from seeing some of Oprah's prior broadcasts, she absolutely detested gum chewing, too. I looked at the girls and thought "Oprah's gonna have a bird," but I didn't want to start bossing these people around or running things—so I kept my mouth shut and prayed the young lady was planning to chew it temporarily, and get rid of it when the sugar was gone.

We finally pulled up at the studio and were led in. The lobby was beautiful and boasted a giant staircase. After we were checked in, we were escorted by a member of her Oprah's staff up the stairs to the second floor. We were given a little tour and shown a great cafeteria area with loads of goodies, pastries, coffees and juices which were offered free of charge to us. Next we were introduced to a makeup artist and a hair stylist. It was their job to determine if we needed any work done to ourselves. I was surprised and impressed with the scenery. I loved the beautiful arrangements of fresh flowers. We were standing around checking everything out when a pretty blond woman approached me. "Adrienne and Alia—right?" she asked.

Alia and I both smiled at the same time. I blurted out "Miranda—you're Miranda, aren't you?" She answered, "Yes."

I hugged her. Because of everything I had gone through the day before, and having so many conversations with her, I felt I had known her for a hundred years. Alia was grinning and gave her a hug. "You guys look great!" she said. "Look, you're going to be situated in this room," she said pointing behind her. "Just go in a take a seat and I'll be back. There will be some other families in there. We'll do some more talking soon."

Alia and I took our seats. This room resembled a tiny intimate movie theater. When we got situated we realized there were a total of four families participating in this taping—much to my surprise. I'd really thought the day before that it would only be Alia, me and Oprah doing this show.

The particulars had never been explained to me. We had fun listening to the other families' reasons for being selected. Every family had a different set of problems in a mother/daughter relationship. The families were all from different parts of the country. Each mother was a single parent and all the daughters had different issues which caused problems in their relationships. It was interesting to be hearing the stories and meeting the other daughters. We had a pleasant time together and one family and I had a similar thought—we had determined our situations with our daughters were so bad that Oprah was going to send us to Dr. Phil for counseling. Also that same mother/daughter duo had a huge fight on the plane and the mother threatened to go back home before the taping. Our two families had a lot in common.

We were interrupted when members of Oprah's staff came in to have us fill out forms, address cards and give us instructions on the taping. It was explained that we would stick to the questions during the interview and then there would be an opportunity during breaks and the after show where we could really hash things out. We would have a chance to speak a bit more freely at that time. Then it was explained that we would be leaving the area soon to have our hair and makeup checked and eventually be taken into the studio taping room.

The hair stylist let me know that I didn't need a thing done to my hair. That made me feel good—like I had done a good job. Alia needed some curls and plopped down in the chair. My make-up artist decided I needed deeper eyebrows and that my wine colored lips should actually be more of an orange, so she fixed those things. I found her quiet unless I asked questions or made small talk. I'm more relaxed talking so we ended up having a nice conversation about cosmetology training and my being a writer. **When Alia was done, her makeup was touched up. We were wondering** where Oprah and Miranda were. I was a bit nervous about Alia in those jeans, boots and sweater and wondered if Oprah would disagree with the outfit.

After hair and makeup was over, I checked the cafeteria out. I really was not hungry—I usually ate my first meal around one in the afternoon. I wanted to skip the coffee, knowing that would send me to the bathroom. Alia hadn't had any more episodes of diarrhea and wasn't going near anything to eat.

✳ ✳ ✳

"Okay everybody. I need the forms I asked you to fill out. I hope you didn't forget to fill the address card out, too so we can keep up with you when you return home." A member of the staff announced when we were all back in the theater room. After Alia and I completed our paperwork, Miranda appeared. "Come on with me," she said to Alia and me.

We followed her into the hall and we all sat at a table. I immediately told her what kind of night I had and what that psychic had told me over a year and a half ago. Then Alia chimed in with some conversation and the three of us were laughing. I showed her the letter I had written in the bar and told her I needed to give it to Oprah. I then showed her my two treasures which were the novels I had written and my own favorite book by R.M. Johnson. Miranda looked at my gifts and then decided to look over the letter. She began laughing and said. "This letter is something—and wonderful. You should definitely have a copy of it for your memories. Give this to me later, before you leave and I'll copy it for you. I'll give Oprah the original. I can take the books now."

"Take a look at this. This is from a year and a half ago. My psychic told me I'd end up here. Look, read it."

Alia and Miranda were looking at me and cracking up. Miranda glanced at the text about the psychic and gave me a weird look. "Don't you tell Oprah anything about any physic stuff. You hear me?" she said.

"Okay. Where's Oprah?" I asked.

"She's not ready yet. Listen, this is the plan. Maria Shriver is going to be on the show today. She has a new book out about parenting. Maria and Oprah are really good friends. Best buddies. Time-wise because they are so happy to see each other when they get together, we may run out of time. There are four families here and some people will not be on the main show. They won't make it because there may be a lot of conversation between Maria and Oprah. Oprah can choose what family is going on first. The families who don't make it on will be seen on a program called *Oxygen* which comes on at night."

"Okay—no problem. I understand that." I said.

"Well, it looks like you and Alia may make it on the regular daytime show. You see, you're scheduled midway through the show. So, that may get you on. We'll see."

"Okay, Miranda." Alia said.

We then returned to the theater room and conversed with the families. In about ten minutes security came for all four families. They first checked to see if we needed a bathroom break. Some did. When they returned all eight of us were hooked up with microphones at our waist around our butts and marched in a line through the studio.

There was a packed audience and a staff member on stage to entertain and prep everyone for the show. She was certainly good at her job. I sat on the front row next to my daughter. I was having a good time. I had been part of a studio audience twenty seven years ago—but that was "Good Times."

I was in a good mood—the entire audience was. We had been warmed up well by Oprah's *Host Before the Real Host Comes On*. Forgive me my readers, I have forgotten her name. Anyway, I sat front row, a little to the right. I was right in front of the couch and I thought "That couch sure looks little. It seems so big when I watch the show from home." Alia was beside me, a mom and daughter guest was beside her and the two other families just behind us. There we were—all eight of us waiting to meet Oprah. I really was surprised we hadn't met her before we were brought in. I hope Alia having those jeans and sweater and boots on was going to be okay. The girl from the other family still had that chewing gum in her mouth and I was thinking "Oprah's not going to like that." I sat and waited. I figured Oprah would be out in a minute, look us all over, say hello and then we'd tape the show. There were TV cameras and gadgets all over the place. I sat patiently. I wasn't very excited or overwhelmed. To be a guest, I was pretty laid back. Alia was looking around, checking things out. It sure was early in the morning. It must have been a little before 9:00 a.m. I had to pee. Damn. Well, it wasn't going to happen because I would have to get security to take me to the ladies room and I had my mike on my butt. You know, it would just be my luck that the mike fell in the toilet. I didn't want to have to say "excuse me" and make it out of my seat—so—I had to hold it until after the show was taped.

The announcement came that Oprah was getting ready to come out. We all stood, applauded and screamed. She was wearing a skirt and sweater and a pair of gold pumps. She had no stockings on. Her hair with all those curls was absolutely beautiful. She was a hell of a lot thinner than I anticipated and her make-up was divine. She was beautiful—and it seemed a natural beauty. She wore a giant smile boasting gorgeous white teeth. She calmed the audience down and we were seated. She then began to explain the days' agenda for the taping. It had *begun* for me. This was *it* for me.

I could not take my eyes off her. I sat in that seat and for some reason I was totally mesmerized. It was her presence. It was something I did not understand—something I was totally unfamiliar with. There is something about Oprah that allows something—vibes or rays or something to radiate off her. They hit me like a ton of bricks. This is my take on it. I don't quite understand it myself so I'm giving you this the best I can. I began listening to her every word as she explained that her dear friend Maria Shriver would soon be joining us. I sat and waited and once Maria came out, she and Oprah shared many delightful stories. They also discussed Maria's newly released book titled *"And One More Thing Before You Go."* This book was written as a tribute to Maria's mother, Eunice Kennedy Shriver, and also touched upon mother daughter relationships and parenting. Mrs. Kennedy Shriver would be joining Oprah and Maria on the couch later in the taping.

After I returned home from Chicago, I tried to calm down from all the hoopla and excitement of being on the show. I dove into the arrangements of my launch party for Connecting, getting head counts for the restaurants, going over the menus and designating places in my home for out of town guests to sleep. The party would take place in nine days on April 3, 2005. Life was a whirlwind.

The Oprah Show taping would be aired on April 8, 2005. A week before the scheduled air time, Alia and I began getting calls from people across the country. They were friends, classmates from her prior university, The University of Maryland at College Park and family who had seen Alia on a "commercial for the Oprah show." People were asking if she really spent 29K. Alia and I were so busy we hadn't caught the commercial. All who telephoned were excited. I'd had a lot to do around the house, so I would leave the TV's on throughout the house trying to catch this commercial that everyone was laughing about. It took a while—a few days—but I finally saw it pop up on the TV one evening. I stood and shook my head. It was a welcome treat and unbelievable seeing the Black American Princess on TV again—this time having fun and not being sick and not talking about the debilitating symptoms of having Crohn's Disease. The BAP was instead talking about spending cold cash and purchasing pretty things—including picturesque settings—on her vacations. That's a Leo for you—when they show off they show off big time—on The Oprah Show.

The launch party went off without a hitch to a full house. My books sold **well and it was announced that Alia and I had made the Oprah Show and** everyone was informed of the date it would air. People were so excited to have an opportunity to see it in five days. Our local TV news station was coming to our house to view it with us, as well as a couple of Barnes and Noble executives, my neighbors and Carolyn Perry, a close friend who had watched Alia grow up. Some friends were planning Oprah parties the day the tape would be aired. Temple University, Alia's college was as proud as could be. Alia and I were quite the buzz of Philly and our suburban town of Elkins Park, and Jenkintown, Pennsylvania. We were loving it.

Alia sat on the end of my bed. For the past three days since we had been back home from the taping in Chicago, she had been on the computer a lot more than usual. This particular night as she sat on the bed, she said to me softly, "She's been through a lot. Did you know all that she has been through?" I knew she was talking about Oprah. Everything had been Oprah since we got home. Alia was getting her hair done like Oprah's. She was going to work for her. She was going to call her before April 24, 2005. She was crossing days off the calendar until she got to April 24th—yep, that's when Oprah told her to call her—one month to the day. She was going to watch her money. She was going to do better. You name it—Alia was going to do it for Oprah. Alia was absolutely Oprah drunk.

I looked over at my daughter and I knew she was genuinely concerned. I didn't want to baby Alia about this subject. If I given her too much sympathy, she'd find some money somehow and show up at Oprah's studio to comfort her. I approached the problem by saying to this twenty year old strong willed Leo the Lion, King of the Jungle who had fought a lot of battles herself at an early age by saying "Yep, sweetie. I realize she has been through a lot. I know. I have some pain regarding what she's gone through, too. Alia—she's strong—she's gonna make it through it all. Care—but don't stress too much about it. Remember—what does not kill us—will make us stronger. Oprah's holding her own. You just remember the things she said to you. She had very little time with you but she tried to use it wisely by directing you."

THE POWERHOUSES

I sat in the audience, front row, so very close to Maria Shriver, Eunice Kennedy Shriver and Oprah Winfrey, watching and listening to these three female powerhouses counsel my child. I was grateful and honored. Plugging Departures and Connecting, those novels I'd written, loved, and was so proud of and the possible notoriety I'd receive and the inevitable advancement of my career because of the mere mention of my books became totally irrelevant to me. It was much more important for me to *listen* to these women as they tried to redirect my daughter. I've always had a gregarious personality, had excellent marketing and promotional skills. A boost from Oprah would indeed be wonderful—but I could sell my own books. I have a lot of self confidence. I'd always have the arena of places like Barnes and Noble, Karibu Book Stores, Borders and B. Dalton to get my book thing off. But on *this* day, I knew that the chances were extremely slim that I'd ever be able to sit and watch these three smart and influential women, two of whom having children of their own, and the other the role model of the century, give good, sound advice toward the development of the most important person in my life. Even if this counseling would only be available for a fraction of a mere hour, it was of the utmost importance to me and far more valuable to me than letting the world know I had written a couple of books. I wanted to capitalize on this moment. *This* was what it was all about. *This,* in my opinion was huge conquest as well as an enormous accomplishment for Adrienne and Alia Bellamy. This was a tremendous blessing and my saying that I was thankful and grateful is the understatement of the year. That taping was one of my quietest moments I had ever encountered in my life—and believe me—I can run my mouth a mile a minute. Everyone knows that about me. But I was thirsty—for knowledge and guidance and I was so appreciative for the vehicles God put on that stage, in front of me that day to assist me in my journey to deliver as a parent my daughter, Alia Bellamy, as a whole human being to society—hopefully—some time very soon in her life. She was twenty years old sitting there listening to these women. As I sat mesmerized, I prayed that perhaps Oprah, Maria and Eunice's words would help Alia to be free of an ego, selfishness, and greed. I've always prayed for my daughter to be fit and sound spiritually, mentally, intellectually and financially. God gave me a tall order as a parent and on March 24, 2005 and he handed me some *assistance* and I had the opportunity to watch Oprah and Maria spoon feed the real facts of life to Alia. To a single parent who wants the best for her child—it doesn't come any better than that.

QUESTIONS FOR DISCUSSION

∾

Question 1: Parenting is one of the most important topics in The Bitch Tried To Steal My Husband's Body. What characteristics make a good parent?

Question 2: Lenny seemed to have it all prior to Carolyn. Why do you think he teamed up with her? What do you think he really wanted? Do you think there is any real depth in his relationship with Carolyn or Debbie? Do you think it is fair how he treated Denise?

Question 3: Relationships are a major part of this novel and all are very different. Compare the relationships of Denise and Lenny and Carolyn and Lenny. Which is your favorite and why?

Question 4: How do you feel about Denise's relationship with Dale?

Question 5: Discuss the different ways in which the lives of these characters might progress.

Question 6: Shock us with a statistic relevant to book.

Adrienne Bellamy was born and raised in Philadelphia, Pennsylvania. She wrote her first poem at age six and continued to write the novels titled *Departures* and *Connecting*. Her hobbies are parenting her two daughters, astrology and cooking. She is a Paralegal and a Nanny.

Made in the USA